SONIC ™

THE HEDGEHOG

TANGLE & WHISPER

SEGA ®

Facebook: **facebook.com/idwpublishing**
Twitter: **@idwpublishing**
YouTube: **youtube.com/idwpublishing**
Tumblr: **tumblr.idwpublishing.com**
Instagram: **instagram.com/idwpublishing**

COVER ART BY
JENNIFER HERNANDEZ

SERIES ASSISTANT EDITS BY
MEGAN BROWN

SERIES EDITS BY
DAVID MARIOTTE

COLLECTION EDITS BY
ALONZO SIMON
AND ZAC BOONE

LETTERS BY
SHAWN LEE

PRODUCTION ASSISTANCE BY
CHRISTA MIESNER

ISBN: 978-1-68405-583-8   23 22 21 20   1 2 3 4

Originally published as SONIC THE HEDGEHOG: TANGLE & WHISPER
issues #1–4 and SONIC THE HEDGEHOG ANNUAL 2019.

Chris Ryall, President & Publisher/CCO
Cara Morrison, Chief Financial Officer
Matthew Ruzicka, Chief Accounting Officer
David Hedgecock, Associate Publisher
John Barber, Editor-in-Chief
Justin Eisinger, Editorial Director, Graphic Novels & Collections
Scott Dunbier, Director, Special Projects
Jerry Bennington, VP of New Product Development
Lorelei Bunjes, VP of Technology & Information Services
Jud Meyers, Sales Director
Anna Morrow, Marketing Director
Tara McCrillis, Director of Design & Production
Mike Ford, Director of Operations
Shauna Monteforte, Manufacturing Operations Director
Rebekah Cahalin, General Manager
Ted Adams and Robbie Robbins, IDW Founders

Special thanks to Mai Kiyotaki, Aaron Webber, Michael Cisneros,
Sandra Jo, and everyone at Sega for their invaluable assistance.

BONDS OF FRIENDSHIP

STORY
IAN FLYNN
ART
JENNIFER HERNANDEZ

JET SET TORNADO

STORY
CALEB GOELLNER
ART
JACK LAWRENCE
COLORS
LEONARDO ITO

VICTORY GARDEN

STORY
EVAN STANLEY & GIGI DUTREIX
ART
EVAN STANLEY

CURSE OF THE PYRAMID

STORY
CAVAN SCOTT
ART
DIANA SKELLY
COLORS
PRISCILLA TRAMONTANO

SONIC FAN CLUB

STORY
JAMES KOCHALKA
ART
JONATHAN GRAY
COLORS
REGGIE GRAHAM

TANGLE & WHISPER

STORY
IAN FLYNN
ART
EVAN STANLEY
COLORS
LEONARDO ITO AND MATT HERMS

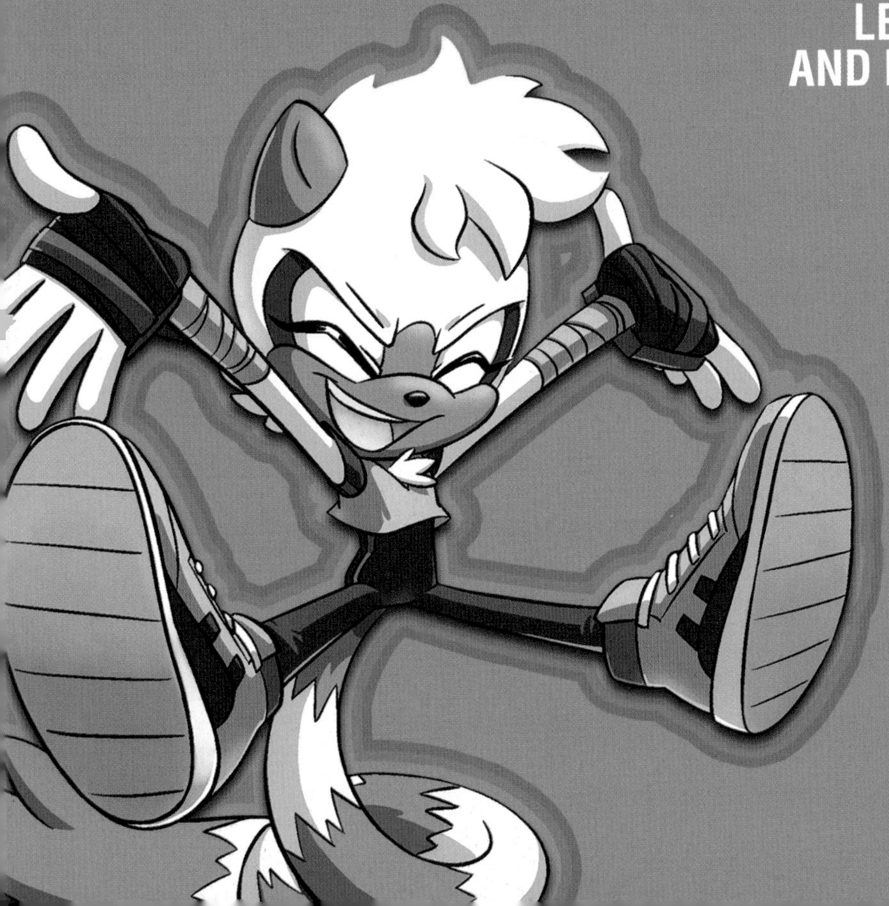

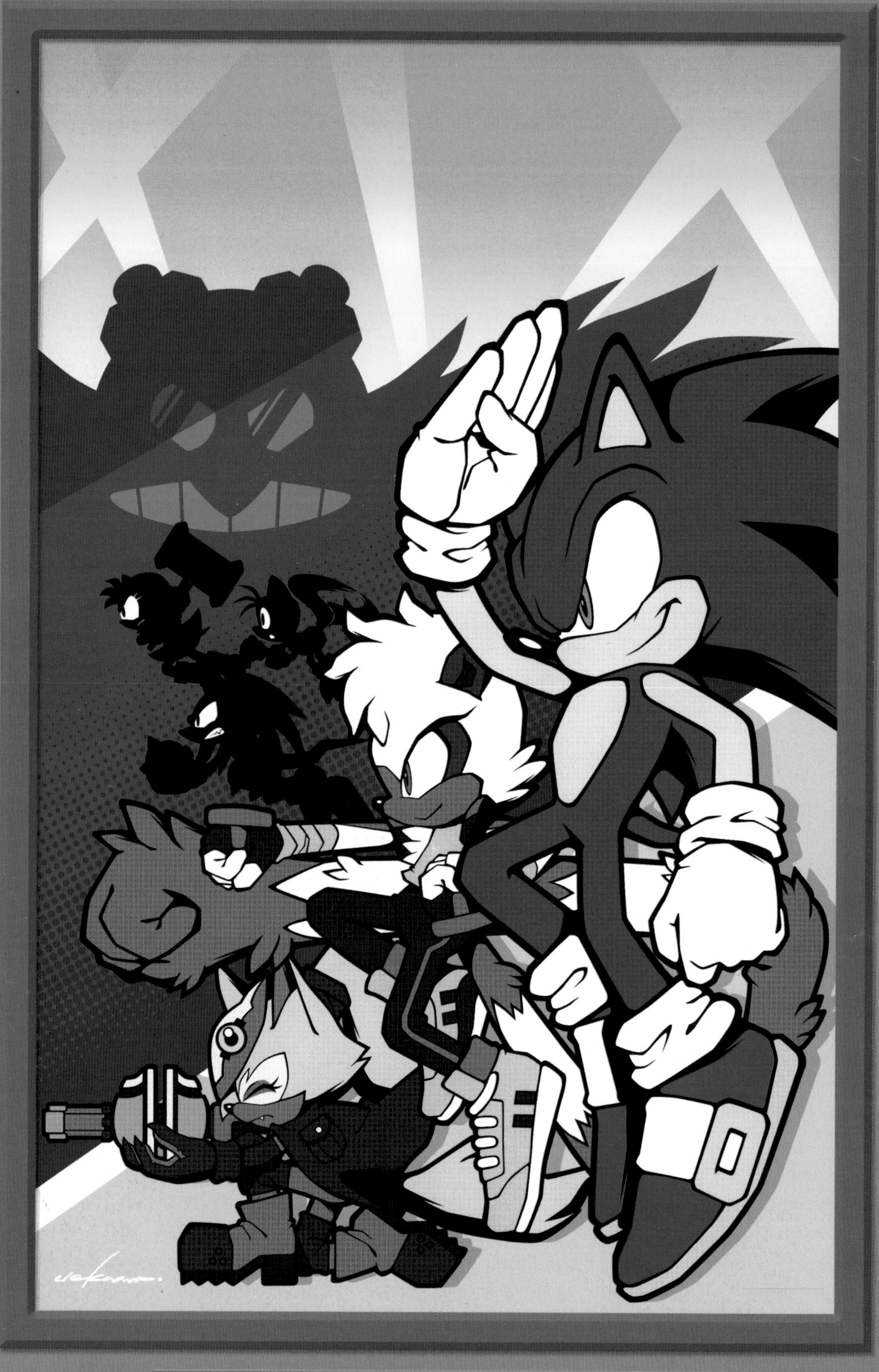

ART BY **YUJI UEKAWA OF SONIC TEAM**

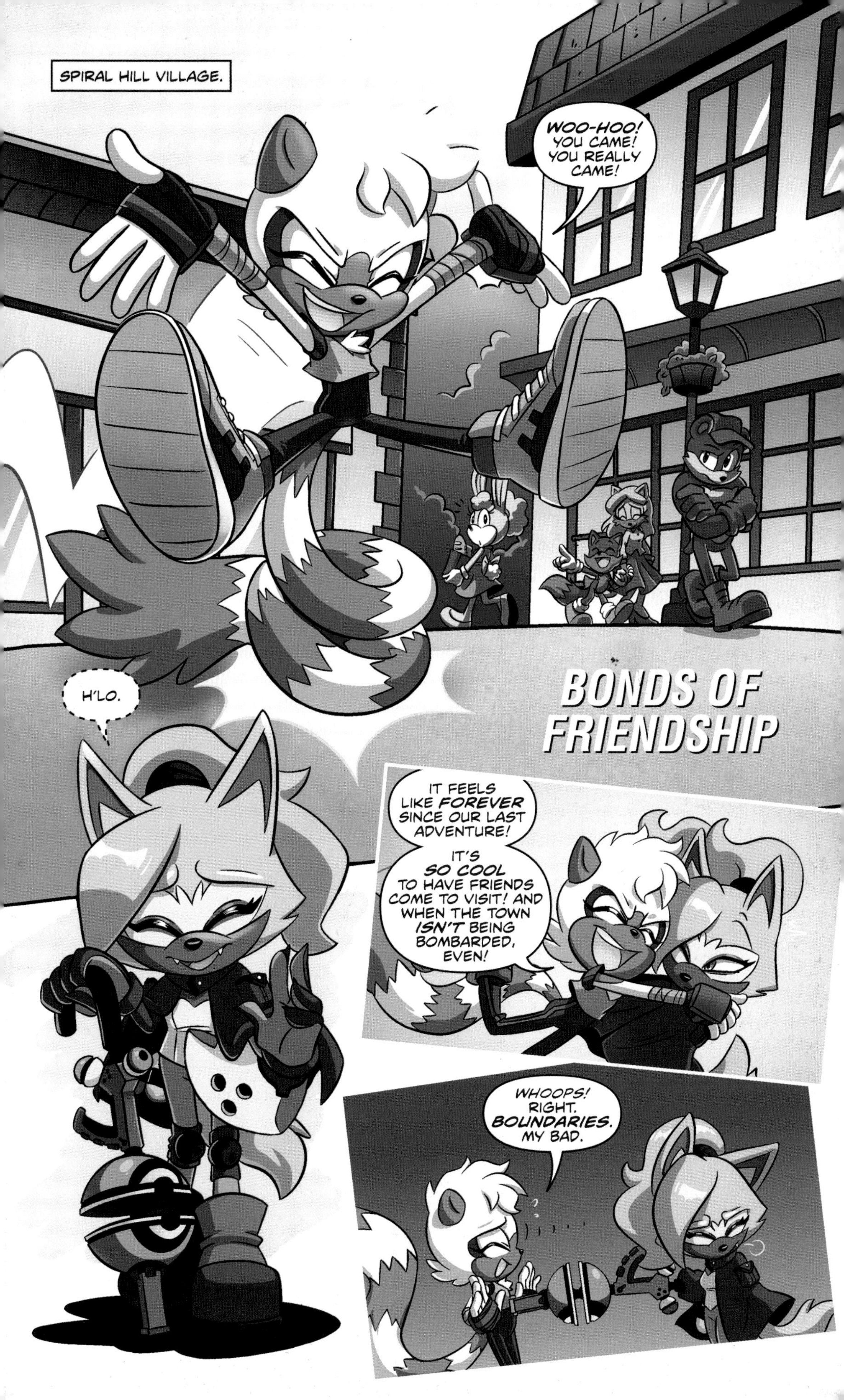
SPIRAL HILL VILLAGE.
WOO-HOO! YOU CAME! YOU REALLY CAME!
H'LO.
BONDS OF FRIENDSHIP
IT FEELS LIKE FOREVER SINCE OUR LAST ADVENTURE!
IT'S SO COOL TO HAVE FRIENDS COME TO VISIT! AND WHEN THE TOWN ISN'T BEING BOMBARDED, EVEN!
WHOOPS! RIGHT. BOUNDARIES. MY BAD.

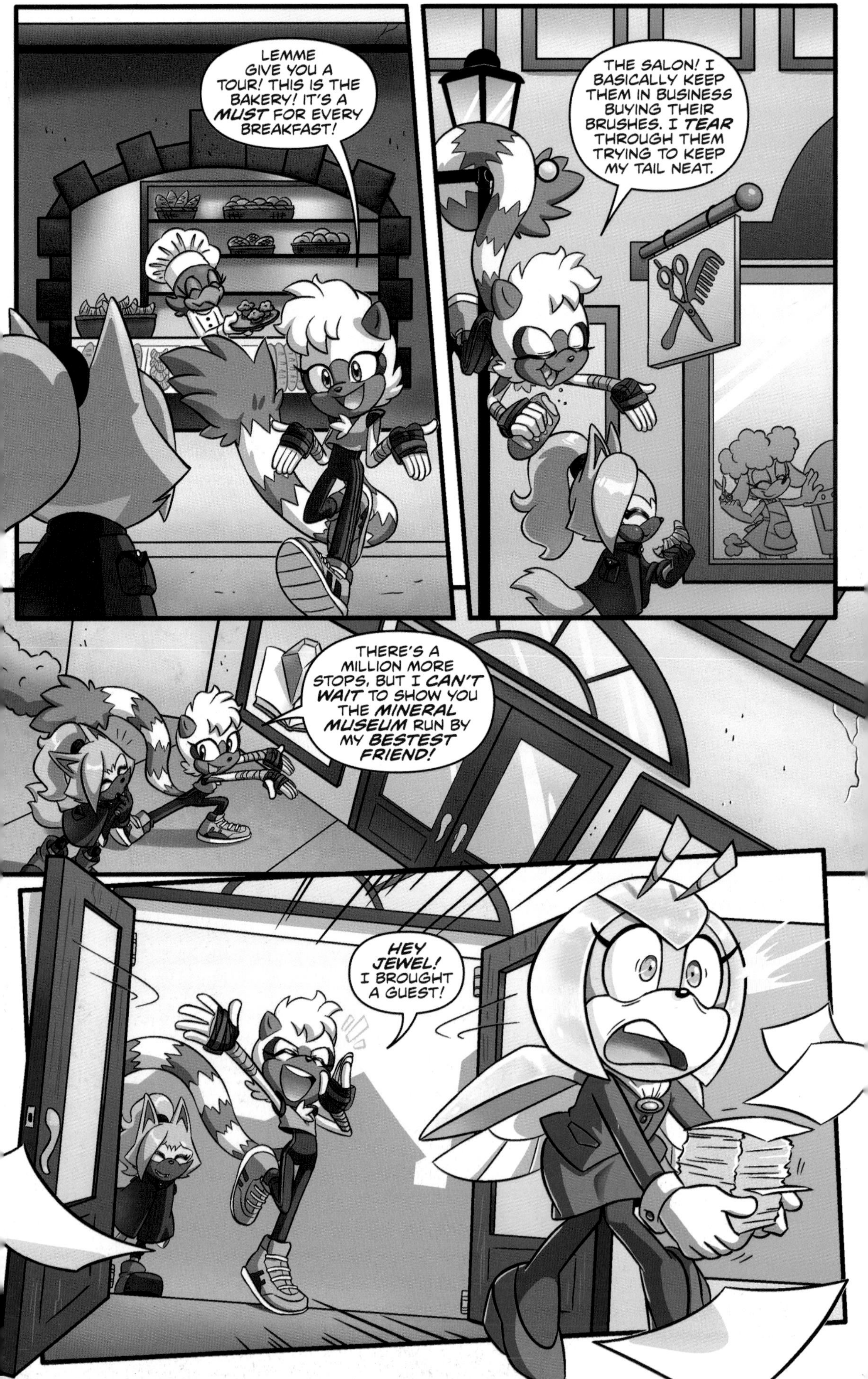
LEMME GIVE YOU A TOUR! THIS IS THE BAKERY! IT'S A MUST FOR EVERY BREAKFAST!
THE SALON! I BASICALLY KEEP THEM IN BUSINESS BUYING THEIR BRUSHES. I TEAR THROUGH THEM TRYING TO KEEP MY TAIL NEAT.
THERE'S A MILLION MORE STOPS, BUT I CAN'T WAIT TO SHOW YOU THE MINERAL MUSEUM RUN BY MY BESTEST FRIEND!
HEY JEWEL! I BROUGHT A GUEST!

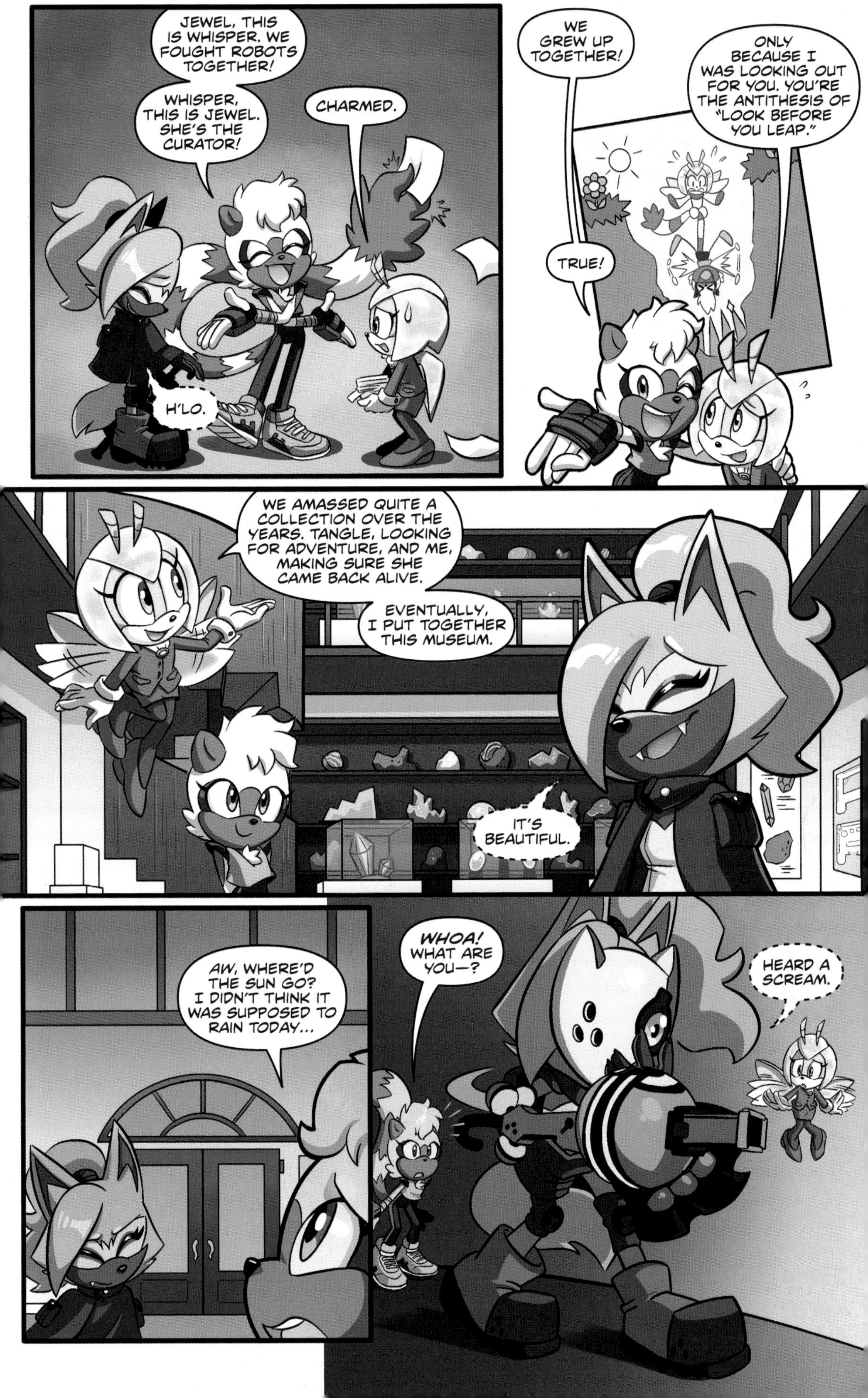
JEWEL, THIS IS WHISPER. WE FOUGHT ROBOTS TOGETHER!
WHISPER, THIS IS JEWEL. SHE'S THE CURATOR!
CHARMED.
H'LO.
WE GREW UP TOGETHER!
ONLY BECAUSE I WAS LOOKING OUT FOR YOU. YOU'RE THE ANTITHESIS OF "LOOK BEFORE YOU LEAP."
TRUE!
WE AMASSED QUITE A COLLECTION OVER THE YEARS. TANGLE, LOOKING FOR ADVENTURE, AND ME, MAKING SURE SHE CAME BACK ALIVE.
EVENTUALLY, I PUT TOGETHER THIS MUSEUM.
IT'S BEAUTIFUL.
AW, WHERE'D THE SUN GO? I DIDN'T THINK IT WAS SUPPOSED TO RAIN TODAY...
WHOA! WHAT ARE YOU—?
HEARD A SCREAM.

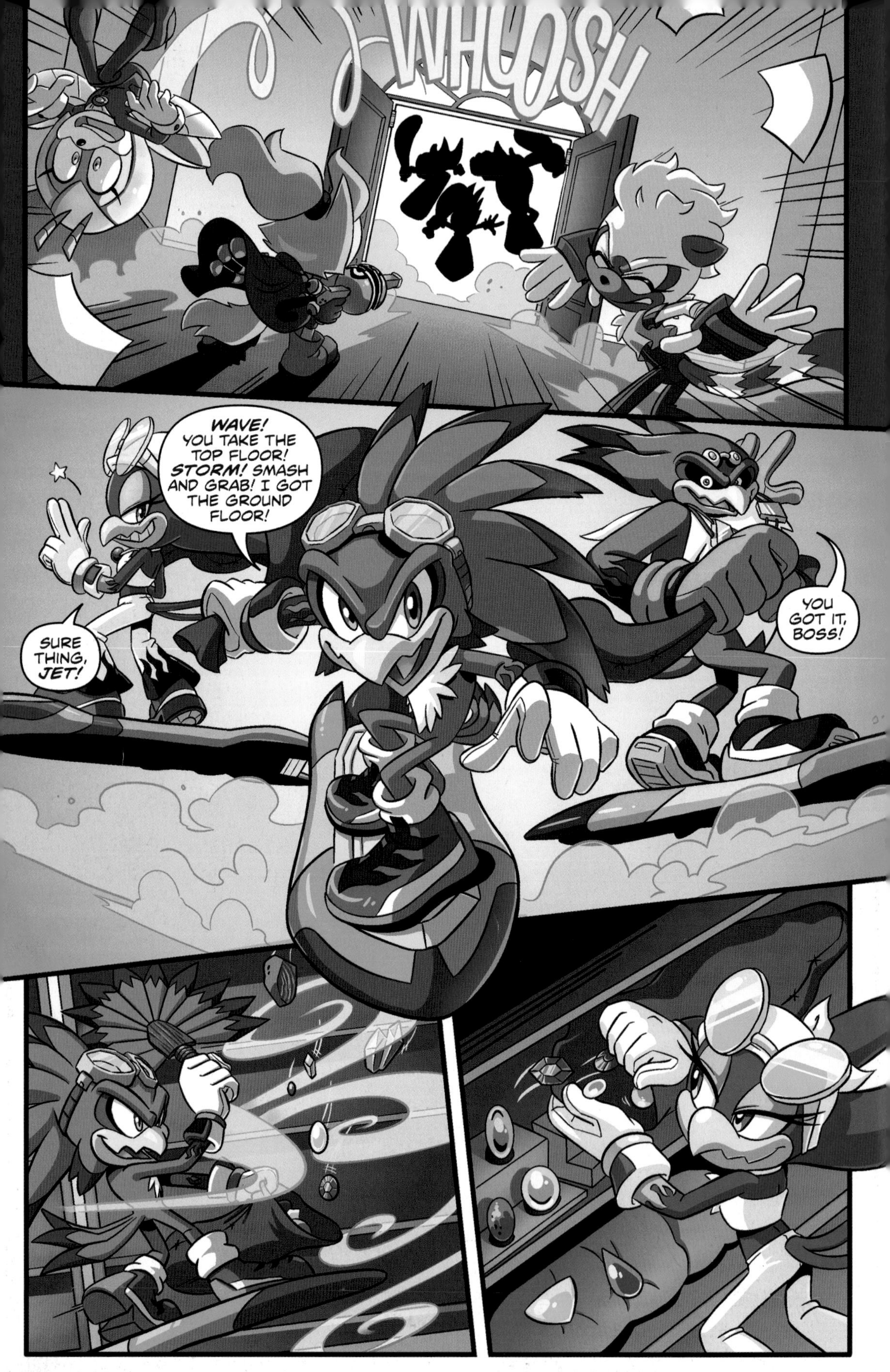
WHUOOSH
WAVE! YOU TAKE THE TOP FLOOR! STORM! SMASH AND GRAB! I GOT THE GROUND FLOOR!
SURE THING, JET!
YOU GOT IT, BOSS!

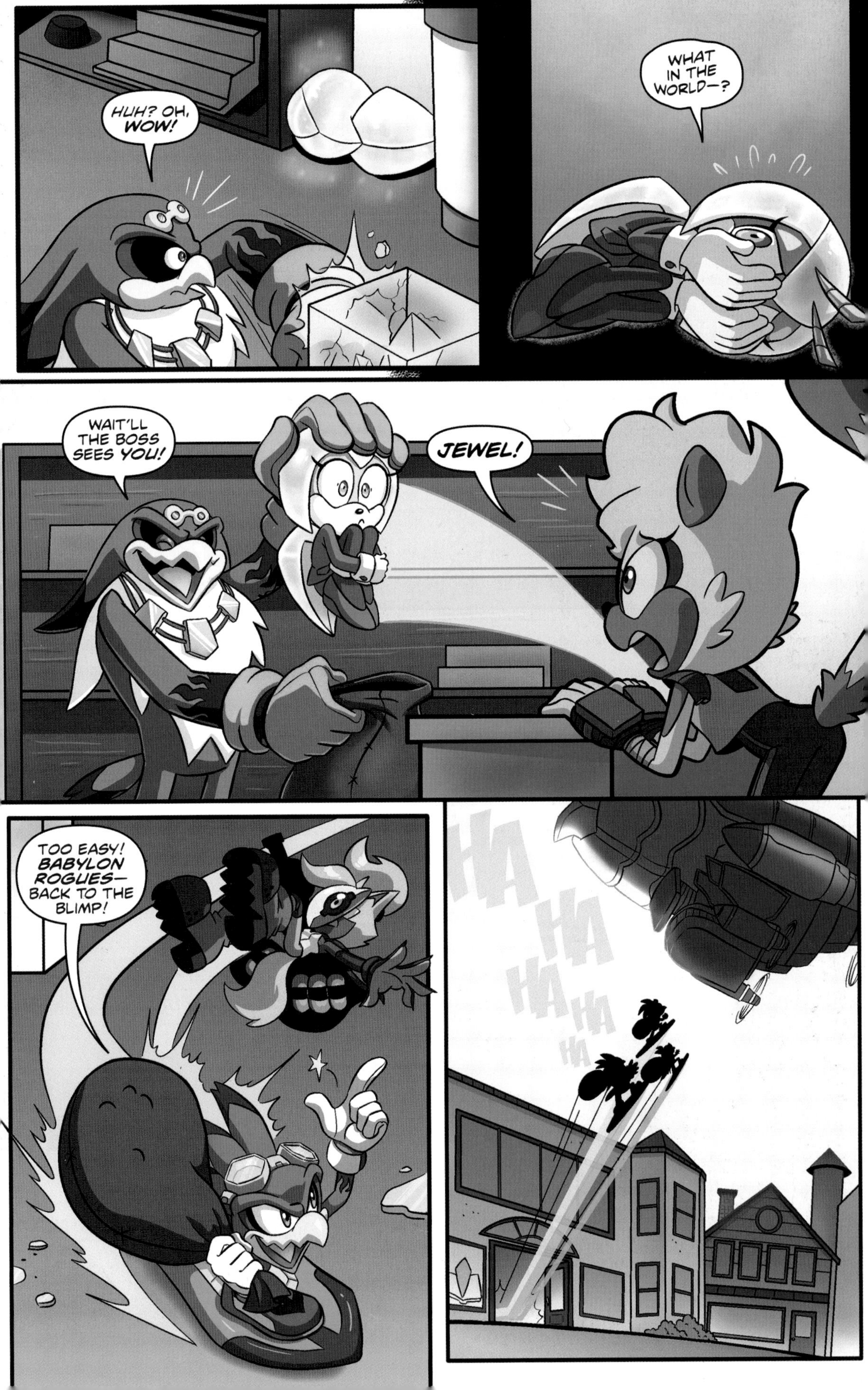
HUH? OH, WOW!
WHAT IN THE WORLD—?
WAIT'LL THE BOSS SEES YOU!
JEWEL!
TOO EASY! BABYLON ROGUES— BACK TO THE BLIMP!
HA HA HA HA HA

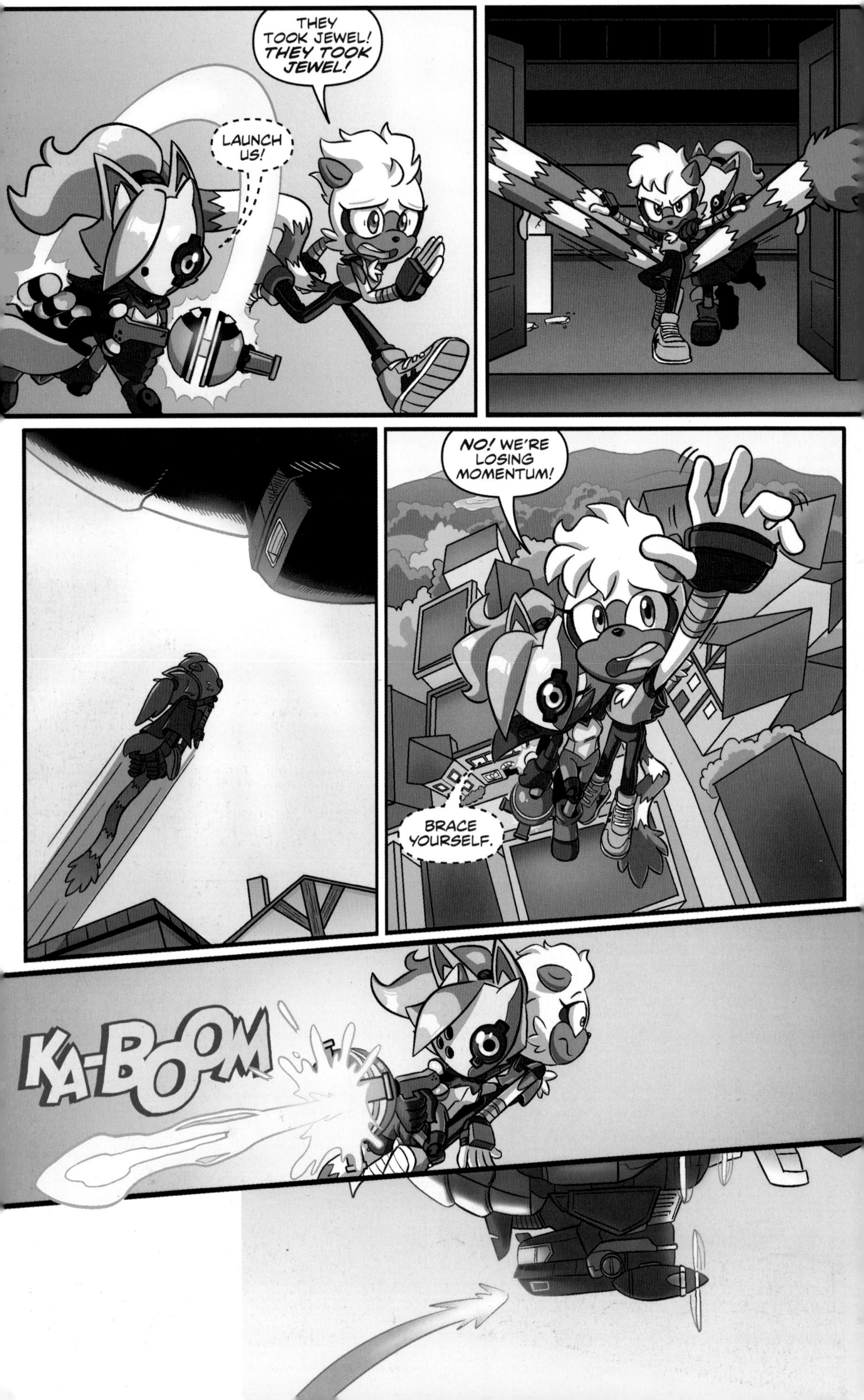
THEY TOOK JEWEL! THEY TOOK JEWEL!
LAUNCH US!
NO! WE'RE LOSING MOMENTUM!
BRACE YOURSELF.
KA-BOOM

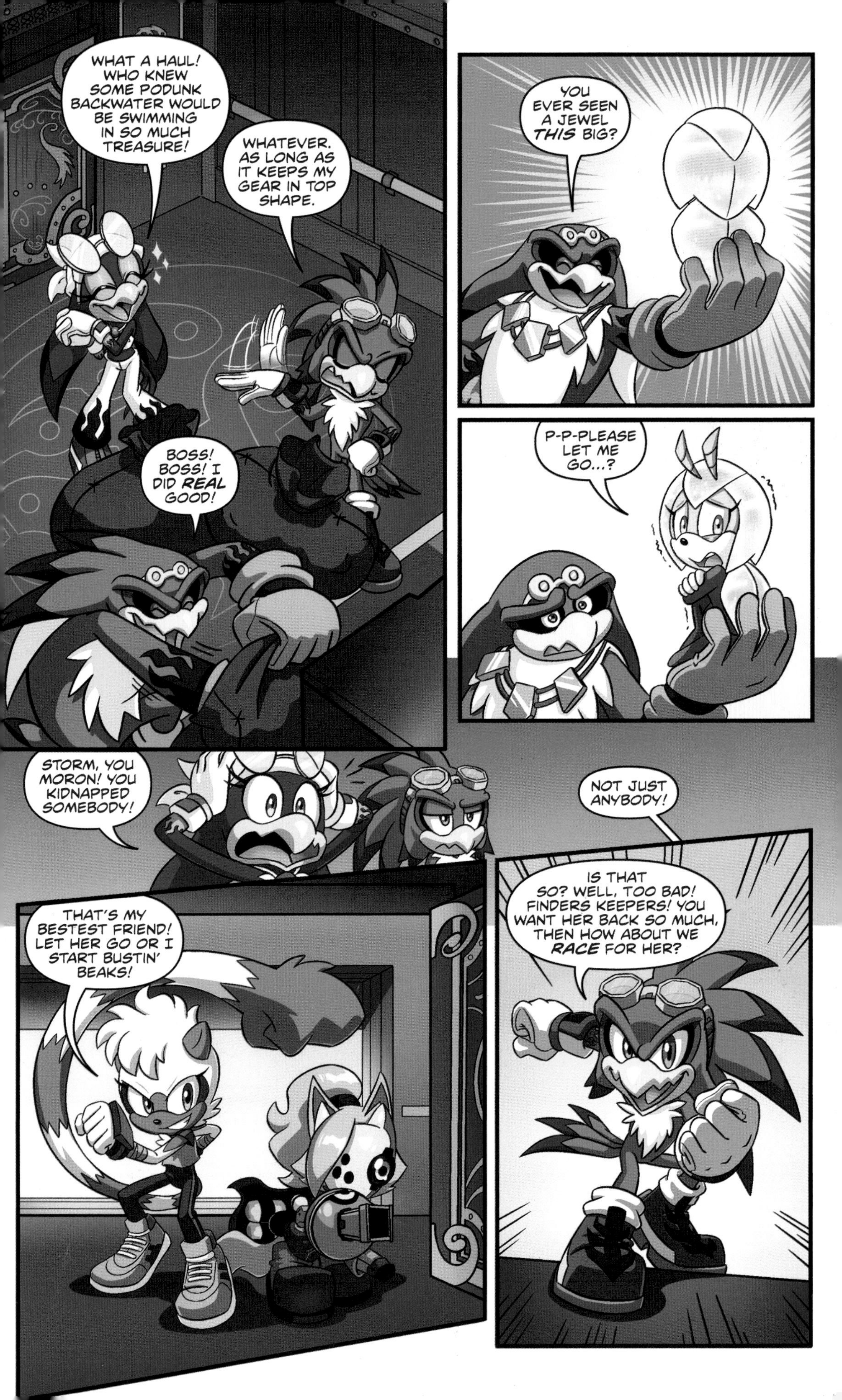
WHAT A HAUL! WHO KNEW SOME PODUNK BACKWATER WOULD BE SWIMMING IN SO MUCH TREASURE!
WHATEVER. AS LONG AS IT KEEPS MY GEAR IN TOP SHAPE.
BOSS! BOSS! I DID REAL GOOD!
YOU EVER SEEN A JEWEL THIS BIG?
P-P-PLEASE LET ME GO...?
STORM, YOU MORON! YOU KIDNAPPED SOMEBODY!
NOT JUST ANYBODY!
THAT'S MY BESTEST FRIEND! LET HER GO OR I START BUSTIN' BEAKS!
IS THAT SO? WELL, TOO BAD! FINDERS KEEPERS! YOU WANT HER BACK SO MUCH, THEN HOW ABOUT WE RACE FOR HER?

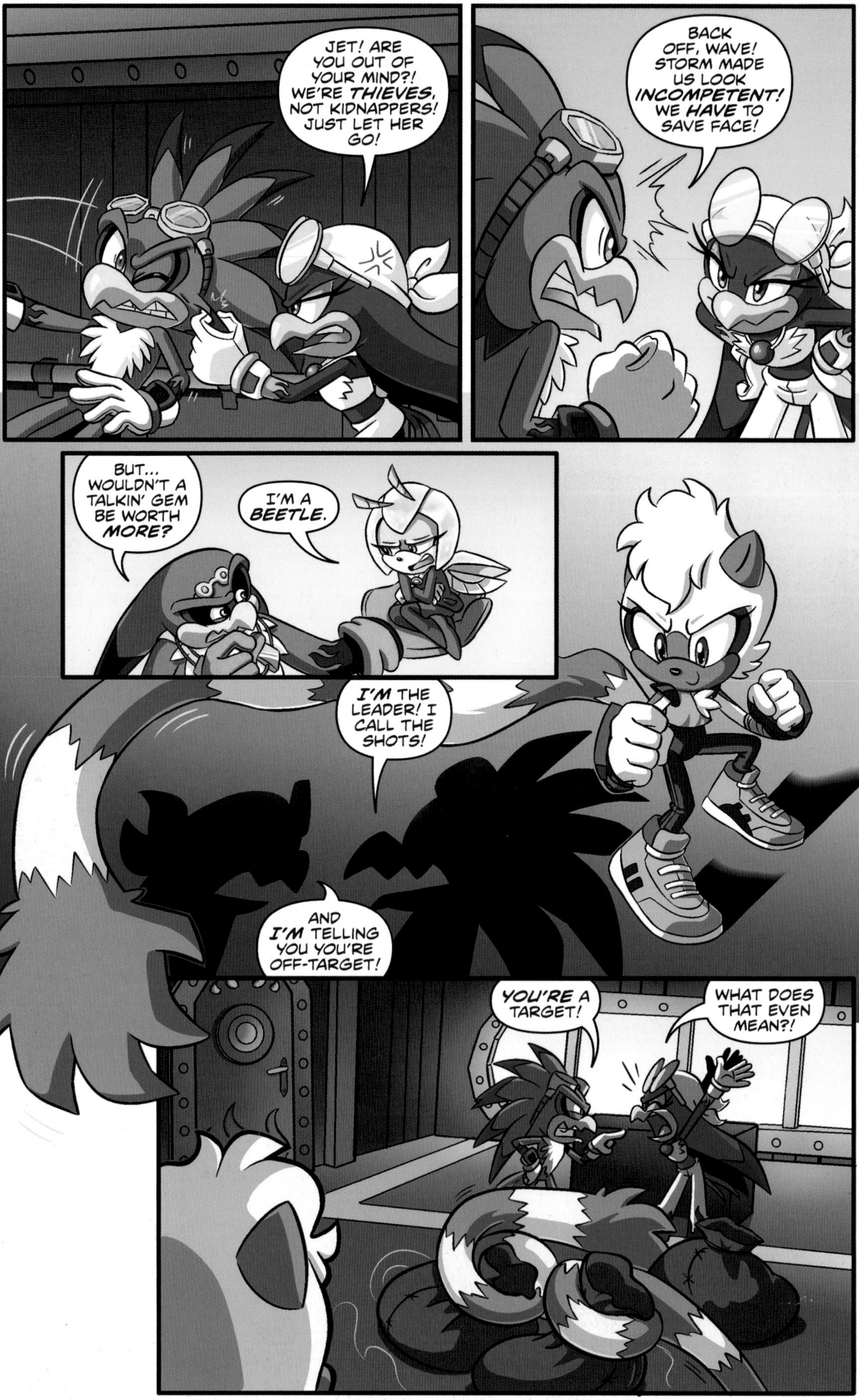

JET! ARE YOU OUT OF YOUR MIND?! WE'RE *THIEVES*, NOT KIDNAPPERS! JUST LET HER GO!
BACK OFF, WAVE! STORM MADE US LOOK *INCOMPETENT!* WE *HAVE* TO SAVE FACE!
BUT... WOULDN'T A TALKIN' GEM BE WORTH *MORE?*
I'M A *BEETLE*.
I'M THE LEADER! I CALL THE SHOTS!
AND *I'M* TELLING YOU YOU'RE OFF-TARGET!
YOU'RE A TARGET!
WHAT DOES THAT EVEN MEAN?!

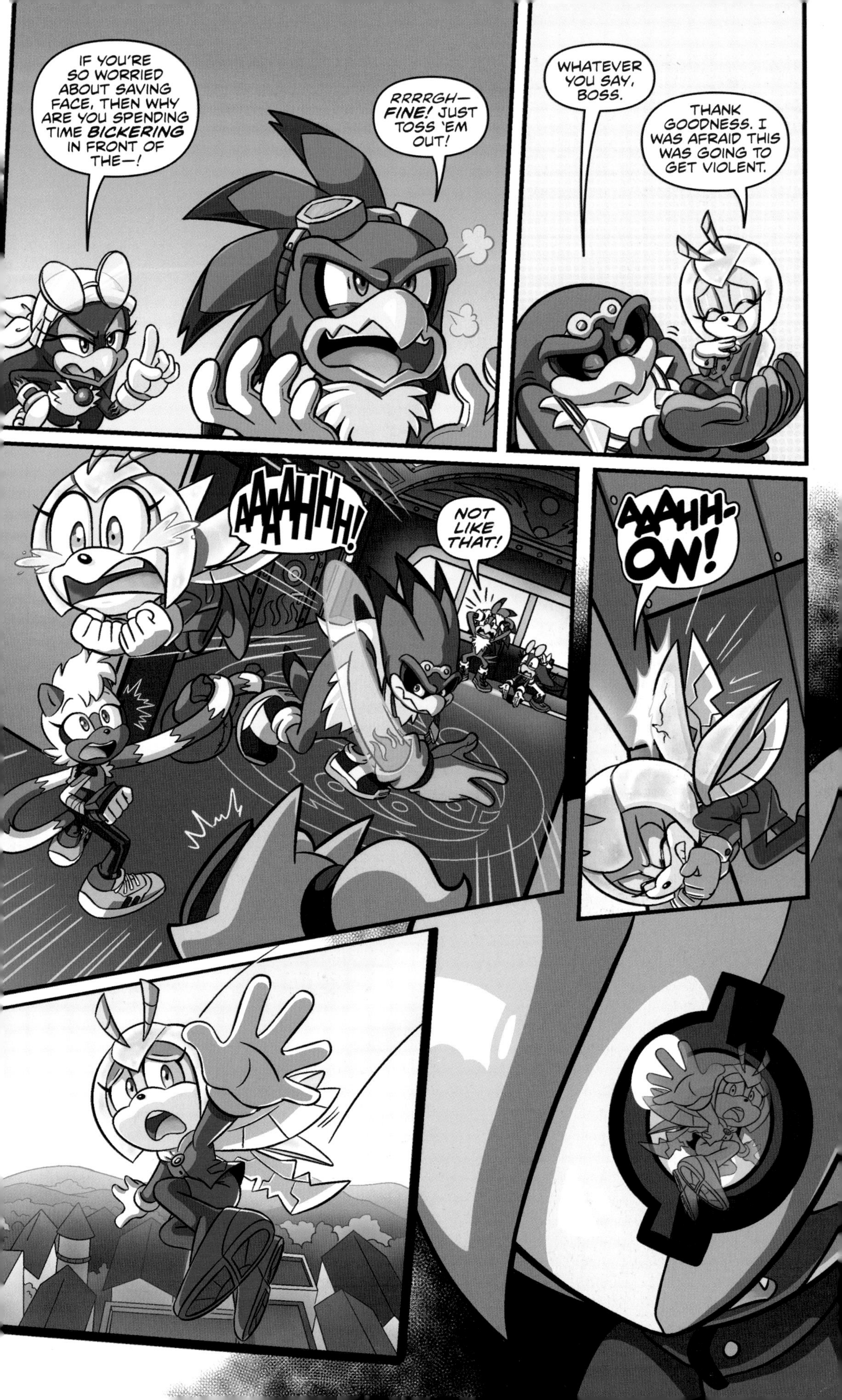
IF YOU'RE SO WORRIED ABOUT SAVING FACE, THEN WHY ARE YOU SPENDING TIME BICKERING IN FRONT OF THE—!
RRRRGH— FINE! JUST TOSS 'EM OUT!
WHATEVER YOU SAY, BOSS.
THANK GOODNESS. I WAS AFRAID THIS WAS GOING TO GET VIOLENT.
AAAAHHHH!
NOT LIKE THAT!
AAAHH-OW!

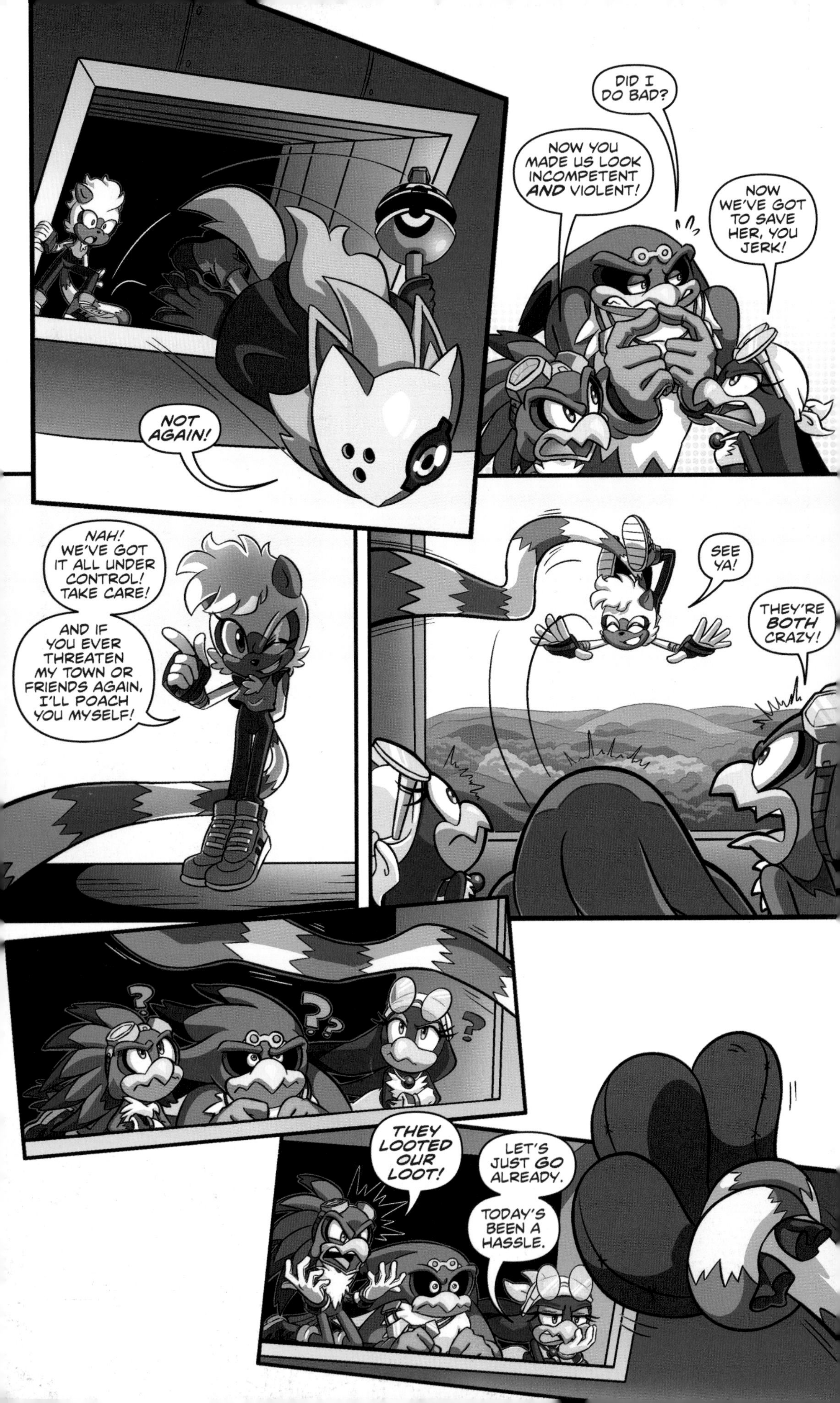
NOT AGAIN!
DID I DO BAD?
NOW YOU MADE US LOOK INCOMPETENT **AND** VIOLENT!
NOW WE'VE GOT TO SAVE HER, YOU JERK!
NAH! WE'VE GOT IT ALL UNDER CONTROL! TAKE CARE!
AND IF YOU EVER THREATEN MY TOWN OR FRIENDS AGAIN, I'LL POACH YOU MYSELF!
SEE YA!
THEY'RE ***BOTH*** CRAZY!
?
??
?
THEY LOOTED OUR LOOT!
LET'S JUST ***GO*** ALREADY.
TODAY'S BEEN A HASSLE.

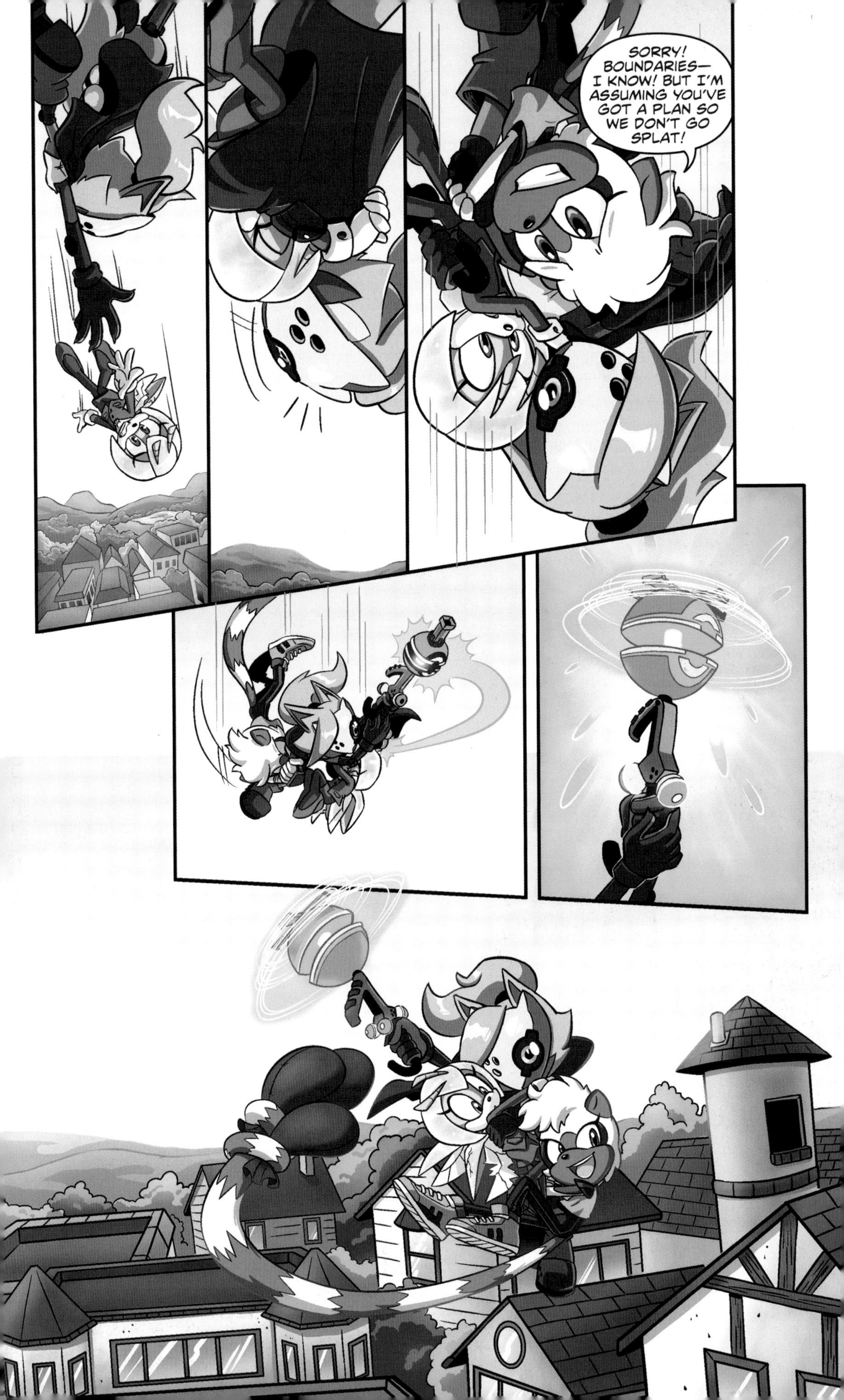
SORRY! BOUNDARIES— I KNOW! BUT I'M ASSUMING YOU'VE GOT A PLAN SO WE DON'T GO SPLAT!

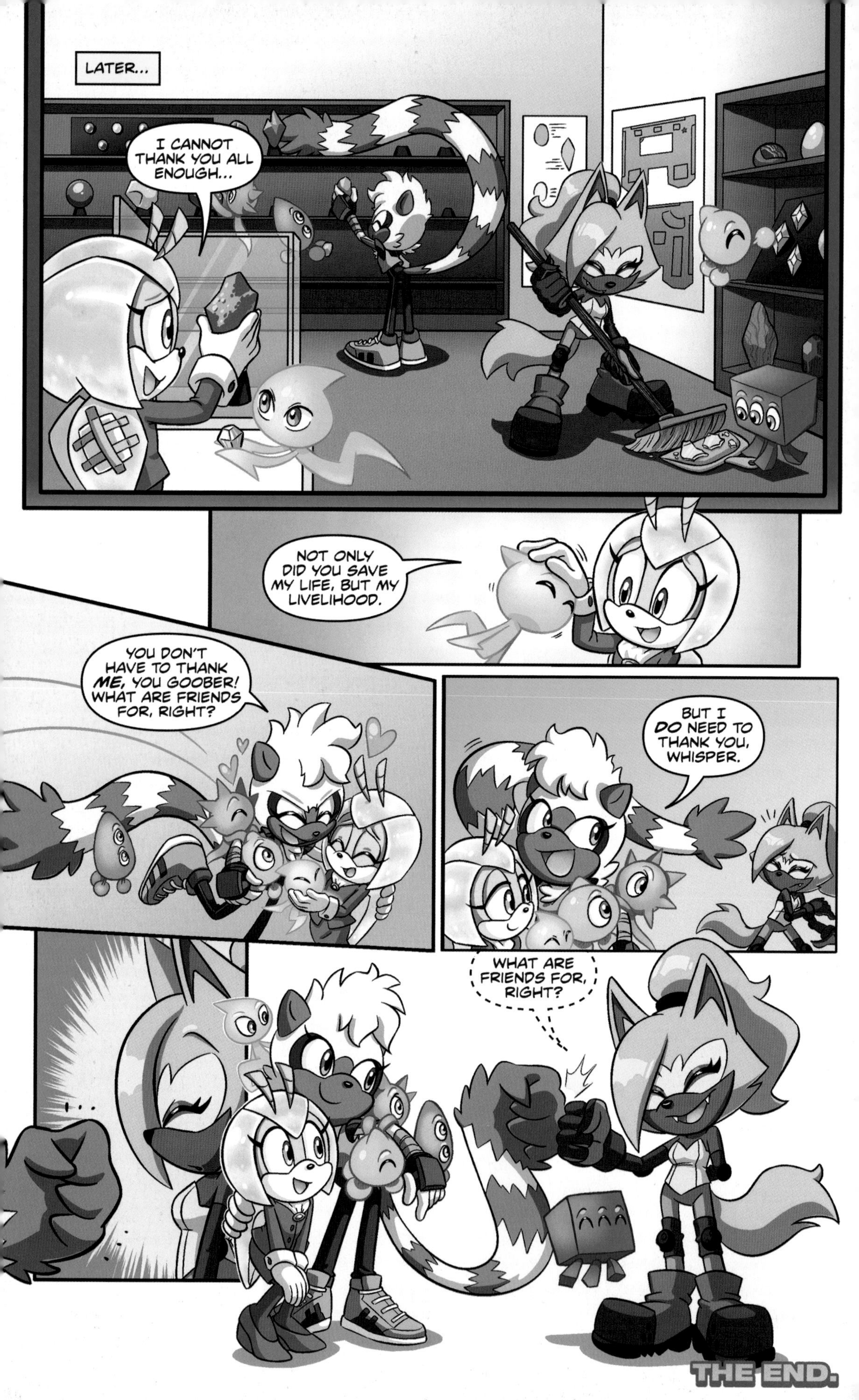
LATER...
I CANNOT THANK YOU ALL ENOUGH...
NOT ONLY DID YOU SAVE MY LIFE, BUT MY LIVELIHOOD.
YOU DON'T HAVE TO THANK *ME*, YOU GOOBER! WHAT ARE FRIENDS FOR, RIGHT?
BUT I *DO* NEED TO THANK YOU, WHISPER.
...
WHAT ARE FRIENDS FOR, RIGHT?
THE END.

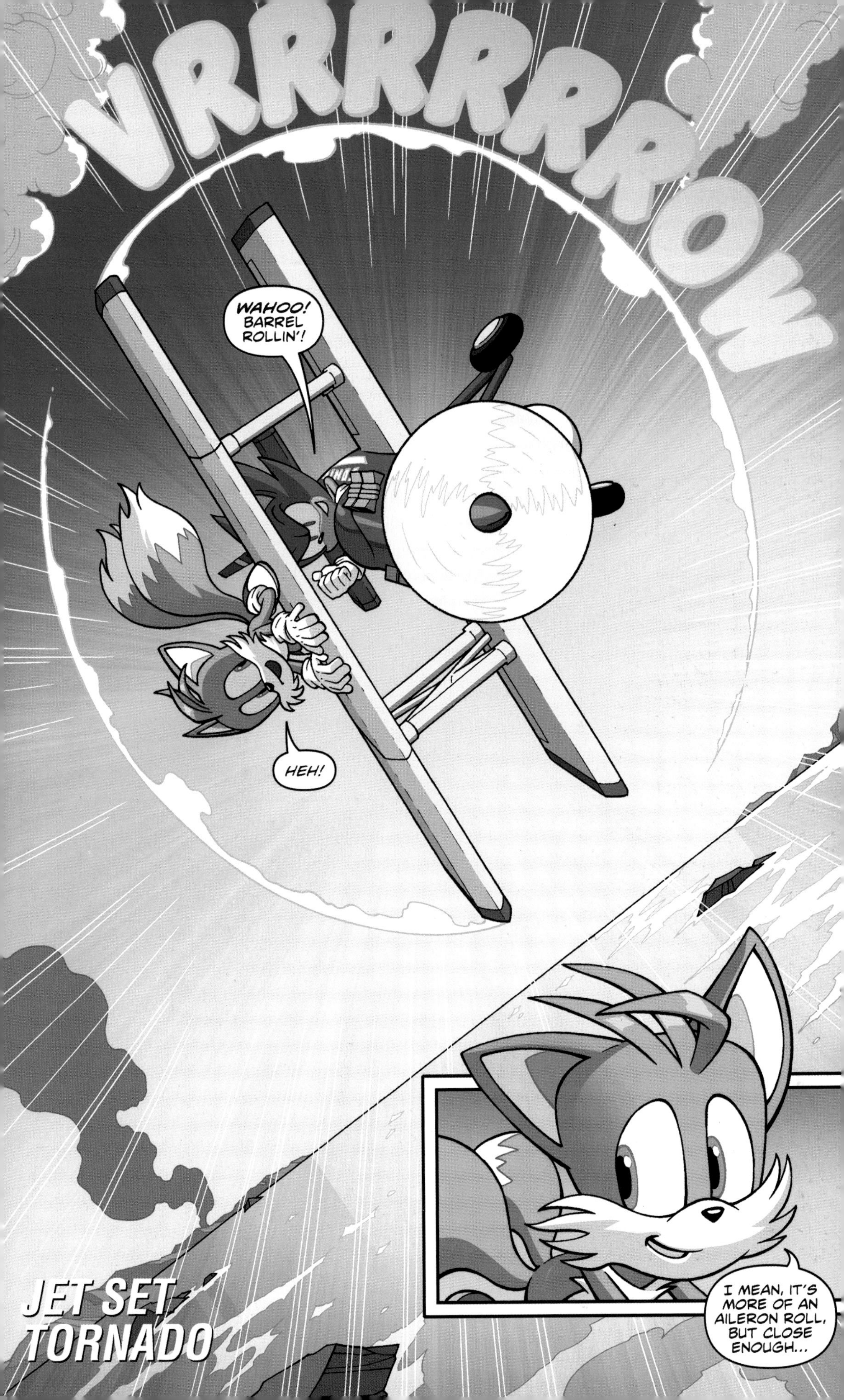
VRRRRRROW
WAHOO! BARREL ROLLIN'!
HEH!
I MEAN, IT'S MORE OF AN AILERON ROLL, BUT CLOSE ENOUGH...
JET SET TORNADO

THANKS FOR TAKING ME UP IN THE TORNADO, TAILS!

IT'S BEEN *WAY* TOO LONG SINCE I'VE SAT IN THE COCKPIT!

WELL, WE HAVEN'T HAD A LOT OF PEACETIME IN THE SKIES LATELY.

I WANT TO GET READY FOR WHATEVER WE MIGHT FACE NEXT, AND THAT MEANS NEW TECH.

PLUS, WHO BETTER TO HELP TEST MY NEW JET BOOSTER PROTOTYPE FOR SPEED?

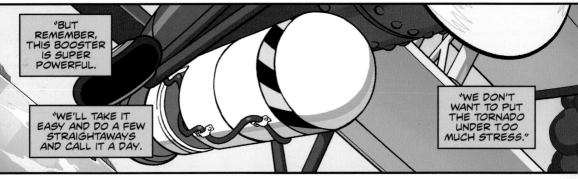

"BUT REMEMBER, THIS BOOSTER IS SUPER POWERFUL.

"WE'LL TAKE IT EASY AND DO A FEW STRAIGHTAWAYS AND CALL IT A DAY.

"WE DON'T WANT TO PUT THE TORNADO UNDER TOO MUCH STRESS."

STRESS? ME? I DON'T KNOW THE MEANING OF THE WOR—

GAH!

VWOOSH

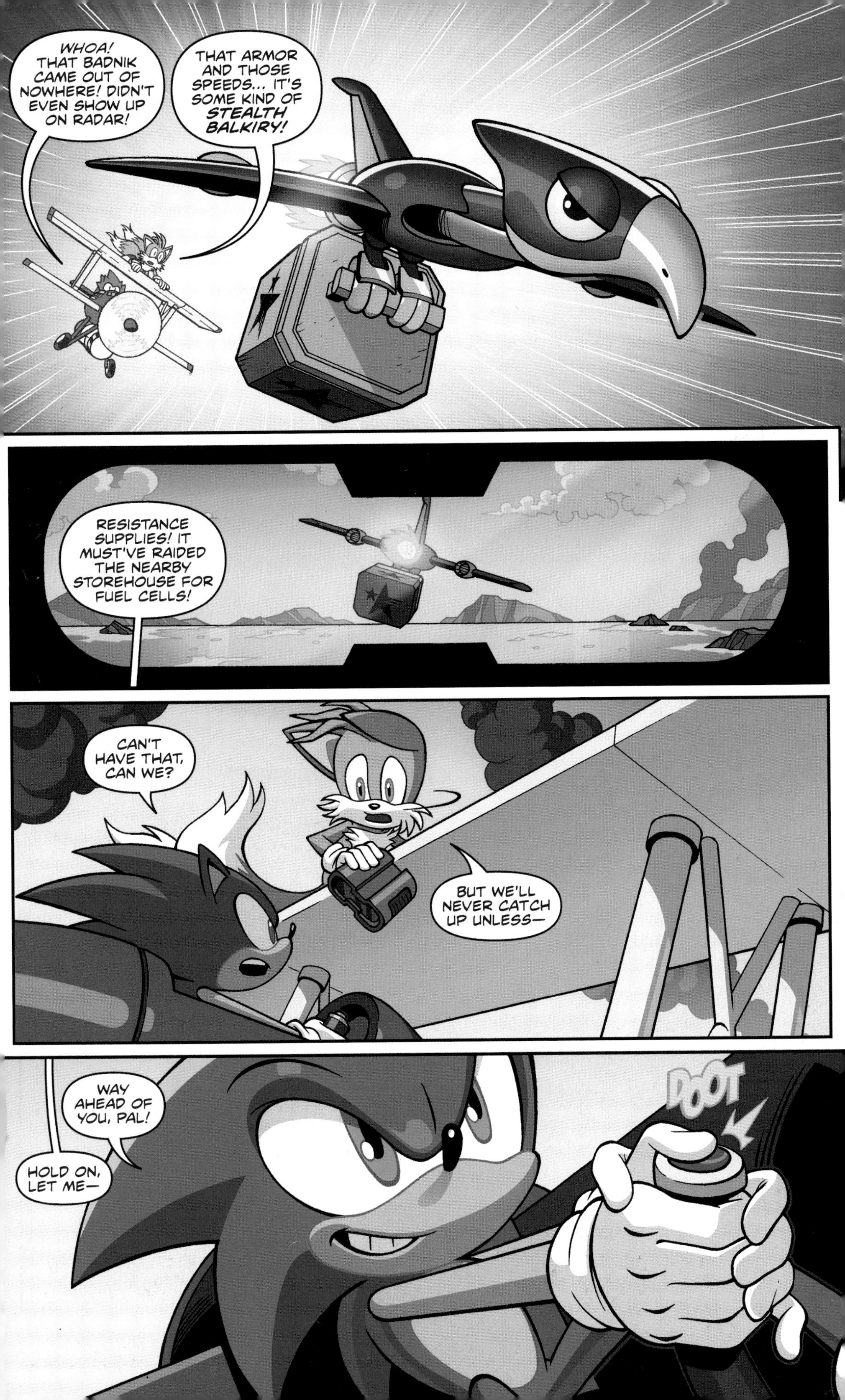
WHOA! THAT BADNIK CAME OUT OF NOWHERE! DIDN'T EVEN SHOW UP ON RADAR!
THAT ARMOR AND THOSE SPEEDS... IT'S SOME KIND OF STEALTH BALKIRY!
RESISTANCE SUPPLIES! IT MUST'VE RAIDED THE NEARBY STOREHOUSE FOR FUEL CELLS!
CAN'T HAVE THAT, CAN WE?
BUT WE'LL NEVER CATCH UP UNLESS—
HOLD ON, LET ME—
WAY AHEAD OF YOU, PAL!
DOOT

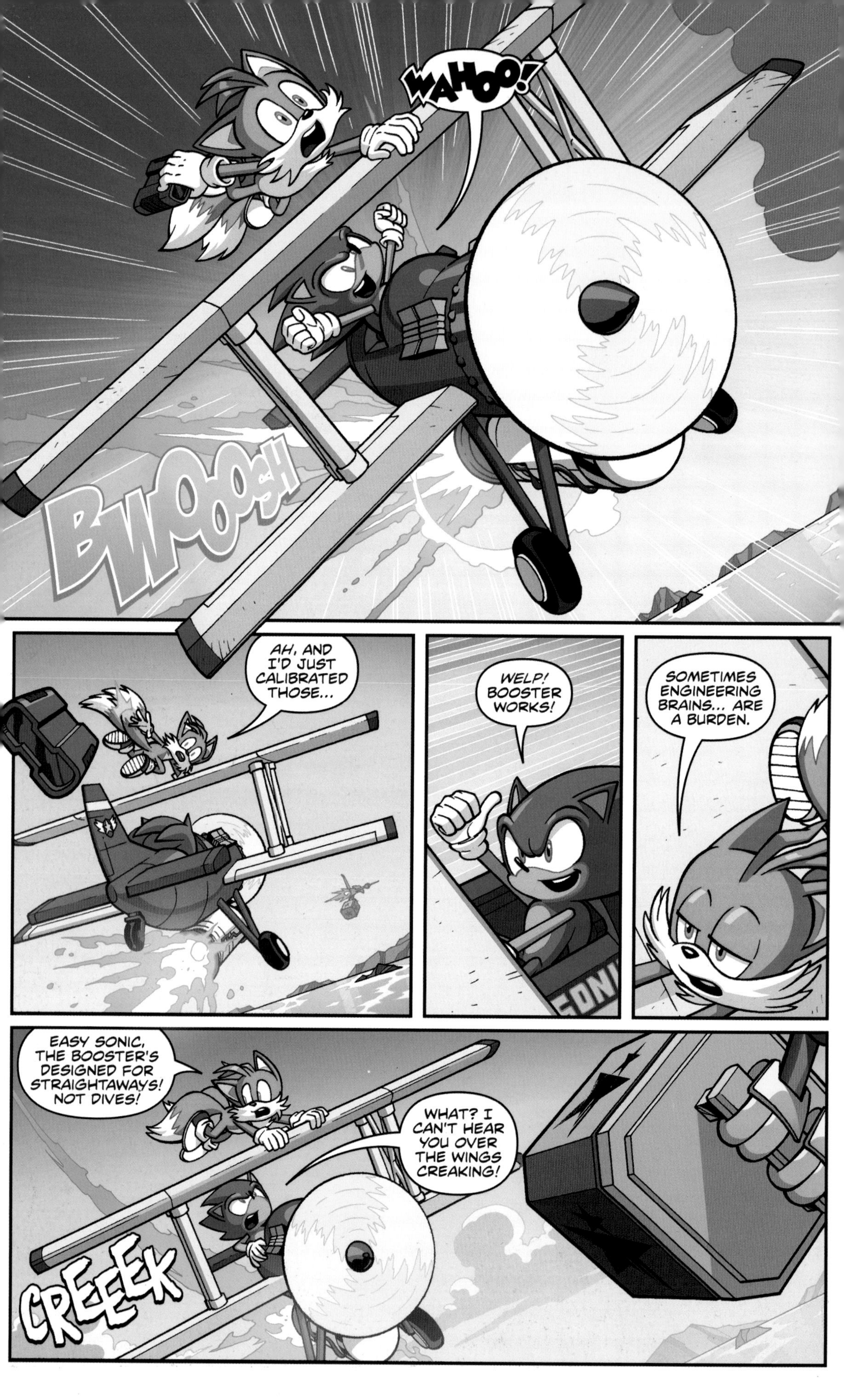
WAHOO!
BWOOOSH
AH, AND I'D JUST CALIBRATED THOSE...
WELP! BOOSTER WORKS!
SOMETIMES ENGINEERING BRAINS... ARE A BURDEN.
EASY SONIC, THE BOOSTER'S DESIGNED FOR STRAIGHTAWAYS! NOT DIVES!
WHAT? I CAN'T HEAR YOU OVER THE WINGS CREAKING!
CREEEEK

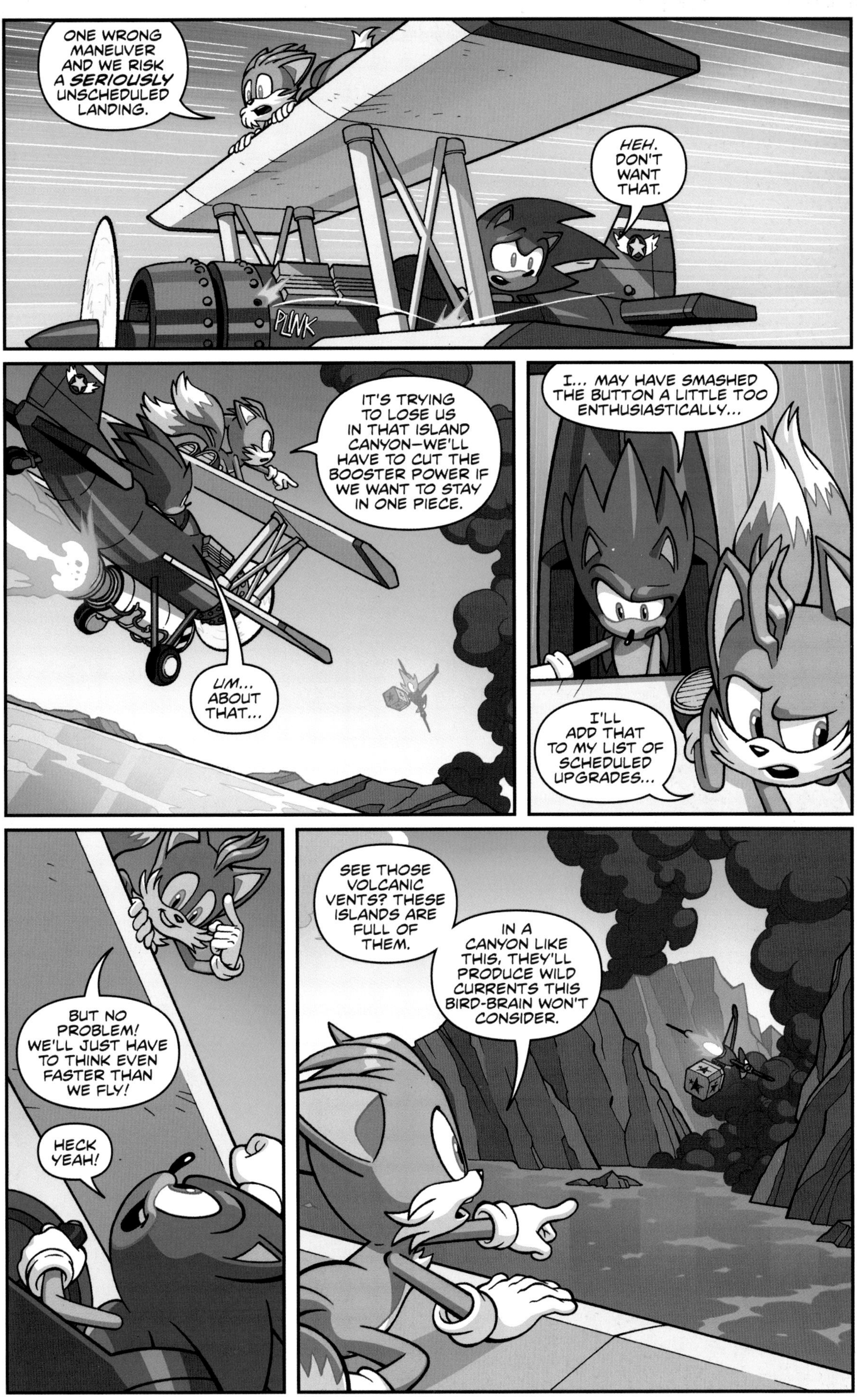
ONE WRONG MANEUVER AND WE RISK A *SERIOUSLY* UNSCHEDULED LANDING.
HEH. DON'T WANT THAT.
PLINK
IT'S TRYING TO LOSE US IN THAT ISLAND CANYON—WE'LL HAVE TO CUT THE BOOSTER POWER IF WE WANT TO STAY IN ONE PIECE.
UM... ABOUT THAT...
I... MAY HAVE SMASHED THE BUTTON A LITTLE TOO ENTHUSIASTICALLY...
I'LL ADD THAT TO MY LIST OF SCHEDULED UPGRADES...
BUT NO PROBLEM! WE'LL JUST HAVE TO THINK EVEN FASTER THAN WE FLY!
HECK YEAH!
SEE THOSE VOLCANIC VENTS? THESE ISLANDS ARE FULL OF THEM.
IN A CANYON LIKE THIS, THEY'LL PRODUCE WILD CURRENTS THIS BIRD-BRAIN WON'T CONSIDER.

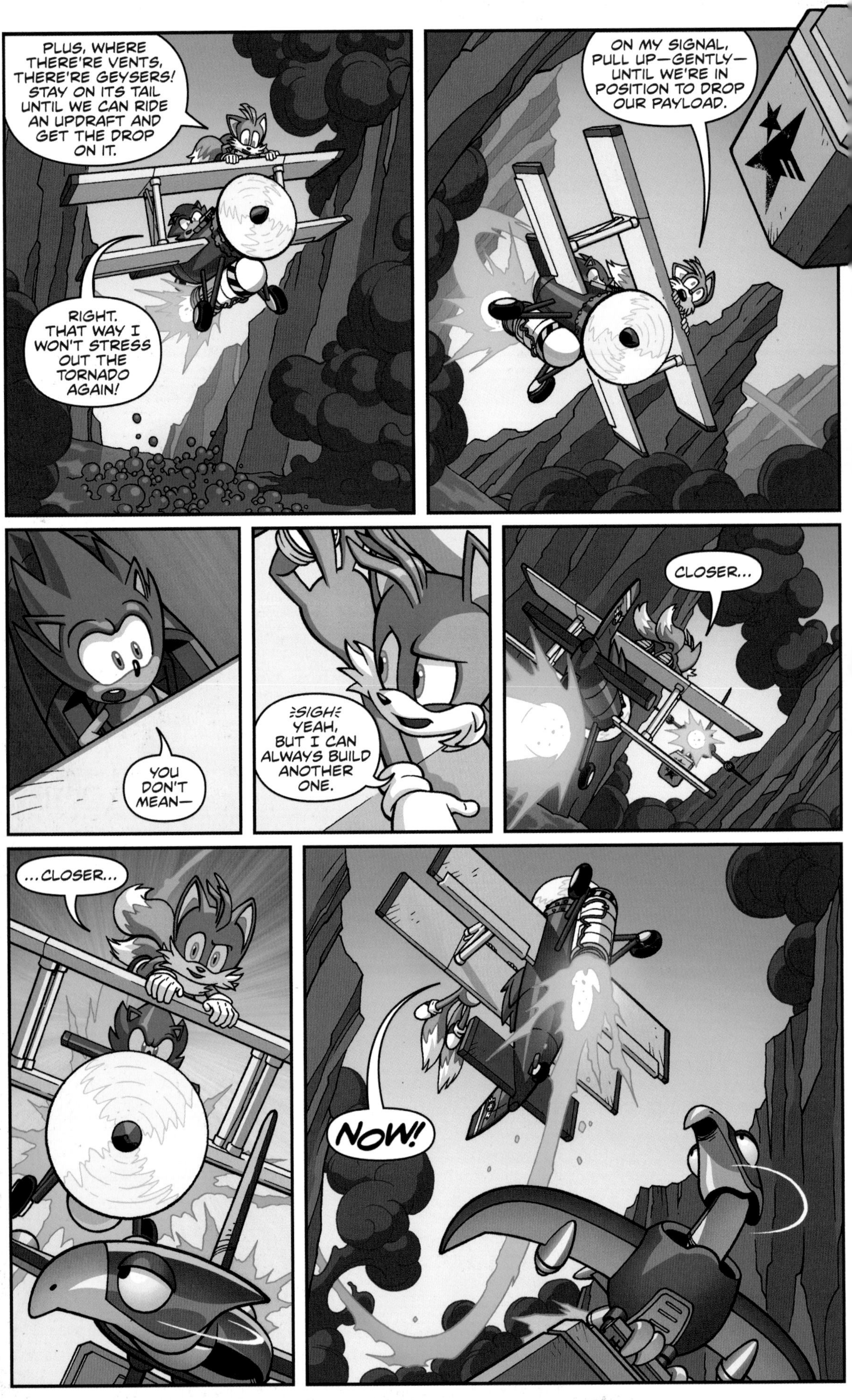
PLUS, WHERE THERE'RE VENTS, THERE'RE GEYSERS! STAY ON ITS TAIL UNTIL WE CAN RIDE AN UPDRAFT AND GET THE DROP ON IT.
RIGHT. THAT WAY I WON'T STRESS OUT THE TORNADO AGAIN!
ON MY SIGNAL, PULL UP—GENTLY—UNTIL WE'RE IN POSITION TO DROP OUR PAYLOAD.
YOU DON'T MEAN—
SIGH YEAH, BUT I CAN ALWAYS BUILD ANOTHER ONE.
CLOSER...
...CLOSER...
NOW!

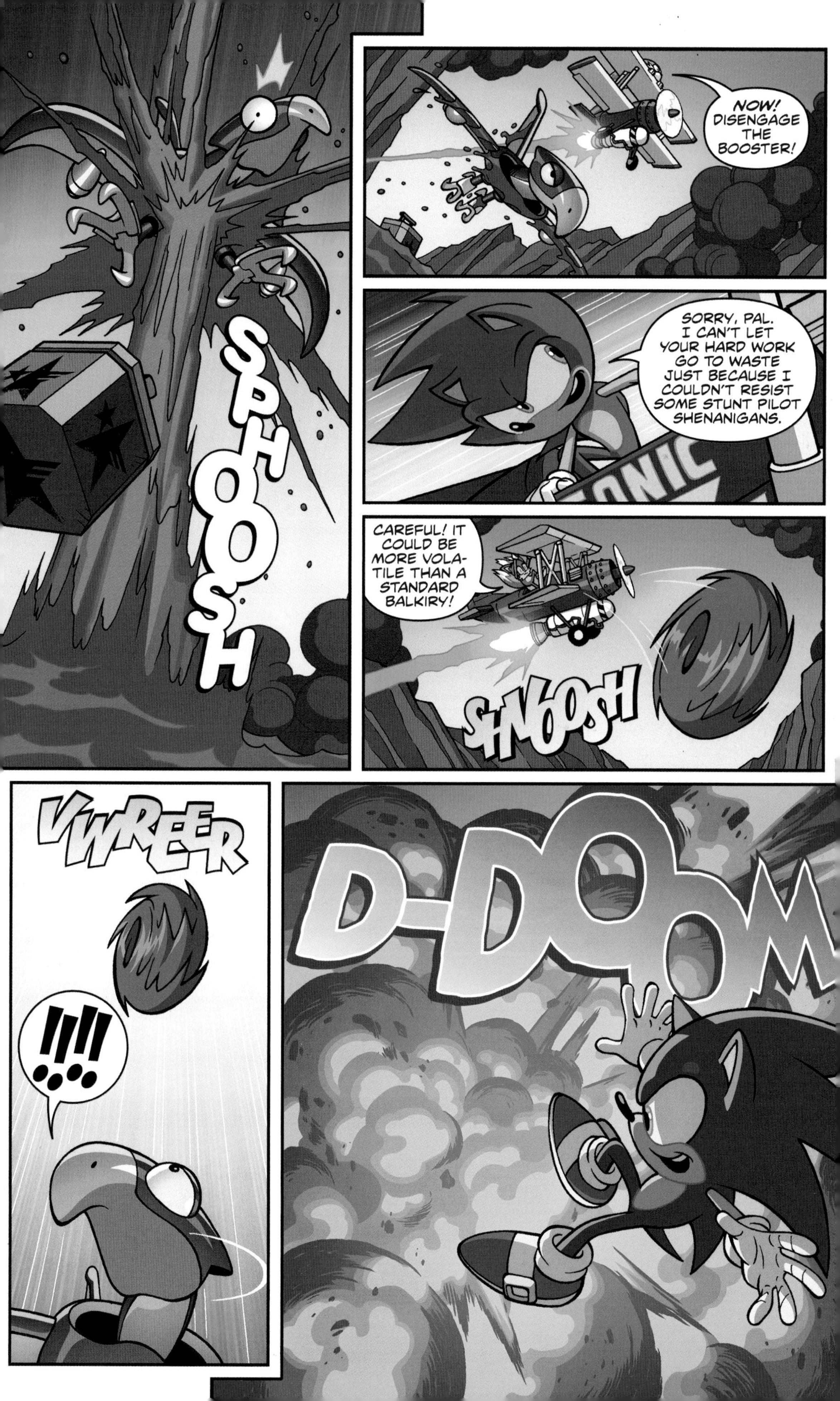
SPHOOSH
NOW! DISENGAGE THE BOOSTER!
SONIC
SORRY, PAL. I CAN'T LET YOUR HARD WORK GO TO WASTE JUST BECAUSE I COULDN'T RESIST SOME STUNT PILOT SHENANIGANS.
CAREFUL! IT COULD BE MORE VOLA-TILE THAN A STANDARD BALKIRY!
SHOOSH
VWREER
!!!!
D-DOOOM

I'VE GOT YOU!

≋COUGH≋ THANKS, BUD. IT **WAS** MORE VOLATILE. HOW'S THE BOOSTER?

WELL, WE'LL HAVE TO KEEP FLYING UNTIL IT RUNS OUT OF FUEL, BUT THIS TEST PROVED IT'S CAPABLE.

ALL THAT'S LEFT TO DO IS RADIO THE RESISTANCE TO RECOVER THE CRATE AND STICK OUR LANDING.

YOU WANT BACK AT THE CONTROLS? YOU SEEM TO HAVE LEARNED YOUR PILOTING LESSON.

I WOULD, IT'S JUST...

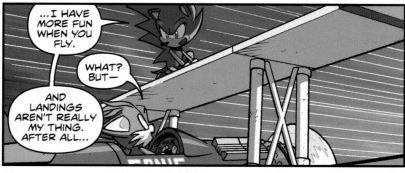

...I HAVE MORE FUN WHEN YOU FLY.

WHAT? BUT—

AND LANDINGS AREN'T REALLY MY THING. AFTER ALL...

...YOU GOTTA GO SLOW.

THE END.

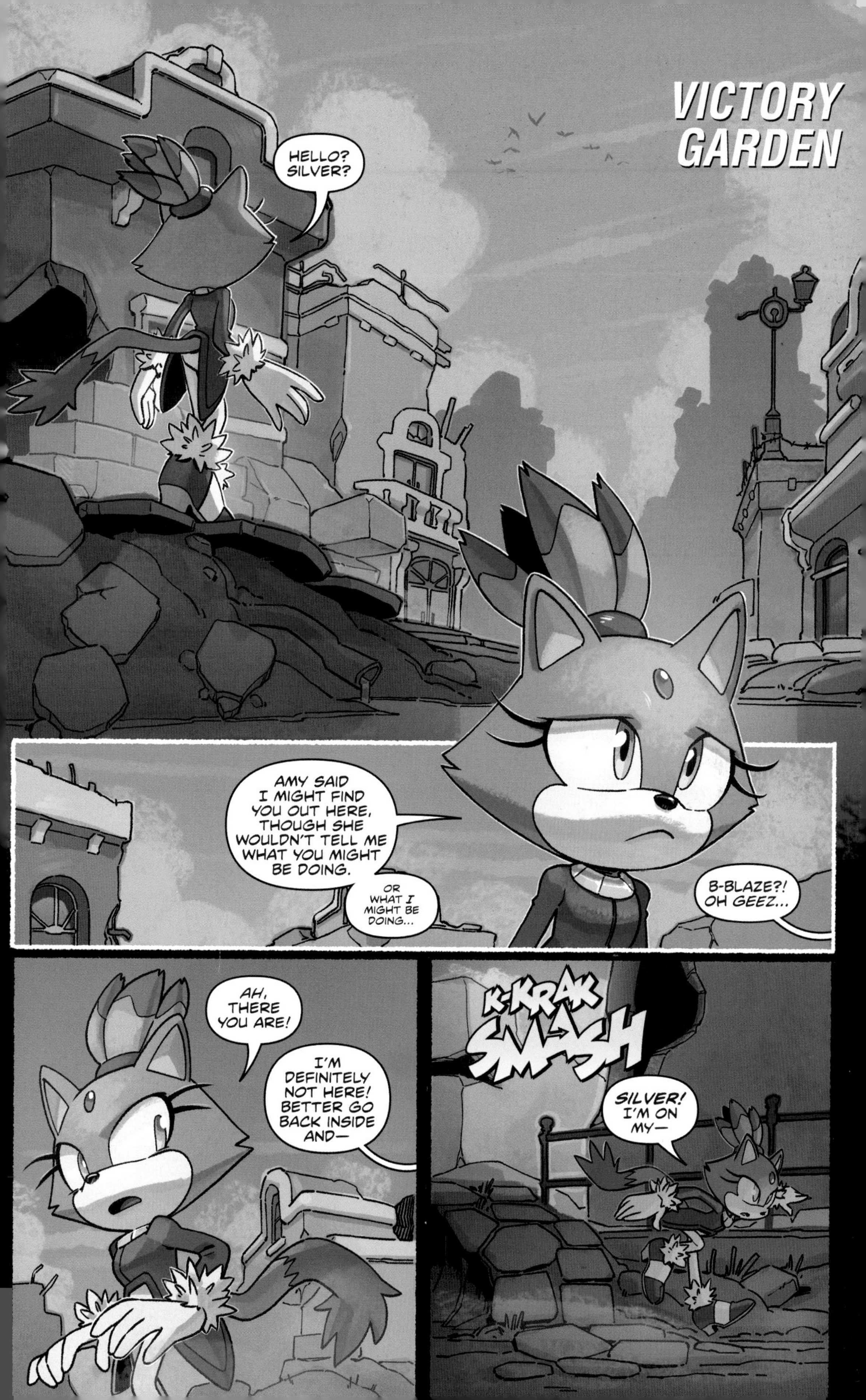
VICTORY GARDEN
HELLO? SILVER?
AMY SAID I MIGHT FIND YOU OUT HERE, THOUGH SHE WOULDN'T TELL ME WHAT YOU MIGHT BE DOING.
OR WHAT I MIGHT BE DOING...
B-BLAZE?! OH GEEZ...
AH, THERE YOU ARE!
I'M DEFINITELY NOT HERE! BETTER GO BACK INSIDE AND—
K-KRAK SMASH
SILVER! I'M ON MY—

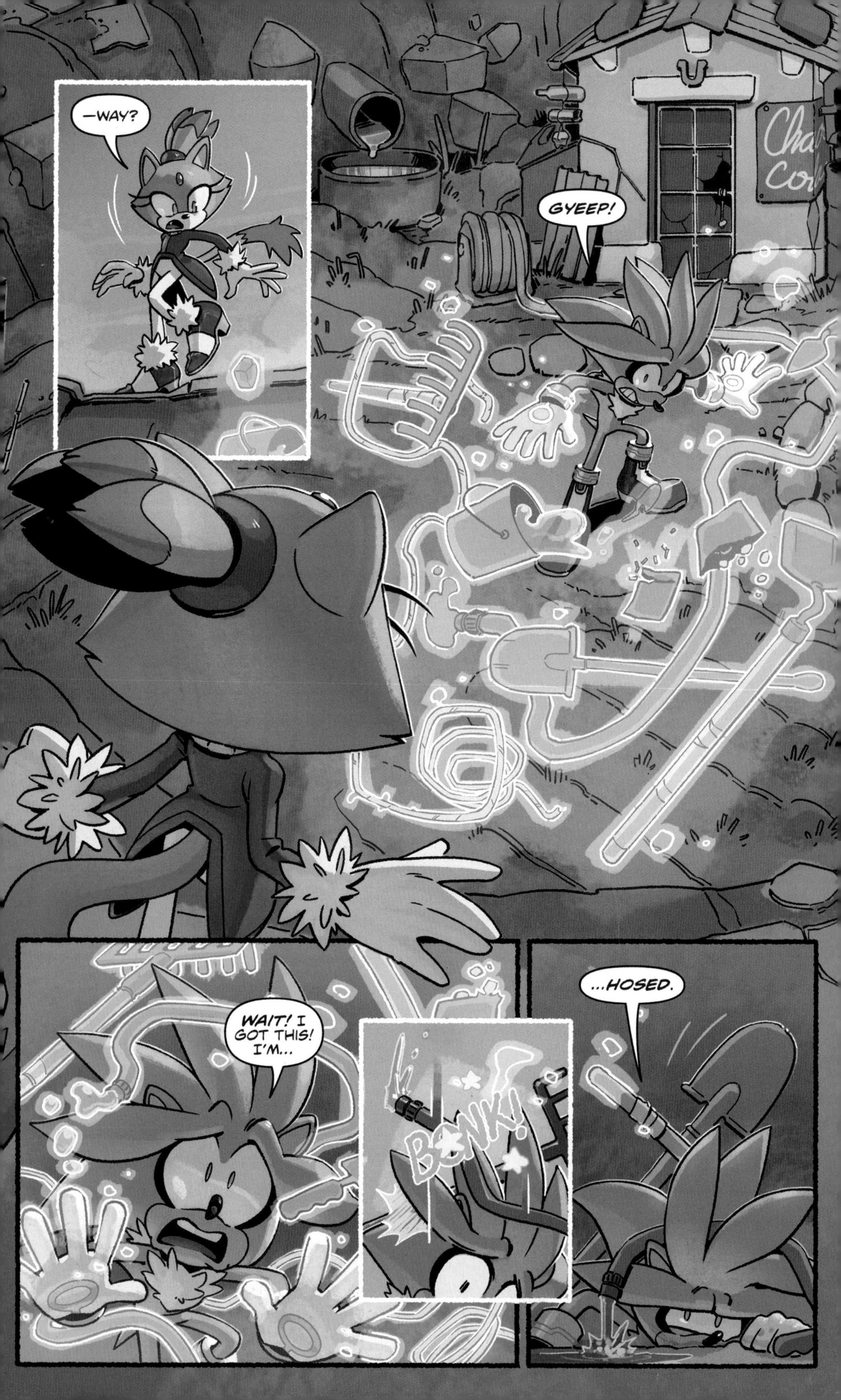
—WAY?
GYEEP!
WAIT! I GOT THIS! I'M...
BONK!
...HOSED.

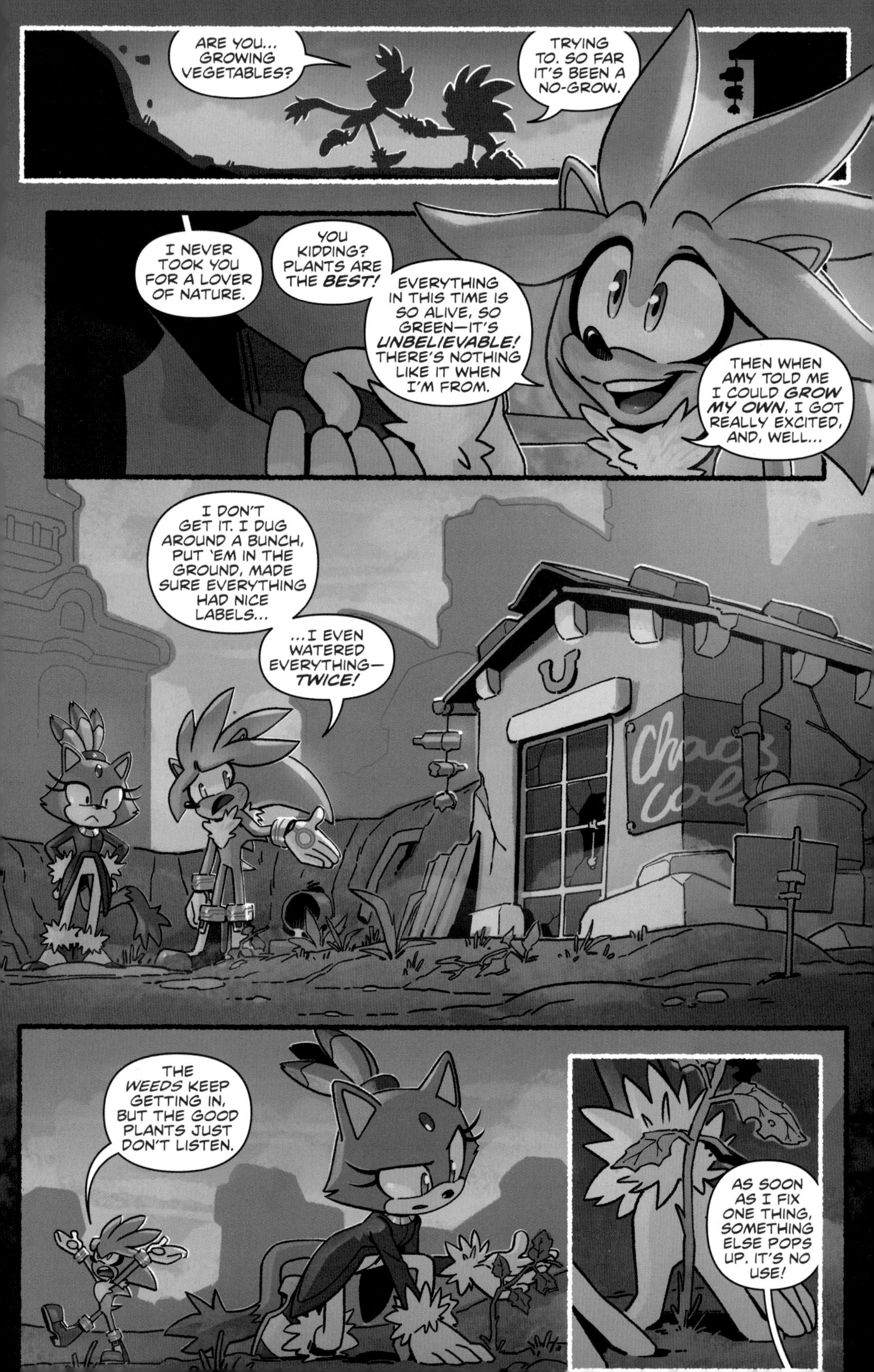
ARE YOU... GROWING VEGETABLES?
TRYING TO. SO FAR IT'S BEEN A NO-GROW.
I NEVER TOOK YOU FOR A LOVER OF NATURE.
YOU KIDDING? PLANTS ARE THE *BEST!*
EVERYTHING IN THIS TIME IS SO ALIVE, SO GREEN—IT'S *UNBELIEVABLE!* THERE'S NOTHING LIKE IT WHEN I'M FROM.
THEN WHEN AMY TOLD ME I COULD *GROW MY OWN*, I GOT REALLY EXCITED, AND, WELL...
I DON'T GET IT. I DUG AROUND A BUNCH, PUT 'EM IN THE GROUND, MADE SURE EVERYTHING HAD NICE LABELS...
...I EVEN WATERED EVERYTHING—*TWICE!*
THE *WEEDS* KEEP GETTING IN, BUT THE GOOD PLANTS JUST DON'T LISTEN.
AS SOON AS I FIX ONE THING, SOMETHING ELSE POPS UP. IT'S NO USE!

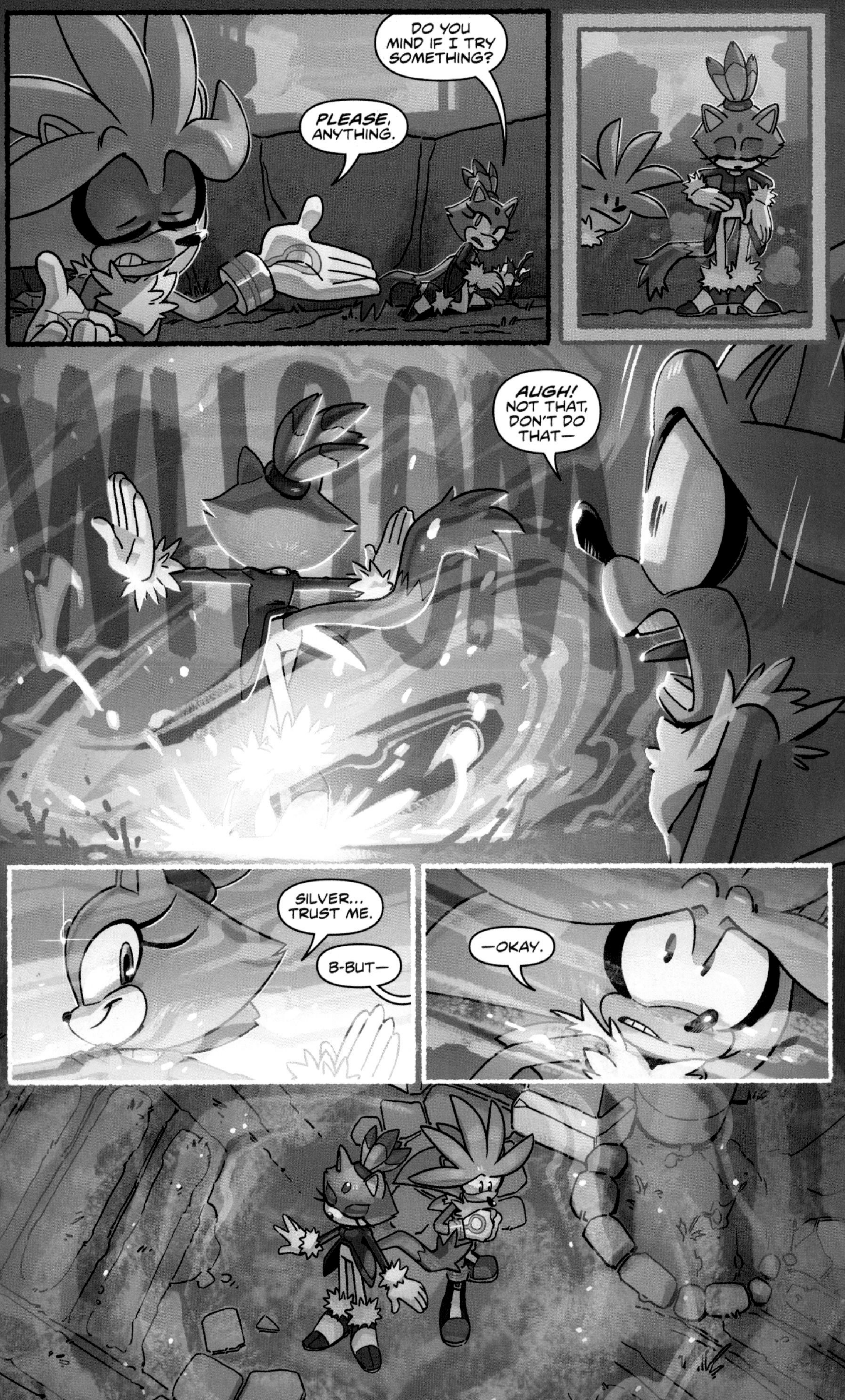
DO YOU MIND IF I TRY SOMETHING?
PLEASE, ANYTHING.
AUGH! NOT THAT, DON'T DO THAT—
SILVER... TRUST ME.
B-BUT—
—OKAY.

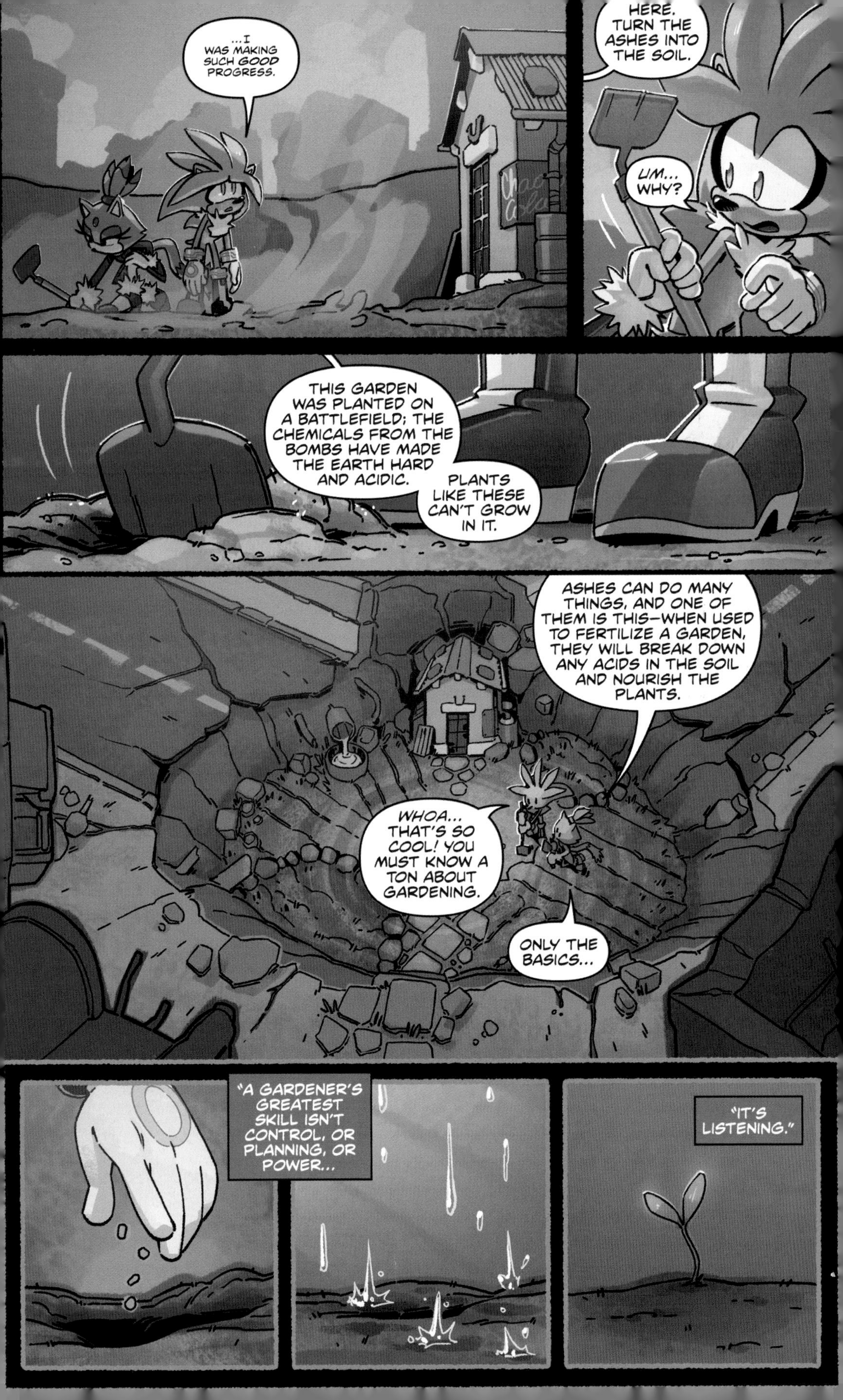
...I WAS MAKING SUCH GOOD PROGRESS.
HERE. TURN THE ASHES INTO THE SOIL.
UM... WHY?
THIS GARDEN WAS PLANTED ON A BATTLEFIELD; THE CHEMICALS FROM THE BOMBS HAVE MADE THE EARTH HARD AND ACIDIC.
PLANTS LIKE THESE CAN'T GROW IN IT.
ASHES CAN DO MANY THINGS, AND ONE OF THEM IS THIS—WHEN USED TO FERTILIZE A GARDEN, THEY WILL BREAK DOWN ANY ACIDS IN THE SOIL AND NOURISH THE PLANTS.
WHOA... THAT'S SO COOL! YOU MUST KNOW A TON ABOUT GARDENING.
ONLY THE BASICS...
"A GARDENER'S GREATEST SKILL ISN'T CONTROL, OR PLANNING, OR POWER...
"IT'S LISTENING."

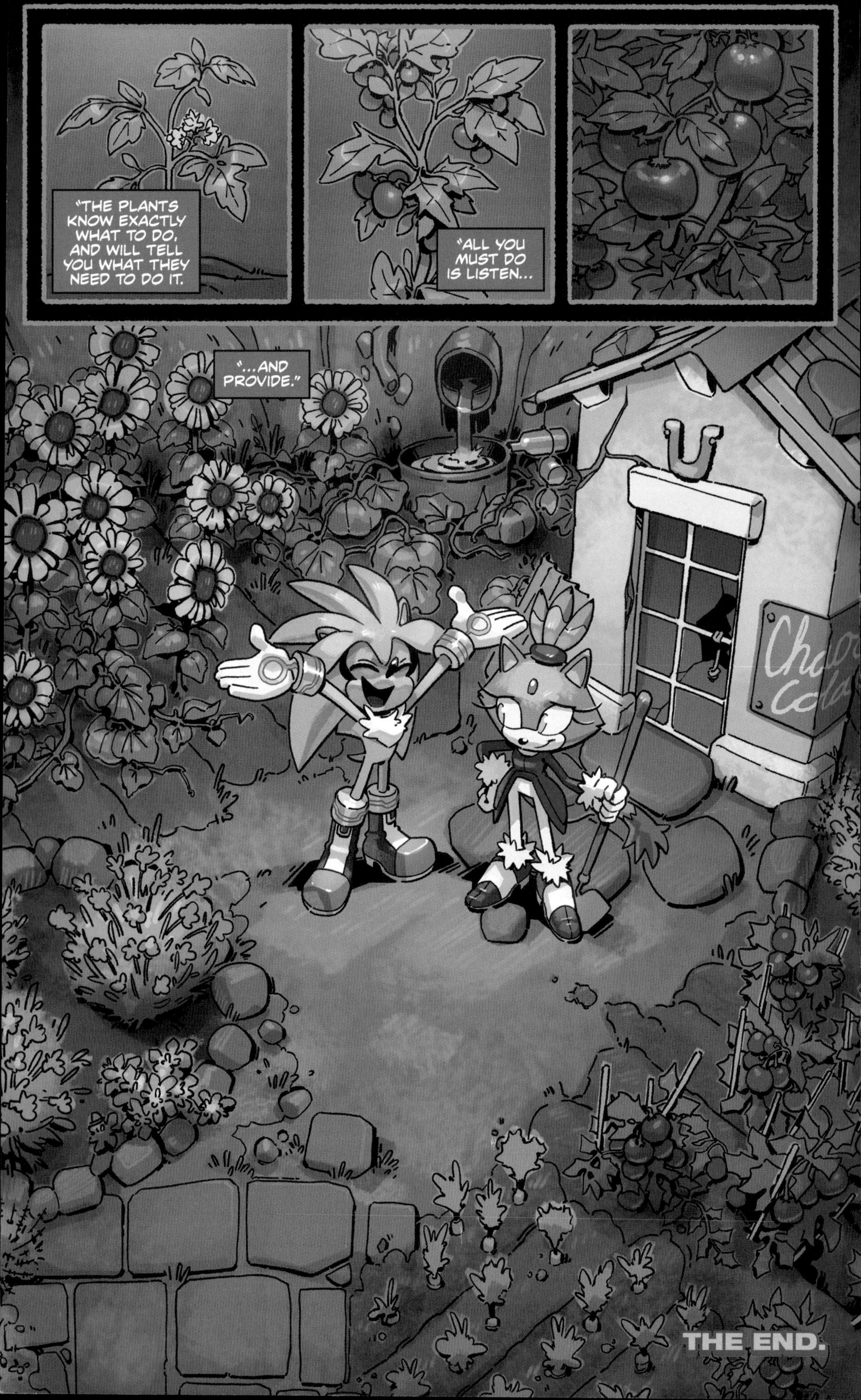
"THE PLANTS KNOW EXACTLY WHAT TO DO, AND WILL TELL YOU WHAT THEY NEED TO DO IT.
"ALL YOU MUST DO IS LISTEN...
"...AND PROVIDE."
THE END.

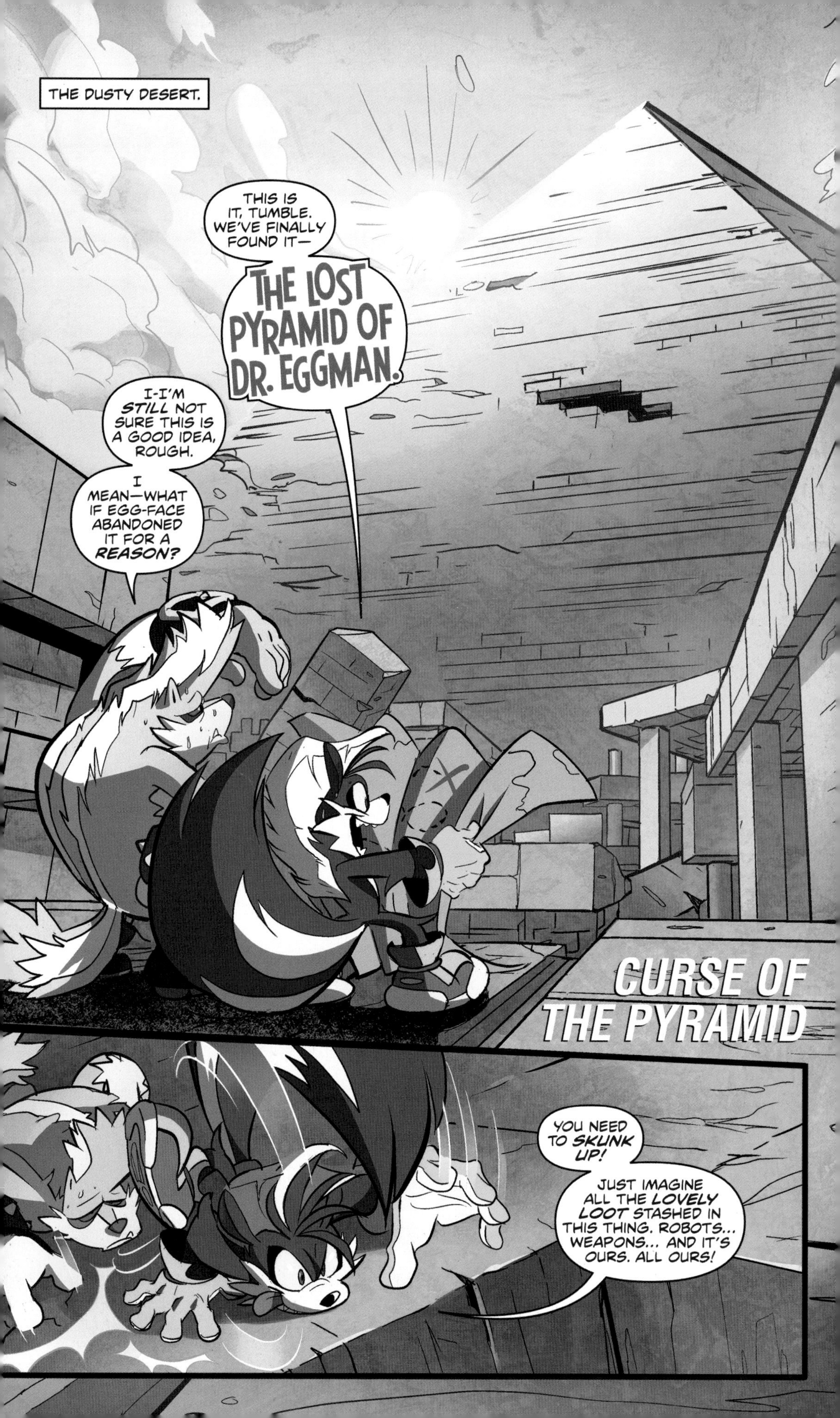
THE DUSTY DESERT.
THIS IS IT, TUMBLE. WE'VE FINALLY FOUND IT—
THE LOST PYRAMID OF DR. EGGMAN.
I-I'M STILL NOT SURE THIS IS A GOOD IDEA, ROUGH.
I MEAN—WHAT IF EGG-FACE ABANDONED IT FOR A REASON?
CURSE OF THE PYRAMID
YOU NEED TO SKUNK UP!
JUST IMAGINE ALL THE LOVELY LOOT STASHED IN THIS THING. ROBOTS... WEAPONS... AND IT'S OURS. ALL OURS!

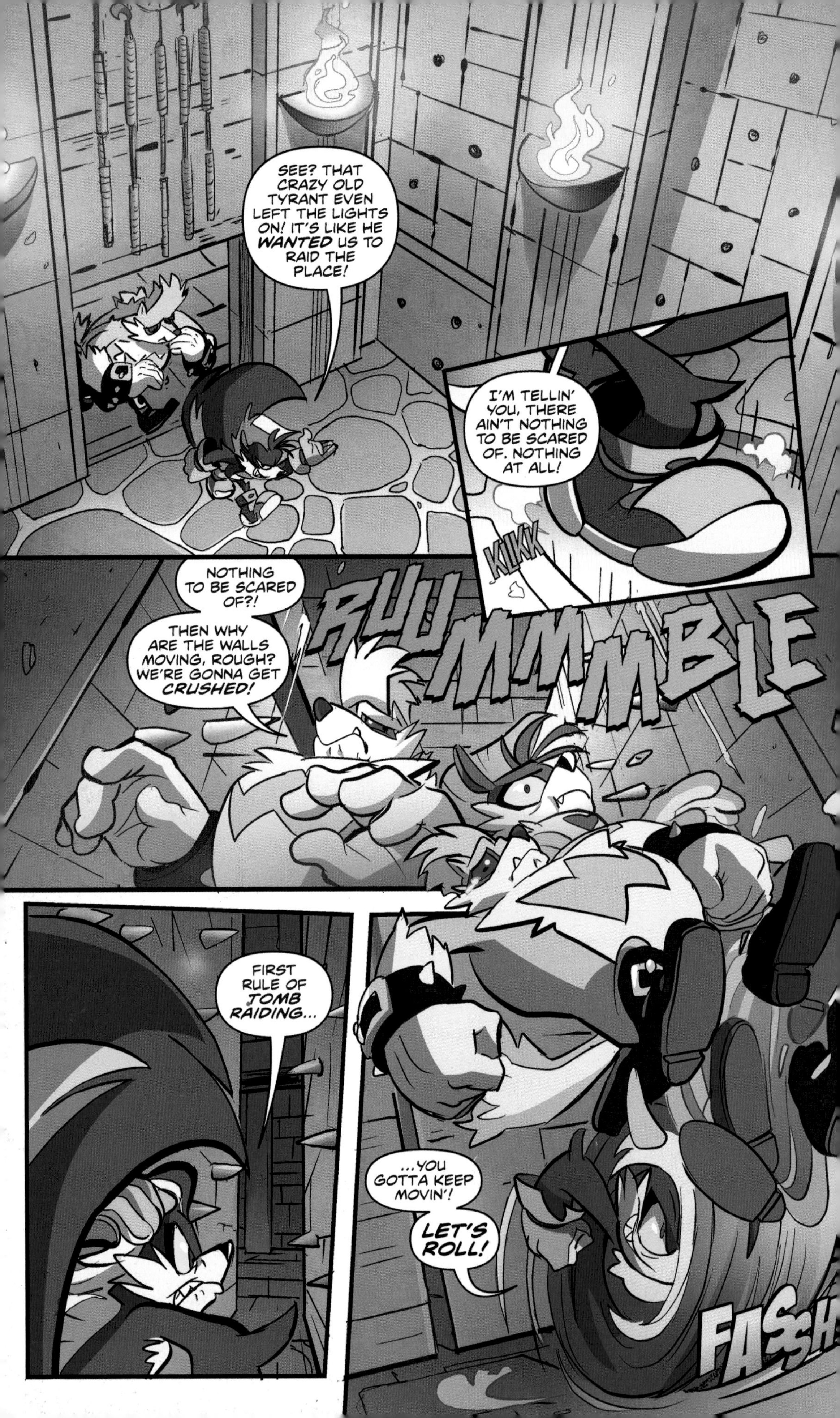
SEE? THAT CRAZY OLD TYRANT EVEN LEFT THE LIGHTS ON! IT'S LIKE HE *WANTED* US TO RAID THE PLACE!
I'M TELLIN' YOU, THERE AIN'T NOTHING TO BE SCARED OF. NOTHING AT ALL!
KLIKK
NOTHING TO BE SCARED OF?!
THEN WHY ARE THE WALLS MOVING, ROUGH? WE'RE GONNA GET *CRUSHED!*
RUUMMMMBLE
FIRST RULE OF *TOMB RAIDING*...
...YOU GOTTA KEEP MOVIN'!
LET'S ROLL!
FASSH

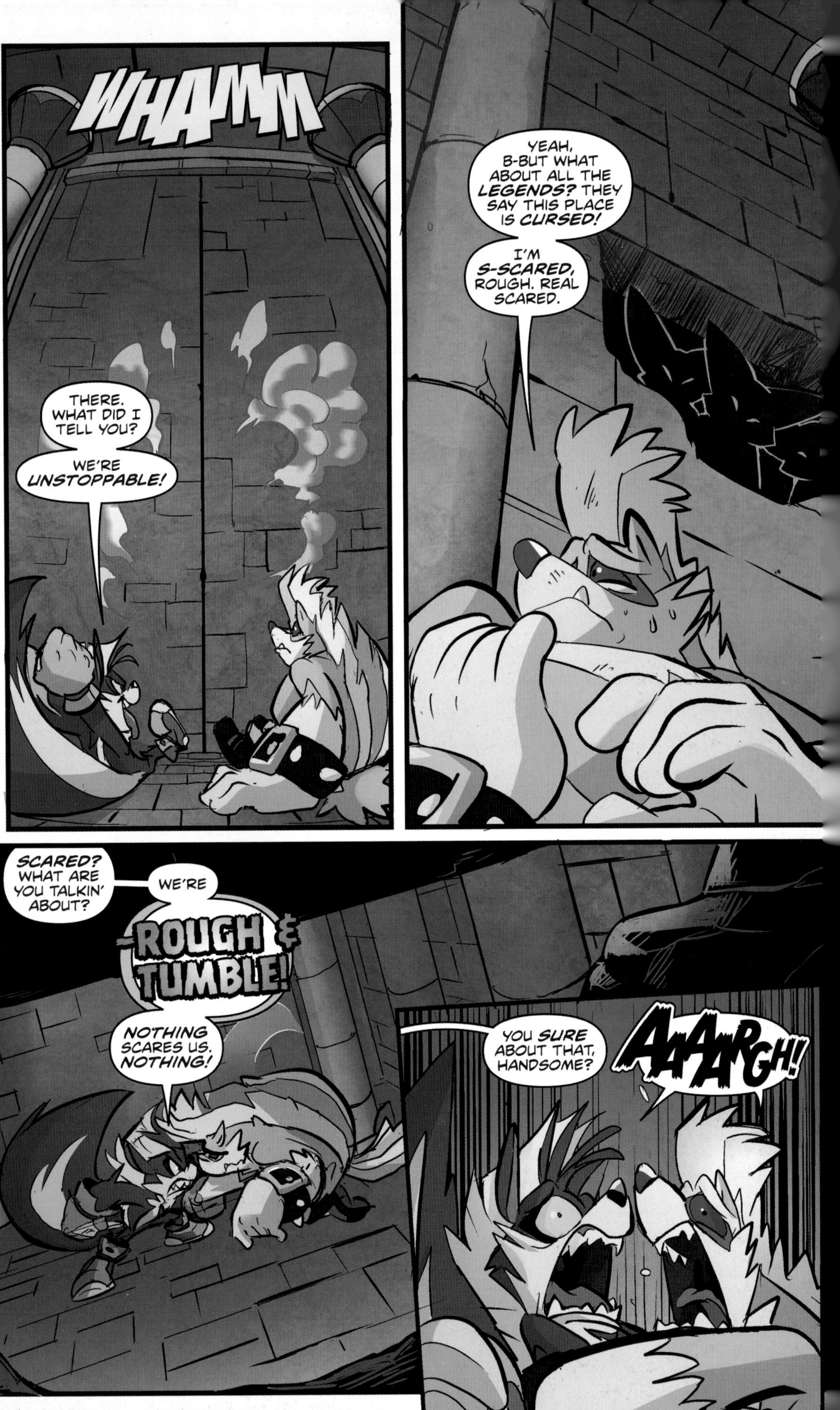
WHAMM
THERE. WHAT DID I TELL YOU?
WE'RE UNSTOPPABLE!
YEAH, B-BUT WHAT ABOUT ALL THE LEGENDS? THEY SAY THIS PLACE IS CURSED!
I'M S-SCARED, ROUGH. REAL SCARED.
SCARED? WHAT ARE YOU TALKIN' ABOUT?
WE'RE
ROUGH & TUMBLE!
NOTHING SCARES US. NOTHING!
YOU SURE ABOUT THAT, HANDSOME?
AAAARGH!

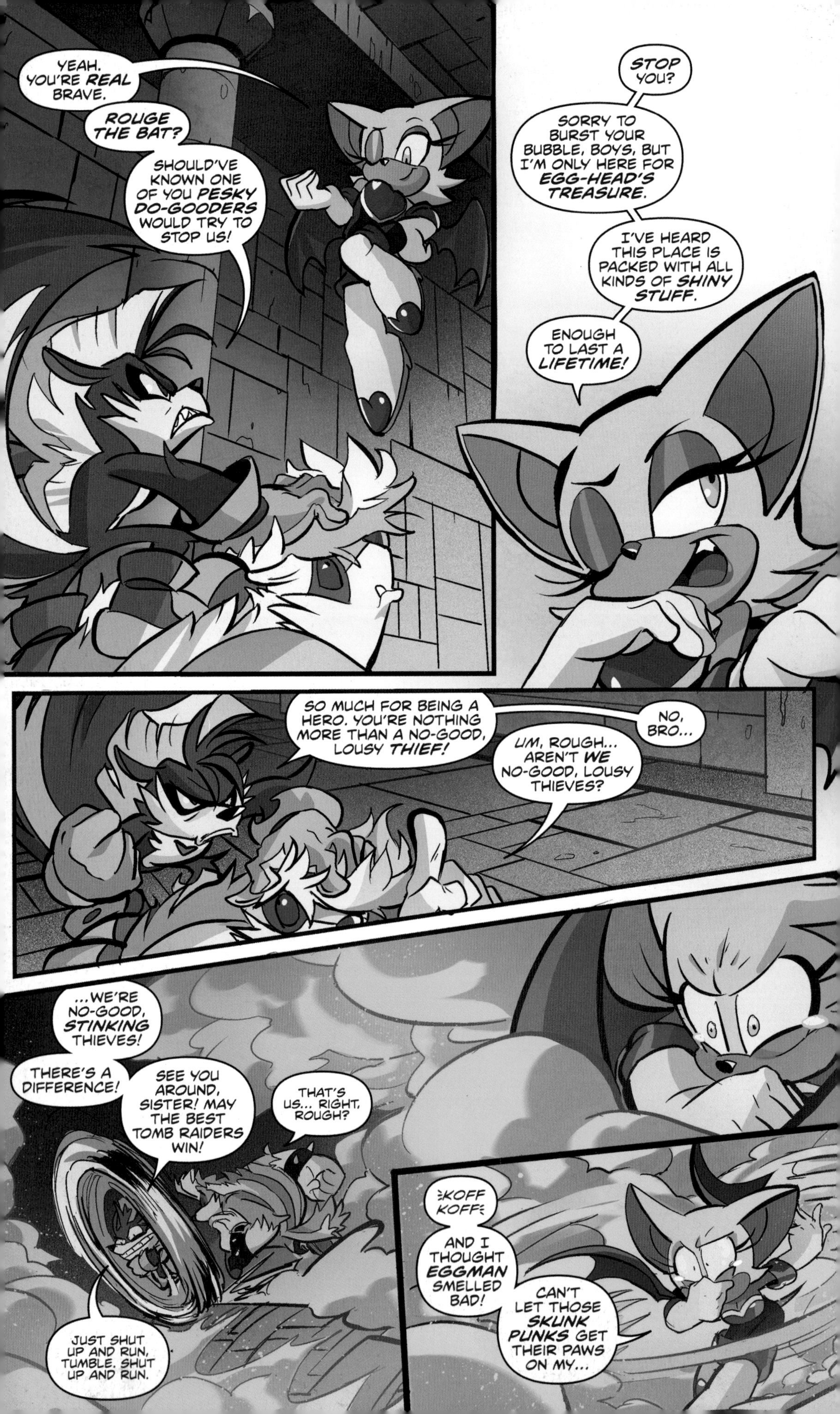
YEAH. YOU'RE REAL BRAVE.
ROUGE THE BAT?
SHOULD'VE KNOWN ONE OF YOU PESKY DO-GOODERS WOULD TRY TO STOP US!
STOP YOU?
SORRY TO BURST YOUR BUBBLE, BOYS, BUT I'M ONLY HERE FOR EGG-HEAD'S TREASURE.
I'VE HEARD THIS PLACE IS PACKED WITH ALL KINDS OF SHINY STUFF.
ENOUGH TO LAST A LIFETIME!
SO MUCH FOR BEING A HERO. YOU'RE NOTHING MORE THAN A NO-GOOD, LOUSY THIEF!
UM, ROUGH... AREN'T WE NO-GOOD, LOUSY THIEVES?
NO, BRO...
...WE'RE NO-GOOD, STINKING THIEVES!
THERE'S A DIFFERENCE!
SEE YOU AROUND, SISTER! MAY THE BEST TOMB RAIDERS WIN!
THAT'S US... RIGHT, ROUGH?
JUST SHUT UP AND RUN, TUMBLE. SHUT UP AND RUN.
KOFF KOFF
AND I THOUGHT EGGMAN SMELLED BAD!
CAN'T LET THOSE SKUNK PUNKS GET THEIR PAWS ON MY...

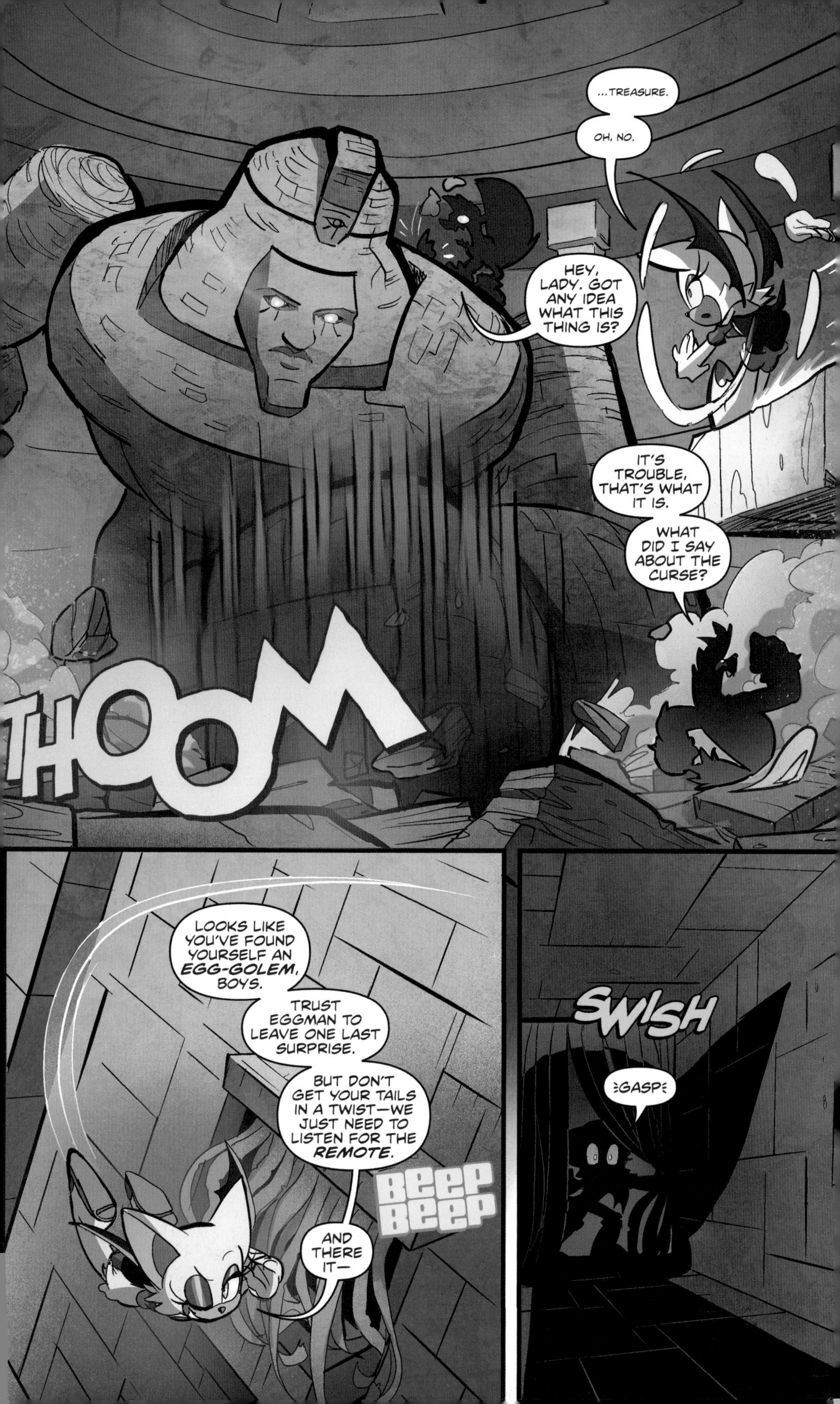
...TREASURE.
OH, NO.
HEY, LADY. GOT ANY IDEA WHAT THIS THING IS?
IT'S TROUBLE, THAT'S WHAT IT IS.
WHAT DID I SAY ABOUT THE CURSE?
THOOM
LOOKS LIKE YOU'VE FOUND YOURSELF AN EGG-GOLEM, BOYS.
TRUST EGGMAN TO LEAVE ONE LAST SURPRISE.
BUT DON'T GET YOUR TAILS IN A TWIST—WE JUST NEED TO LISTEN FOR THE REMOTE.
BEEP BEEP
AND THERE IT—
SWISH
GASP

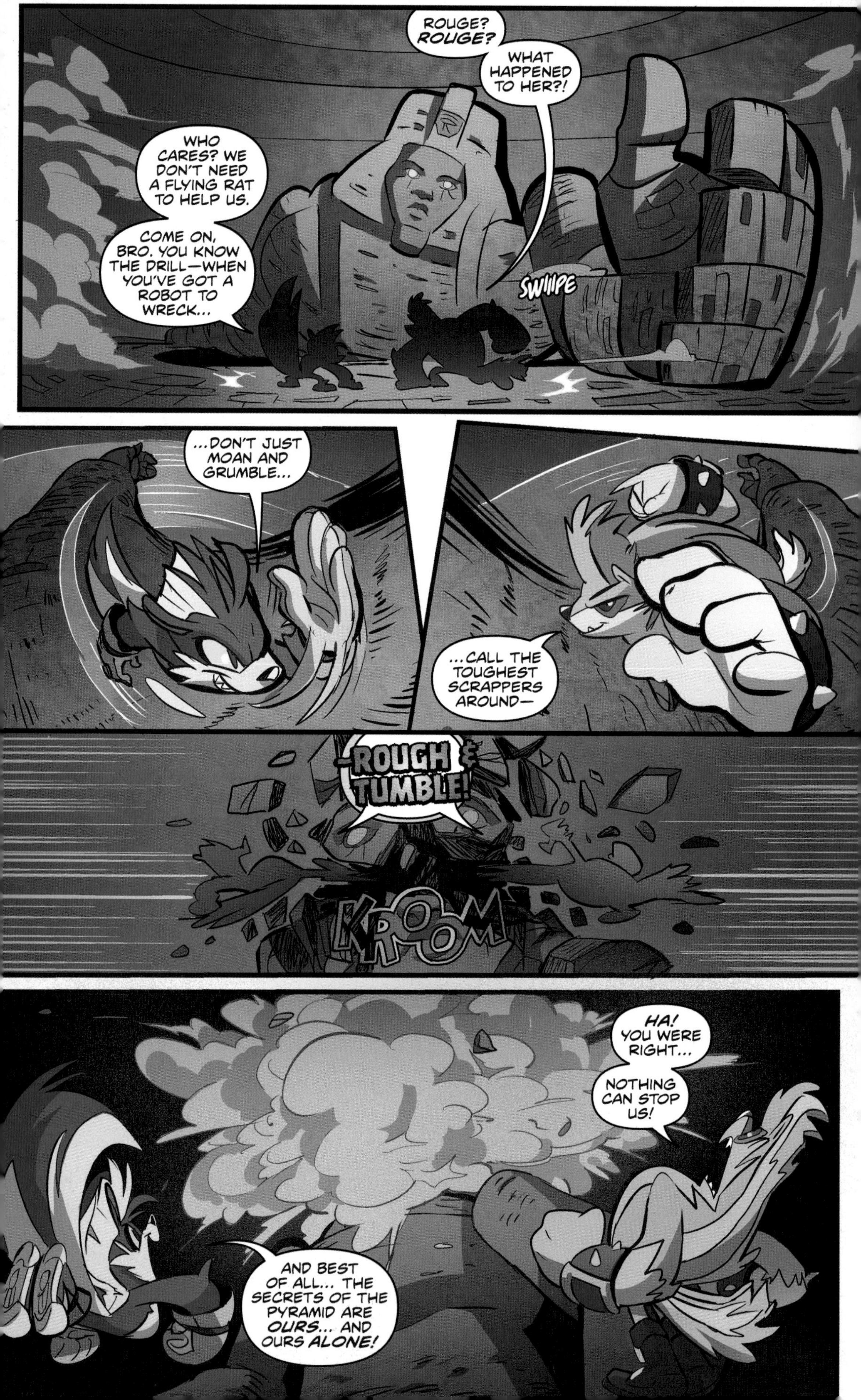
ROUGE? ROUGE?
WHAT HAPPENED TO HER?!
WHO CARES? WE DON'T NEED A FLYING RAT TO HELP US.
COME ON, BRO. YOU KNOW THE DRILL—WHEN YOU'VE GOT A ROBOT TO WRECK...
SWIIIPE
...DON'T JUST MOAN AND GRUMBLE...
...CALL THE TOUGHEST SCRAPPERS AROUND—
—ROUGH & TUMBLE!
KROOOM
HA! YOU WERE RIGHT...
NOTHING CAN STOP US!
AND BEST OF ALL... THE SECRETS OF THE PYRAMID ARE OURS... AND OURS ALONE!

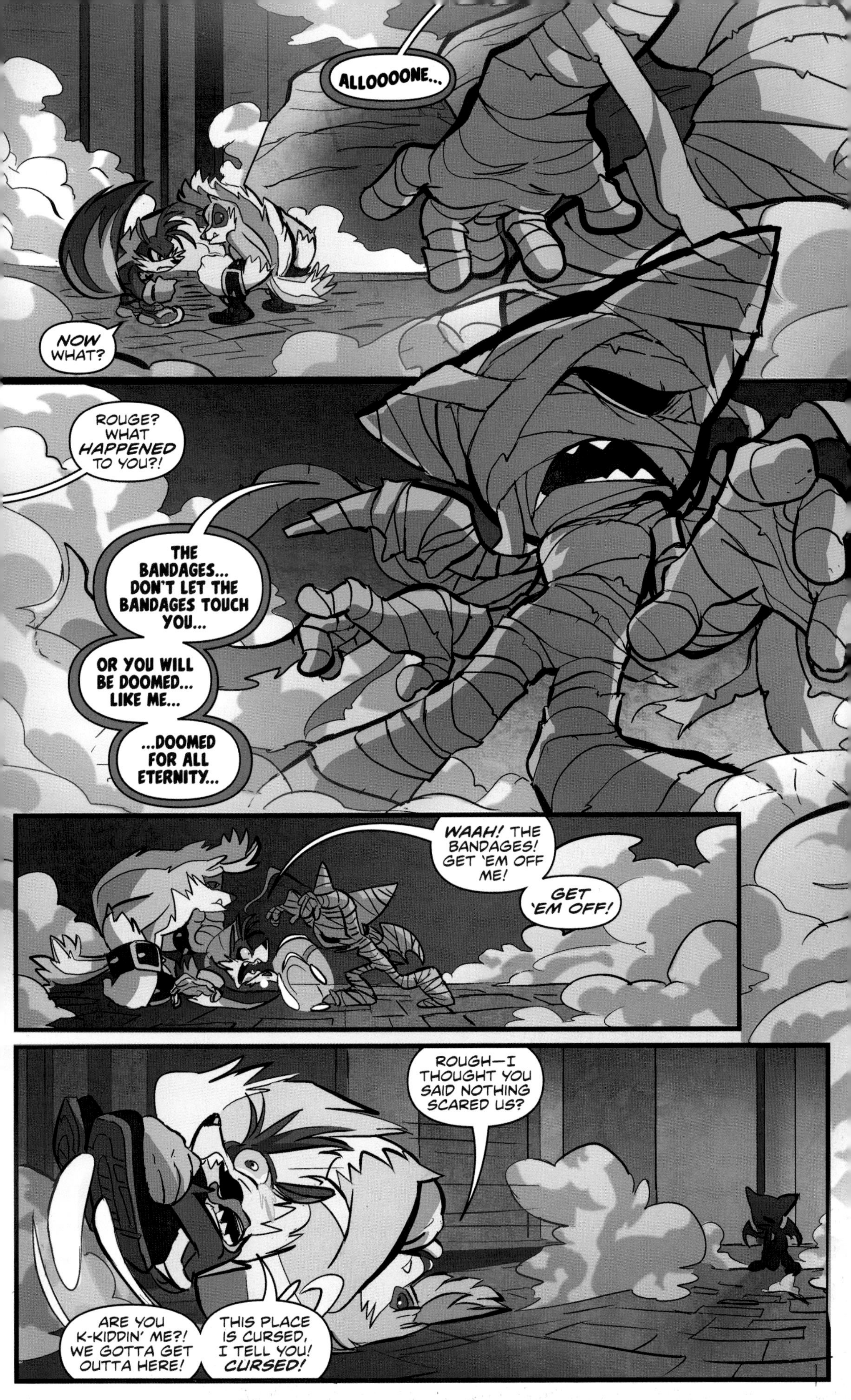
ALLOOOONE...
NOW WHAT?
ROUGE? WHAT HAPPENED TO YOU?!
THE BANDAGES... DON'T LET THE BANDAGES TOUCH YOU...
OR YOU WILL BE DOOMED... LIKE ME...
...DOOMED FOR ALL ETERNITY...
WAAH! THE BANDAGES! GET 'EM OFF ME!
GET 'EM OFF!
ROUGH—I THOUGHT YOU SAID NOTHING SCARED US?
ARE YOU K-KIDDIN' ME?! WE GOTTA GET OUTTA HERE!
THIS PLACE IS CURSED, I TELL YOU! CURSED!

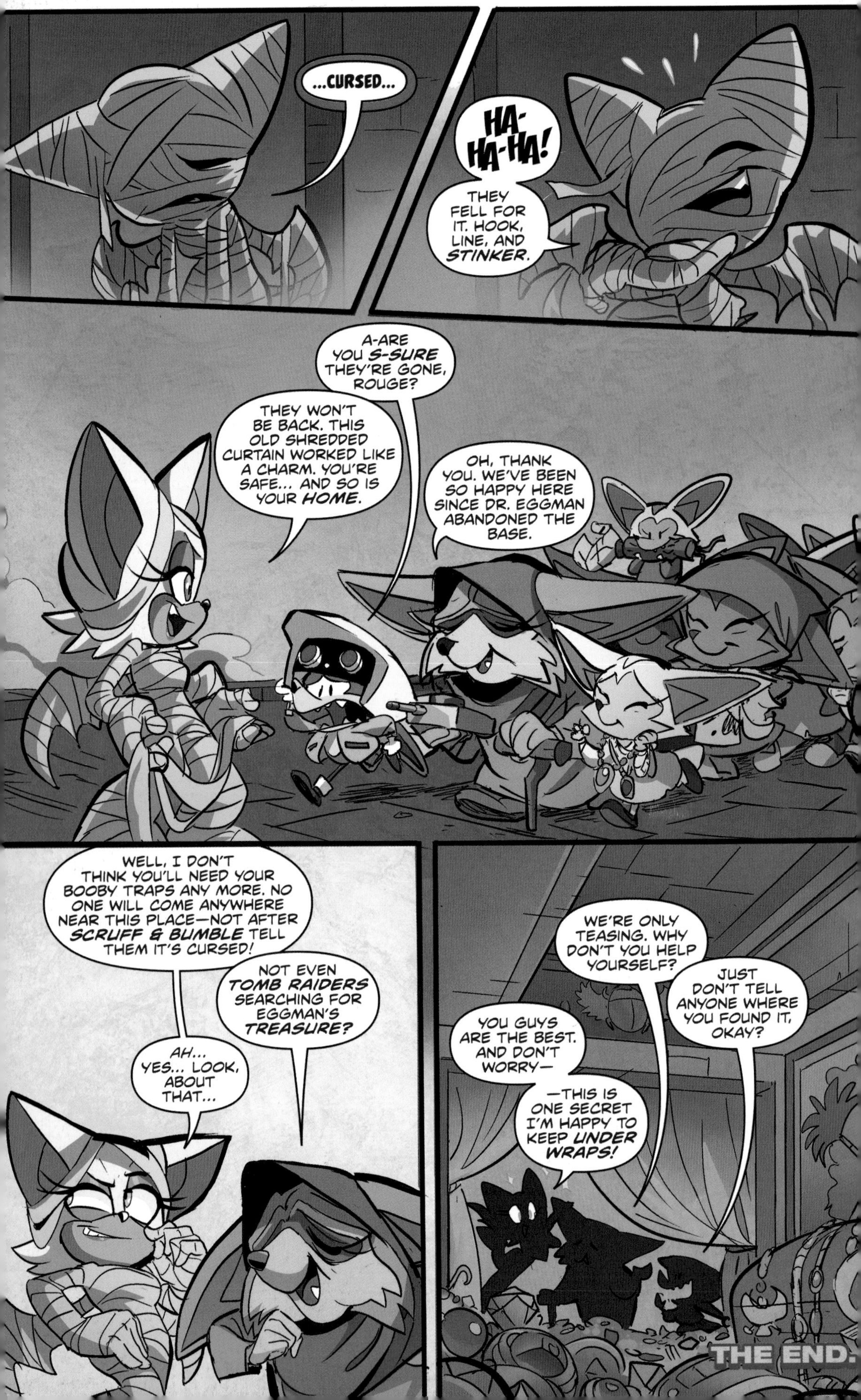
...CURSED...
HA-HA-HA!
THEY FELL FOR IT. HOOK, LINE, AND STINKER.
A-ARE YOU S-SURE THEY'RE GONE, ROUGE?
THEY WON'T BE BACK. THIS OLD SHREDDED CURTAIN WORKED LIKE A CHARM. YOU'RE SAFE... AND SO IS YOUR HOME.
OH, THANK YOU. WE'VE BEEN SO HAPPY HERE SINCE DR. EGGMAN ABANDONED THE BASE.
WELL, I DON'T THINK YOU'LL NEED YOUR BOOBY TRAPS ANY MORE. NO ONE WILL COME ANYWHERE NEAR THIS PLACE—NOT AFTER SCRUFF & BUMBLE TELL THEM IT'S CURSED!
NOT EVEN TOMB RAIDERS SEARCHING FOR EGGMAN'S TREASURE?
AH... YES... LOOK, ABOUT THAT...
WE'RE ONLY TEASING. WHY DON'T YOU HELP YOURSELF?
JUST DON'T TELL ANYONE WHERE YOU FOUND IT, OKAY?
YOU GUYS ARE THE BEST. AND DON'T WORRY—
—THIS IS ONE SECRET I'M HAPPY TO KEEP UNDER WRAPS!
THE END.

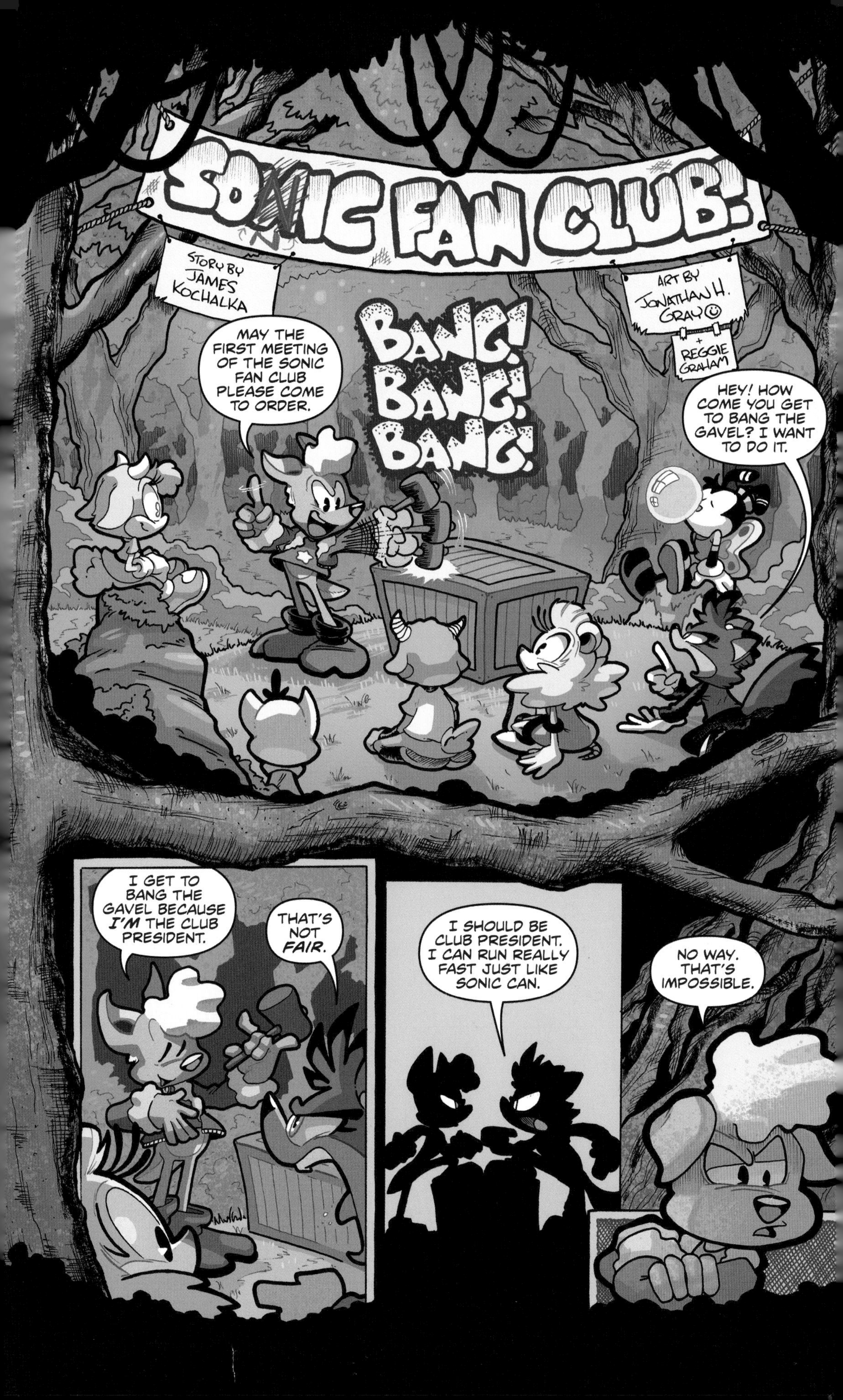
SONIC FAN CLUB!
STORY BY JAMES KOCHALKA
ART BY JONATHAN H. GRAY + REGGIE GRAHAM
MAY THE FIRST MEETING OF THE SONIC FAN CLUB PLEASE COME TO ORDER.
BANG! BANG! BANG!
HEY! HOW COME YOU GET TO BANG THE GAVEL? I WANT TO DO IT.
I GET TO BANG THE GAVEL BECAUSE *I'M* THE CLUB PRESIDENT.
THAT'S NOT *FAIR*.
I SHOULD BE CLUB PRESIDENT. I CAN RUN REALLY FAST JUST LIKE SONIC CAN.
NO WAY. THAT'S IMPOSSIBLE.

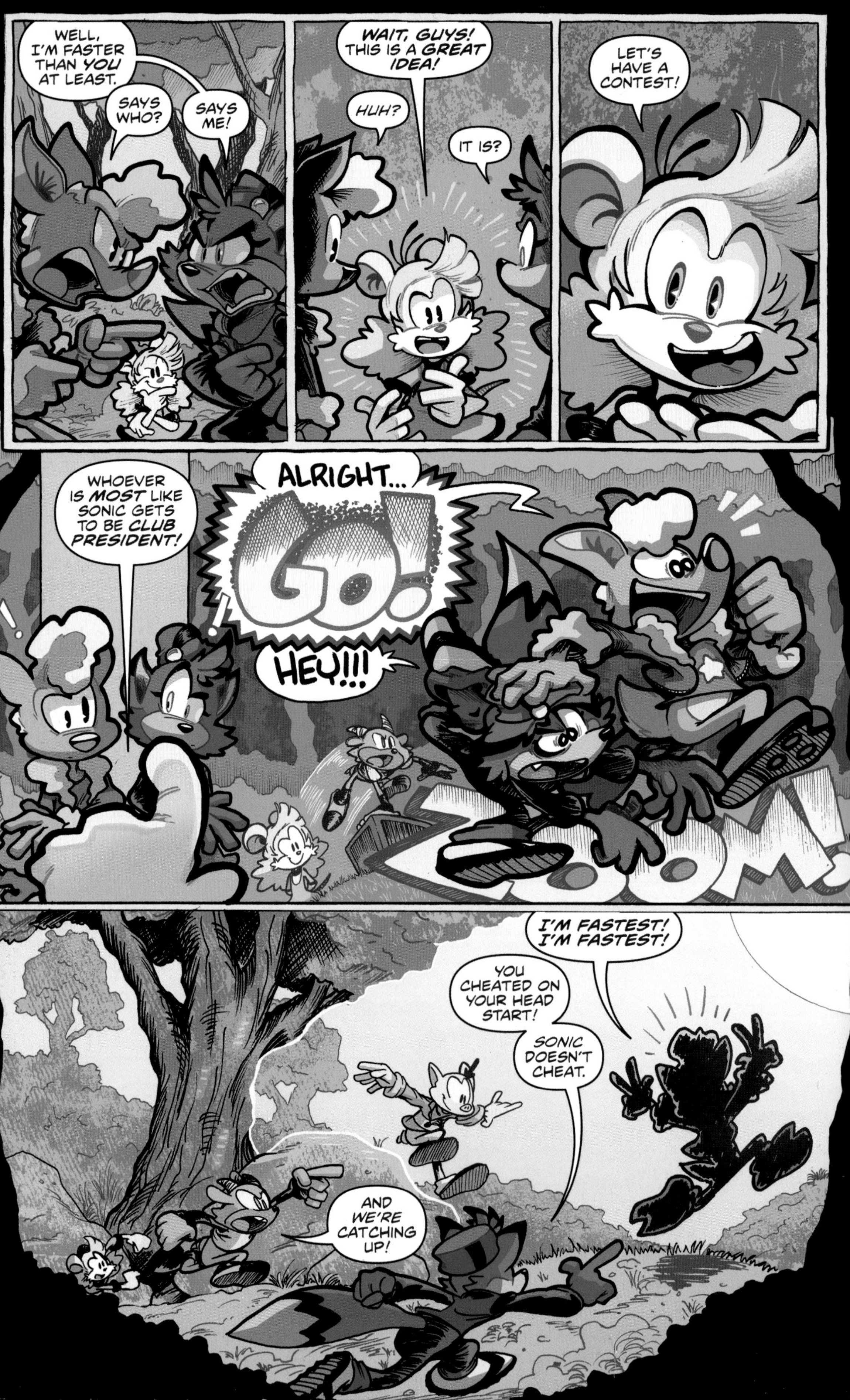

WELL, I'M FASTER THAN YOU AT LEAST.
SAYS WHO?
SAYS ME!
WAIT, GUYS! THIS IS A GREAT IDEA!
HUH?
IT IS?
LET'S HAVE A CONTEST!
WHOEVER IS MOST LIKE SONIC GETS TO BE CLUB PRESIDENT!
ALRIGHT...
GO!
HEY!!!
ZOOM!
I'M FASTEST! I'M FASTEST!
YOU CHEATED ON YOUR HEAD START!
SONIC DOESN'T CHEAT.
AND WE'RE CATCHING UP!

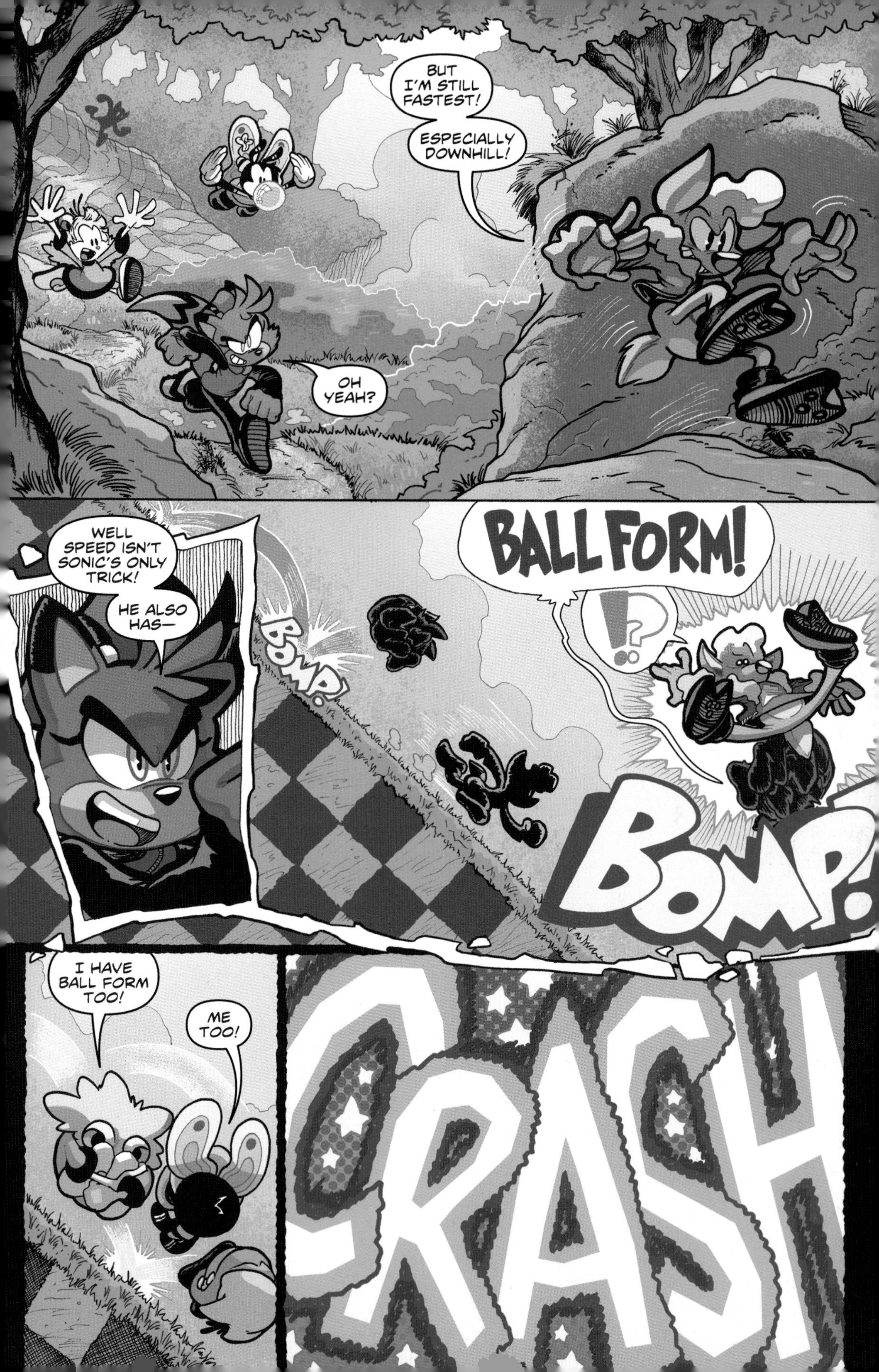

BUT I'M STILL FASTEST!
ESPECIALLY DOWNHILL!
OH YEAH?
WELL SPEED ISN'T SONIC'S ONLY TRICK!
HE ALSO HAS—
BALL FORM!
BOMP!
!?
BOMP!
I HAVE BALL FORM TOO!
ME TOO!
CRASH

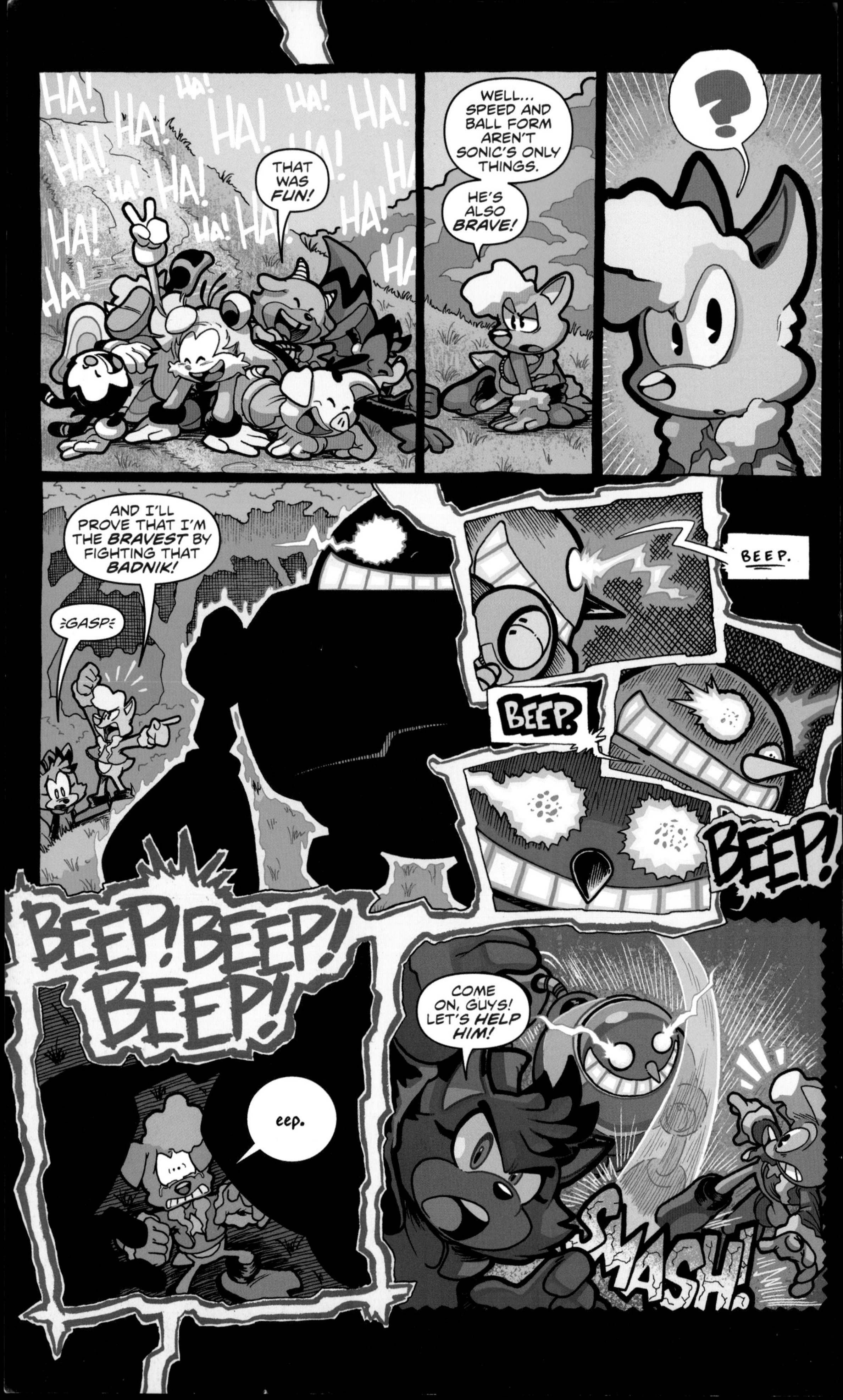
HA! HA! HA! HA! HA! HA! HA! HA! HA! HA! HA! HA! HA! HA! HA! HA!
THAT WAS FUN!
WELL... SPEED AND BALL FORM AREN'T SONIC'S ONLY THINGS.
HE'S ALSO BRAVE!
?
AND I'LL PROVE THAT I'M THE BRAVEST BY FIGHTING THAT BADNIK!
GASP
BEEP.
BEEP.
BEEP!
BEEP! BEEP! BEEP!
eep.
COME ON, GUYS! LET'S HELP HIM!
SMASH!

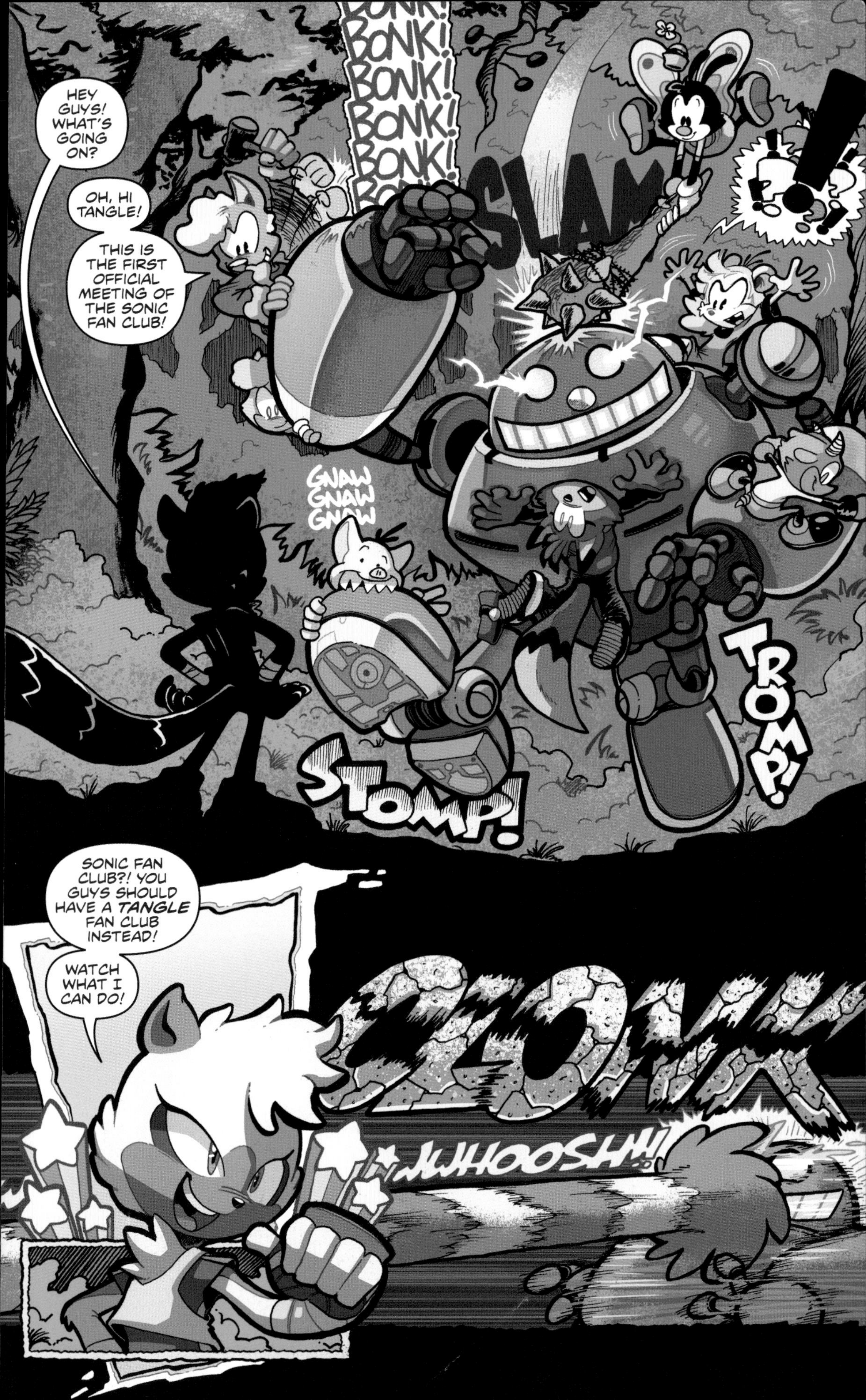
HEY GUYS! WHAT'S GOING ON?
OH, HI TANGLE!
THIS IS THE FIRST OFFICIAL MEETING OF THE SONIC FAN CLUB!
BONK! BONK! BONK! BONK! BONK!
SLAM
GNAW GNAW GNAW
STOMP!
TROMP!
SONIC FAN CLUB?! YOU GUYS SHOULD HAVE A TANGLE FAN CLUB INSTEAD!
WATCH WHAT I CAN DO!
WHOOSH!!

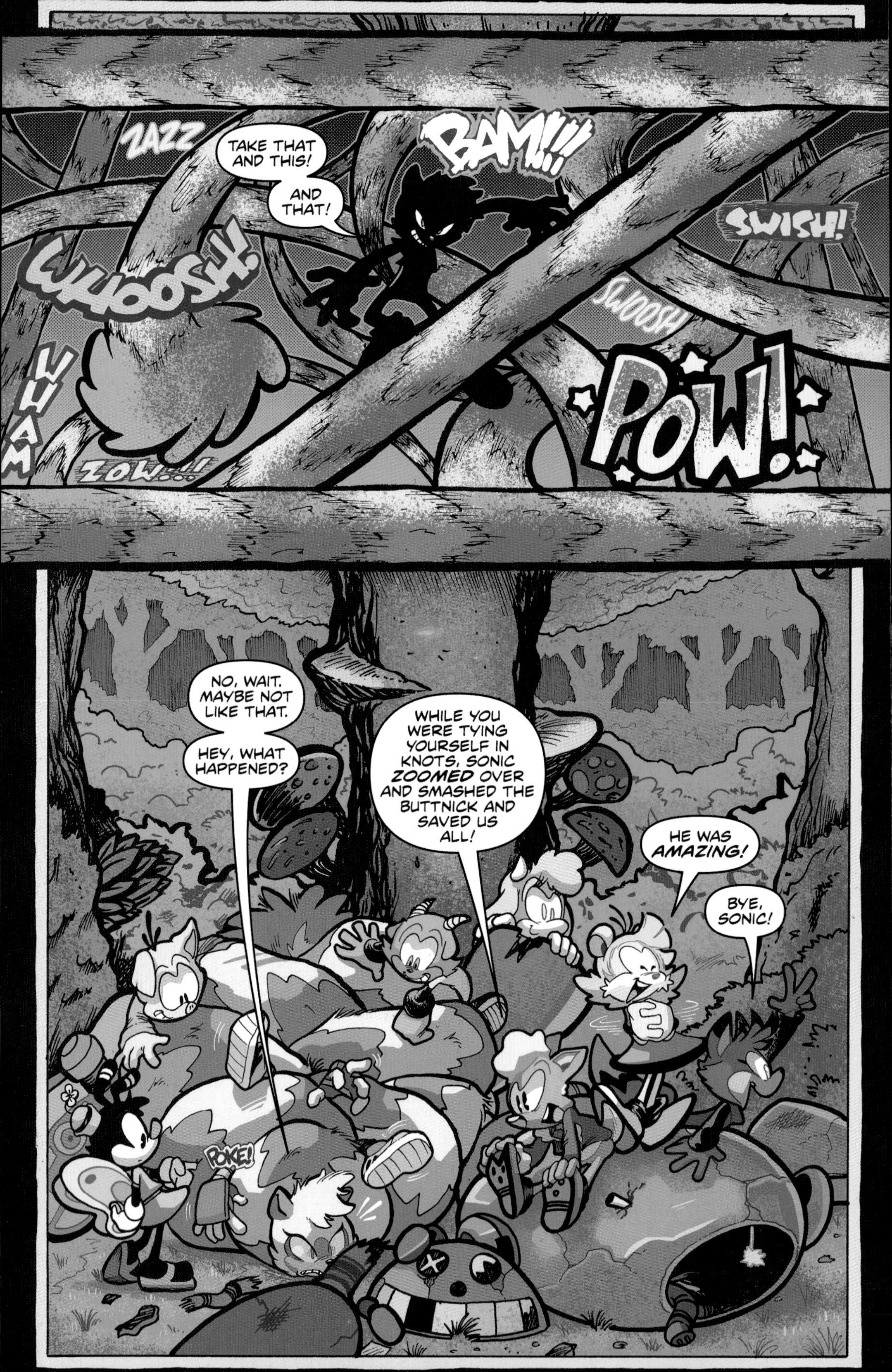
ZAZZ
TAKE THAT AND THIS!
AND THAT!
BAM!!!
SWISH!
WHOOSH!
SWOOSH
WHAM
ZOW...!
POW!
NO, WAIT. MAYBE NOT LIKE THAT.
HEY, WHAT HAPPENED?
WHILE YOU WERE TYING YOURSELF IN KNOTS, SONIC *ZOOMED* OVER AND SMASHED THE BUTTNICK AND SAVED US ALL!
HE WAS *AMAZING!*
BYE, SONIC!
POKE!

* the end *

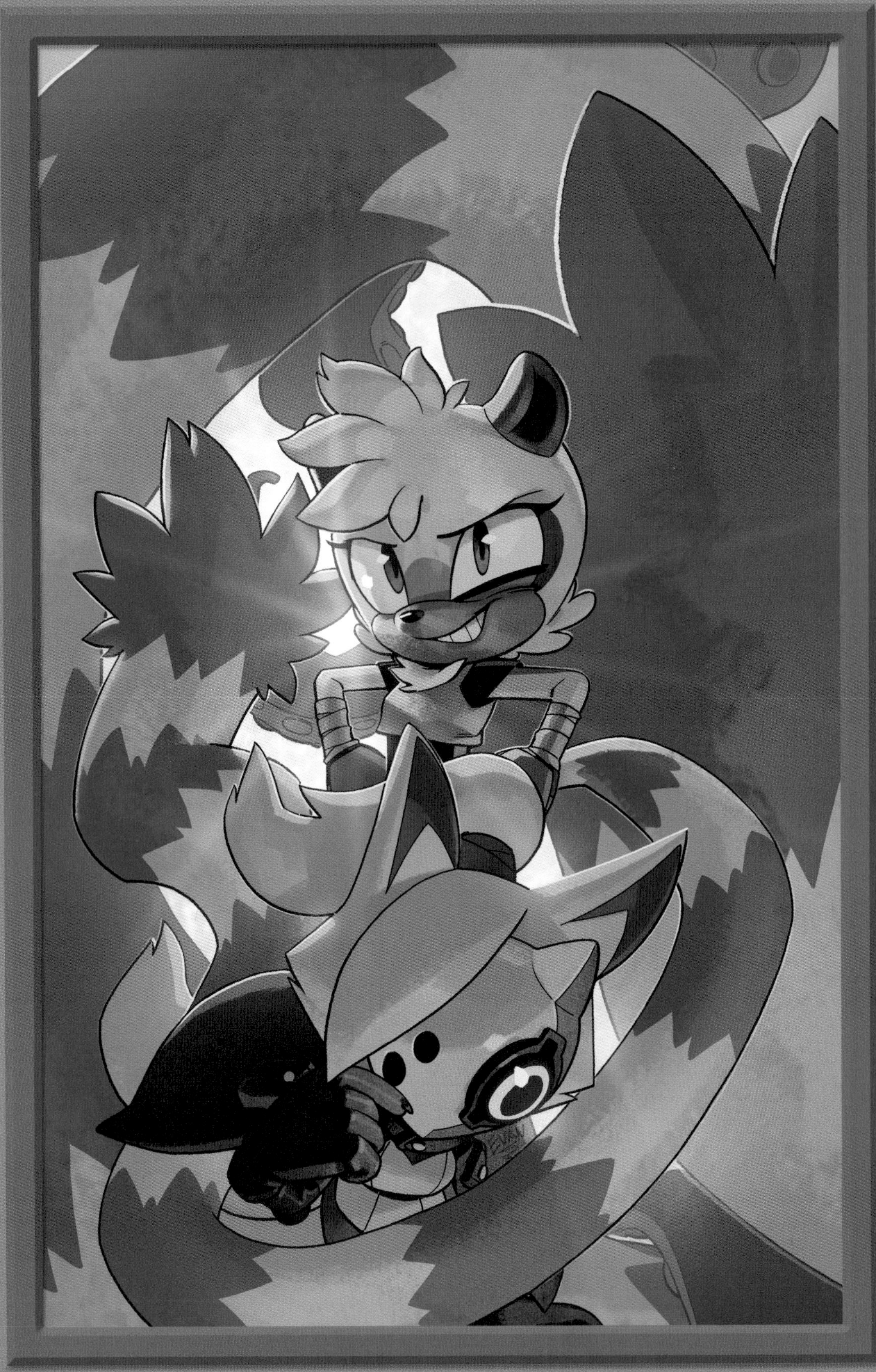

ART BY **EVAN STANLEY**

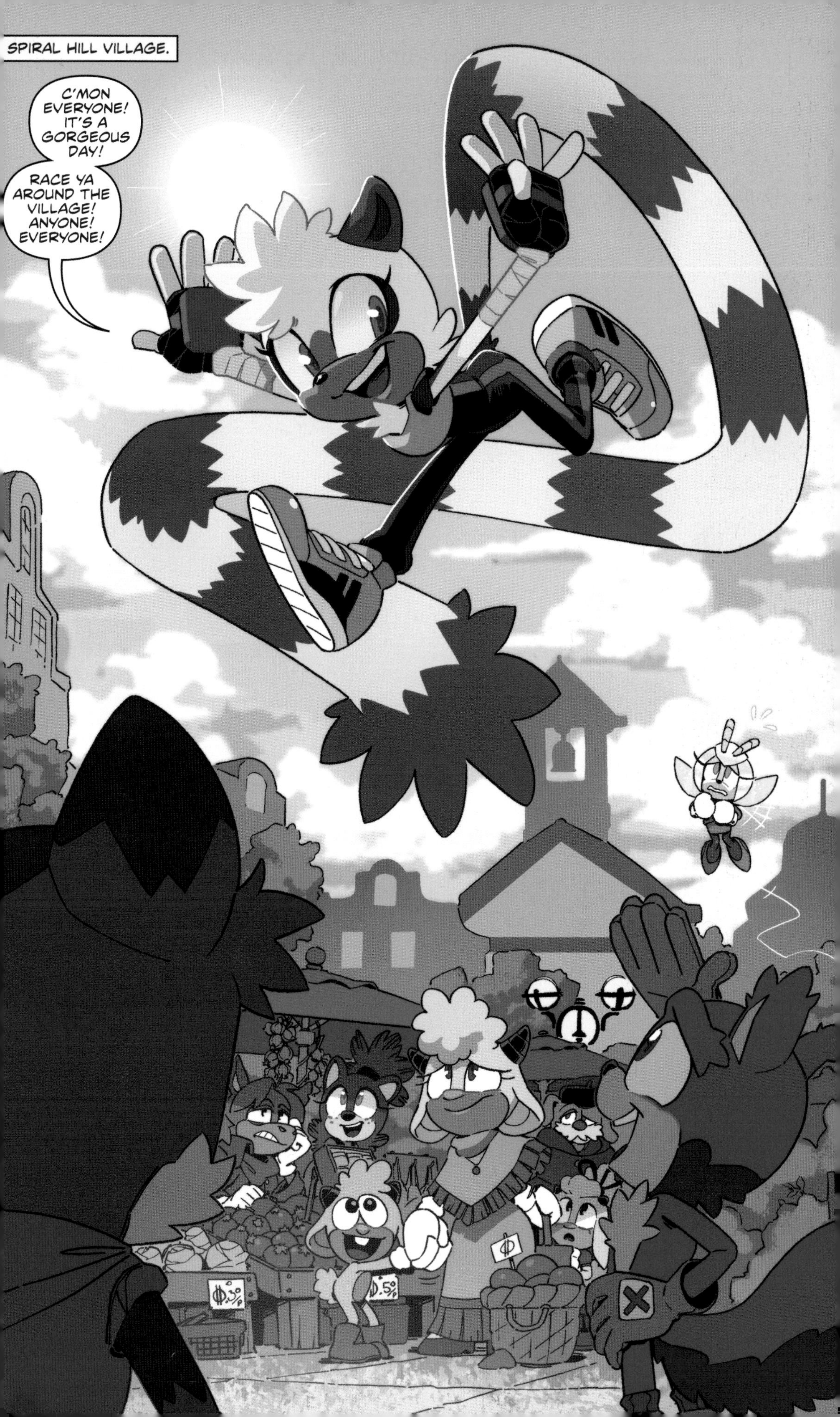
SPIRAL HILL VILLAGE.
C'MON EVERYONE! IT'S A GORGEOUS DAY!
RACE YA AROUND THE VILLAGE! ANYONE! EVERYONE!

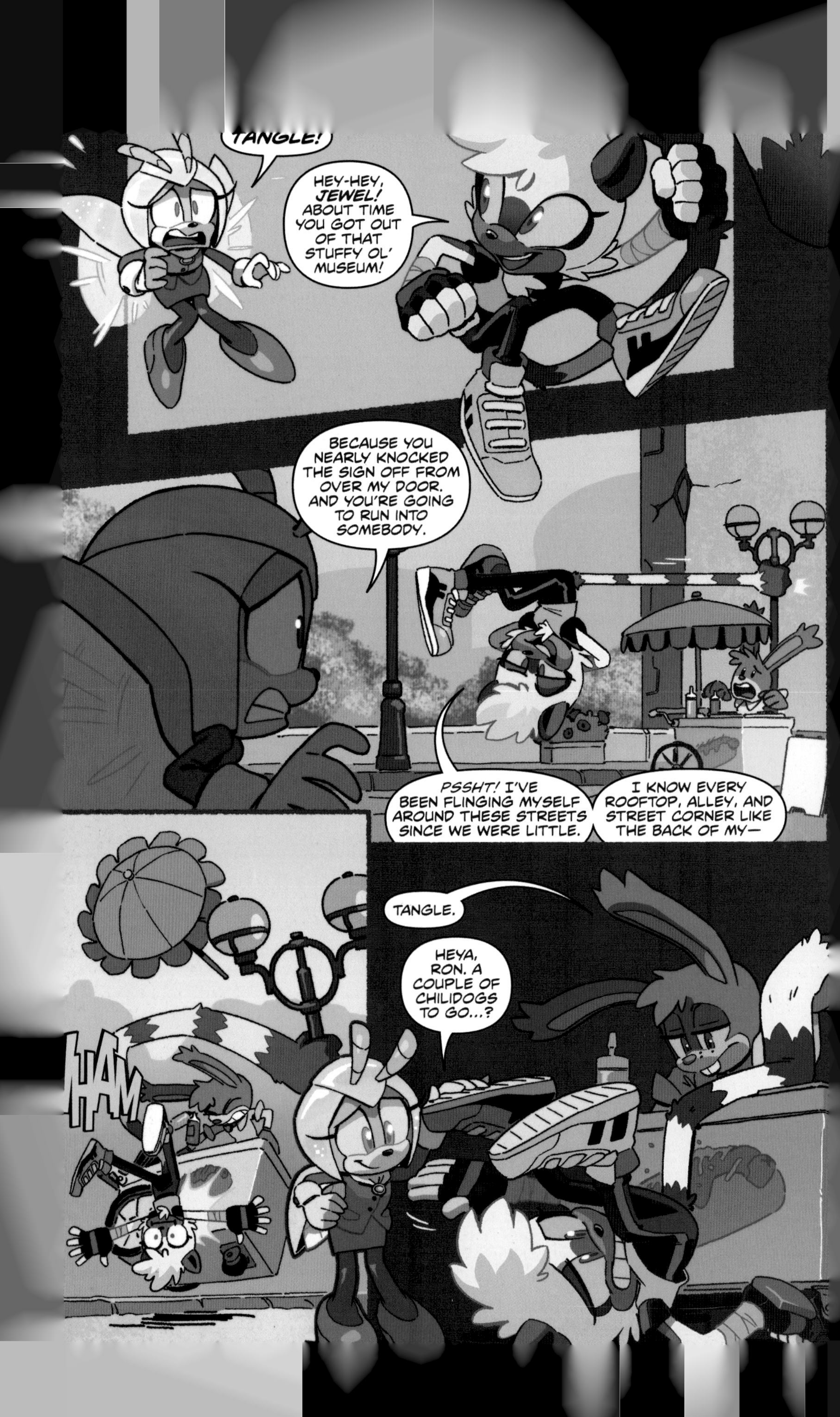
TANGLE!
HEY-HEY, JEWEL! ABOUT TIME YOU GOT OUT OF THAT STUFFY OL' MUSEUM!
BECAUSE YOU NEARLY KNOCKED THE SIGN OFF FROM OVER MY DOOR. AND YOU'RE GOING TO RUN INTO SOMEBODY.
PSSHT! I'VE BEEN FLINGING MYSELF AROUND THESE STREETS SINCE WE WERE LITTLE.
I KNOW EVERY ROOFTOP, ALLEY, AND STREET CORNER LIKE THE BACK OF MY—
WHAM
TANGLE.
HEYA, RON. A COUPLE OF CHILIDOGS TO GO...?

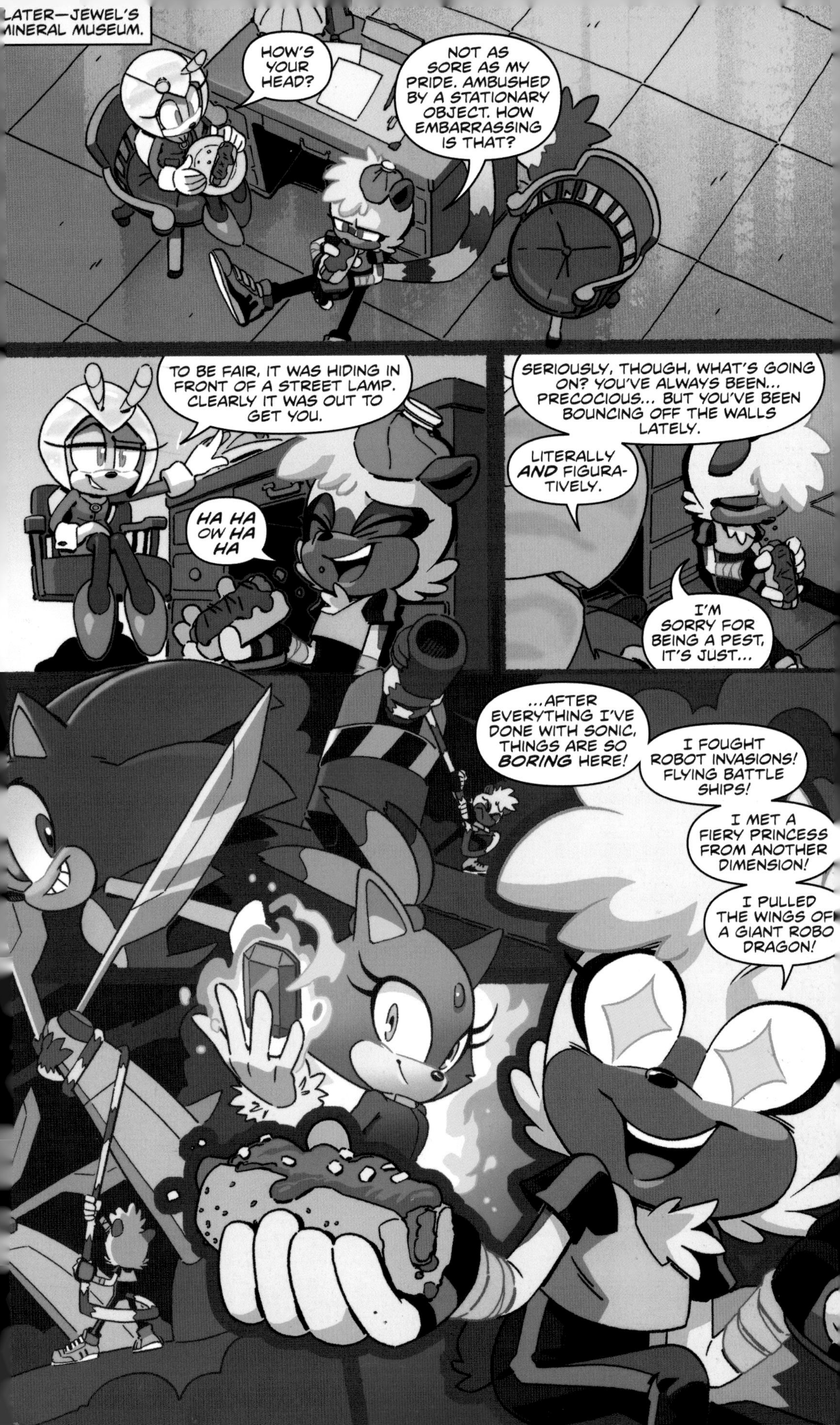
LATER—JEWEL'S MINERAL MUSEUM.
HOW'S YOUR HEAD?
NOT AS SORE AS MY PRIDE. AMBUSHED BY A STATIONARY OBJECT. HOW EMBARRASSING IS THAT?
TO BE FAIR, IT WAS HIDING IN FRONT OF A STREET LAMP. CLEARLY IT WAS OUT TO GET YOU.
HA HA OW HA HA
SERIOUSLY, THOUGH, WHAT'S GOING ON? YOU'VE ALWAYS BEEN... PRECOCIOUS... BUT YOU'VE BEEN BOUNCING OFF THE WALLS LATELY.
LITERALLY AND FIGURATIVELY.
I'M SORRY FOR BEING A PEST, IT'S JUST...
...AFTER EVERYTHING I'VE DONE WITH SONIC, THINGS ARE SO BORING HERE!
I FOUGHT ROBOT INVASIONS! FLYING BATTLE SHIPS!
I MET A FIERY PRINCESS FROM ANOTHER DIMENSION!
I PULLED THE WINGS OF A GIANT ROBO DRAGON!

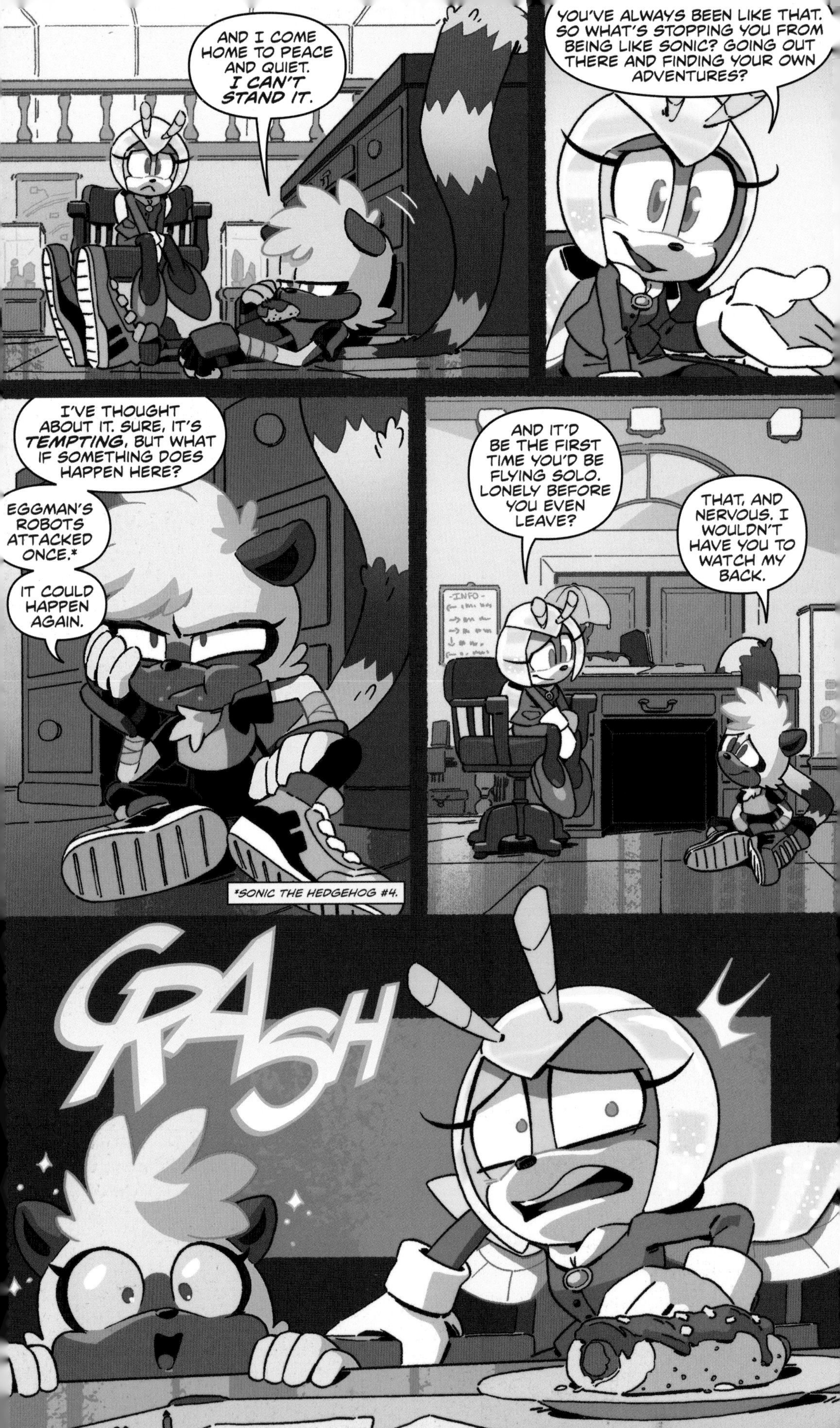
AND I COME HOME TO PEACE AND QUIET. I CAN'T STAND IT.
YOU'VE ALWAYS BEEN LIKE THAT. SO WHAT'S STOPPING YOU FROM BEING LIKE SONIC? GOING OUT THERE AND FINDING YOUR OWN ADVENTURES?
I'VE THOUGHT ABOUT IT. SURE, IT'S TEMPTING, BUT WHAT IF SOMETHING DOES HAPPEN HERE?
EGGMAN'S ROBOTS ATTACKED ONCE.*
IT COULD HAPPEN AGAIN.
*SONIC THE HEDGEHOG #4.
AND IT'D BE THE FIRST TIME YOU'D BE FLYING SOLO. LONELY BEFORE YOU EVEN LEAVE?
THAT, AND NERVOUS. I WOULDN'T HAVE YOU TO WATCH MY BACK.
-INFO-
CRASH

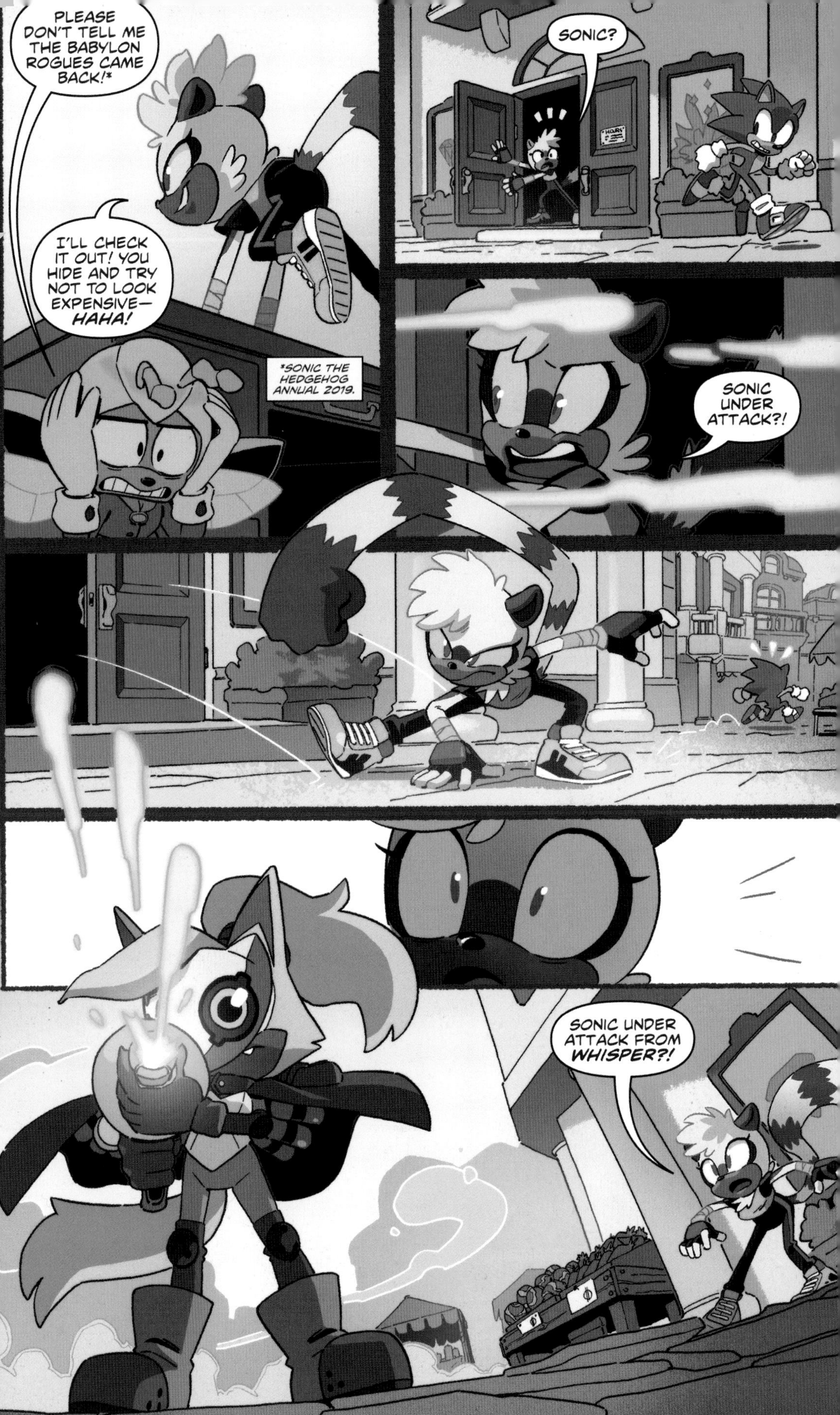
PLEASE DON'T TELL ME THE BABYLON ROGUES CAME BACK!*
I'LL CHECK IT OUT! YOU HIDE AND TRY NOT TO LOOK EXPENSIVE— HAHA!
*SONIC THE HEDGEHOG ANNUAL 2019.
SONIC?
SONIC UNDER ATTACK?!
SONIC UNDER ATTACK FROM WHISPER?!

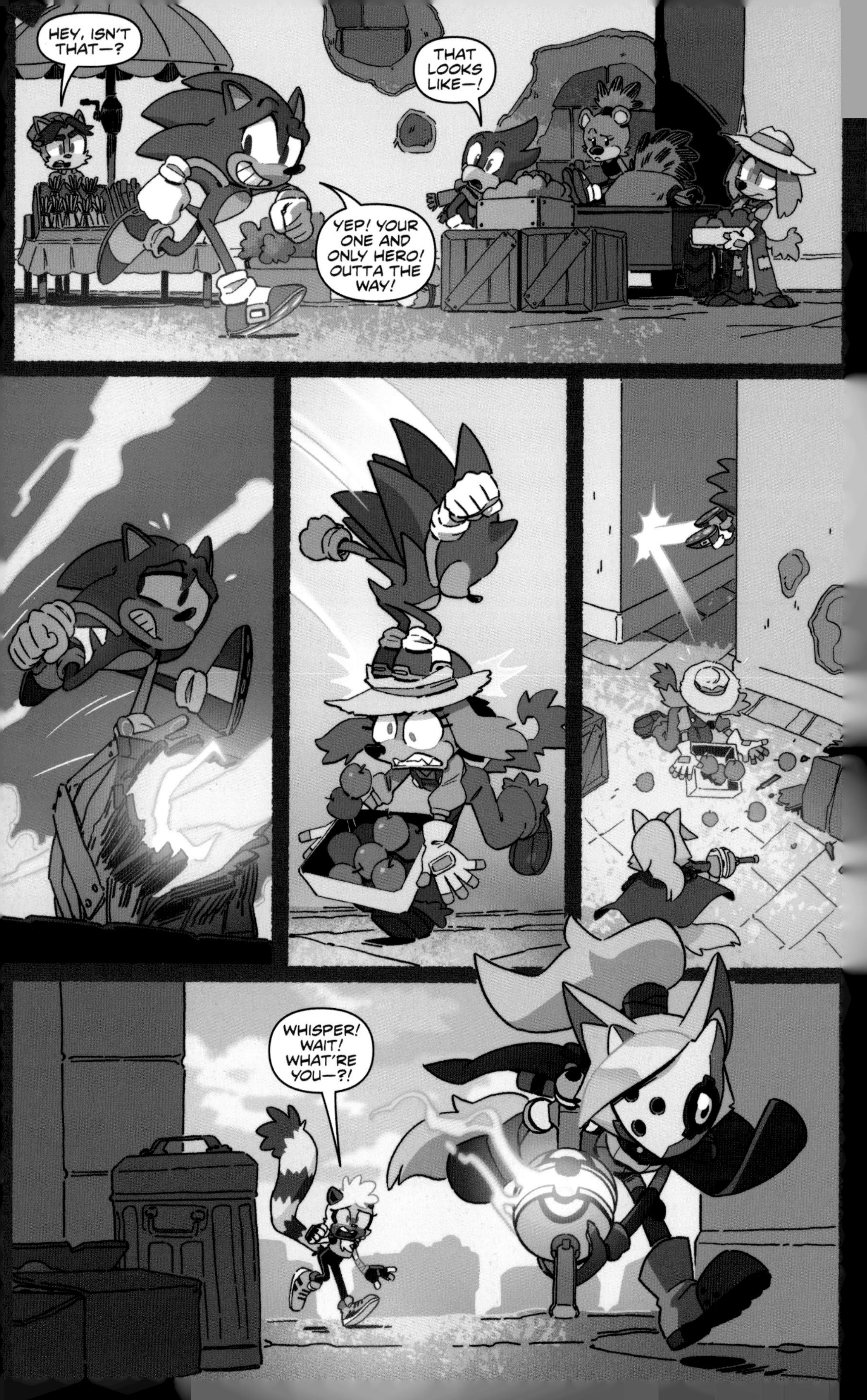
HEY, ISN'T THAT—?
THAT LOOKS LIKE—!
YEP! YOUR ONE AND ONLY HERO! OUTTA THE WAY!
WHISPER! WAIT! WHAT'RE YOU—?!

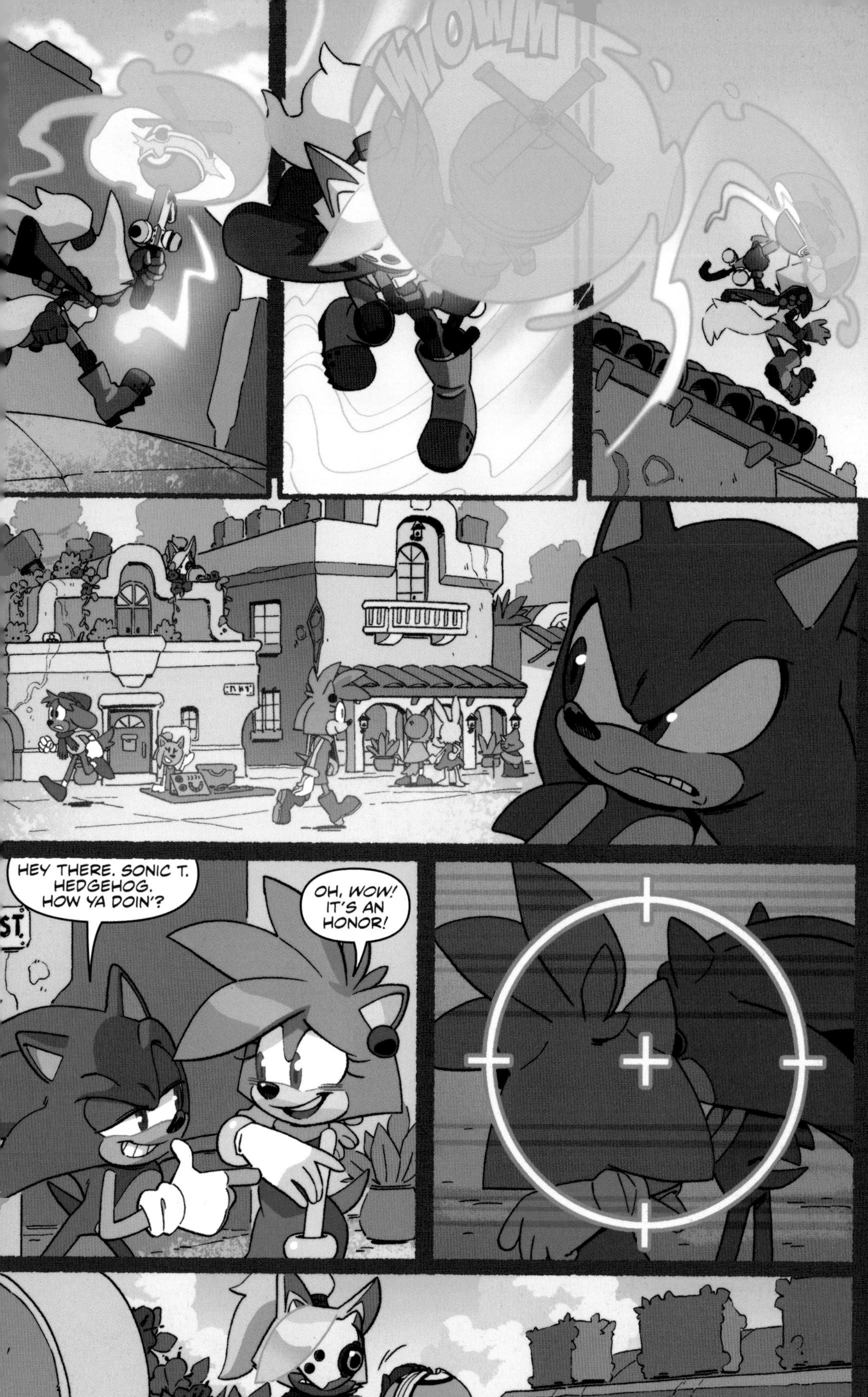
WOWM
HEY THERE. SONIC T. HEDGEHOG. HOW YA DOIN'?
OH, WOW! IT'S AN HONOR!
ST.

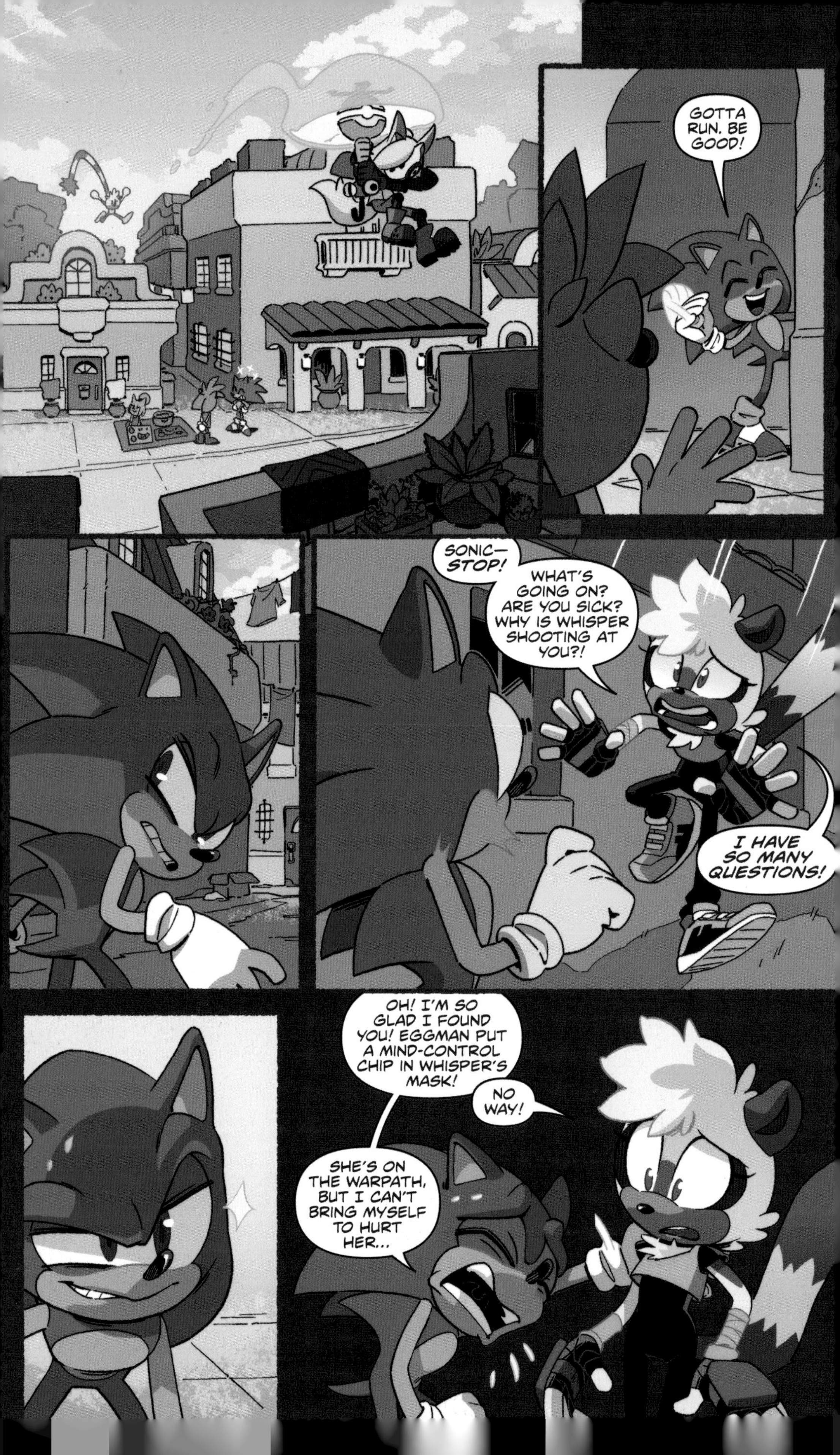
GOTTA RUN. BE GOOD!
SONIC— STOP!
WHAT'S GOING ON? ARE YOU SICK? WHY IS WHISPER SHOOTING AT YOU?!
I HAVE SO MANY QUESTIONS!
OH! I'M SO GLAD I FOUND YOU! EGGMAN PUT A MIND-CONTROL CHIP IN WHISPER'S MASK!
NO WAY!
SHE'S ON THE WARPATH, BUT I CAN'T BRING MYSELF TO HURT HER...

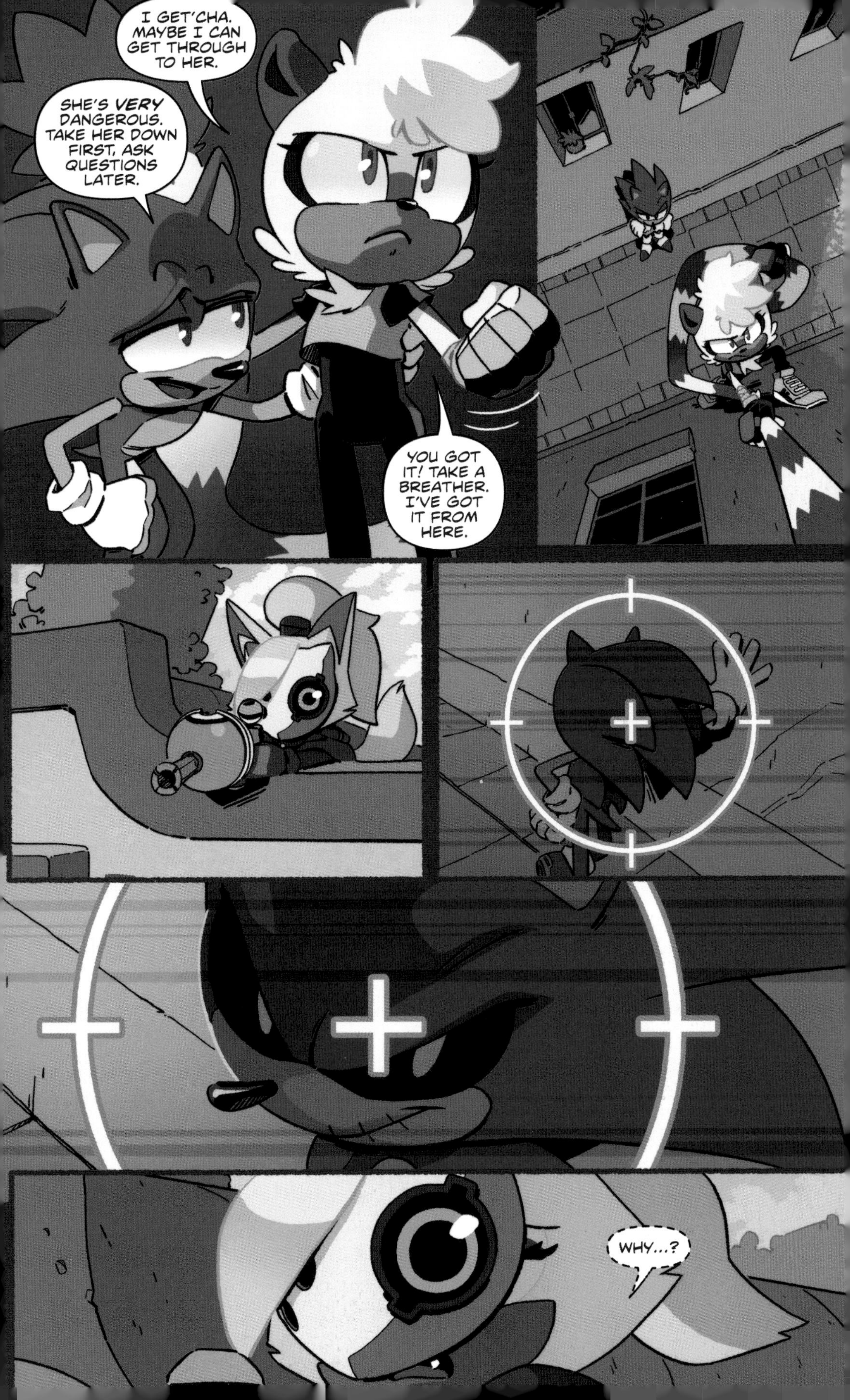

SHE'S VERY DANGEROUS. TAKE HER DOWN FIRST, ASK QUESTIONS LATER.
I GET'CHA. MAYBE I CAN GET THROUGH TO HER.
YOU GOT IT! TAKE A BREATHER. I'VE GOT IT FROM HERE.
WHY...?

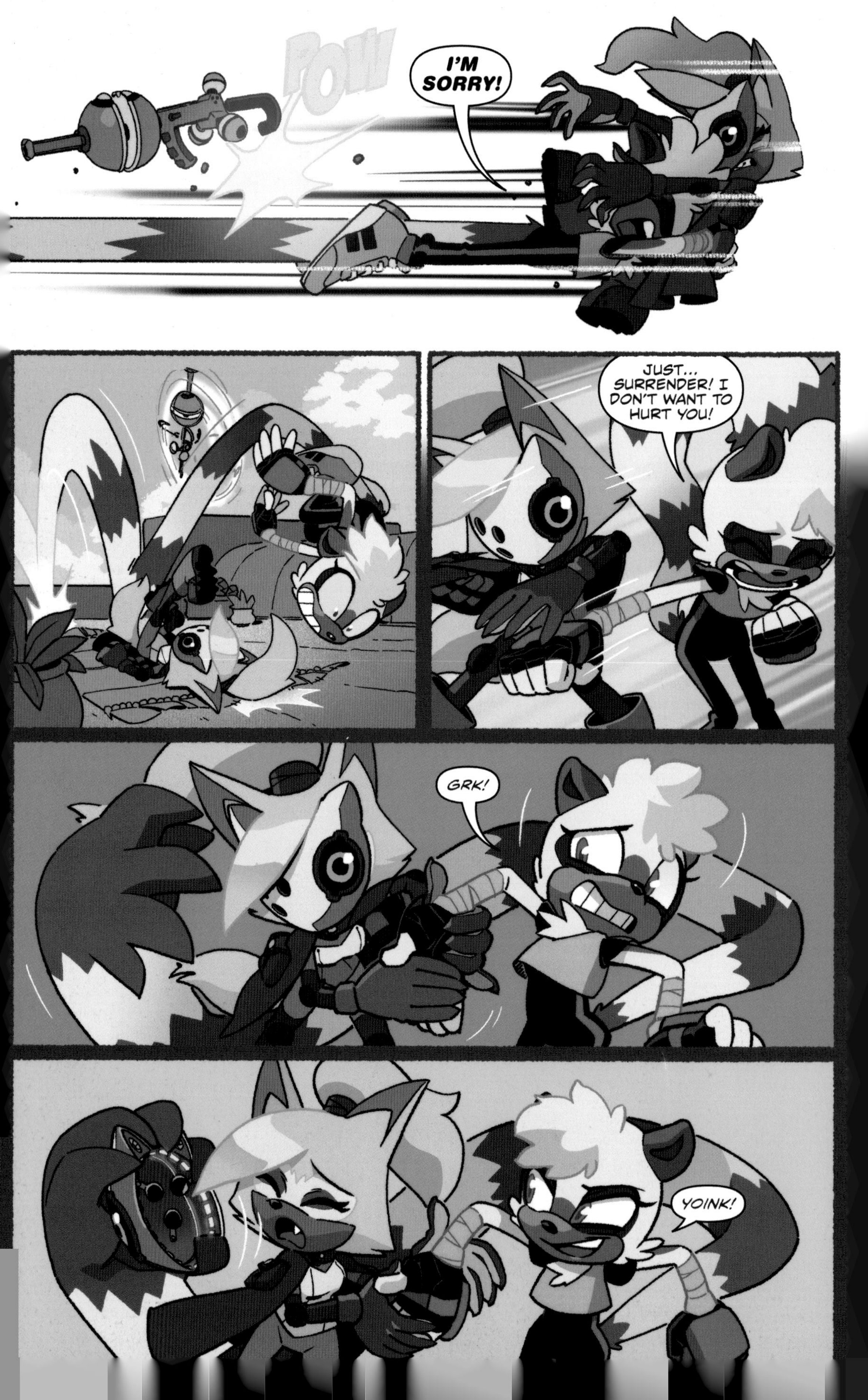
POW
I'M SORRY!
JUST... SURRENDER! I DON'T WANT TO HURT YOU!
GRK!
YOINK!

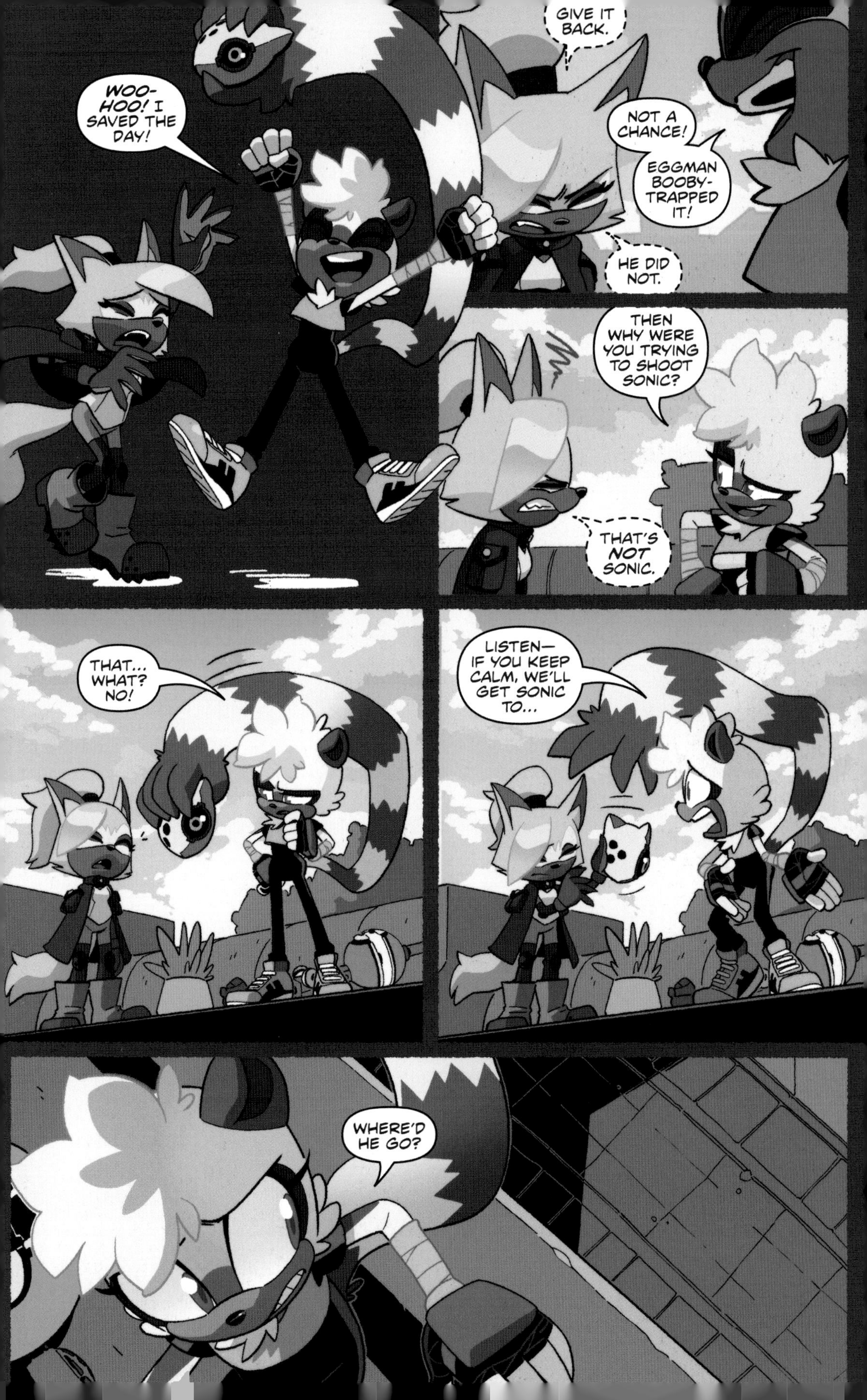
WOO-HOO! I SAVED THE DAY!
GIVE IT BACK.
NOT A CHANCE!
EGGMAN BOOBY-TRAPPED IT!
HE DID NOT.
THEN WHY WERE YOU TRYING TO SHOOT SONIC?
THAT'S NOT SONIC.
THAT... WHAT? NO!
LISTEN— IF YOU KEEP CALM, WE'LL GET SONIC TO...
WHERE'D HE GO?

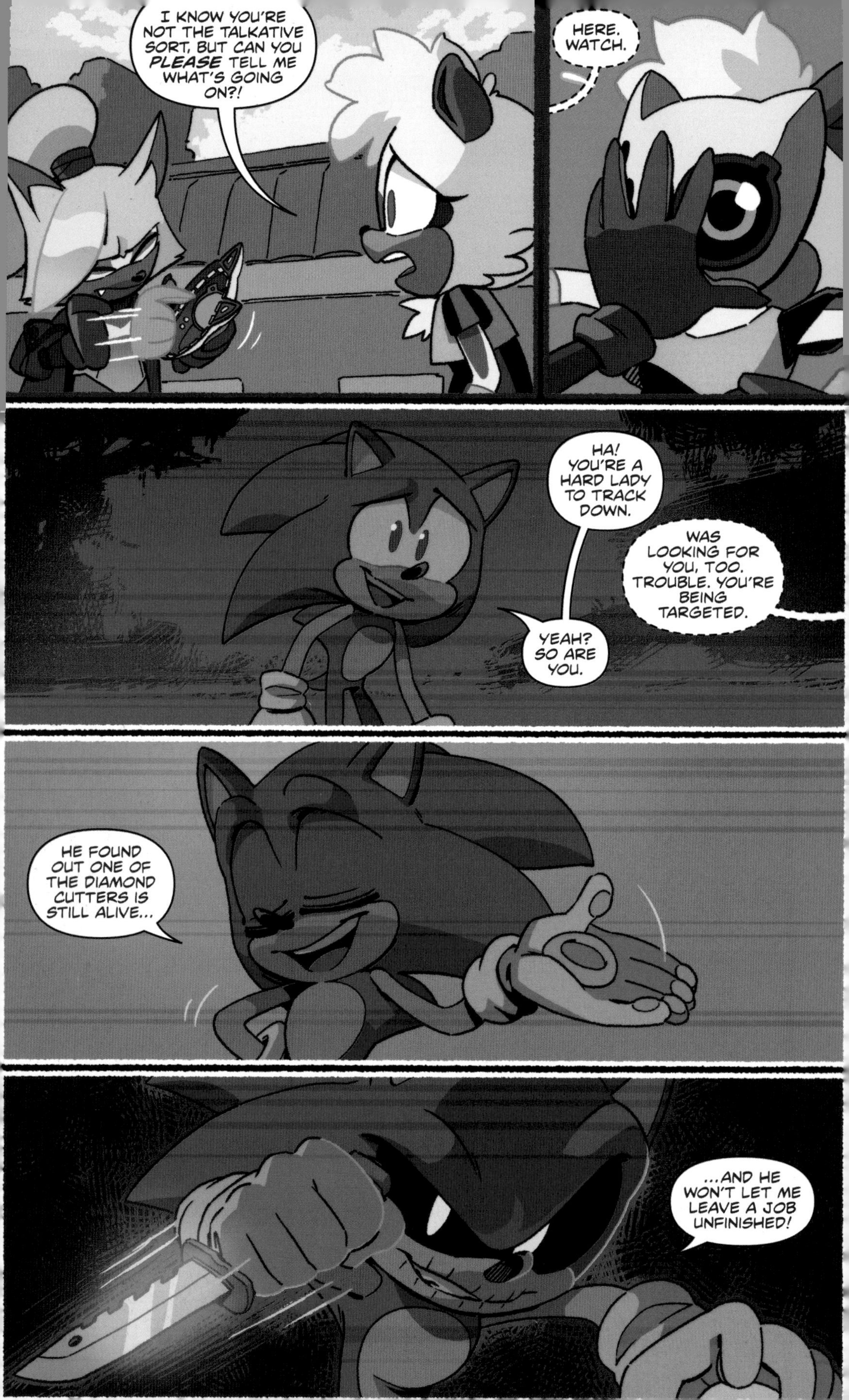
I KNOW YOU'RE NOT THE TALKATIVE SORT, BUT CAN YOU *PLEASE* TELL ME WHAT'S GOING ON?!
HERE. WATCH.
HA! YOU'RE A HARD LADY TO TRACK DOWN.
YEAH? SO ARE YOU.
WAS LOOKING FOR YOU, TOO. TROUBLE. YOU'RE BEING TARGETED.
HE FOUND OUT ONE OF THE DIAMOND CUTTERS IS STILL ALIVE...
...AND HE WON'T LET ME LEAVE A JOB UNFINISHED!

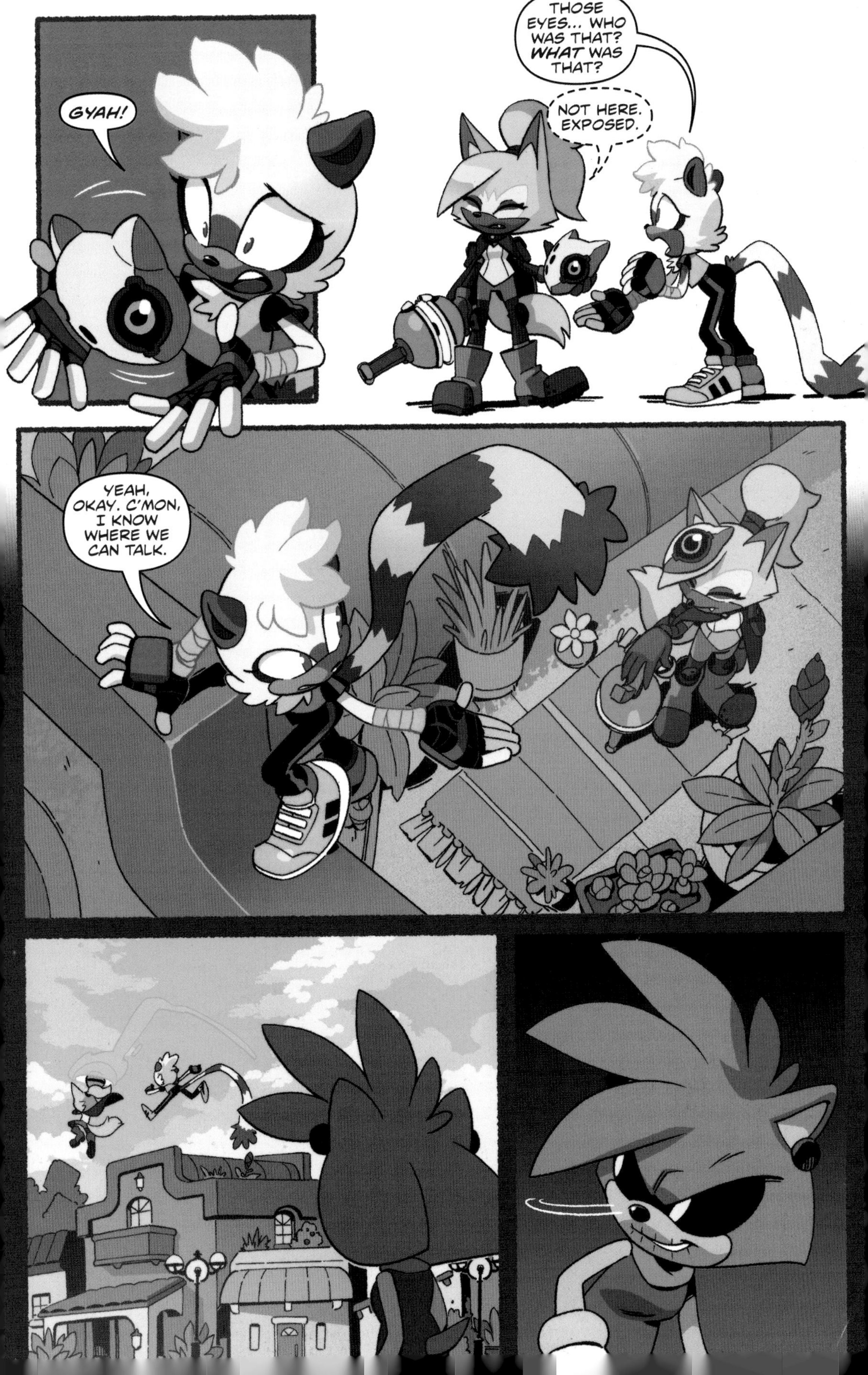
GYAH!
THOSE EYES... WHO WAS THAT? WHAT WAS THAT?
NOT HERE. EXPOSED.
YEAH, OKAY. C'MON, I KNOW WHERE WE CAN TALK.

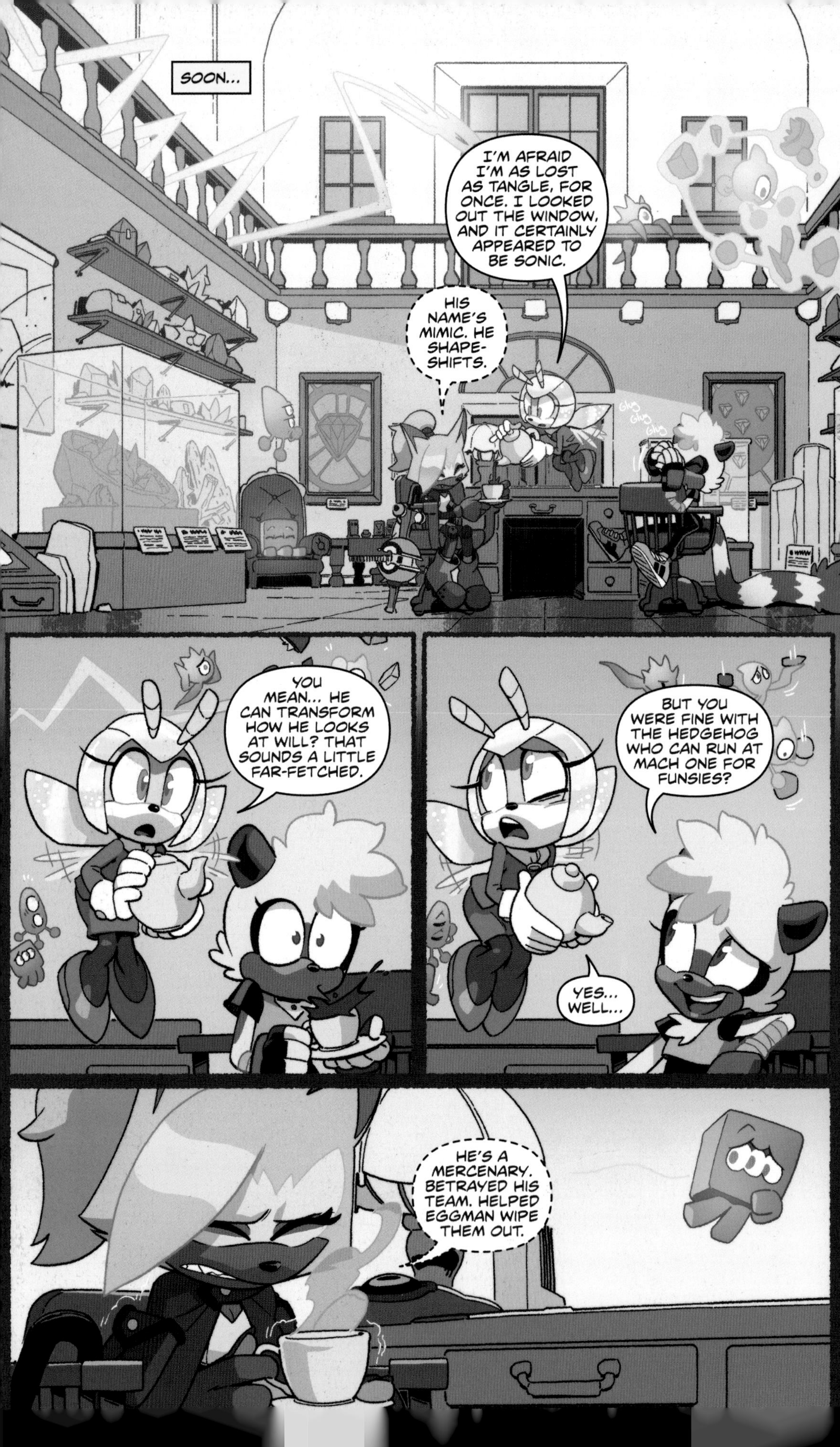

SOON...
I'M AFRAID I'M AS LOST AS TANGLE, FOR ONCE. I LOOKED OUT THE WINDOW, AND IT CERTAINLY APPEARED TO BE SONIC.
HIS NAME'S MIMIC. HE SHAPE-SHIFTS.
Glug Glug Glug
YOU MEAN... HE CAN TRANSFORM HOW HE LOOKS AT WILL? THAT SOUNDS A LITTLE FAR-FETCHED.
BUT YOU WERE FINE WITH THE HEDGEHOG WHO CAN RUN AT MACH ONE FOR FUNSIES?
YES... WELL...
HE'S A MERCENARY. BETRAYED HIS TEAM. HELPED EGGMAN WIPE THEM OUT.

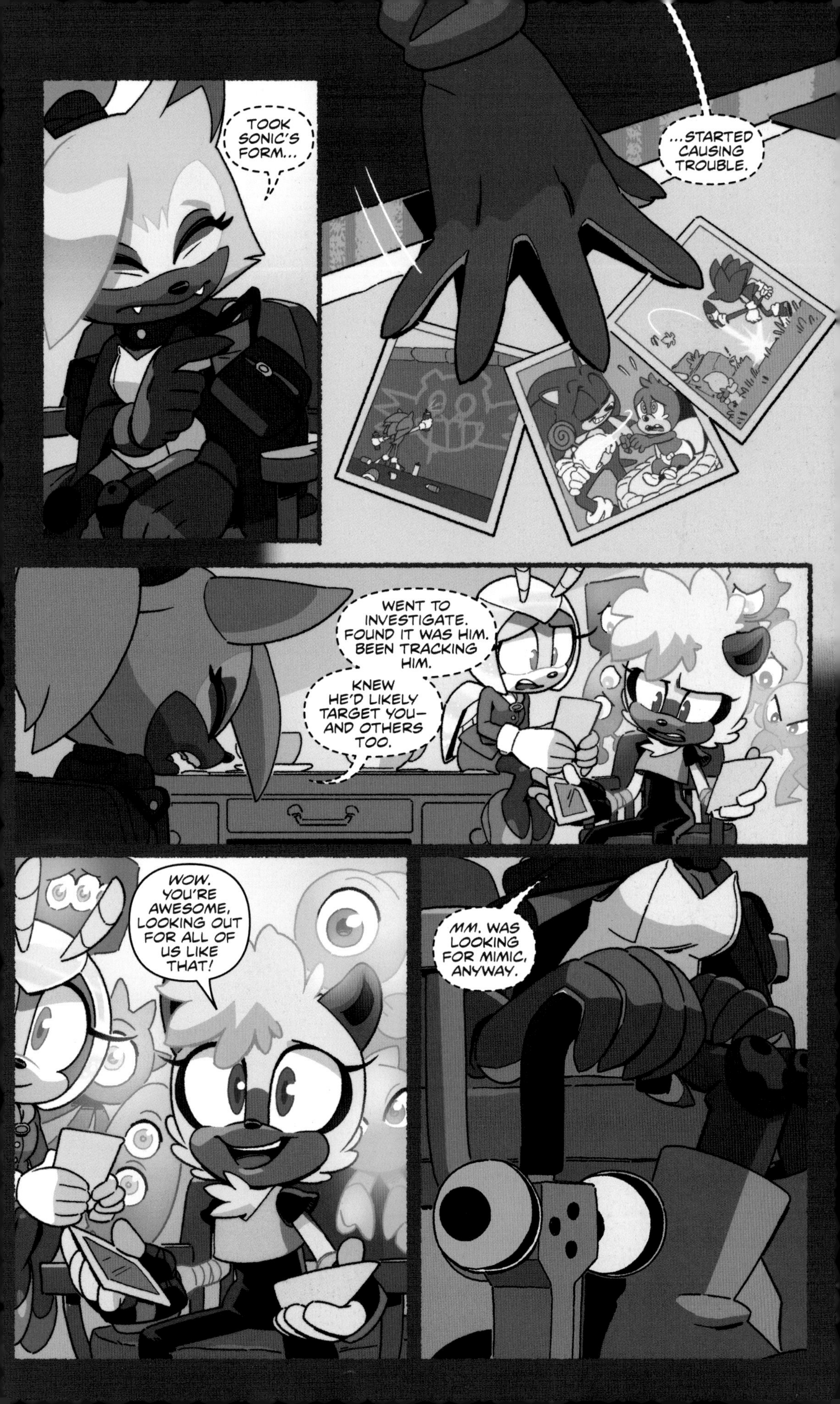
TOOK SONIC'S FORM...
...STARTED CAUSING TROUBLE.
WENT TO INVESTIGATE. FOUND IT WAS HIM. BEEN TRACKING HIM.
KNEW HE'D LIKELY TARGET YOU— AND OTHERS TOO.
WOW. YOU'RE AWESOME, LOOKING OUT FOR ALL OF US LIKE THAT!
MM. WAS LOOKING FOR MIMIC, ANYWAY.

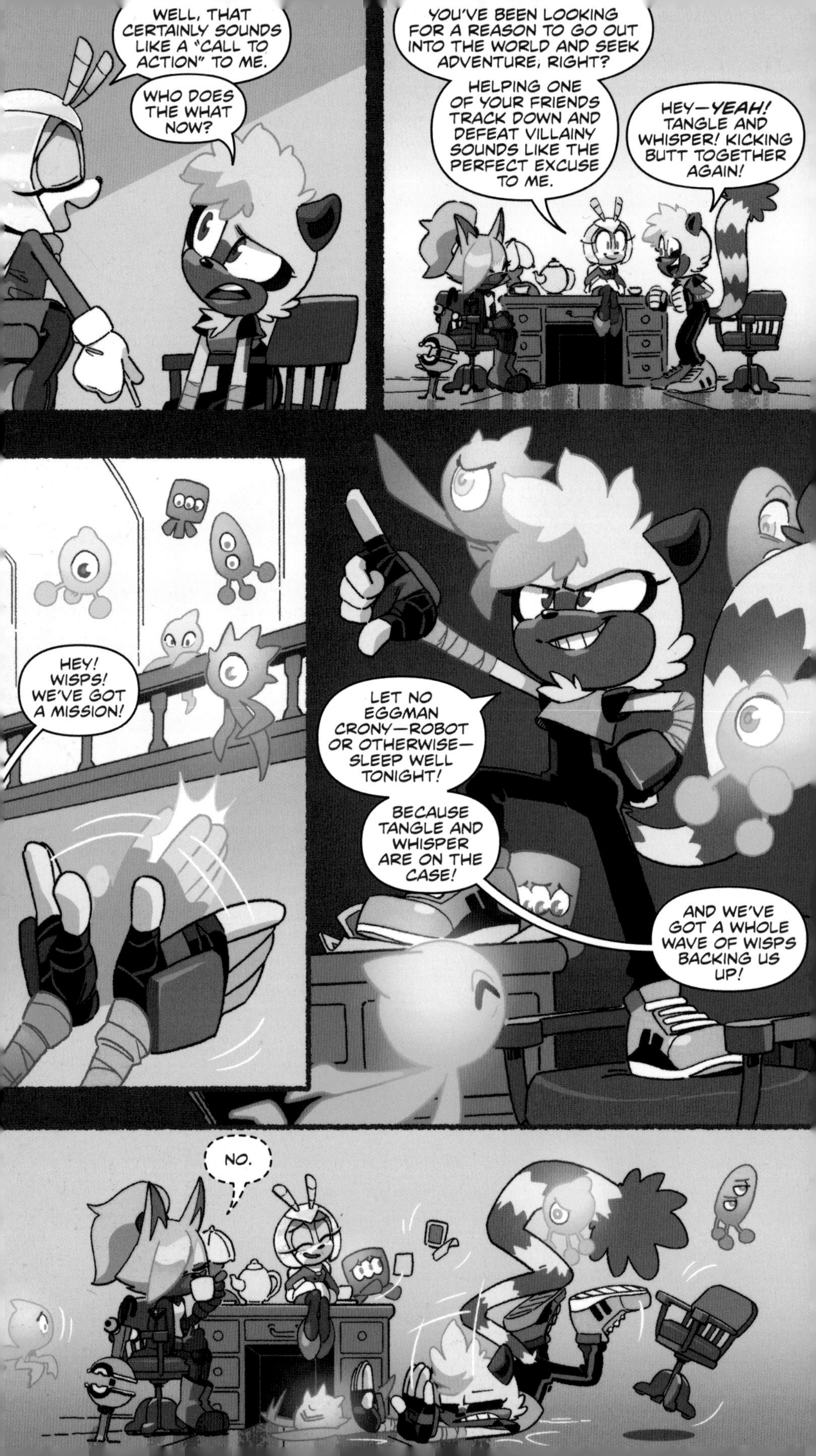
WELL, THAT CERTAINLY SOUNDS LIKE A "CALL TO ACTION" TO ME.
WHO DOES THE WHAT NOW?
YOU'VE BEEN LOOKING FOR A REASON TO GO OUT INTO THE WORLD AND SEEK ADVENTURE, RIGHT?
HELPING ONE OF YOUR FRIENDS TRACK DOWN AND DEFEAT VILLAINY SOUNDS LIKE THE PERFECT EXCUSE TO ME.
HEY—YEAH! TANGLE AND WHISPER! KICKING BUTT TOGETHER AGAIN!
HEY! WISPS! WE'VE GOT A MISSION!
LET NO EGGMAN CRONY—ROBOT OR OTHERWISE—SLEEP WELL TONIGHT!
BECAUSE TANGLE AND WHISPER ARE ON THE CASE!
AND WE'VE GOT A WHOLE WAVE OF WISPS BACKING US UP!
NO.

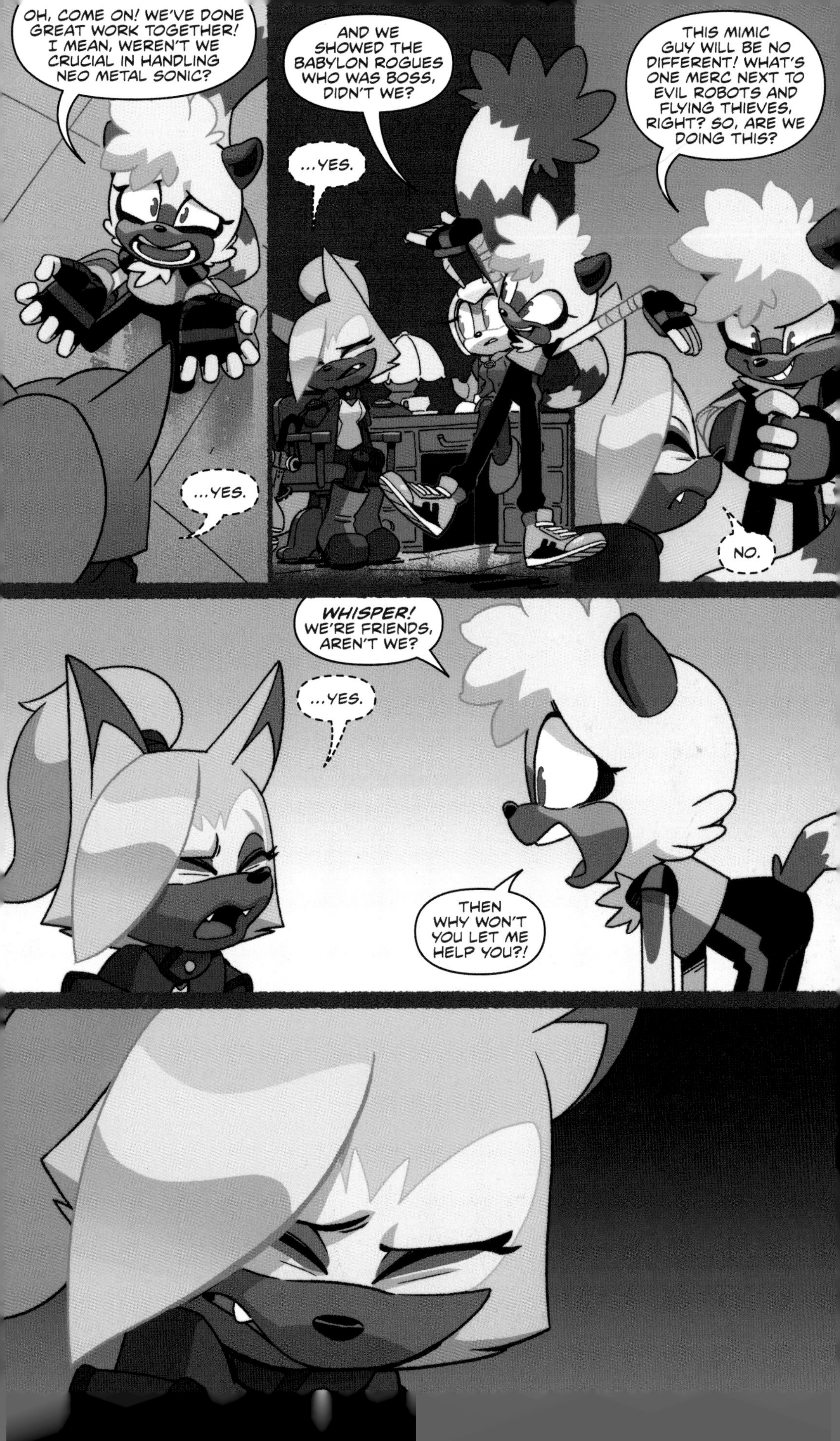

OH, COME ON! WE'VE DONE GREAT WORK TOGETHER! I MEAN, WEREN'T WE CRUCIAL IN HANDLING NEO METAL SONIC?
...YES.
AND WE SHOWED THE BABYLON ROGUES WHO WAS BOSS, DIDN'T WE?
...YES.
THIS MIMIC GUY WILL BE NO DIFFERENT! WHAT'S ONE MERC NEXT TO EVIL ROBOTS AND FLYING THIEVES, RIGHT? SO, ARE WE DOING THIS?
NO.
WHISPER! WE'RE FRIENDS, AREN'T WE?
...YES.
THEN WHY WON'T YOU LET ME HELP YOU?!

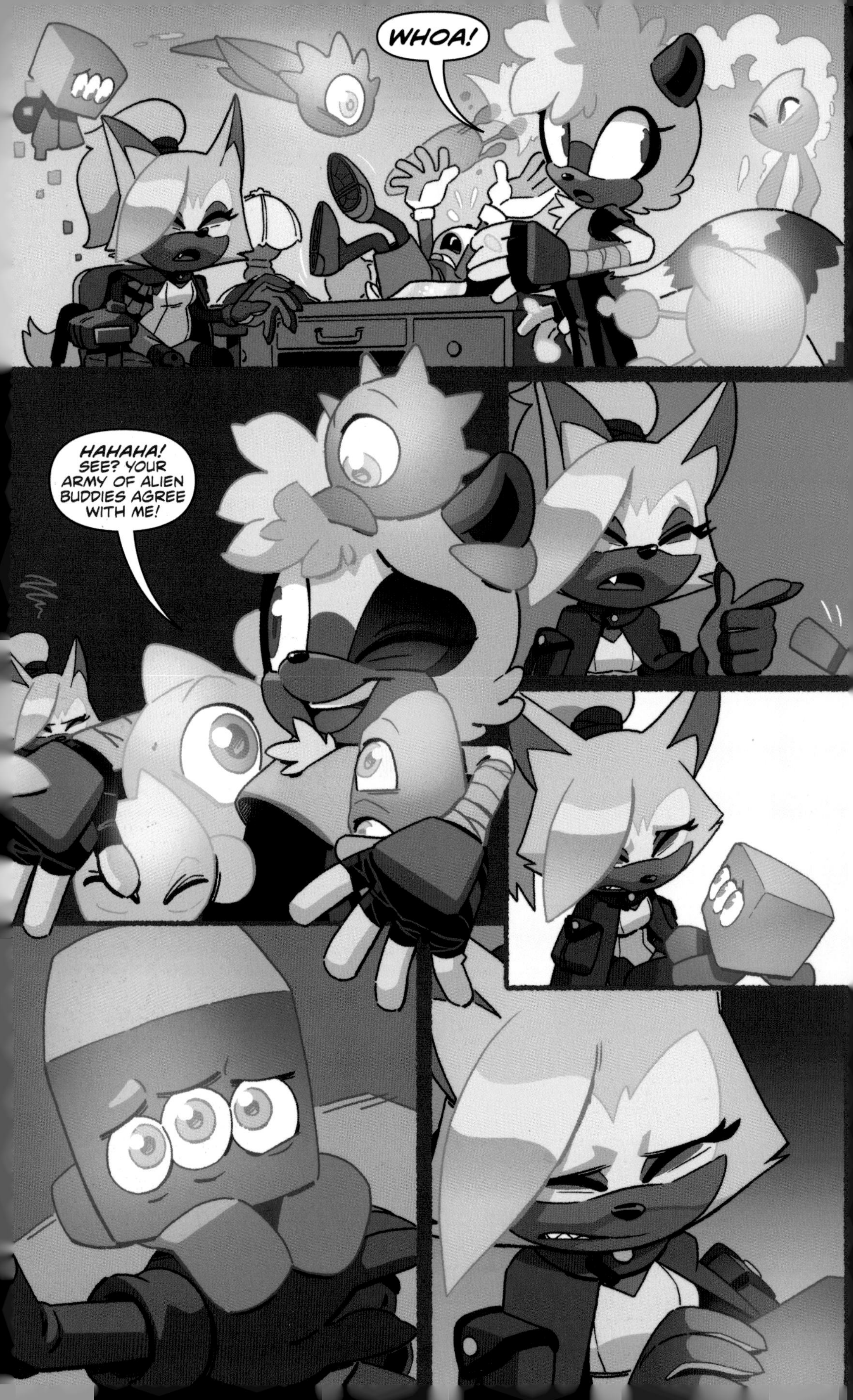
WHOA!
HAHAHA! SEE? YOUR ARMY OF ALIEN BUDDIES AGREE WITH ME!

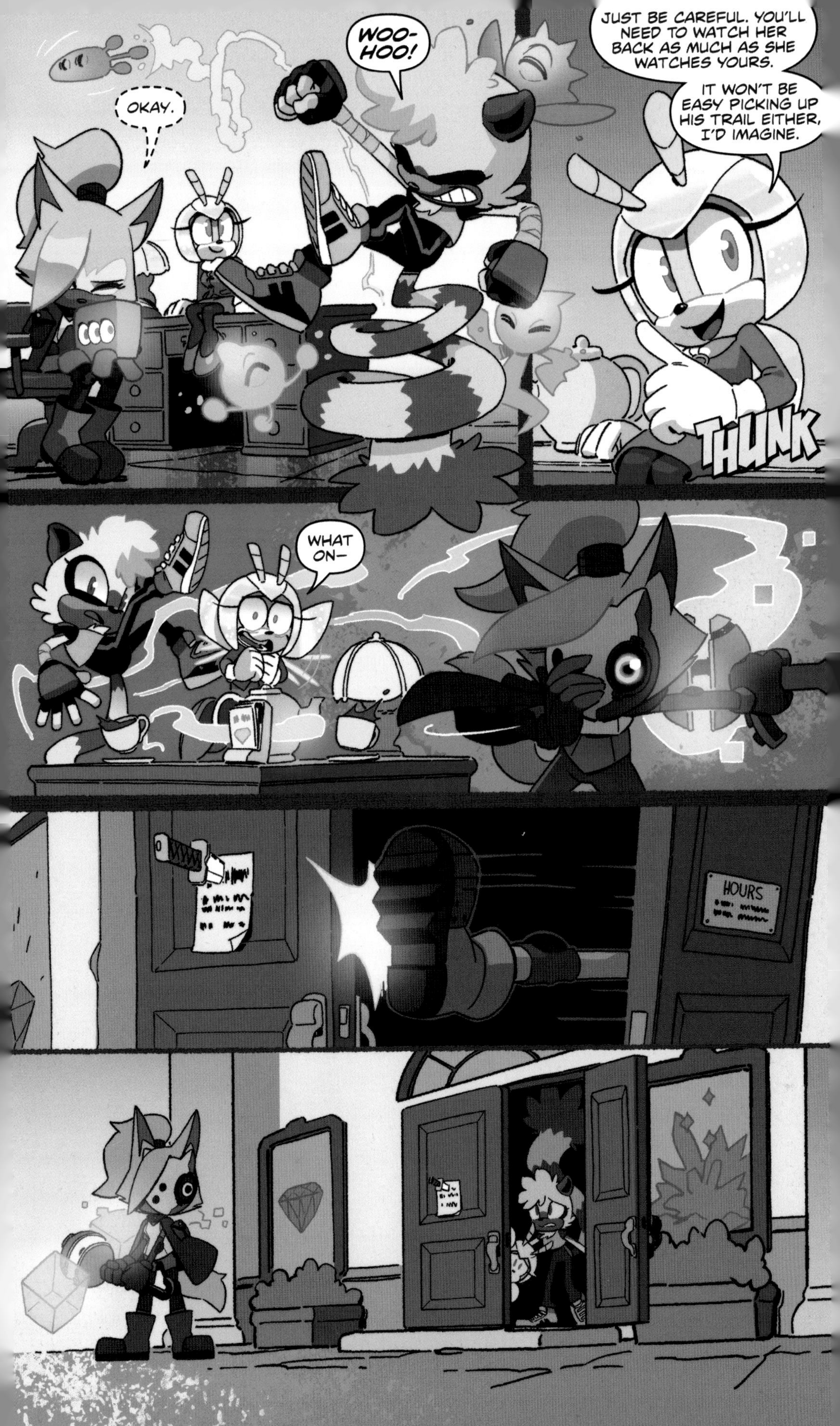
OKAY.
WOO-HOO!
JUST BE CAREFUL. YOU'LL NEED TO WATCH HER BACK AS MUCH AS SHE WATCHES YOURS.
IT WON'T BE EASY PICKING UP HIS TRAIL EITHER, I'D IMAGINE.
THUNK
WHAT ON—
HOURS

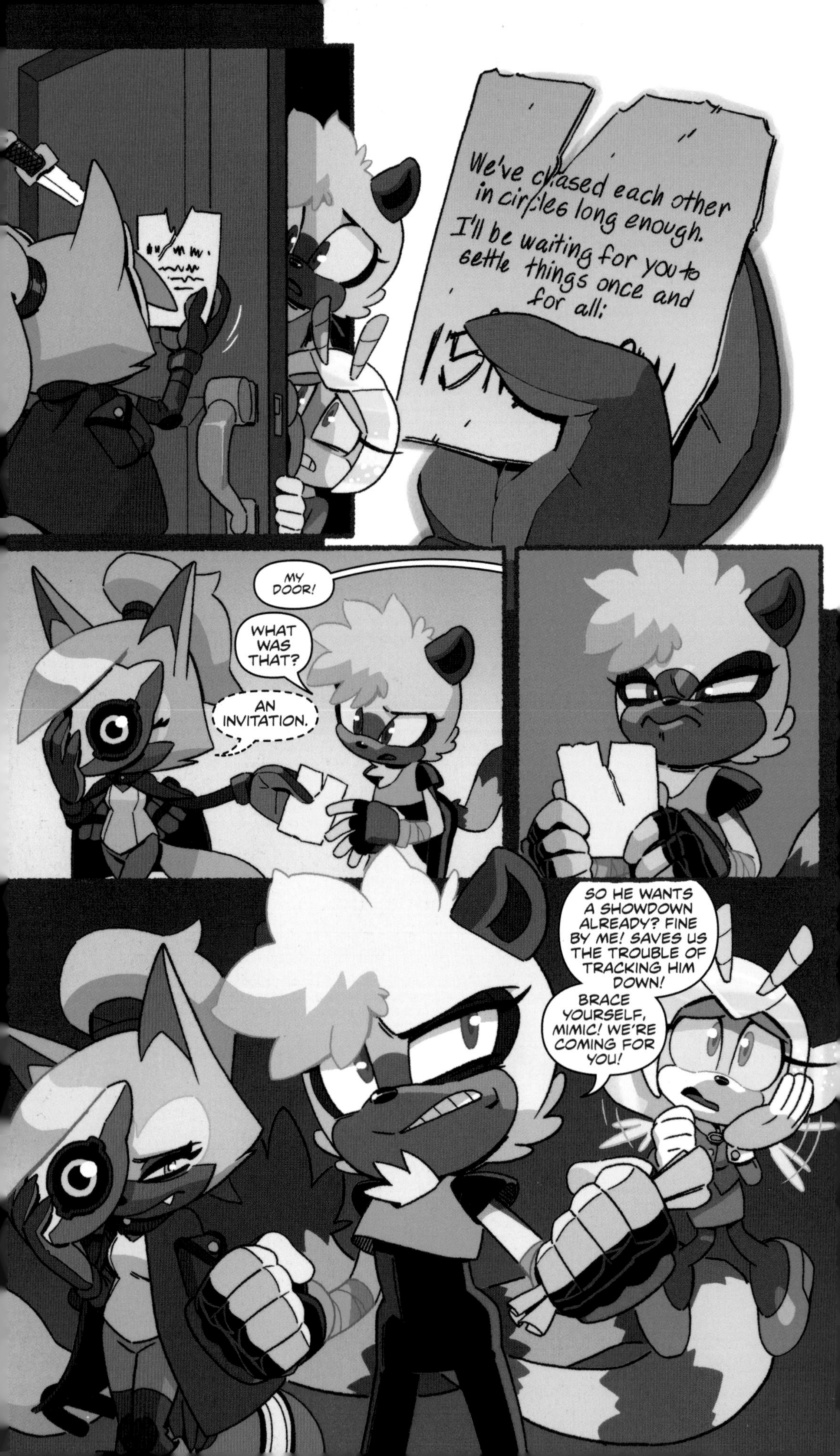
We've chased each other in circles long enough.
I'll be waiting for you to settle things once and for all:
MY DOOR!
WHAT WAS THAT?
AN INVITATION.
SO HE WANTS A SHOWDOWN ALREADY? FINE BY ME! SAVES US THE TROUBLE OF TRACKING HIM DOWN!
BRACE YOURSELF, MIMIC! WE'RE COMING FOR YOU!

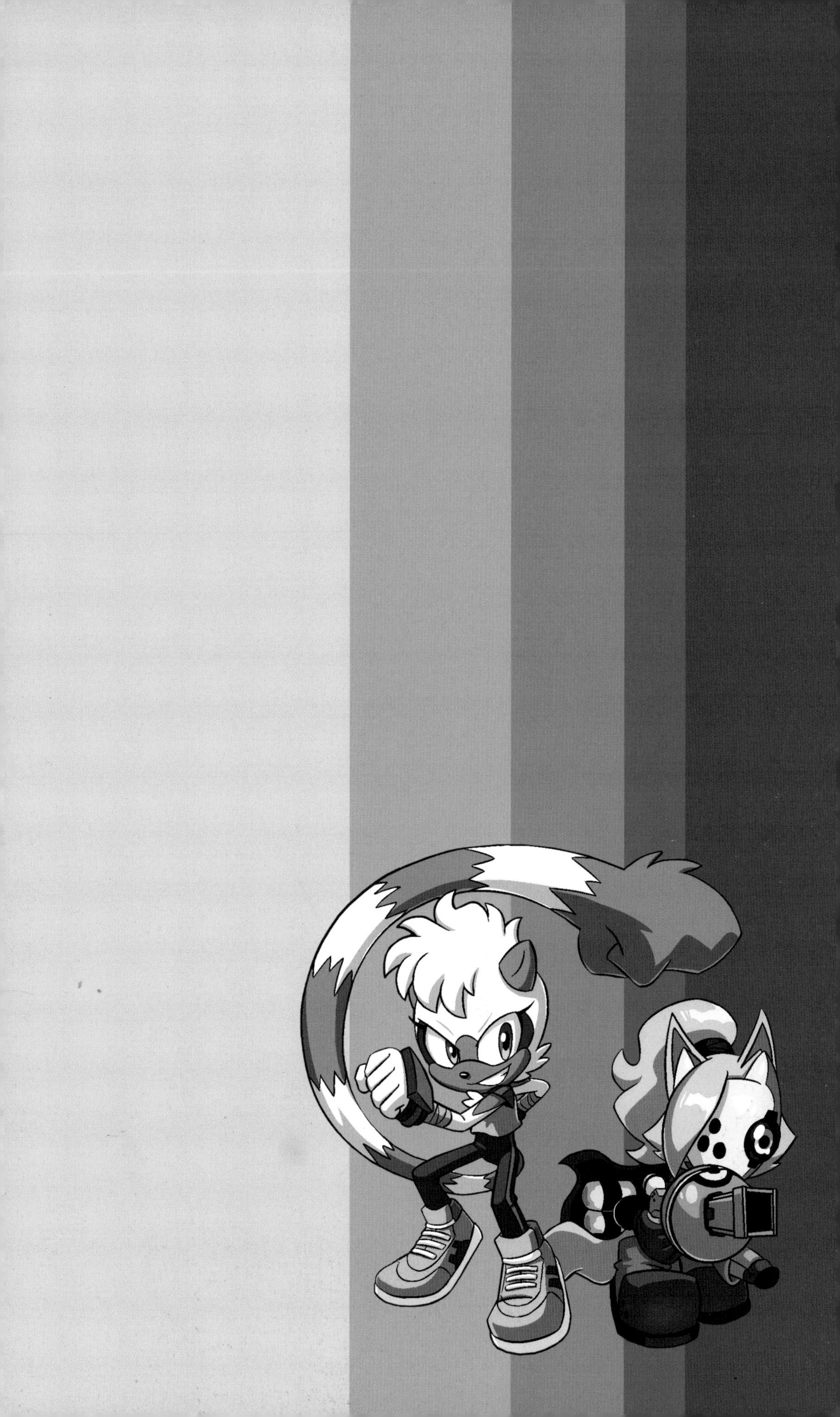

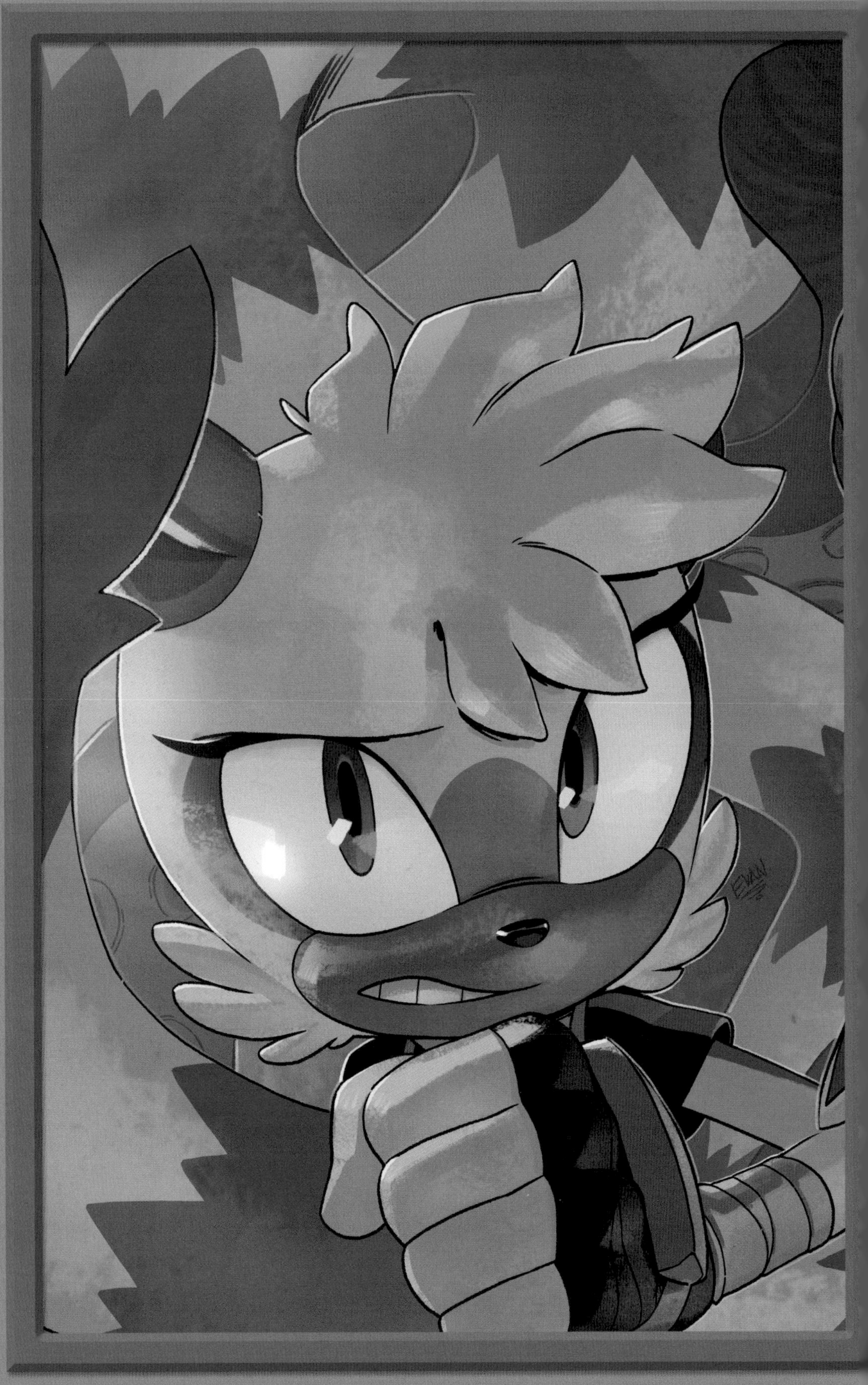

ART BY **EVAN STANLEY**

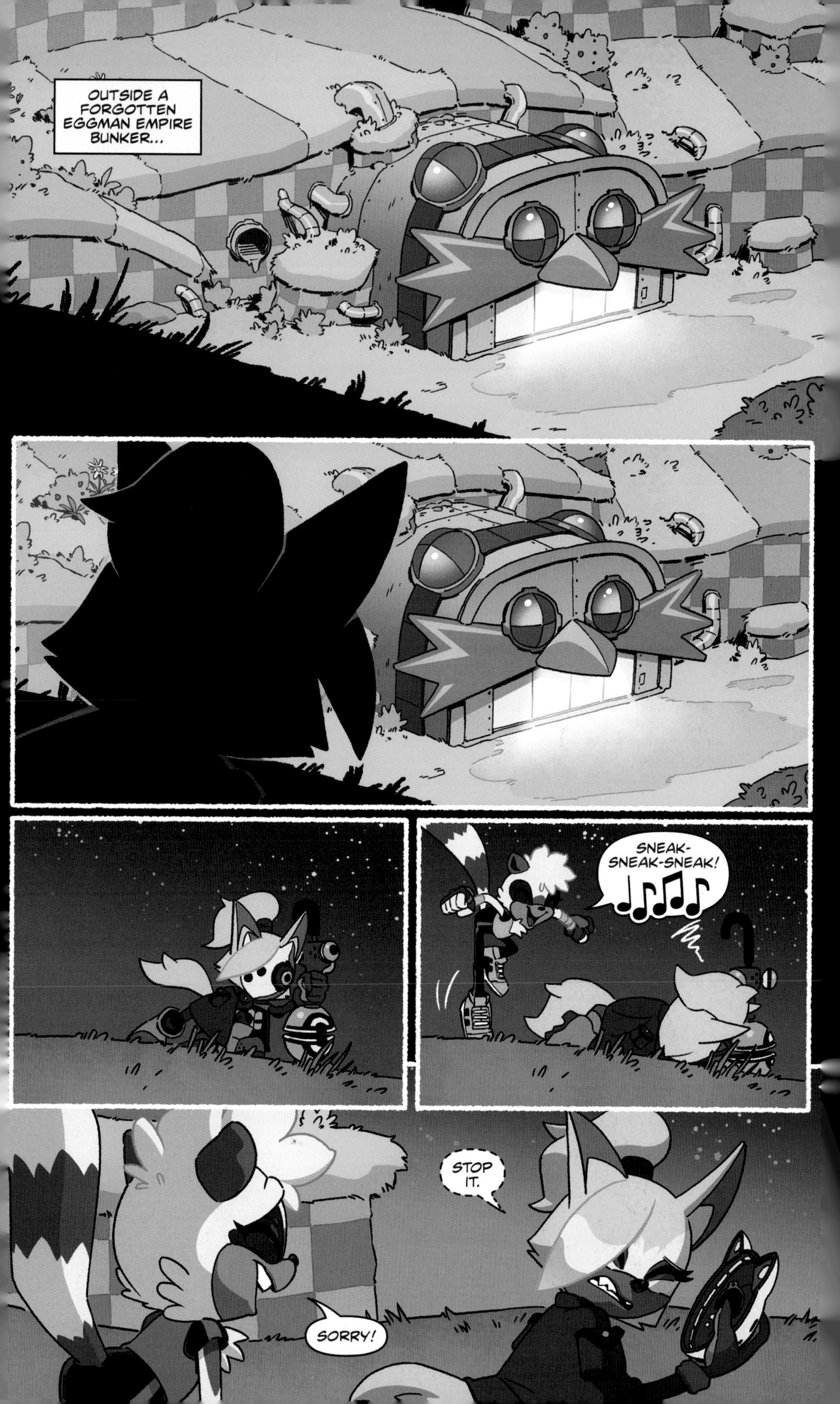
OUTSIDE A FORGOTTEN EGGMAN EMPIRE BUNKER...
SNEAK-SNEAK-SNEAK!
STOP IT.
SORRY!

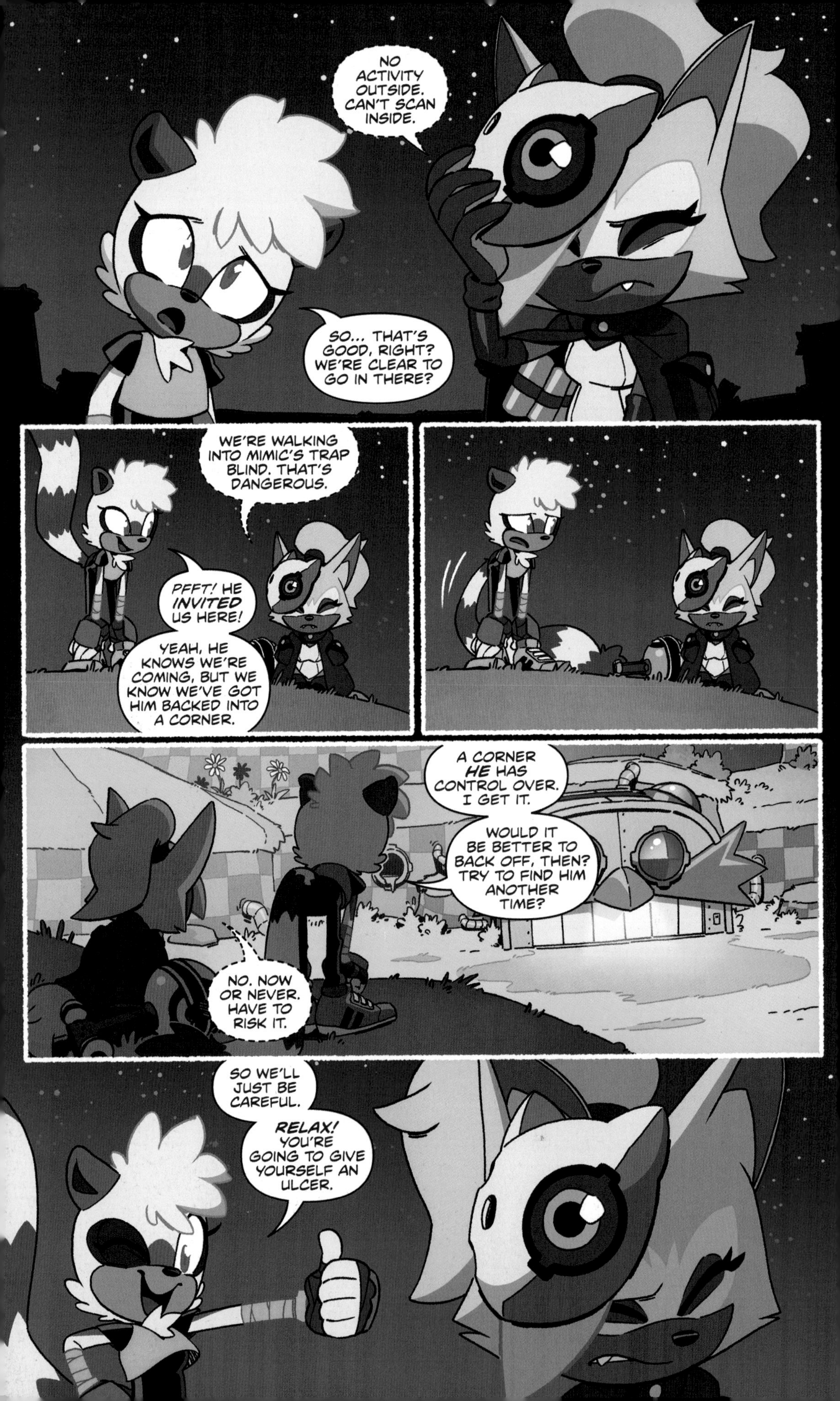

NO ACTIVITY OUTSIDE. CAN'T SCAN INSIDE.
SO... THAT'S GOOD, RIGHT? WE'RE CLEAR TO GO IN THERE?
WE'RE WALKING INTO MIMIC'S TRAP BLIND. THAT'S DANGEROUS.
PFFT! HE *INVITED* US HERE!
YEAH, HE KNOWS WE'RE COMING, BUT WE KNOW WE'VE GOT HIM BACKED INTO A CORNER.
A CORNER *HE* HAS CONTROL OVER. I GET IT.
WOULD IT BE BETTER TO BACK OFF, THEN? TRY TO FIND HIM ANOTHER TIME?
NO. NOW OR NEVER. HAVE TO RISK IT.
SO WE'LL JUST BE CAREFUL.
RELAX! YOU'RE GOING TO GIVE YOURSELF AN ULCER.

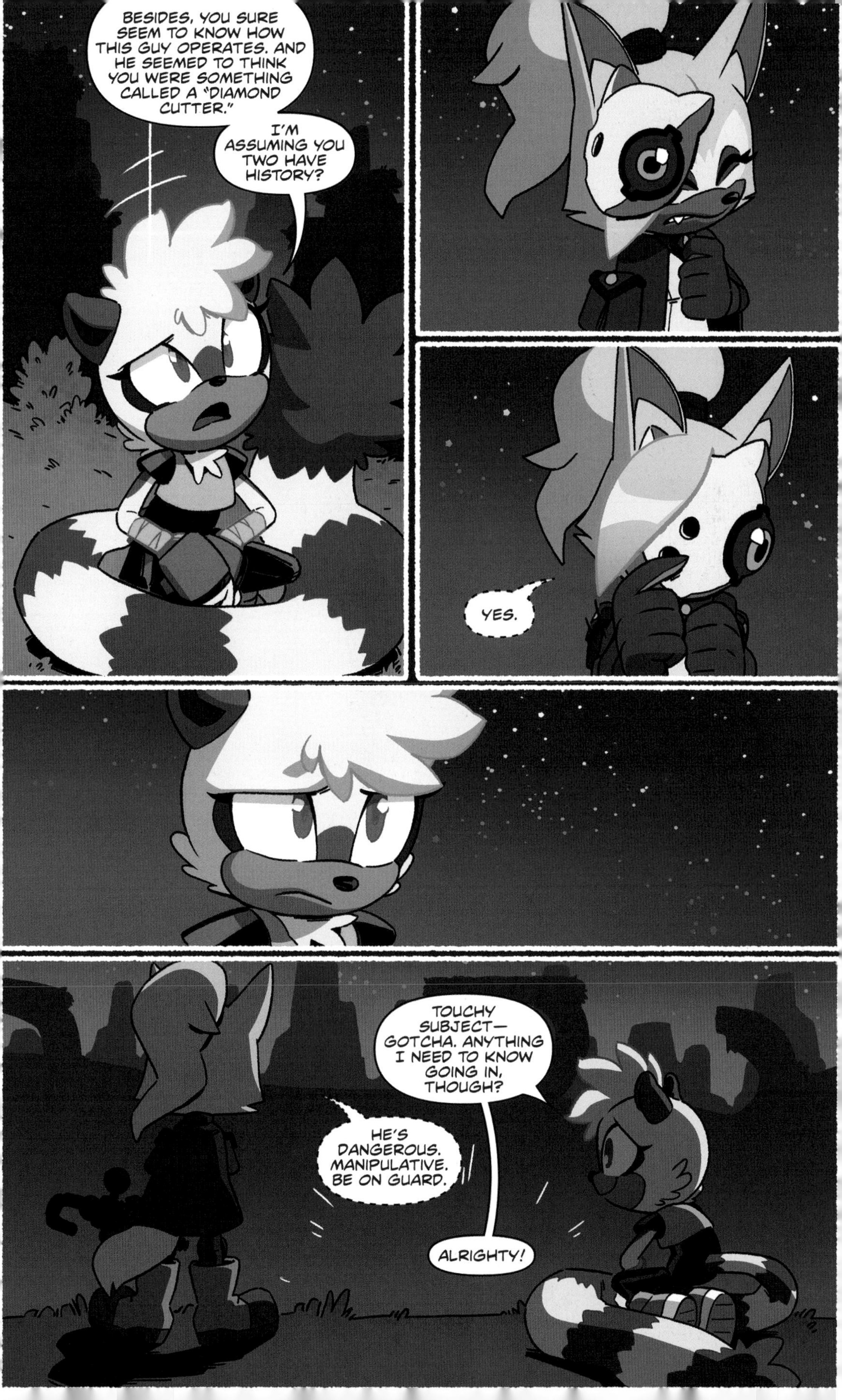
BESIDES, YOU SURE SEEM TO KNOW HOW THIS GUY OPERATES. AND HE SEEMED TO THINK YOU WERE SOMETHING CALLED A "DIAMOND CUTTER."
I'M ASSUMING YOU TWO HAVE HISTORY?
YES.
TOUCHY SUBJECT— GOTCHA. ANYTHING I NEED TO KNOW GOING IN, THOUGH?
HE'S DANGEROUS. MANIPULATIVE. BE ON GUARD.
ALRIGHTY!

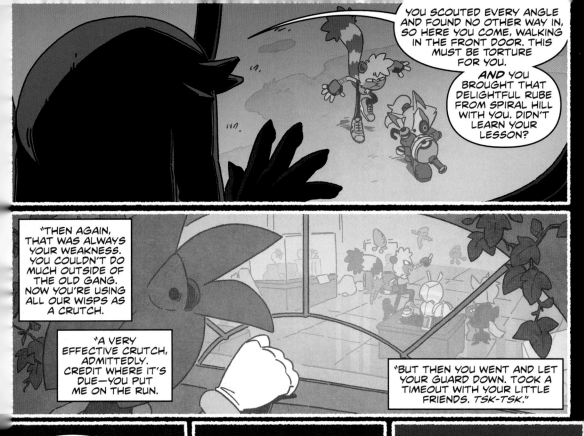

YOU SCOUTED EVERY ANGLE AND FOUND NO OTHER WAY IN, SO HERE YOU COME, WALKING IN THE FRONT DOOR. THIS MUST BE TORTURE FOR YOU.

AND YOU BROUGHT THAT DELIGHTFUL RUBE FROM SPIRAL HILL WITH YOU. DIDN'T LEARN YOUR LESSON?

"THEN AGAIN, THAT WAS ALWAYS YOUR WEAKNESS. YOU COULDN'T DO MUCH OUTSIDE OF THE OLD GANG. NOW YOU'RE USING ALL OUR WISPS AS A CRUTCH.

"A VERY EFFECTIVE CRUTCH, ADMITTEDLY. CREDIT WHERE IT'S DUE—YOU PUT ME ON THE RUN.

"BUT THEN YOU WENT AND LET YOUR GUARD DOWN. TOOK A TIMEOUT WITH YOUR LITTLE FRIENDS. *TSK-TSK.*"

PART OF ME WISHES WE COULD SETTLE THIS JUST BETWEEN US...

...BUT SINCE YOU *INSIST* ON BRINGING ALONG THE YOKEL...

...I'LL JUST HAVE TO LET *YOU* HANDICAP YOURSELF.

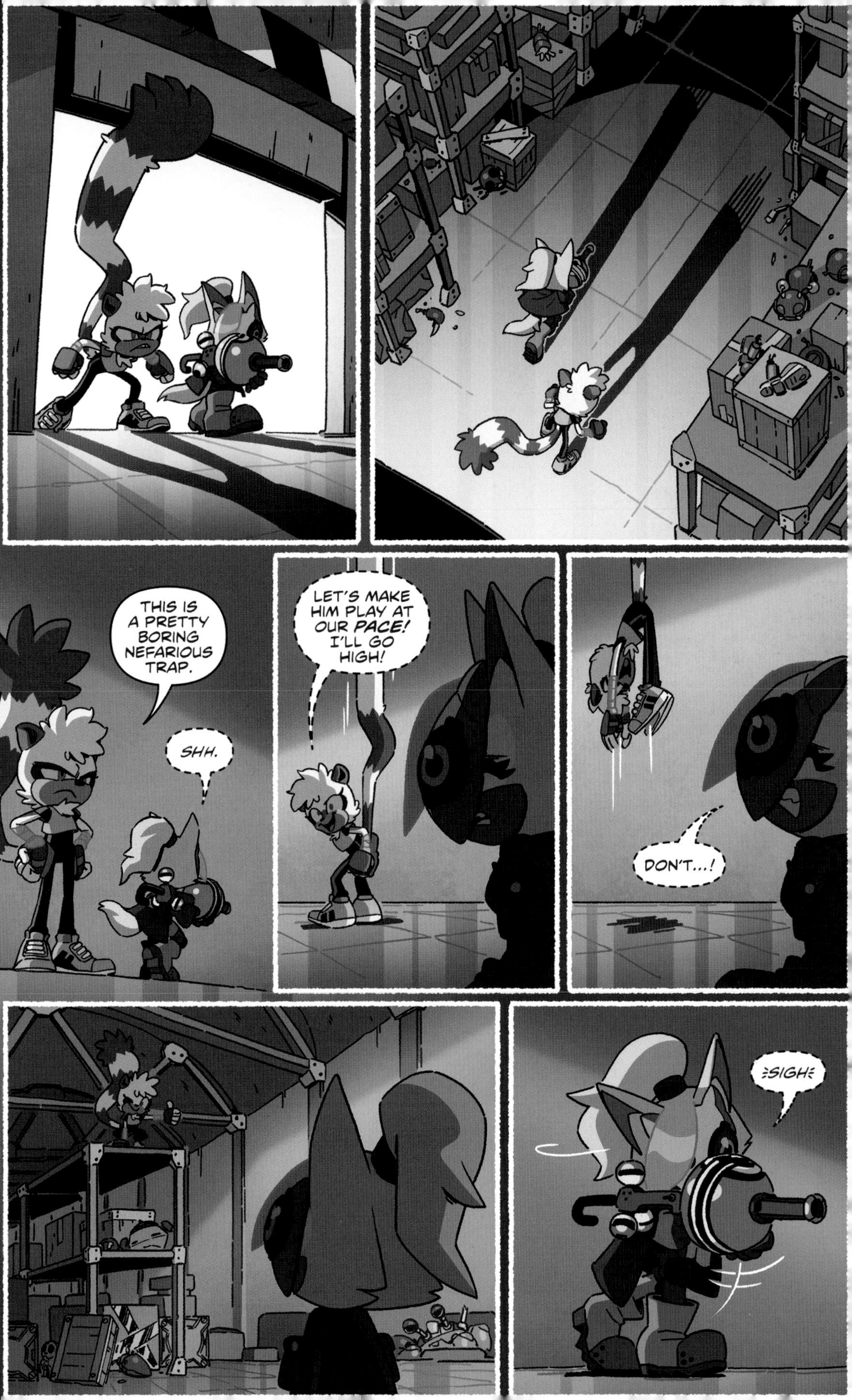
THIS IS A PRETTY BORING NEFARIOUS TRAP.
SHH.
LET'S MAKE HIM PLAY AT OUR PACE! I'LL GO HIGH!
DON'T...!
≈SIGH≈

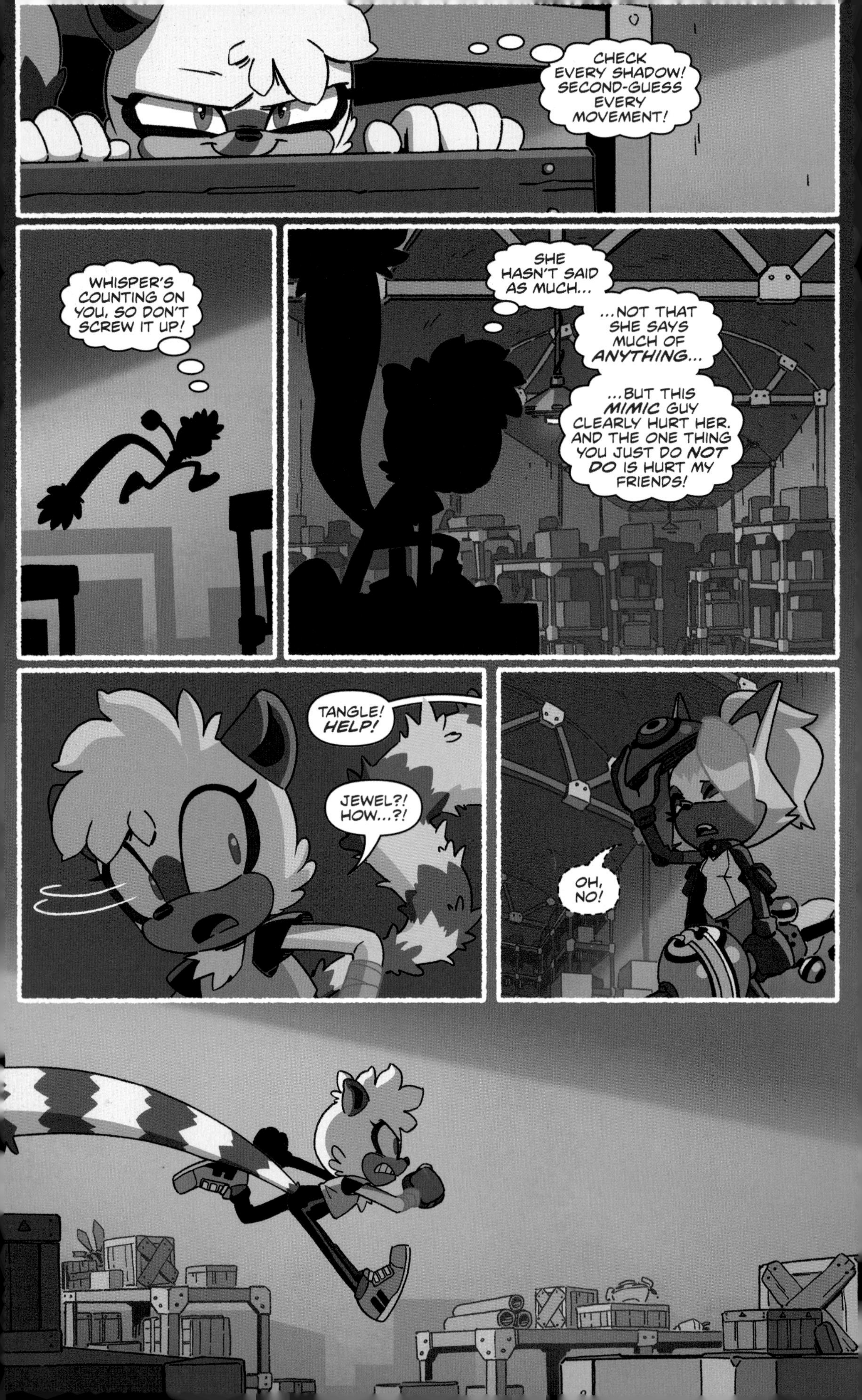
CHECK EVERY SHADOW! SECOND-GUESS EVERY MOVEMENT!
WHISPER'S COUNTING ON YOU, SO DON'T SCREW IT UP!
SHE HASN'T SAID AS MUCH...
...NOT THAT SHE SAYS MUCH OF ANYTHING...
...BUT THIS MIMIC GUY CLEARLY HURT HER. AND THE ONE THING YOU JUST DO NOT DO IS HURT MY FRIENDS!
TANGLE! HELP!
JEWEL?! HOW...?!
OH, NO!

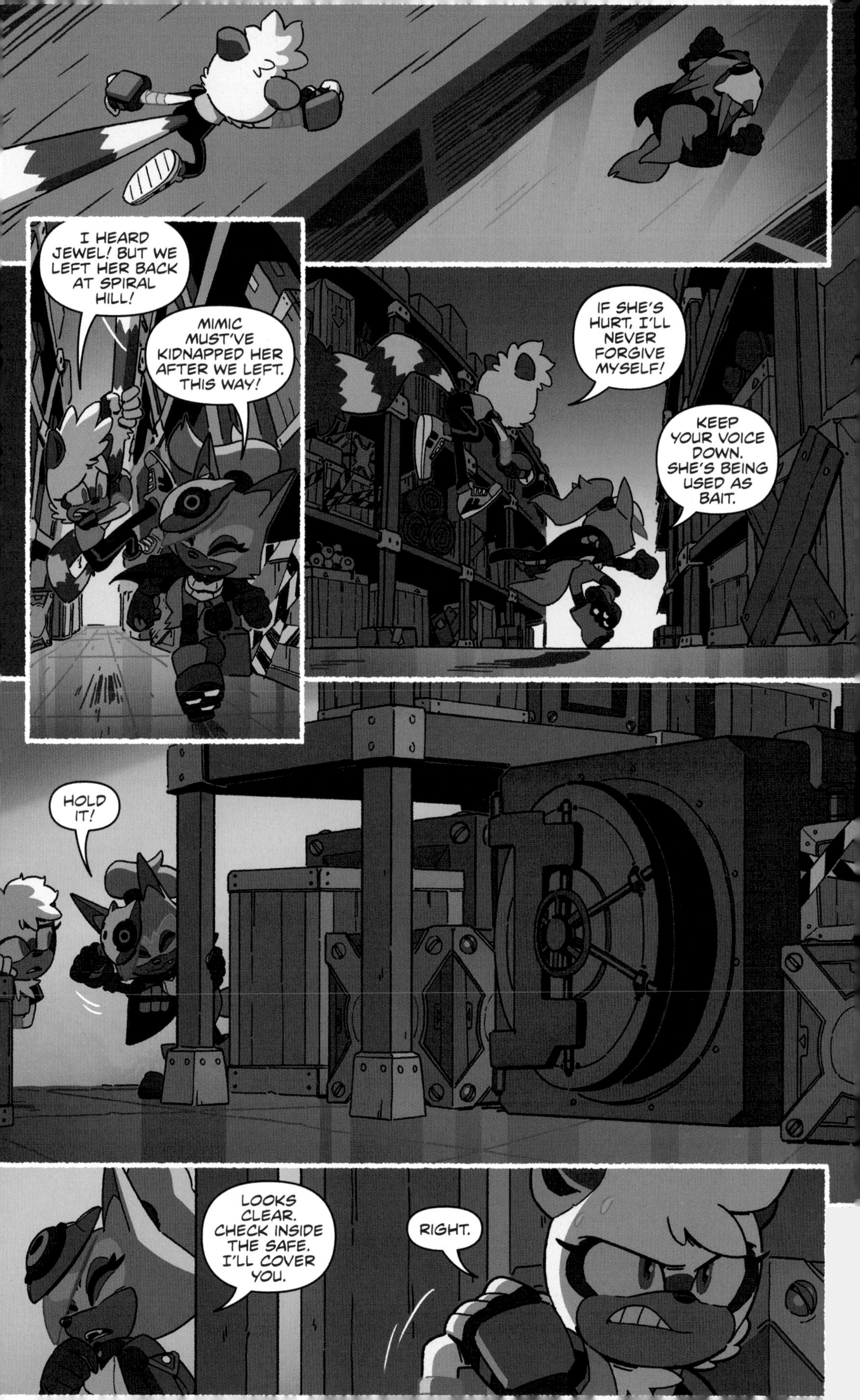
I HEARD JEWEL! BUT WE LEFT HER BACK AT SPIRAL HILL!
MIMIC MUST'VE KIDNAPPED HER AFTER WE LEFT. THIS WAY!
IF SHE'S HURT, I'LL NEVER FORGIVE MYSELF!
KEEP YOUR VOICE DOWN. SHE'S BEING USED AS BAIT.
HOLD IT!
LOOKS CLEAR. CHECK INSIDE THE SAFE. I'LL COVER YOU.
RIGHT.

HEH... WHISPER MUST BE WORRIED, TOO. I'VE NEVER HEARD HER SPEAK SO PLAINLY...

WAIT. DID SHE NOT HAVE HER WISPON?

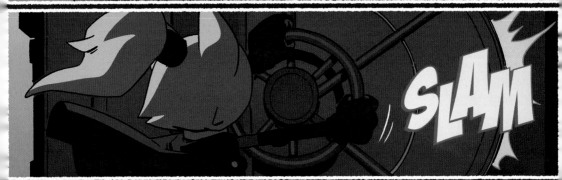

SLAM

NO-NO-NO!

LET ME OUT! F-FIGHT M-ME IN TH-THE O-OPEN!

HELLO?! YOU JERK! OPEN UP RIGHT NOW!

DON'T. CAN'T PASS OUT AGAIN. CAN'T USE UP THE AIR. IT'S DARK. JUST... FORGET YOU'RE ENCLOSED AND... UM...

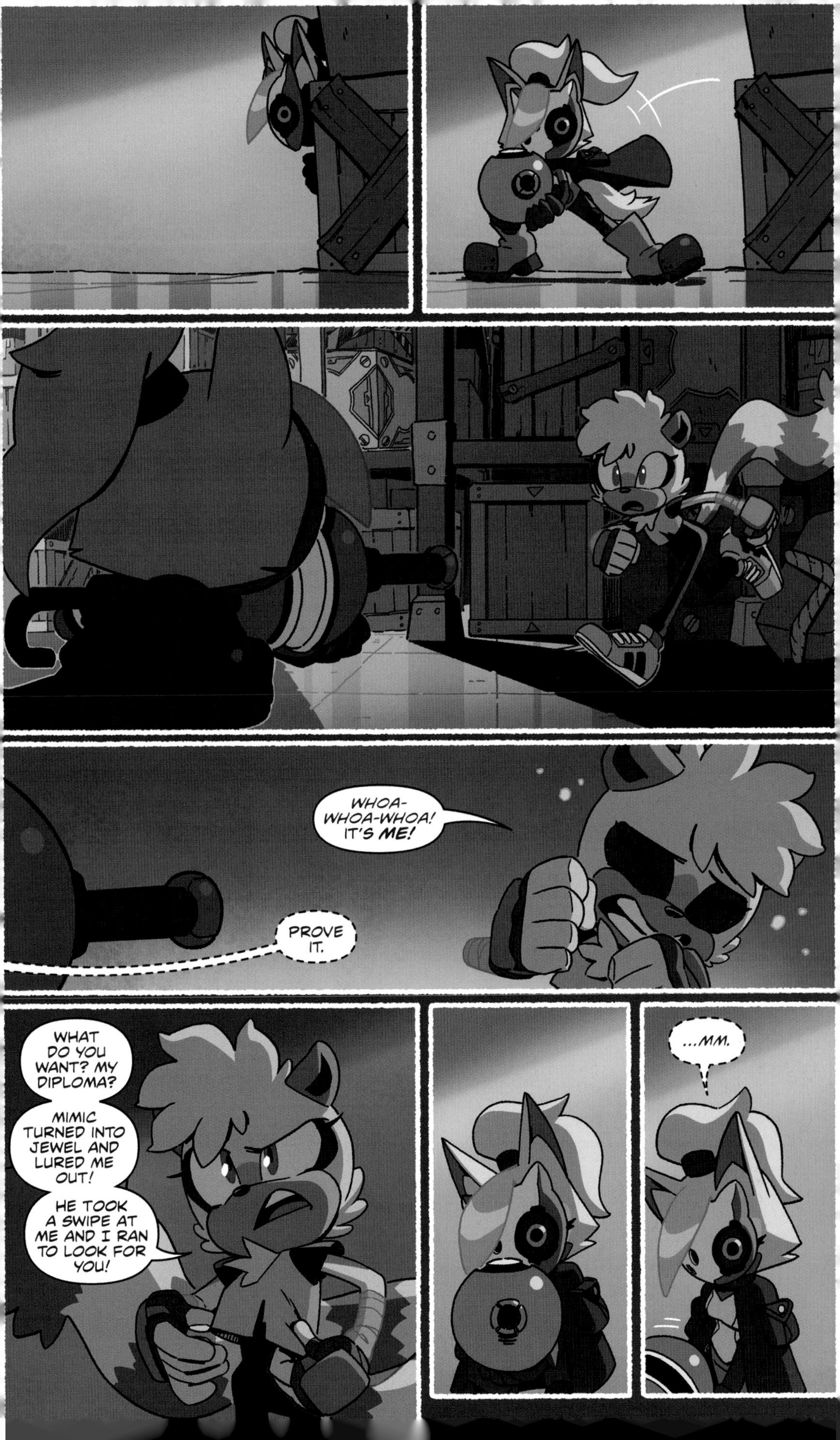
WHOA-
WHOA-WHOA!
IT'S ***ME!***
PROVE IT.
WHAT DO YOU WANT? MY DIPLOMA?
MIMIC TURNED INTO JEWEL AND LURED ME OUT!
HE TOOK A SWIPE AT ME AND I RAN TO LOOK FOR YOU!
...MM.

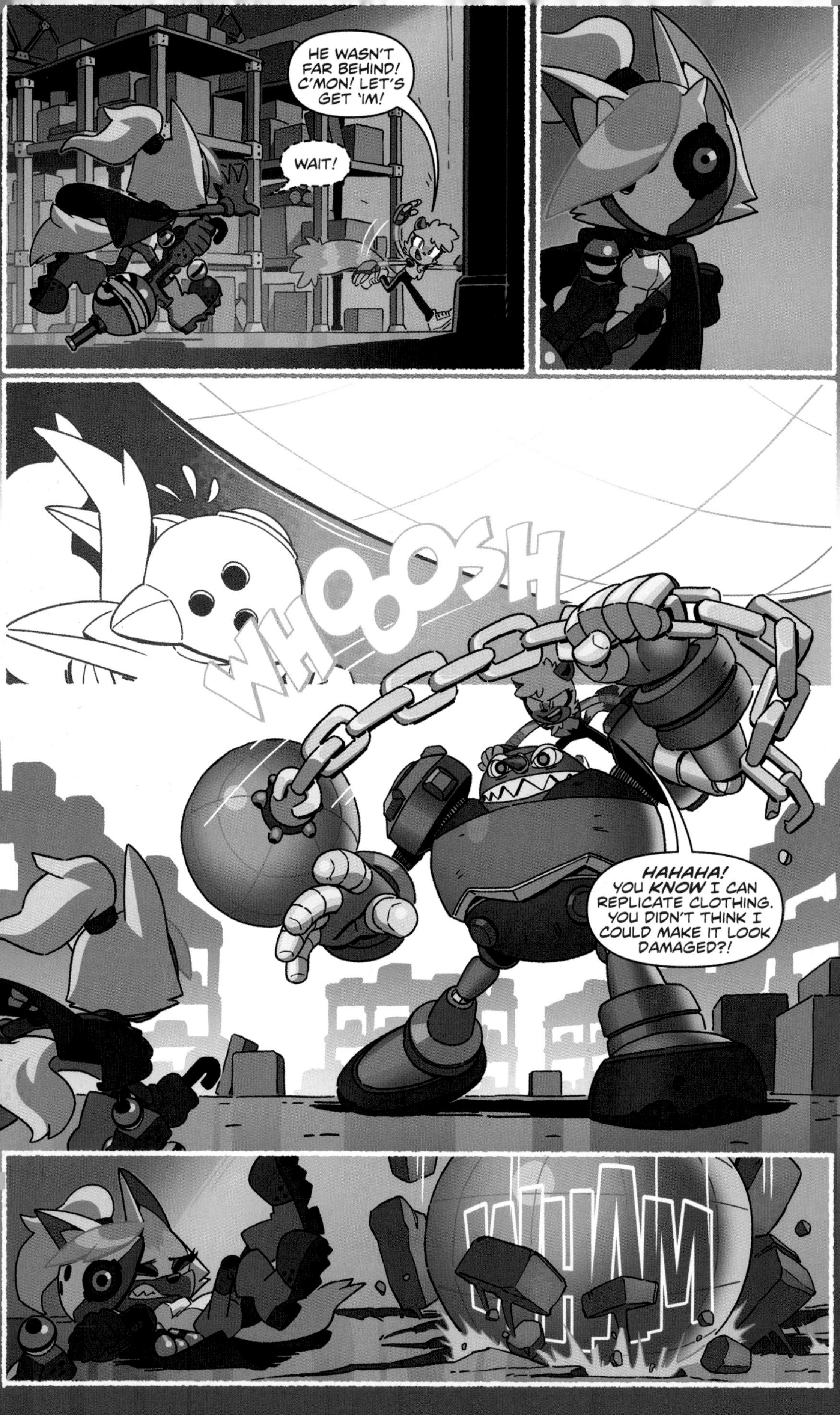
HE WASN'T FAR BEHIND! C'MON! LET'S GET 'IM!
WAIT!
WHOOOSH
HAHAHA! YOU KNOW I CAN REPLICATE CLOTHING. YOU DIDN'T THINK I COULD MAKE IT LOOK DAMAGED?!
WHAM

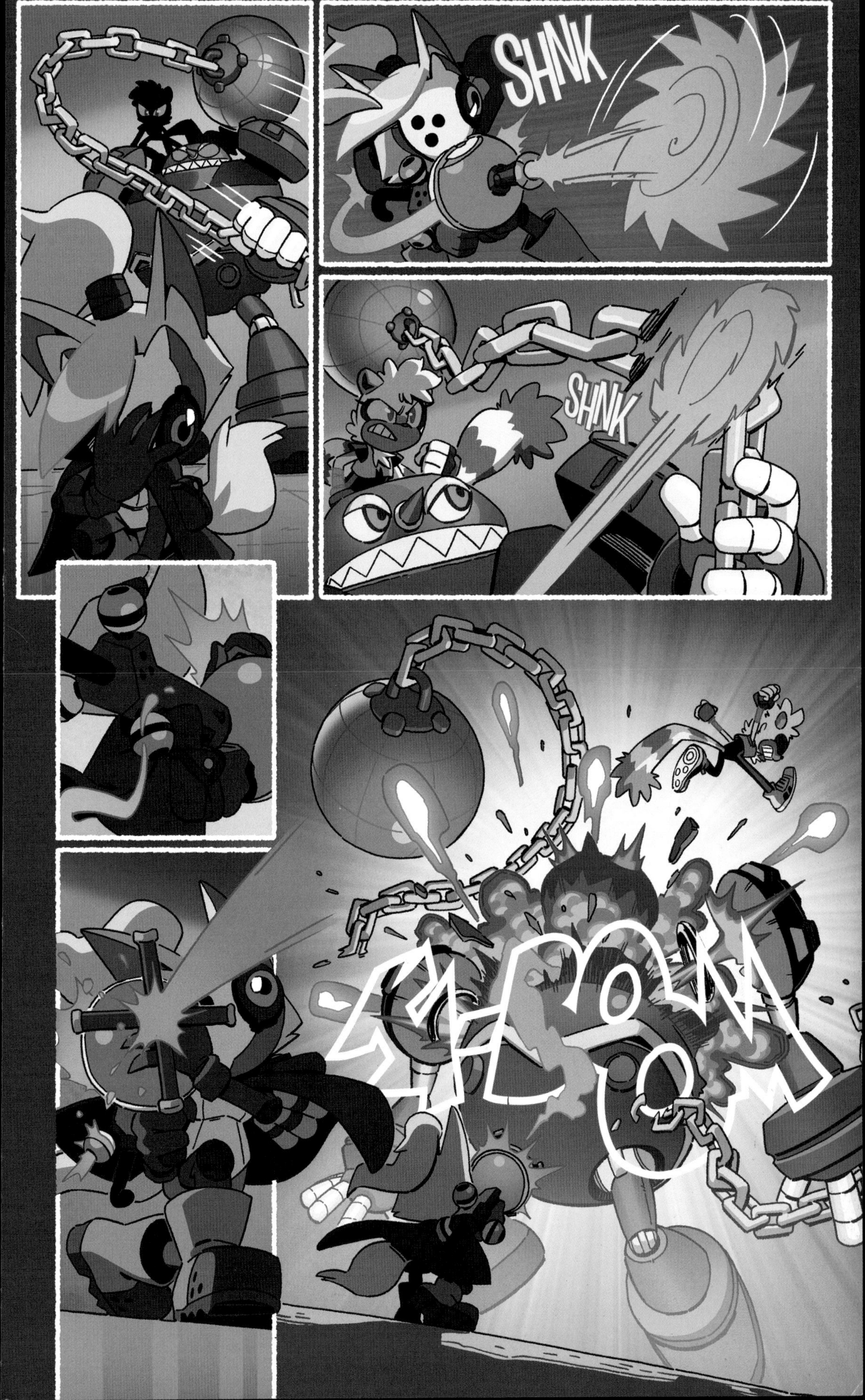
SHNK
SHNK
CHOOM

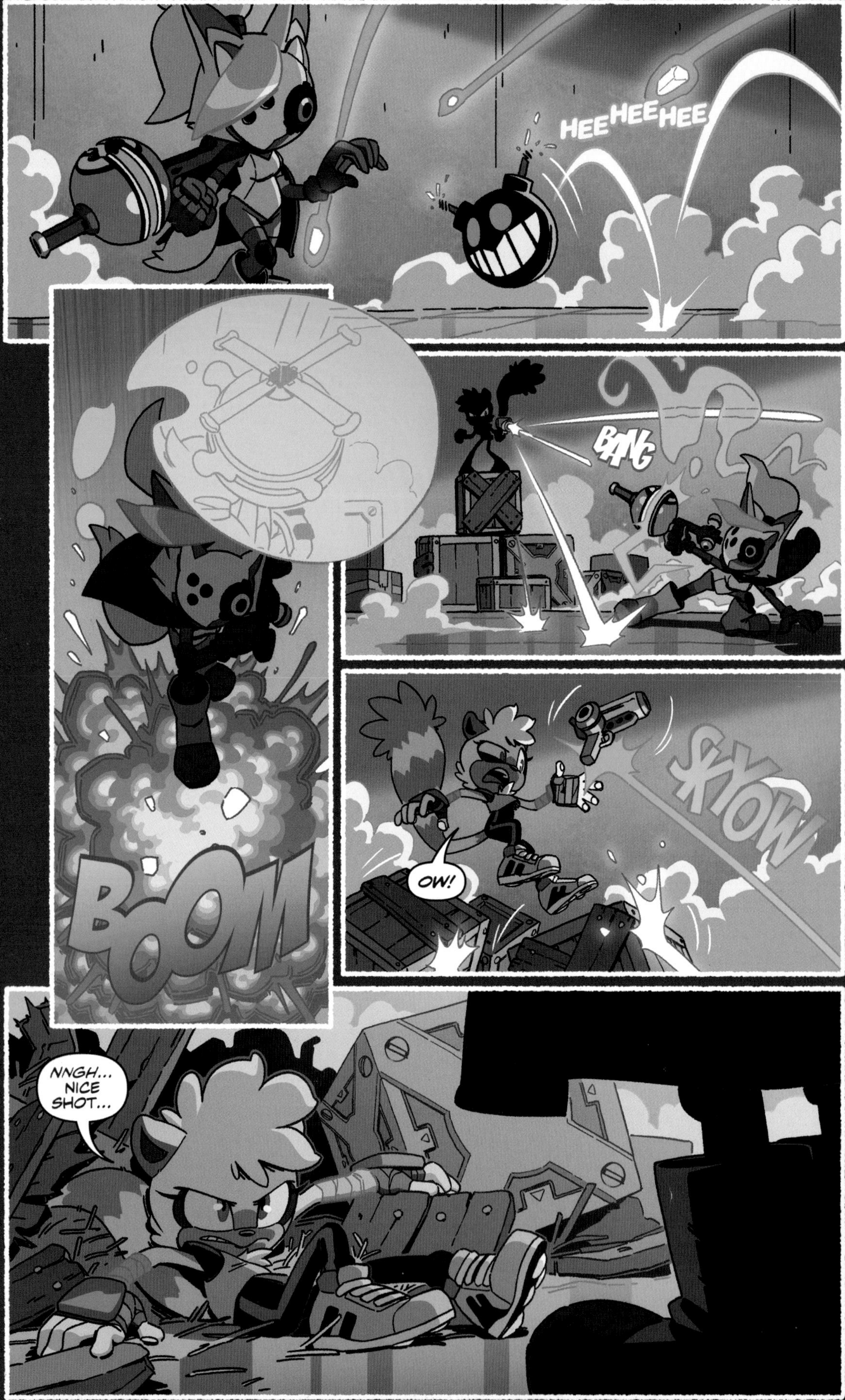
HEEHEEHEE
BOOM
BANG
SKYOW
OW!
NNGH... NICE SHOT...

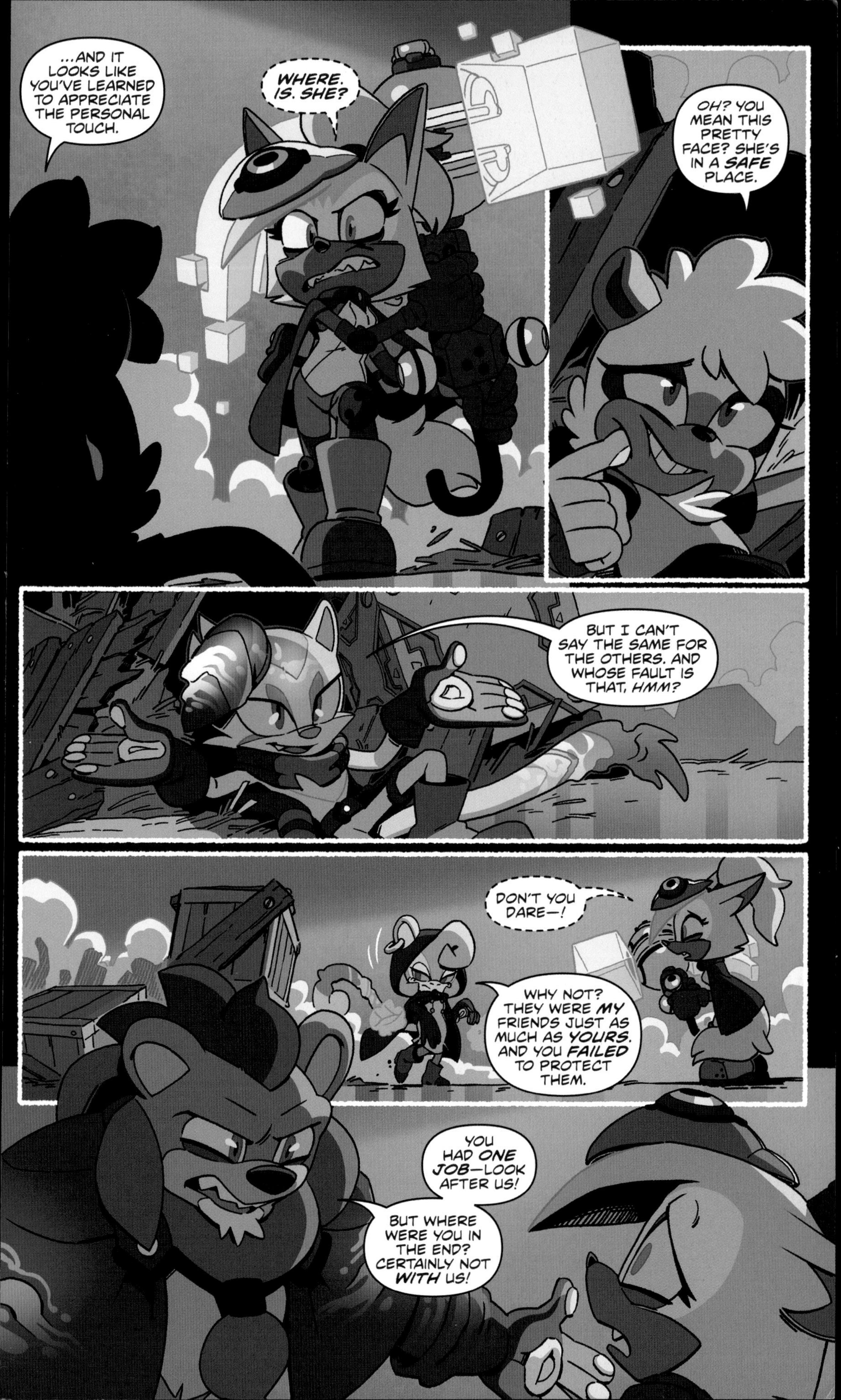
...AND IT LOOKS LIKE YOU'VE LEARNED TO APPRECIATE THE PERSONAL TOUCH.
WHERE. IS. SHE?
OH? YOU MEAN THIS PRETTY FACE? SHE'S IN A SAFE PLACE.
BUT I CAN'T SAY THE SAME FOR THE OTHERS. AND WHOSE FAULT IS THAT, HMM?
DON'T YOU DARE—!
WHY NOT? THEY WERE MY FRIENDS JUST AS MUCH AS YOURS. AND YOU FAILED TO PROTECT THEM.
YOU HAD ONE JOB—LOOK AFTER US!
BUT WHERE WERE YOU IN THE END? CERTAINLY NOT WITH US!

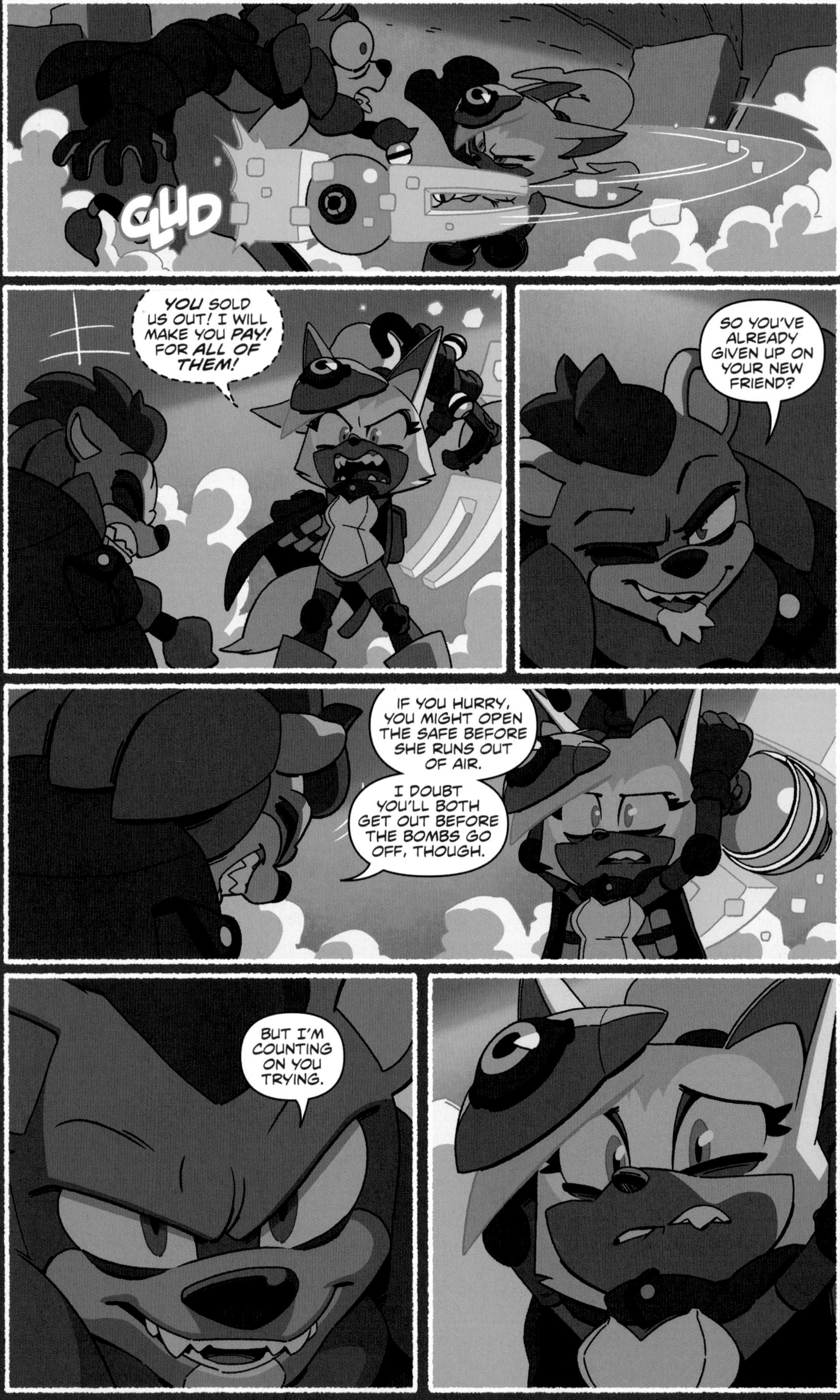
GLUD
YOU SOLD US OUT! I WILL MAKE YOU PAY! FOR ALL OF THEM!
SO YOU'VE ALREADY GIVEN UP ON YOUR NEW FRIEND?
IF YOU HURRY, YOU MIGHT OPEN THE SAFE BEFORE SHE RUNS OUT OF AIR.
I DOUBT YOU'LL BOTH GET OUT BEFORE THE BOMBS GO OFF, THOUGH.
BUT I'M COUNTING ON YOU TRYING.

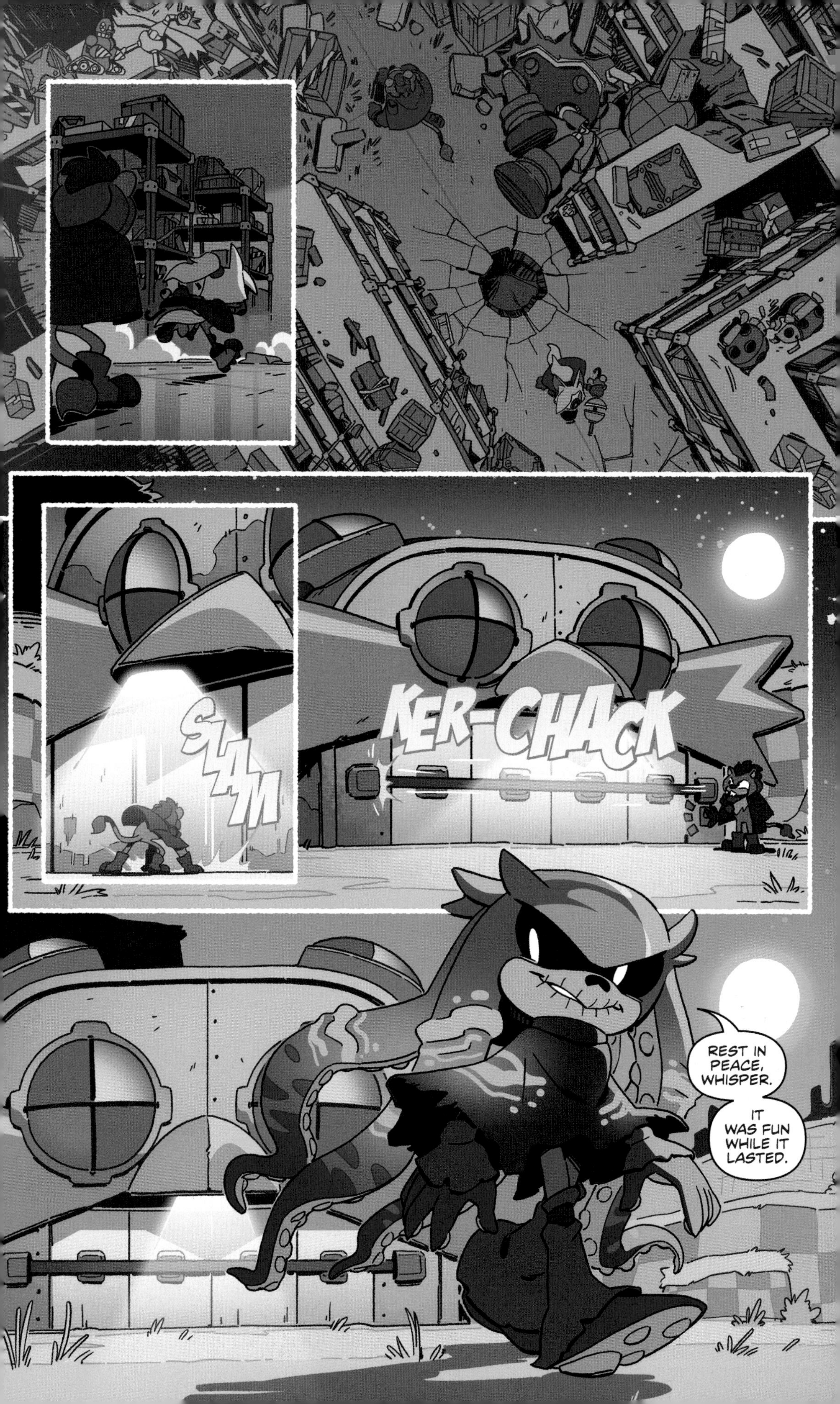
SLAM
KER-CHACK
REST IN PEACE, WHISPER.
IT WAS FUN WHILE IT LASTED.

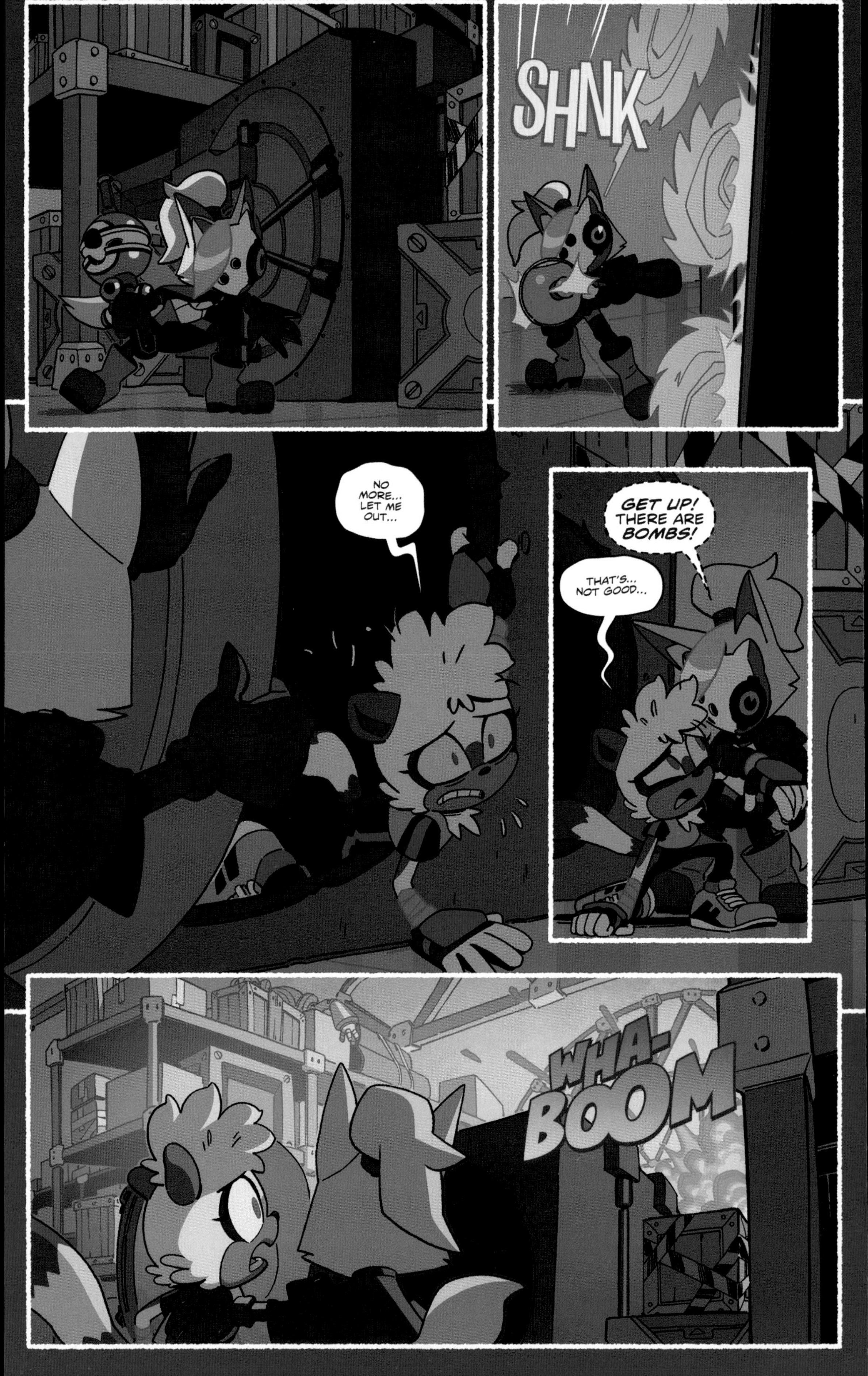
SHNK
NO MORE... LET ME OUT...
GET UP! THERE ARE BOMBS!
THAT'S... NOT GOOD...
WHA-BOOM

WELP... I'M GONNA HATE THIS, BUT...

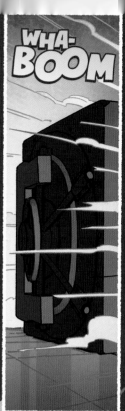

WHA-BOOM

KRA-KA-KOOM

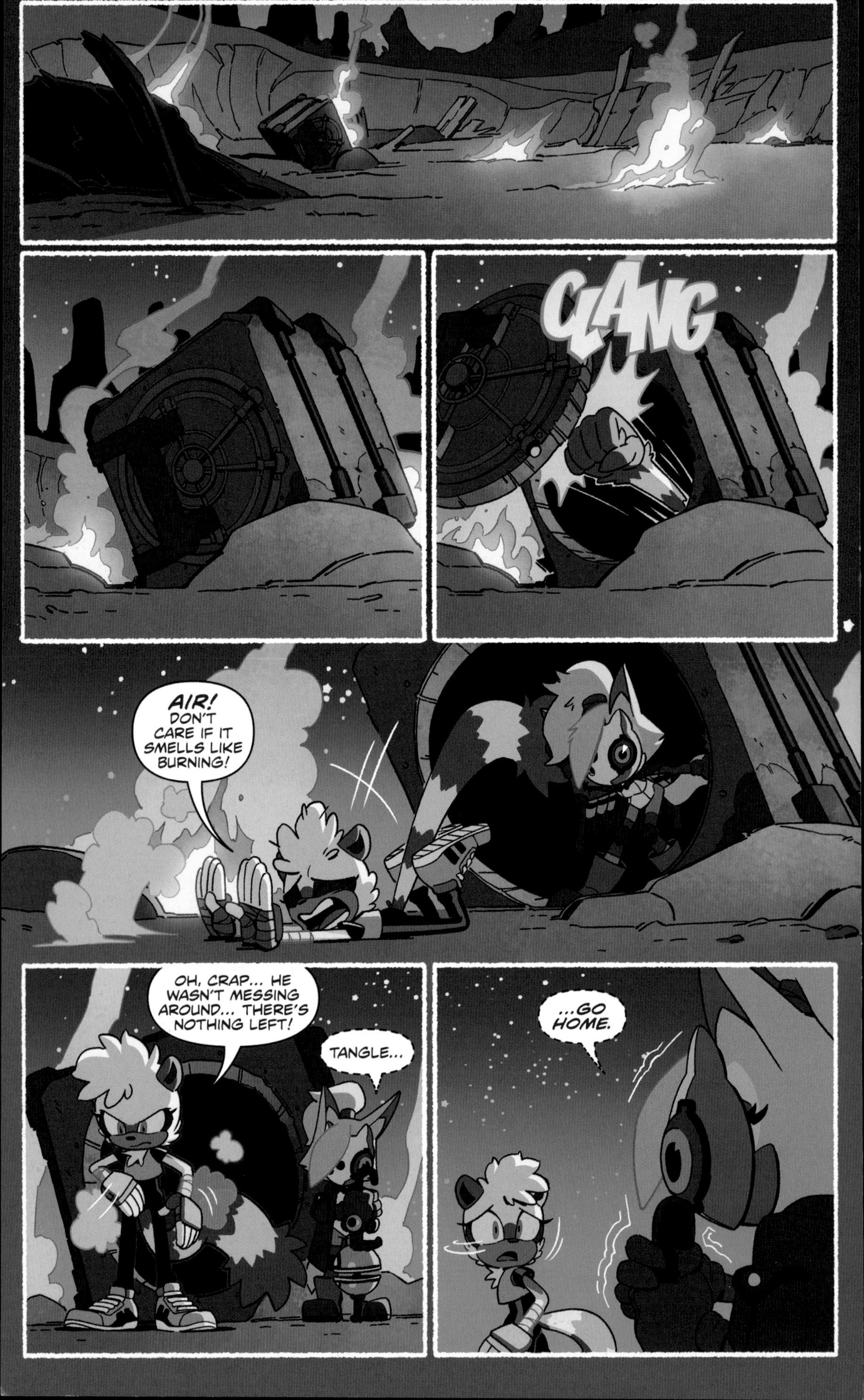
CLANG
AIR! DON'T CARE IF IT SMELLS LIKE BURNING!
OH, CRAP... HE WASN'T MESSING AROUND... THERE'S NOTHING LEFT!
TANGLE...
...GO HOME.

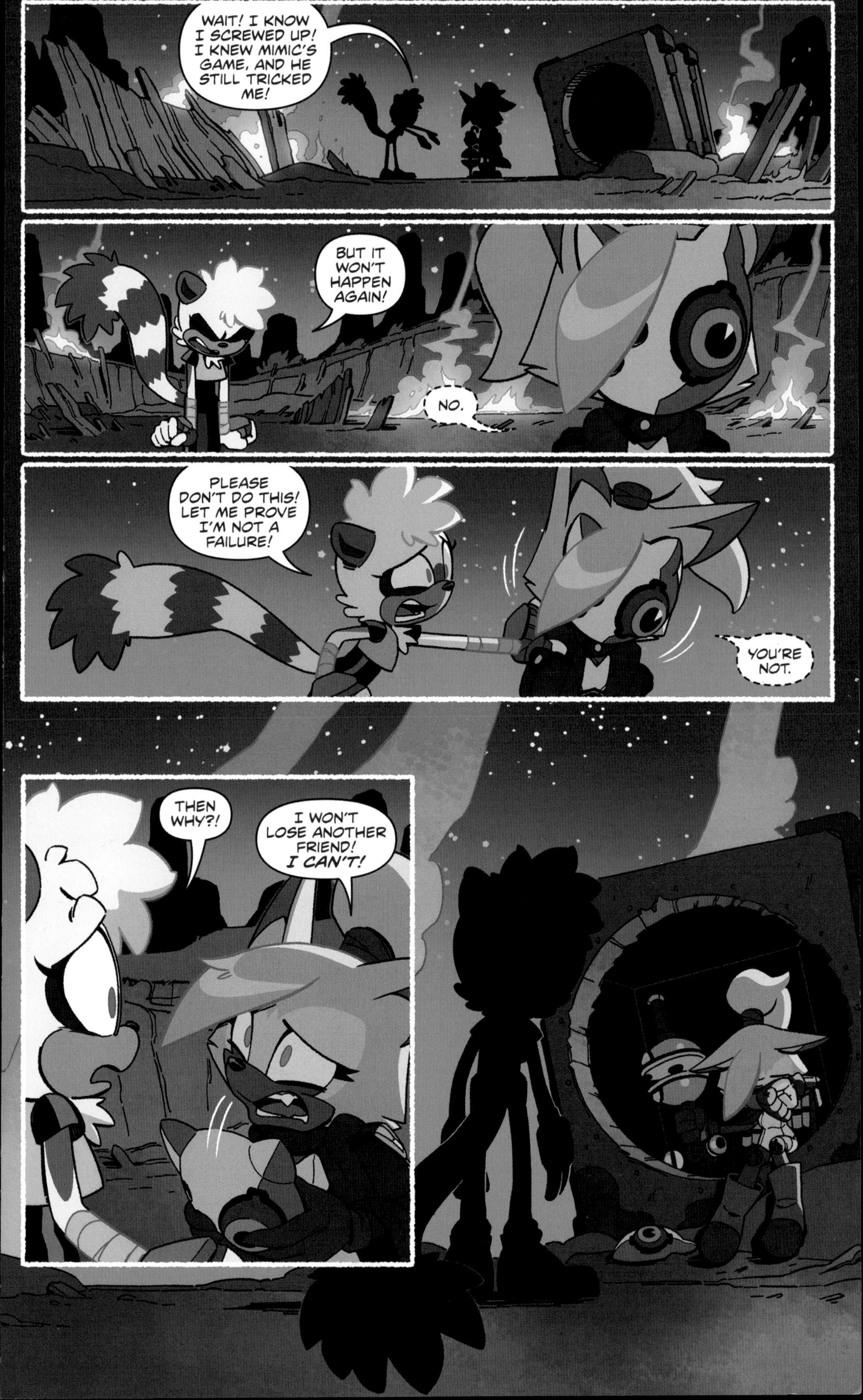
WAIT! I KNOW I SCREWED UP! I KNEW MIMIC'S GAME, AND HE STILL TRICKED ME!
BUT IT WON'T HAPPEN AGAIN!
NO.
PLEASE DON'T DO THIS! LET ME PROVE I'M NOT A FAILURE!
YOU'RE NOT.
THEN WHY?!
I WON'T LOSE ANOTHER FRIEND! I CAN'T!

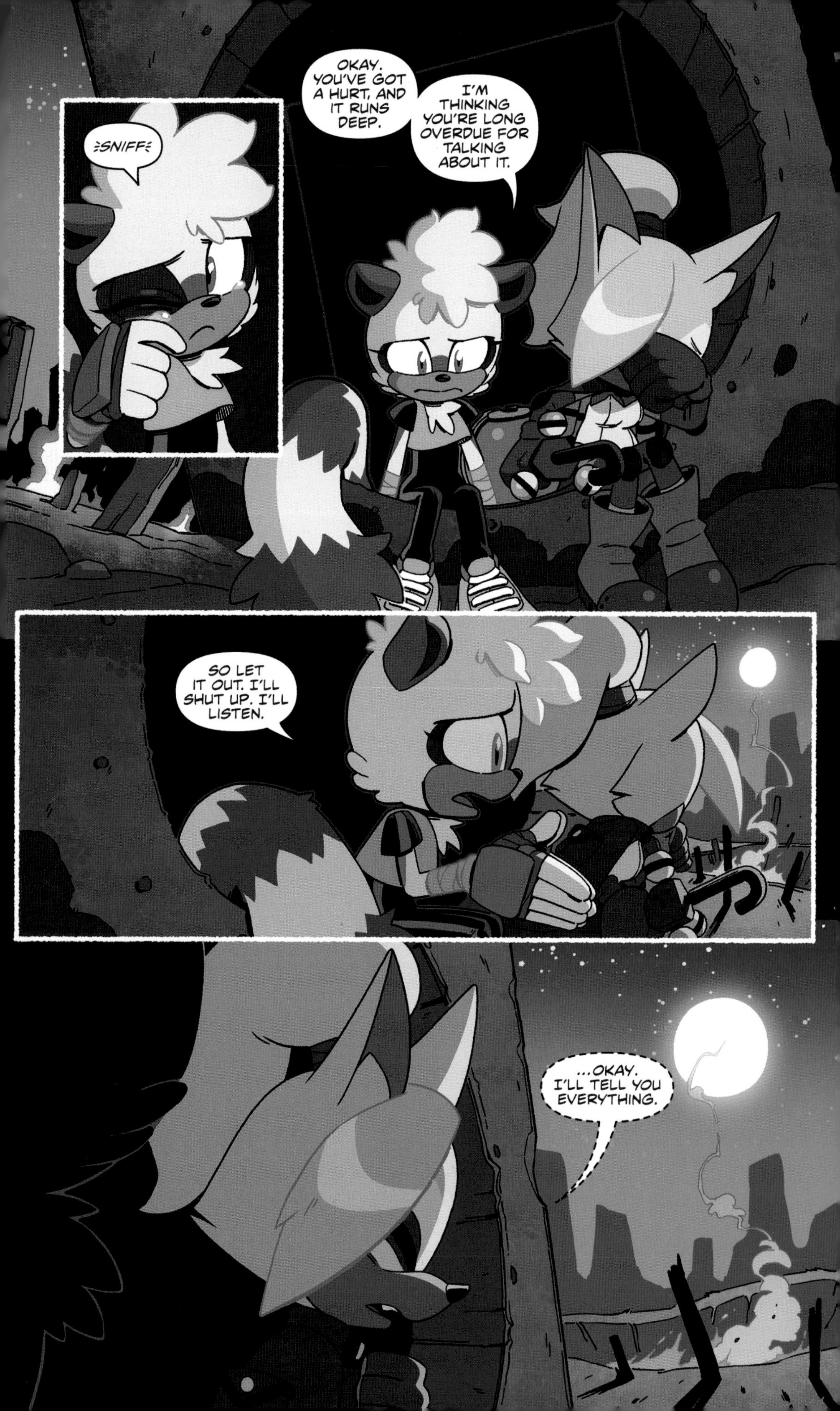

OKAY. YOU'VE GOT A HURT, AND IT RUNS DEEP.
I'M THINKING YOU'RE LONG OVERDUE FOR TALKING ABOUT IT.
SNIFF
SO LET IT OUT. I'LL SHUT UP. I'LL LISTEN.
...OKAY. I'LL TELL YOU EVERYTHING.

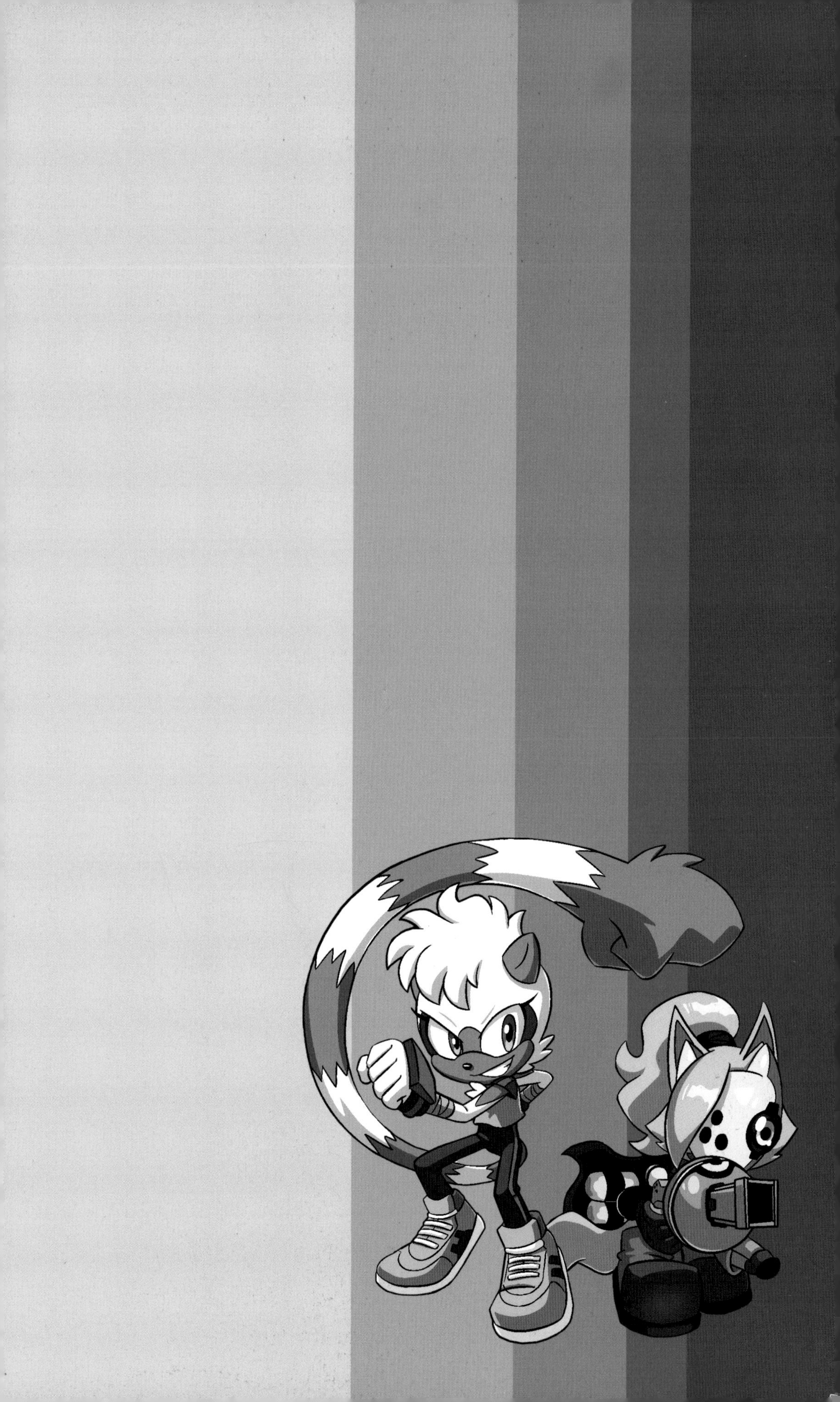

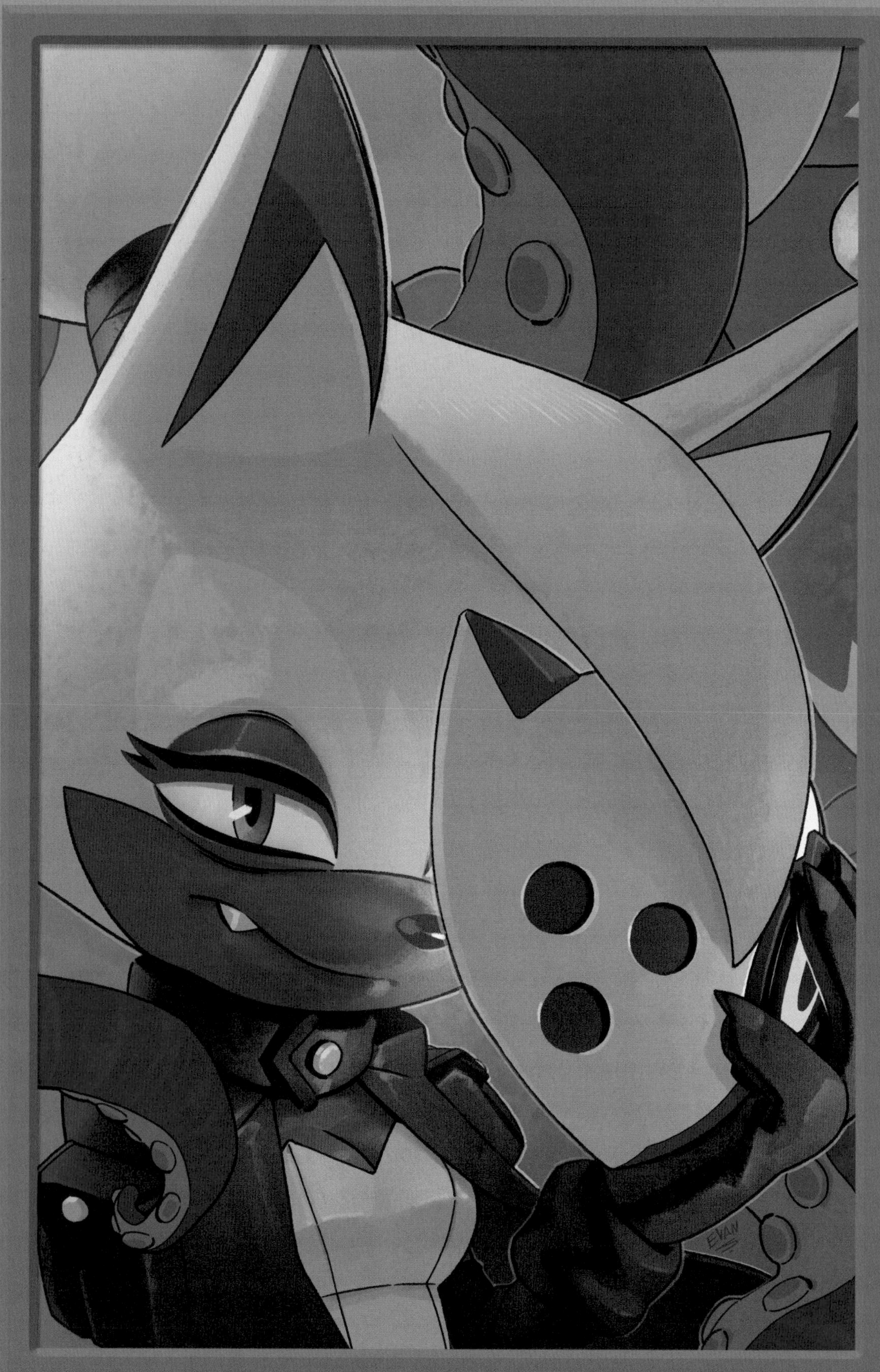
EVAN

ART BY **EVAN STANLEY**

GROUND ZERO OF A FORMER EGGMAN BUNKER...

YOU'VE BEEN CARRYING SOME SERIOUS BAGGAGE ALL ON YOUR OWN. I SEE THAT NOW.

LET ME HELP.

WHAT HAPPENED? WHAT DID MIMIC DO TO YOU?

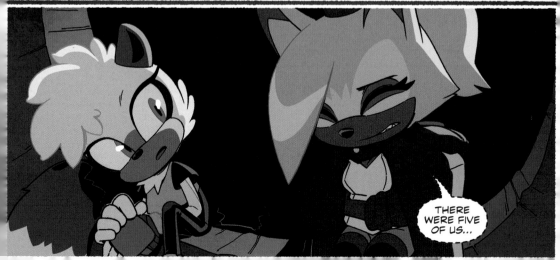

THERE WERE FIVE OF US...

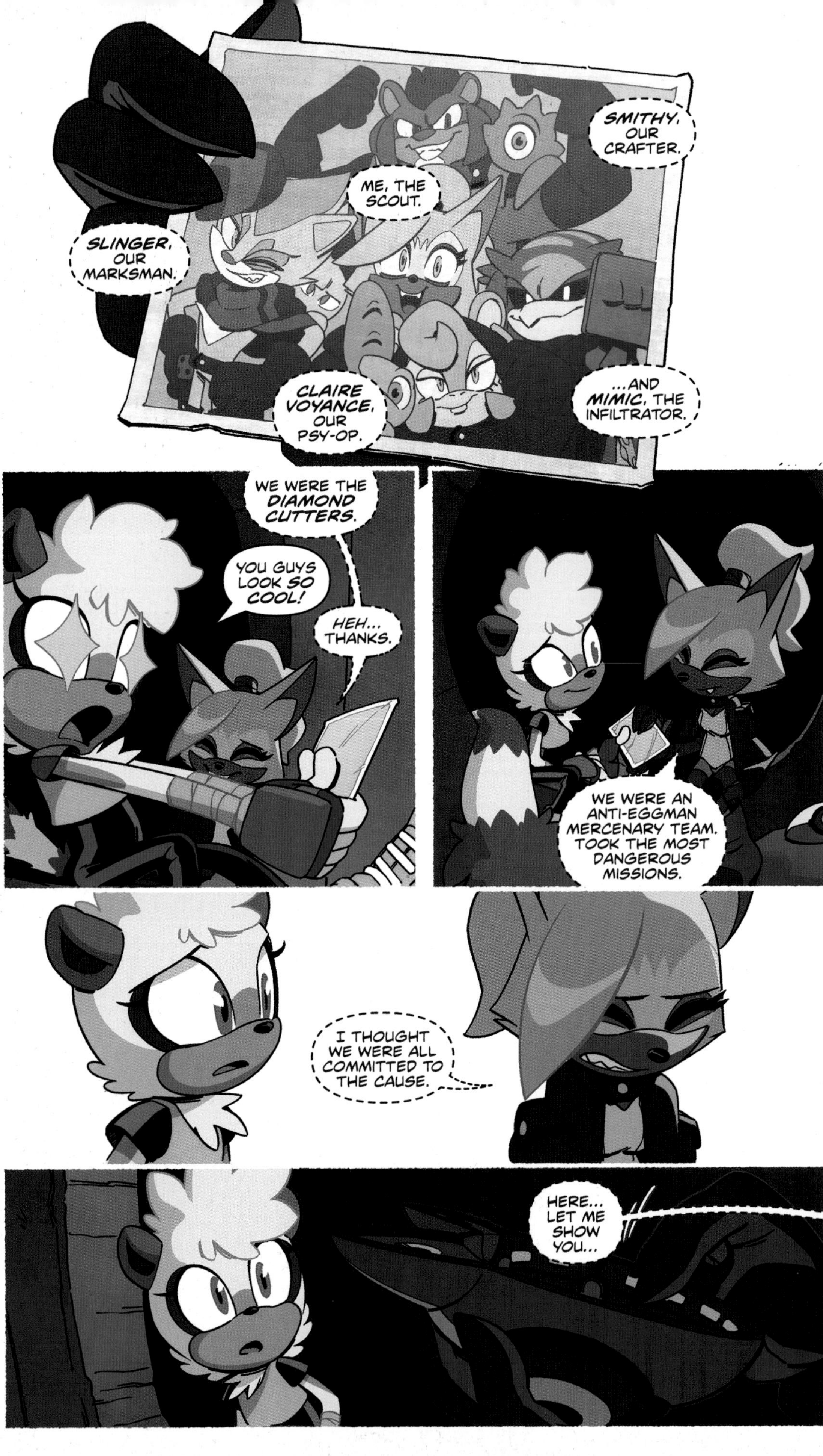
SLINGER, OUR MARKSMAN.
ME, THE SCOUT.
SMITHY, OUR CRAFTER.
CLAIRE VOYANCE, OUR PSY-OP.
...AND MIMIC, THE INFILTRATOR.
WE WERE THE DIAMOND CUTTERS.
YOU GUYS LOOK SO COOL!
HEH... THANKS.
WE WERE AN ANTI-EGGMAN MERCENARY TEAM. TOOK THE MOST DANGEROUS MISSIONS.
I THOUGHT WE WERE ALL COMMITTED TO THE CAUSE.
HERE... LET ME SHOW YOU...

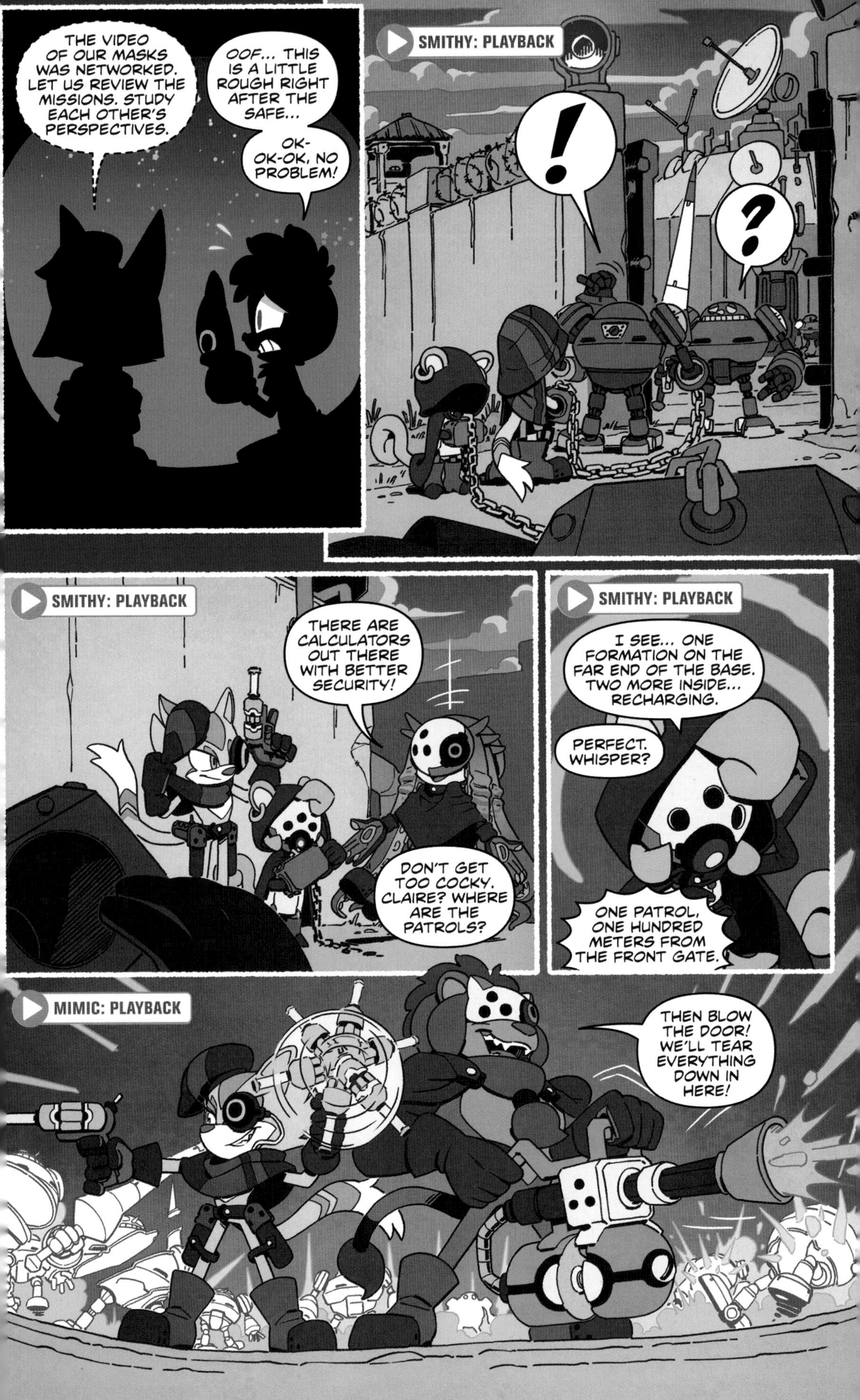
THE VIDEO OF OUR MASKS WAS NETWORKED. LET US REVIEW THE MISSIONS. STUDY EACH OTHER'S PERSPECTIVES.
OOF... THIS IS A LITTLE ROUGH RIGHT AFTER THE SAFE...
OK-OK-OK, NO PROBLEM!
SMITHY: PLAYBACK
!
?
SMITHY: PLAYBACK
THERE ARE CALCULATORS OUT THERE WITH BETTER SECURITY!
DON'T GET TOO COCKY. CLAIRE? WHERE ARE THE PATROLS?
SMITHY: PLAYBACK
I SEE... ONE FORMATION ON THE FAR END OF THE BASE. TWO MORE INSIDE... RECHARGING.
PERFECT. WHISPER?
ONE PATROL, ONE HUNDRED METERS FROM THE FRONT GATE.
MIMIC: PLAYBACK
THEN BLOW THE DOOR! WE'LL TEAR EVERYTHING DOWN IN HERE!

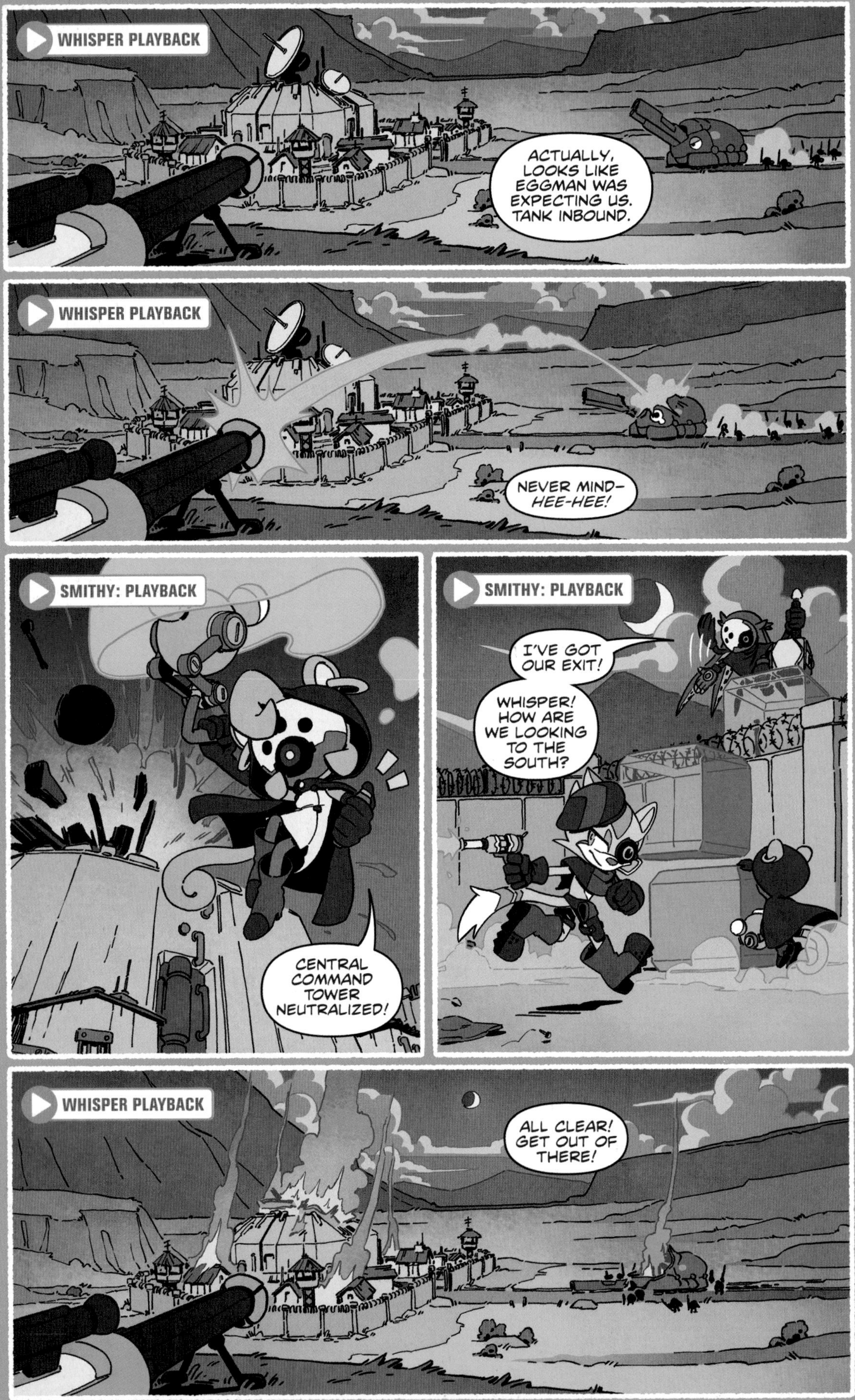
WHISPER PLAYBACK
ACTUALLY, LOOKS LIKE EGGMAN WAS EXPECTING US. TANK INBOUND.
WHISPER PLAYBACK
NEVER MIND— HEE-HEE!
SMITHY: PLAYBACK
CENTRAL COMMAND TOWER NEUTRALIZED!
SMITHY: PLAYBACK
I'VE GOT OUR EXIT!
WHISPER! HOW ARE WE LOOKING TO THE SOUTH?
WHISPER PLAYBACK
ALL CLEAR! GET OUT OF THERE!

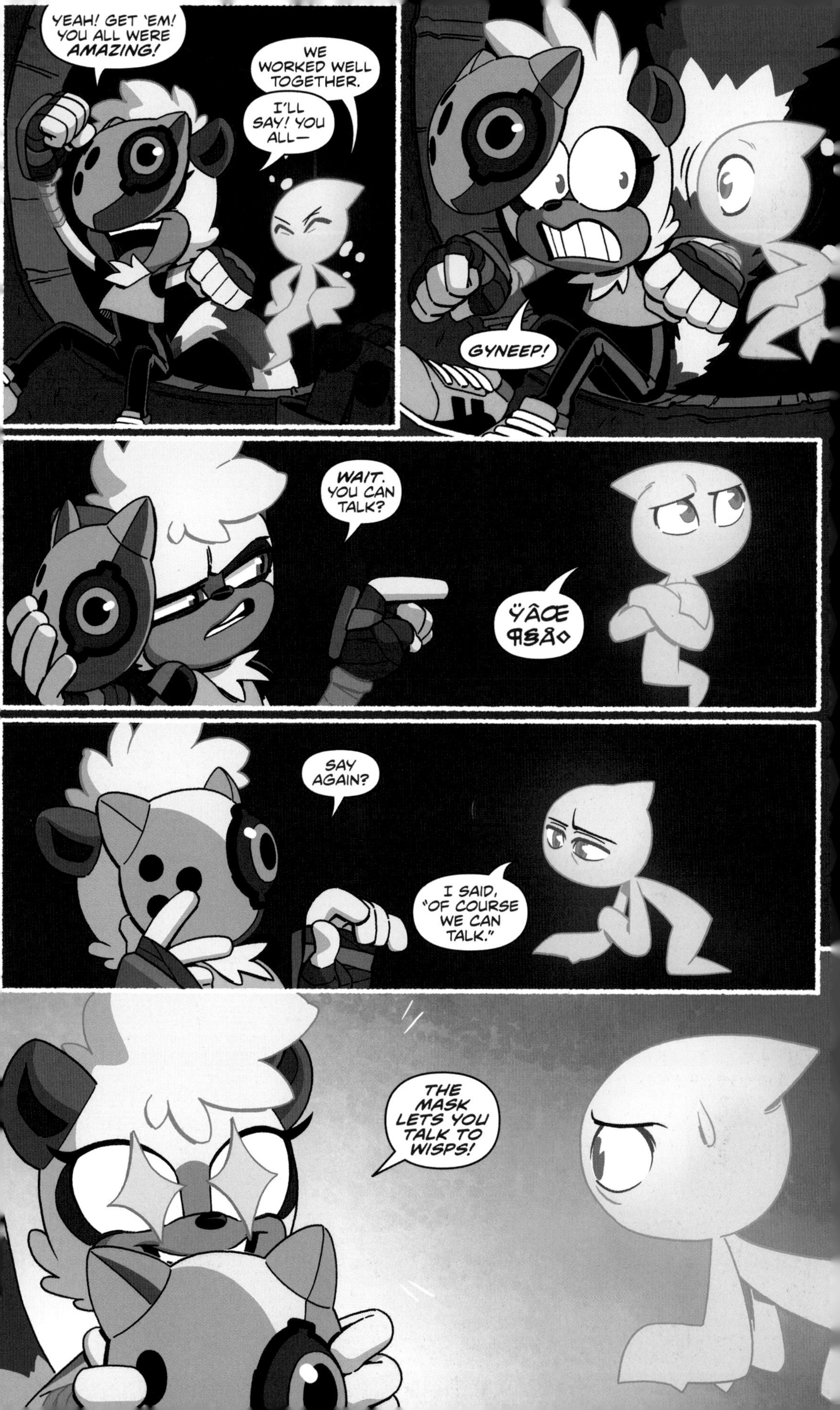
YEAH! GET 'EM! YOU ALL WERE AMAZING!
WE WORKED WELL TOGETHER.
I'LL SAY! YOU ALL—
GYNEEP!
WAIT. YOU CAN TALK?
SAY AGAIN?
I SAID, "OF COURSE WE CAN TALK."
THE MASK LETS YOU TALK TO WISPS!

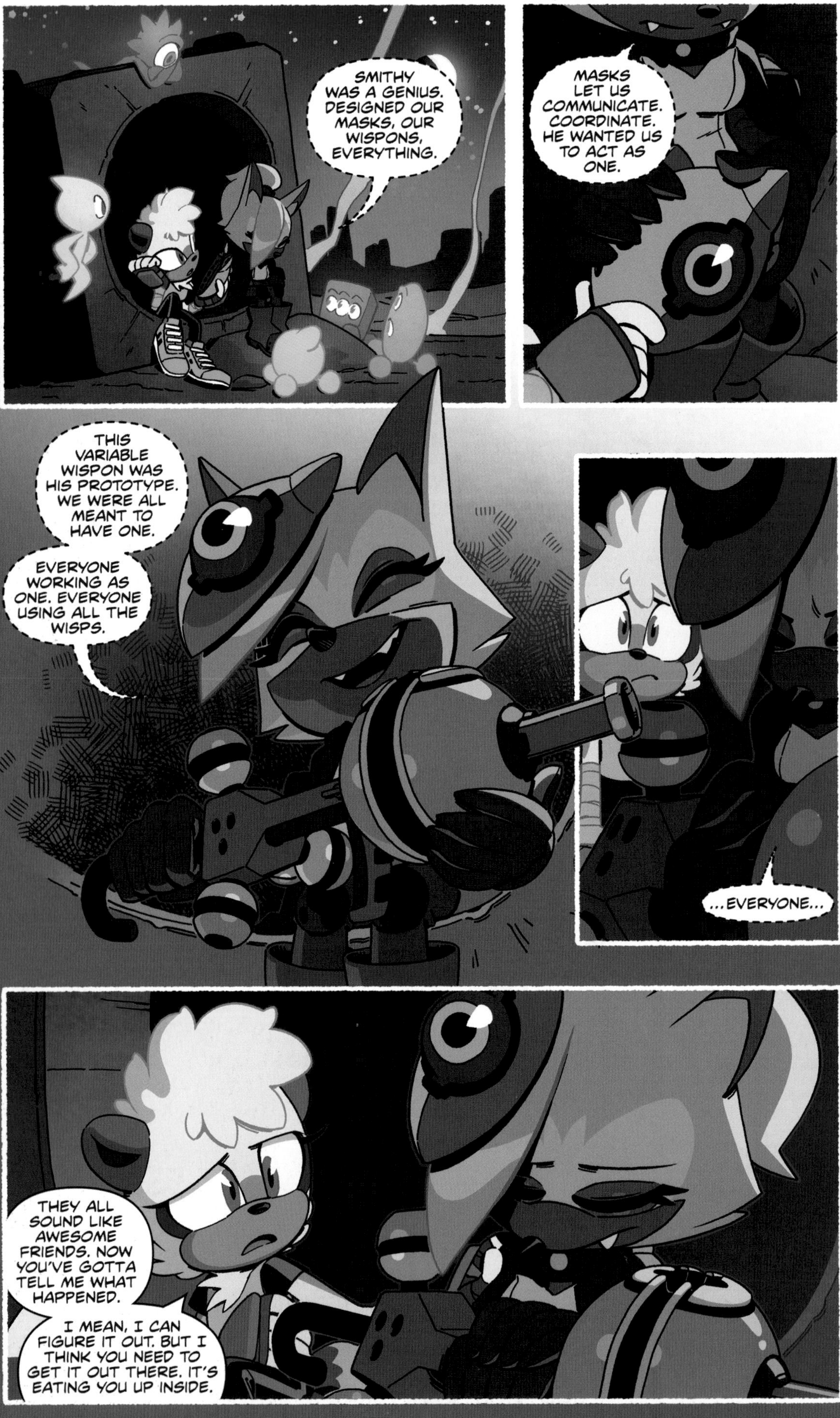
SMITHY WAS A GENIUS. DESIGNED OUR MASKS, OUR WISPONS, EVERYTHING.
MASKS LET US COMMUNICATE. COORDINATE. HE WANTED US TO ACT AS ONE.
THIS VARIABLE WISPON WAS HIS PROTOTYPE. WE WERE ALL MEANT TO HAVE ONE.
EVERYONE WORKING AS ONE. EVERYONE USING ALL THE WISPS.
...EVERYONE...
THEY ALL SOUND LIKE AWESOME FRIENDS. NOW YOU'VE GOTTA TELL ME WHAT HAPPENED.
I MEAN, I CAN FIGURE IT OUT. BUT I THINK YOU NEED TO GET IT OUT THERE. IT'S EATING YOU UP INSIDE.

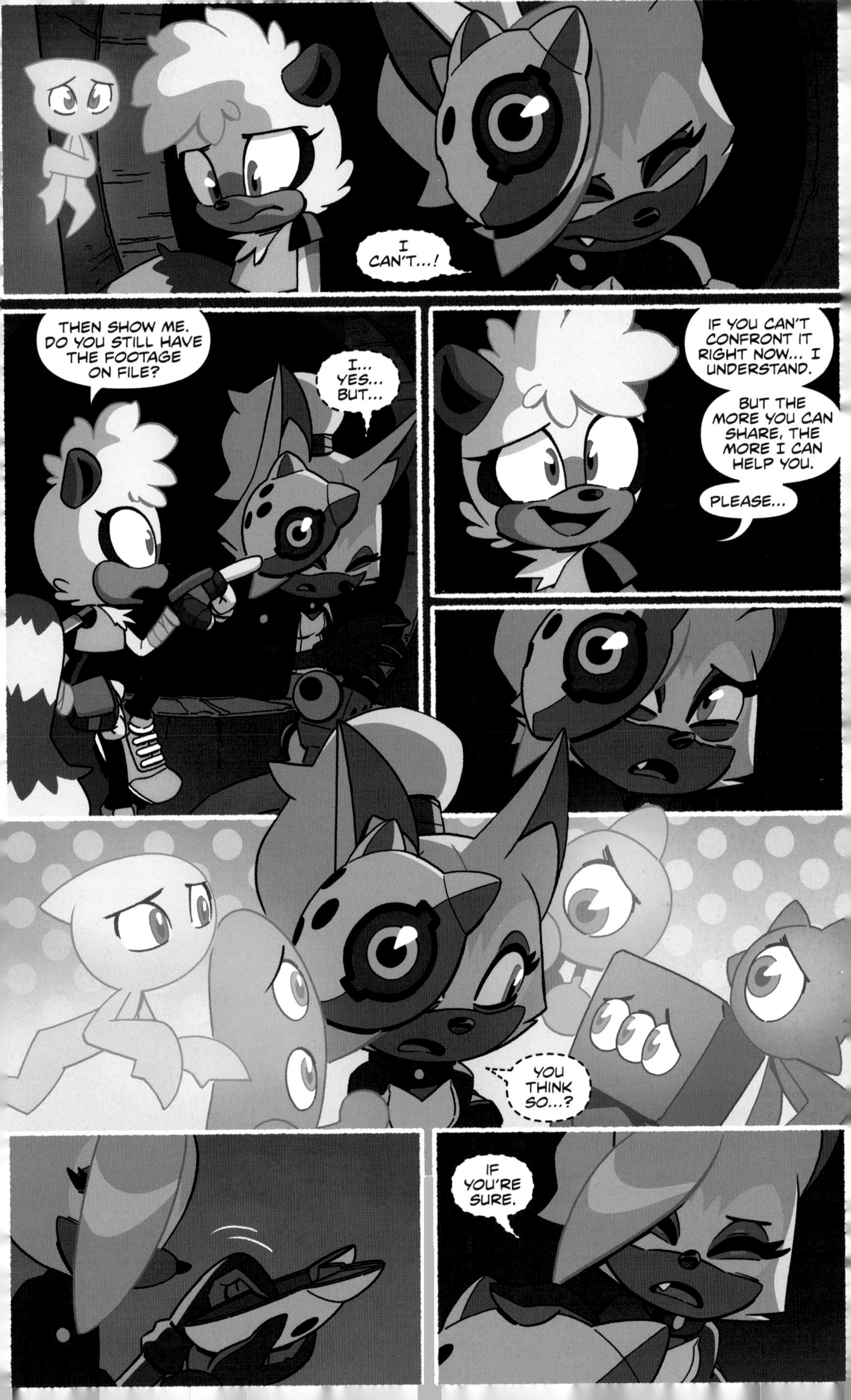
I CAN'T...!
THEN SHOW ME. DO YOU STILL HAVE THE FOOTAGE ON FILE?
I... YES... BUT...
IF YOU CAN'T CONFRONT IT RIGHT NOW... I UNDERSTAND.
BUT THE MORE YOU CAN SHARE, THE MORE I CAN HELP YOU.
PLEASE...
YOU THINK SO...?
IF YOU'RE SURE.

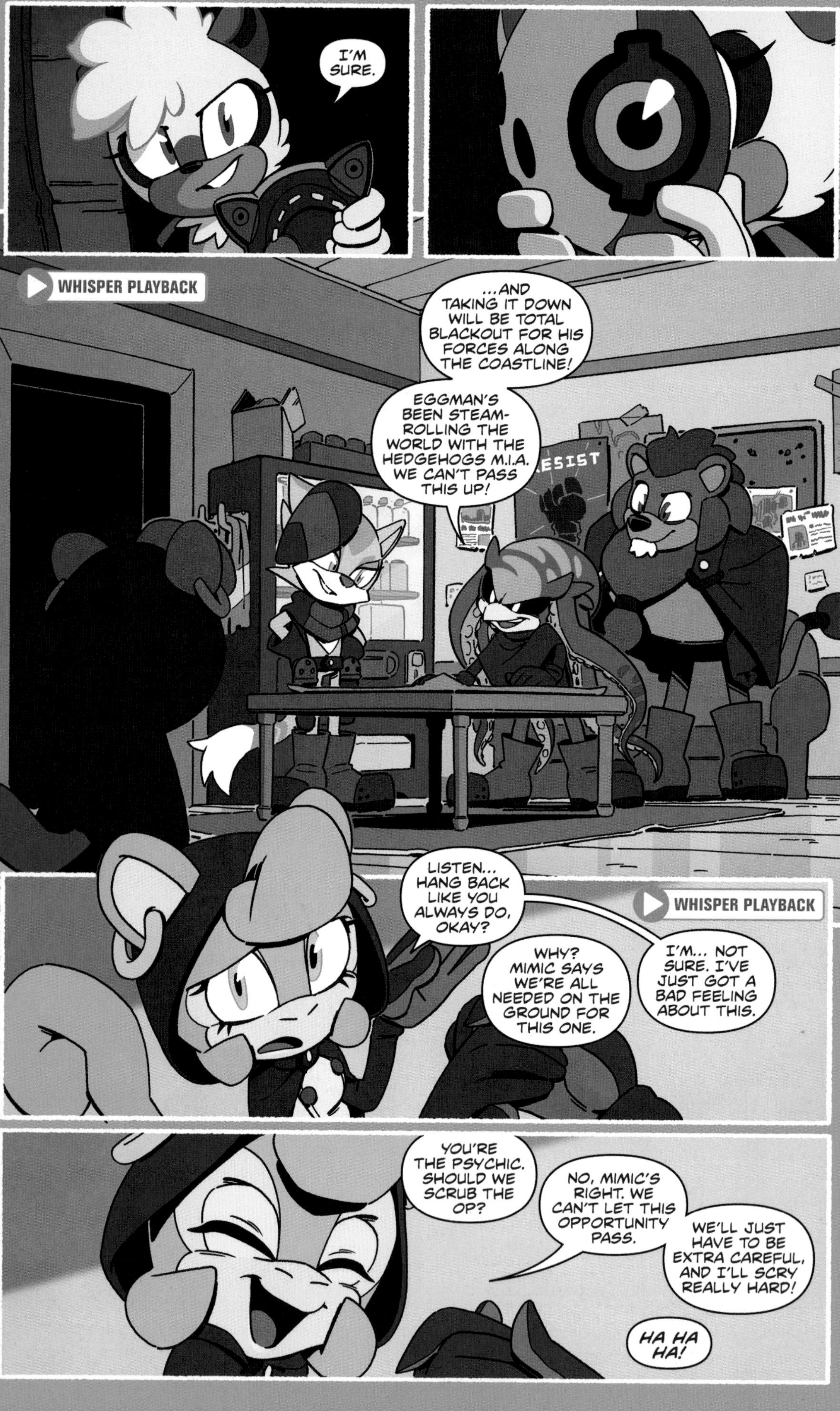
I'M SURE.
WHISPER PLAYBACK
...AND TAKING IT DOWN WILL BE TOTAL BLACKOUT FOR HIS FORCES ALONG THE COASTLINE!
EGGMAN'S BEEN STEAM-ROLLING THE WORLD WITH THE HEDGEHOGS M.I.A. WE CAN'T PASS THIS UP!
RESIST
LISTEN... HANG BACK LIKE YOU ALWAYS DO, OKAY?
WHISPER PLAYBACK
WHY? MIMIC SAYS WE'RE ALL NEEDED ON THE GROUND FOR THIS ONE.
I'M... NOT SURE. I'VE JUST GOT A BAD FEELING ABOUT THIS.
YOU'RE THE PSYCHIC. SHOULD WE SCRUB THE OP?
NO, MIMIC'S RIGHT. WE CAN'T LET THIS OPPORTUNITY PASS.
WE'LL JUST HAVE TO BE EXTRA CAREFUL, AND I'LL SCRY REALLY HARD!
HA HA HA!

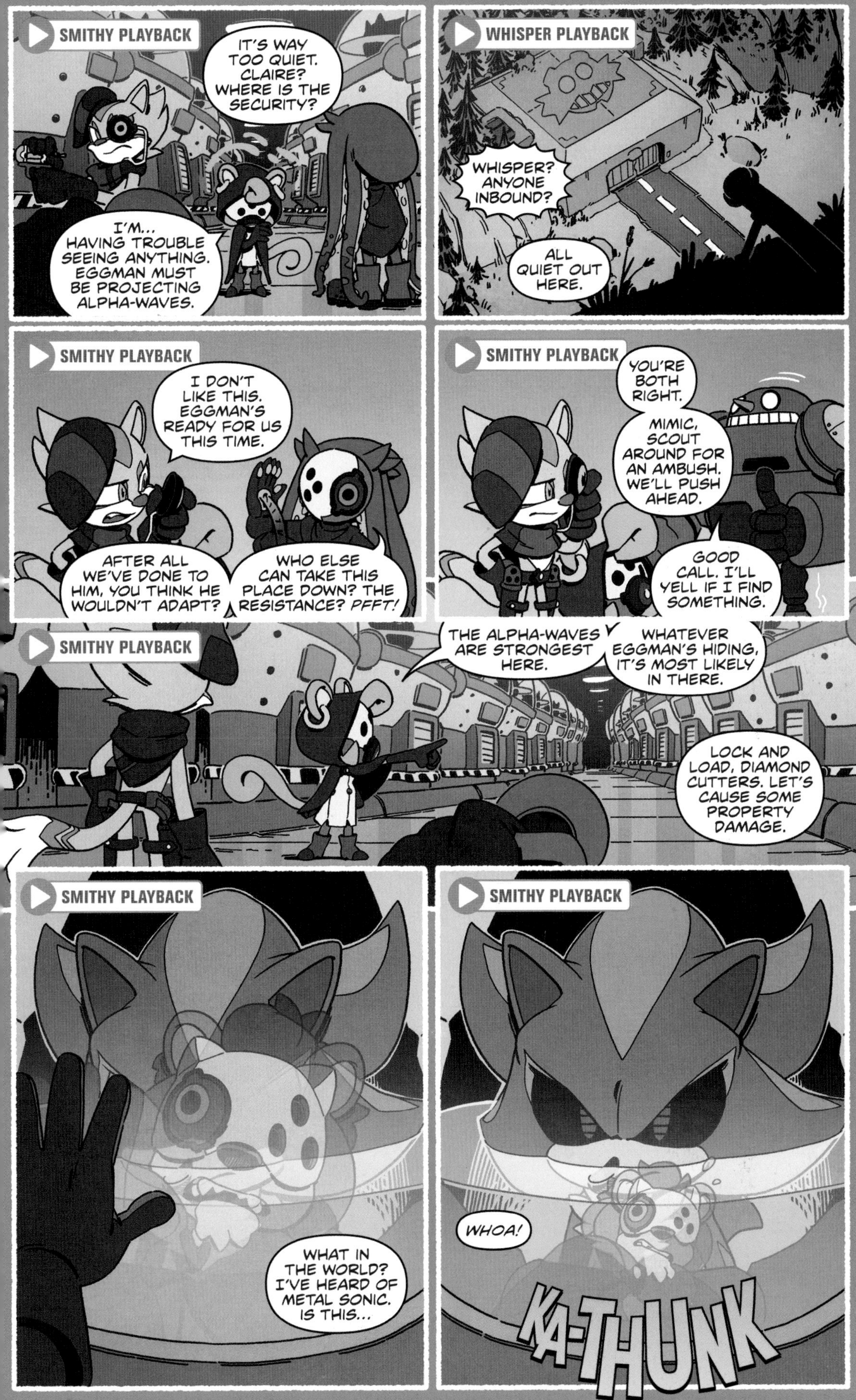

SMITHY PLAYBACK
IT'S WAY TOO QUIET. CLAIRE? WHERE IS THE SECURITY?
I'M... HAVING TROUBLE SEEING ANYTHING. EGGMAN MUST BE PROJECTING ALPHA-WAVES.
WHISPER PLAYBACK
WHISPER? ANYONE INBOUND?
ALL QUIET OUT HERE.
SMITHY PLAYBACK
I DON'T LIKE THIS. EGGMAN'S READY FOR US THIS TIME.
AFTER ALL WE'VE DONE TO HIM, YOU THINK HE WOULDN'T ADAPT?
WHO ELSE CAN TAKE THIS PLACE DOWN? THE RESISTANCE? PFFT!
SMITHY PLAYBACK
YOU'RE BOTH RIGHT.
MIMIC, SCOUT AROUND FOR AN AMBUSH. WE'LL PUSH AHEAD.
GOOD CALL. I'LL YELL IF I FIND SOMETHING.
SMITHY PLAYBACK
THE ALPHA-WAVES ARE STRONGEST HERE.
WHATEVER EGGMAN'S HIDING, IT'S MOST LIKELY IN THERE.
LOCK AND LOAD, DIAMOND CUTTERS. LET'S CAUSE SOME PROPERTY DAMAGE.
SMITHY PLAYBACK
WHAT IN THE WORLD? I'VE HEARD OF METAL SONIC. IS THIS...
SMITHY PLAYBACK
WHOA!
KA-THUNK

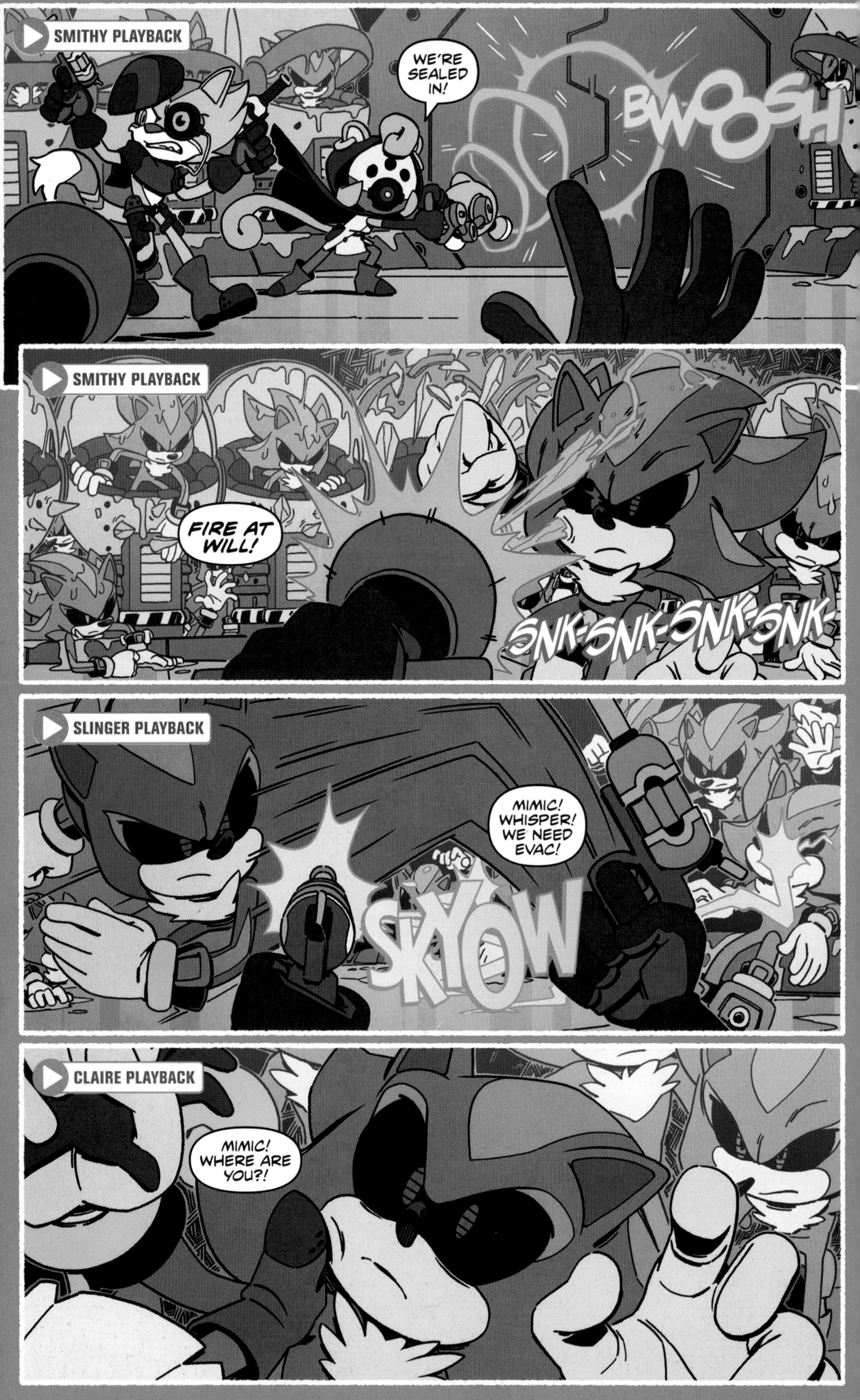
SMITHY PLAYBACK
WE'RE SEALED IN!
BWOOSH
SMITHY PLAYBACK
FIRE AT WILL!
SNK-SNK-SNK-SNK
SLINGER PLAYBACK
MIMIC! WHISPER! WE NEED EVAC!
SKYOW
CLAIRE PLAYBACK
MIMIC! WHERE ARE YOU?!

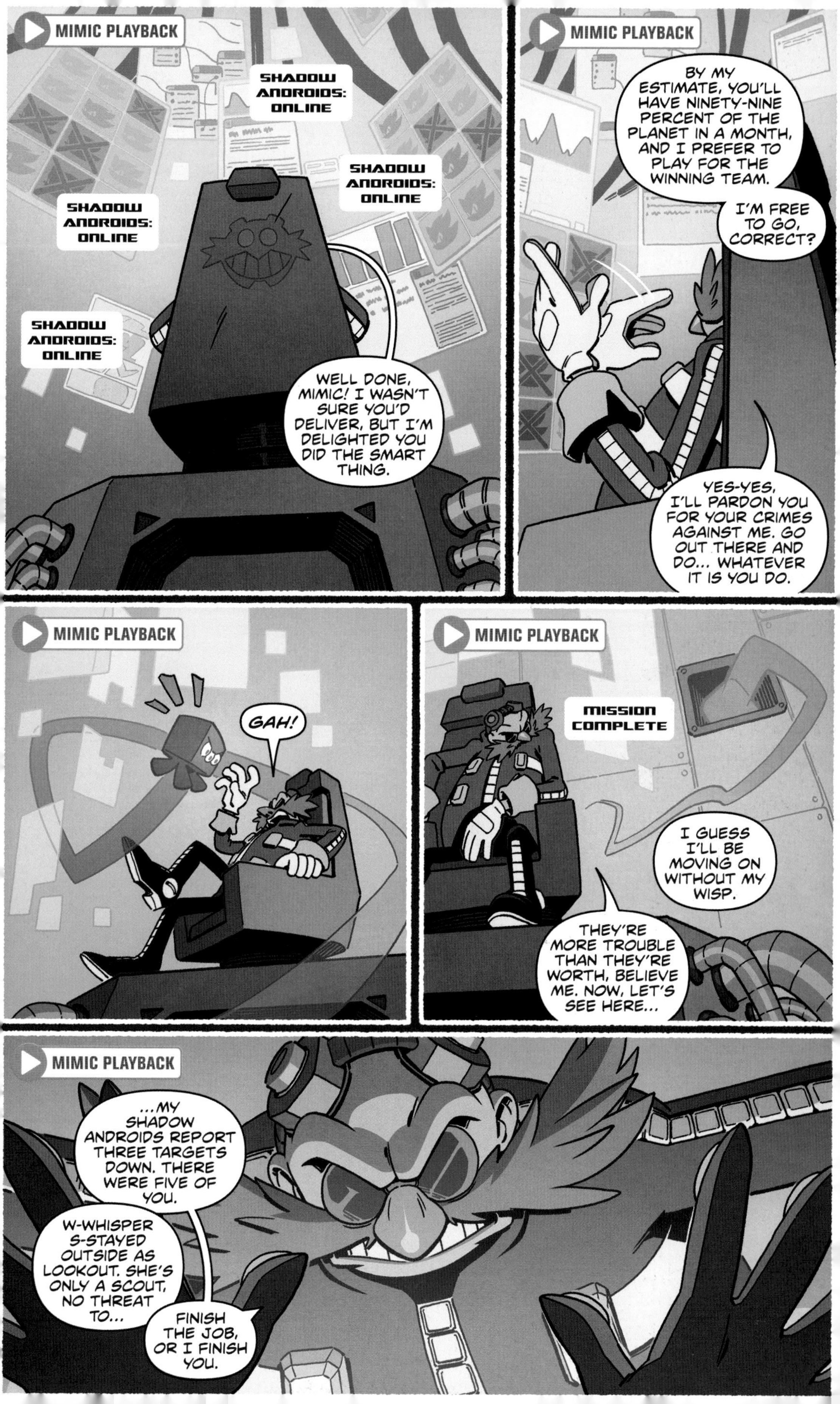
MIMIC PLAYBACK
SHADOW ANDROIDS: ONLINE
SHADOW ANDROIDS: ONLINE
SHADOW ANDROIDS: ONLINE
SHADOW ANDROIDS: ONLINE
WELL DONE, MIMIC! I WASN'T SURE YOU'D DELIVER, BUT I'M DELIGHTED YOU DID THE SMART THING.
MIMIC PLAYBACK
BY MY ESTIMATE, YOU'LL HAVE NINETY-NINE PERCENT OF THE PLANET IN A MONTH, AND I PREFER TO PLAY FOR THE WINNING TEAM.
I'M FREE TO GO, CORRECT?
YES-YES, I'LL PARDON YOU FOR YOUR CRIMES AGAINST ME. GO OUT THERE AND DO... WHATEVER IT IS YOU DO.
MIMIC PLAYBACK
GAH!
MIMIC PLAYBACK
MISSION COMPLETE
I GUESS I'LL BE MOVING ON WITHOUT MY WISP.
THEY'RE MORE TROUBLE THAN THEY'RE WORTH, BELIEVE ME. NOW, LET'S SEE HERE...
MIMIC PLAYBACK
...MY SHADOW ANDROIDS REPORT THREE TARGETS DOWN. THERE WERE FIVE OF YOU.
W-WHISPER S-STAYED OUTSIDE AS LOOKOUT. SHE'S ONLY A SCOUT, NO THREAT TO...
FINISH THE JOB, OR I FINISH YOU.

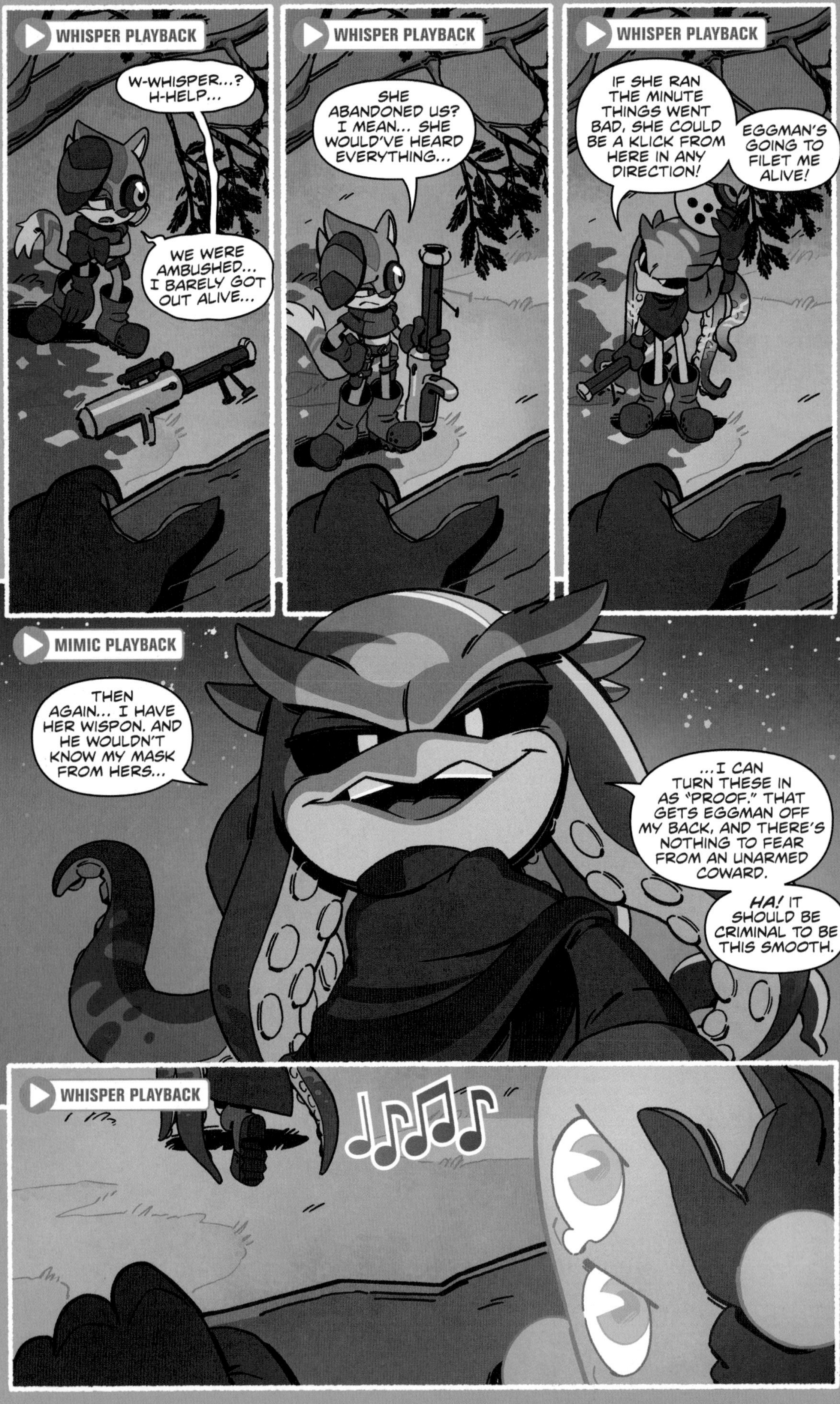
WHISPER PLAYBACK
W-WHISPER...? H-HELP...
WE WERE AMBUSHED... I BARELY GOT OUT ALIVE...
WHISPER PLAYBACK
SHE ABANDONED US? I MEAN... SHE WOULD'VE HEARD EVERYTHING...
WHISPER PLAYBACK
IF SHE RAN THE MINUTE THINGS WENT BAD, SHE COULD BE A KLICK FROM HERE IN ANY DIRECTION!
EGGMAN'S GOING TO FILET ME ALIVE!
MIMIC PLAYBACK
THEN AGAIN... I HAVE HER WISPON. AND HE WOULDN'T KNOW MY MASK FROM HERS...
...I CAN TURN THESE IN AS "PROOF." THAT GETS EGGMAN OFF MY BACK, AND THERE'S NOTHING TO FEAR FROM AN UNARMED COWARD.
HA! IT SHOULD BE CRIMINAL TO BE THIS SMOOTH.
WHISPER PLAYBACK

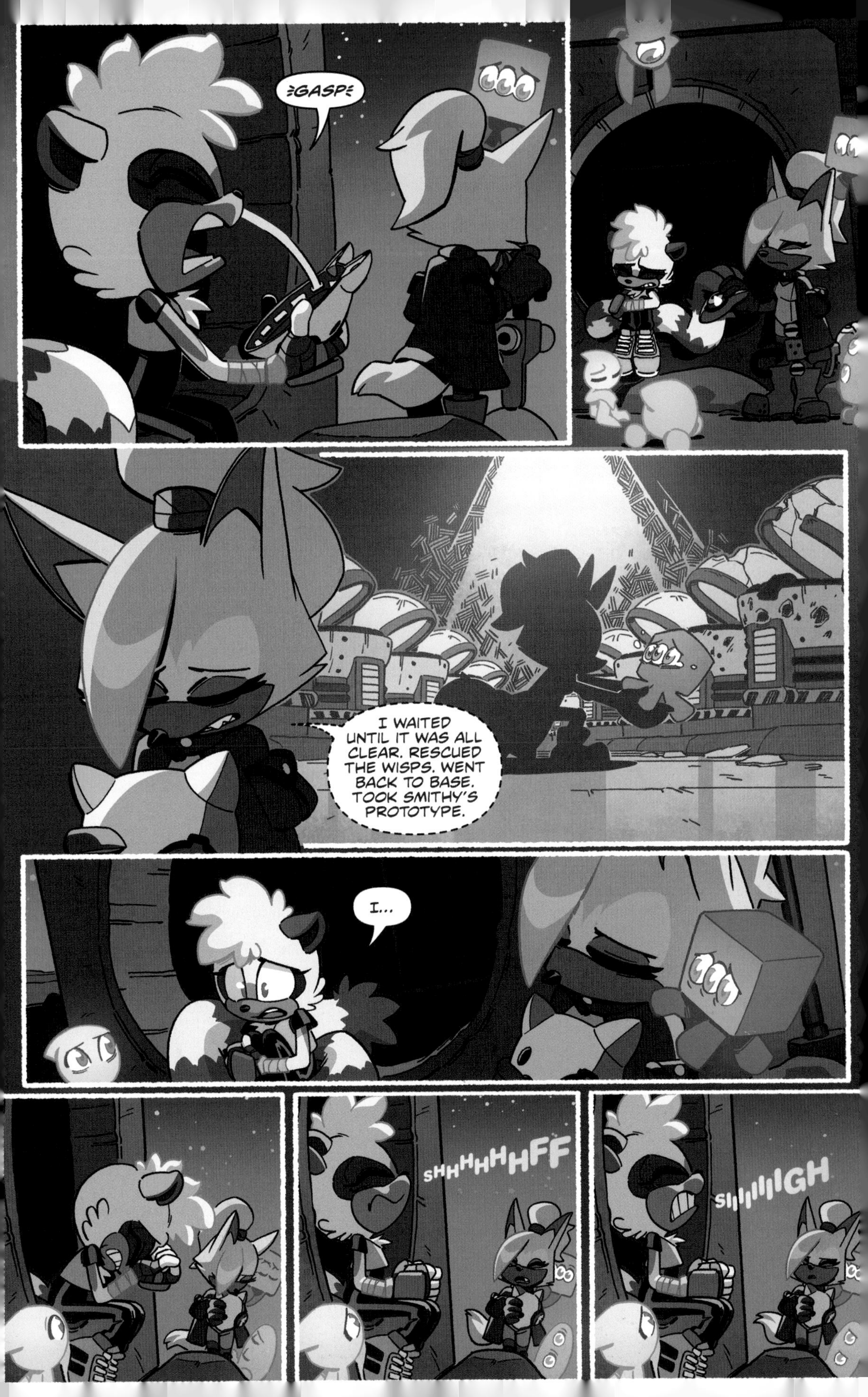
GASP
I WAITED UNTIL IT WAS ALL CLEAR. RESCUED THE WISPS. WENT BACK TO BASE. TOOK SMITHY'S PROTOTYPE.
I...
SHHHHHHHFF
SIIIIIIIGH

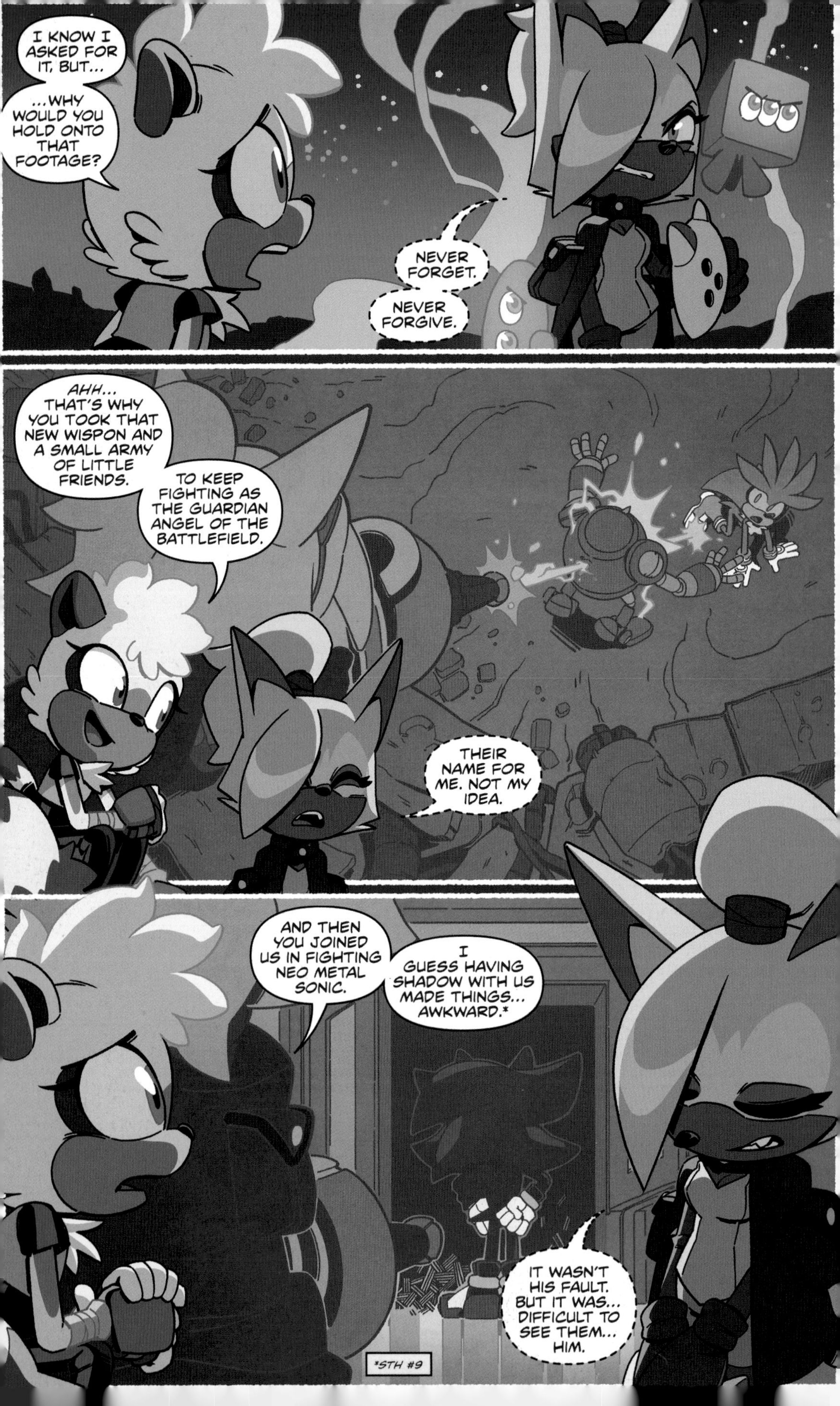
I KNOW I ASKED FOR IT, BUT...
...WHY WOULD YOU HOLD ONTO THAT FOOTAGE?
NEVER FORGET.
NEVER FORGIVE.
AHH... THAT'S WHY YOU TOOK THAT NEW WISPON AND A SMALL ARMY OF LITTLE FRIENDS.
TO KEEP FIGHTING AS THE GUARDIAN ANGEL OF THE BATTLEFIELD.
THEIR NAME FOR ME. NOT MY IDEA.
AND THEN YOU JOINED US IN FIGHTING NEO METAL SONIC.
I GUESS HAVING SHADOW WITH US MADE THINGS... AWKWARD.*
IT WASN'T HIS FAULT. BUT IT WAS... DIFFICULT TO SEE THEM... HIM.
*STH #9

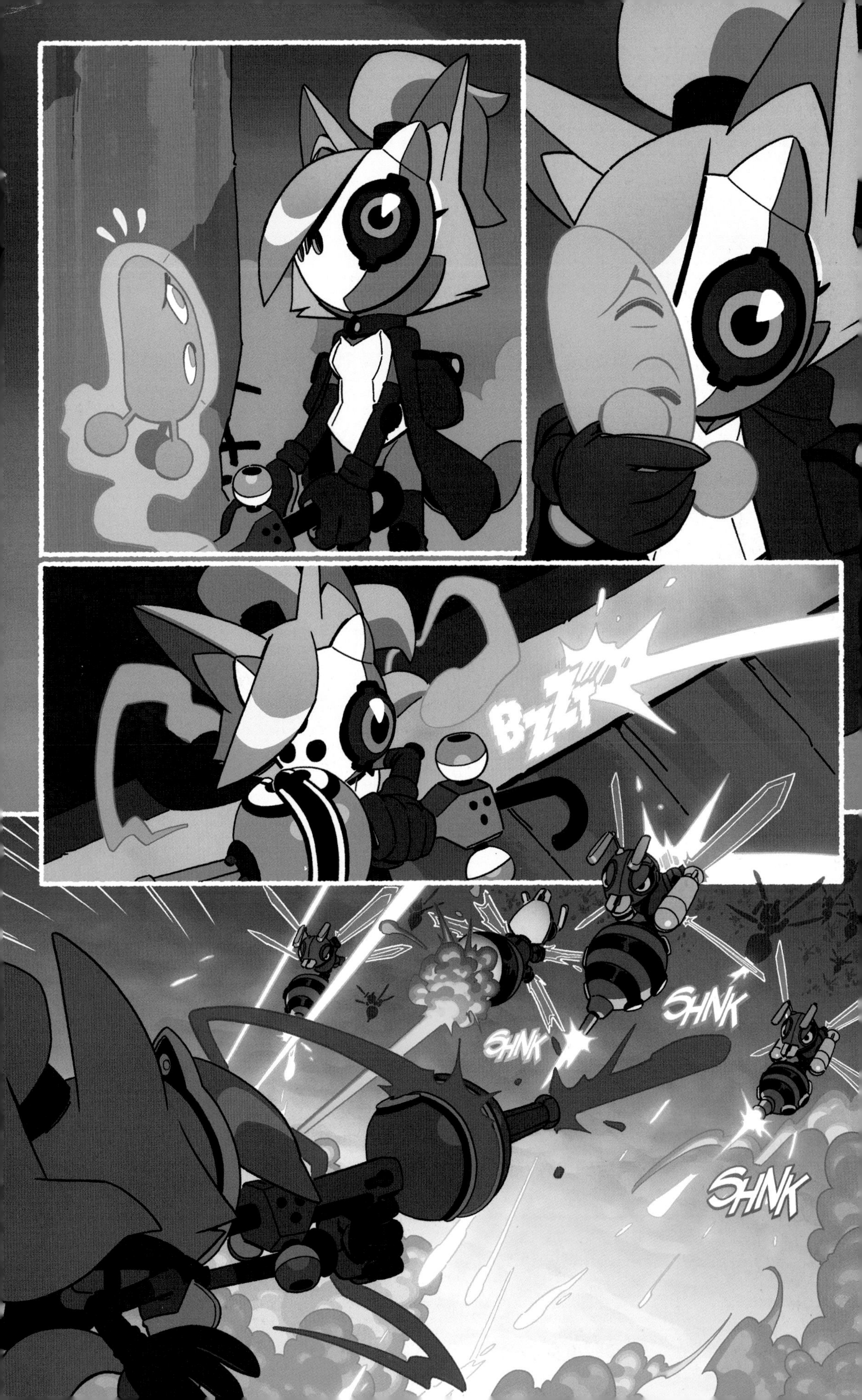
BZZZT
SHNK
SHNK
SHNK

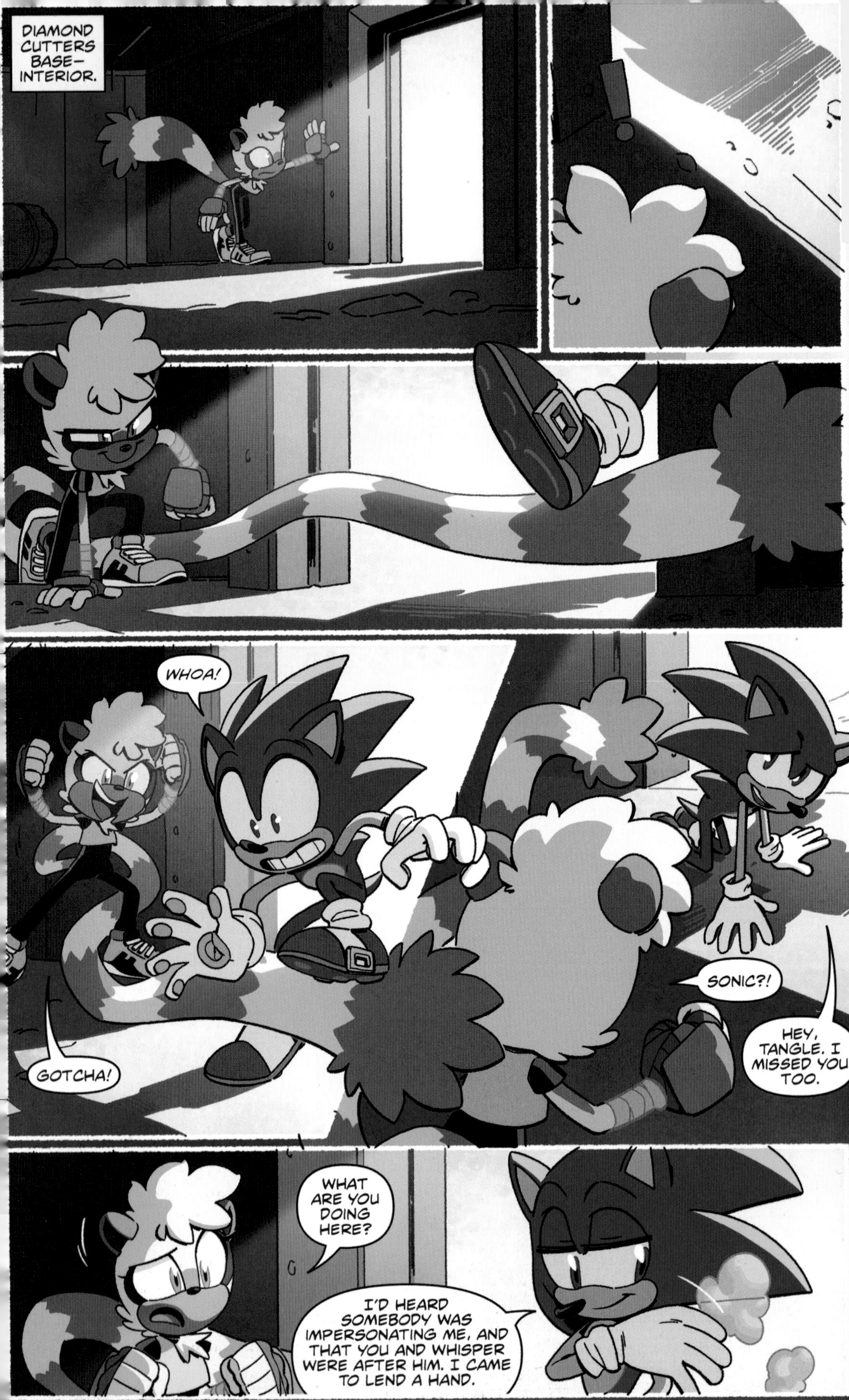
DIAMOND CUTTERS BASE— INTERIOR.
WHOA!
GOTCHA!
SONIC?!
HEY, TANGLE. I MISSED YOU TOO.
WHAT ARE YOU DOING HERE?
I'D HEARD SOMEBODY WAS IMPERSONATING ME, AND THAT YOU AND WHISPER WERE AFTER HIM. I CAME TO LEND A HAND.

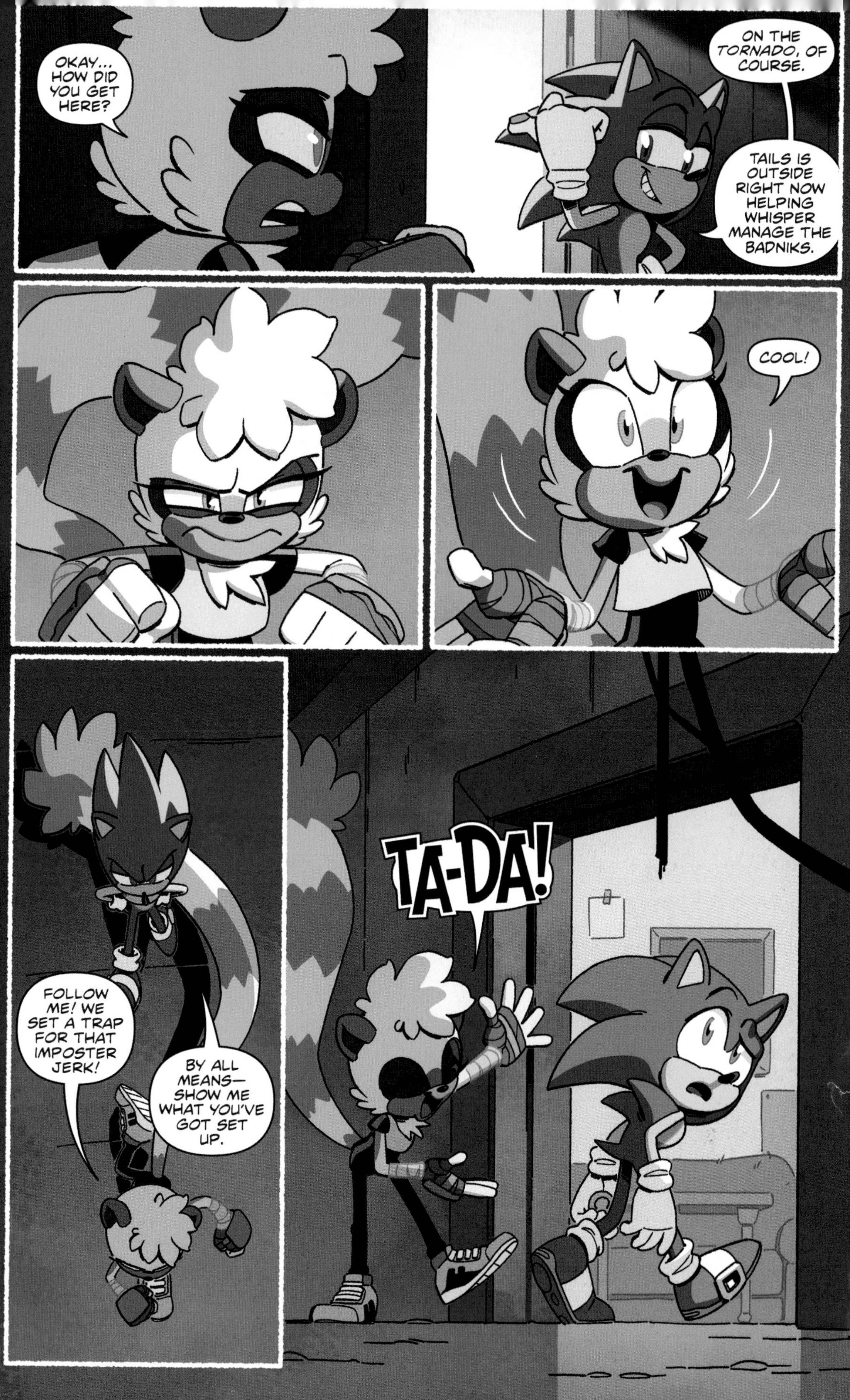
OKAY... HOW DID YOU GET HERE?
ON THE *TORNADO*, OF COURSE.
TAILS IS OUTSIDE RIGHT NOW HELPING WHISPER MANAGE THE BADNIKS.
COOL!
TA-DA!
FOLLOW ME! WE SET A TRAP FOR THAT IMPOSTER JERK!
BY ALL MEANS—SHOW ME WHAT YOU'VE GOT SET UP.

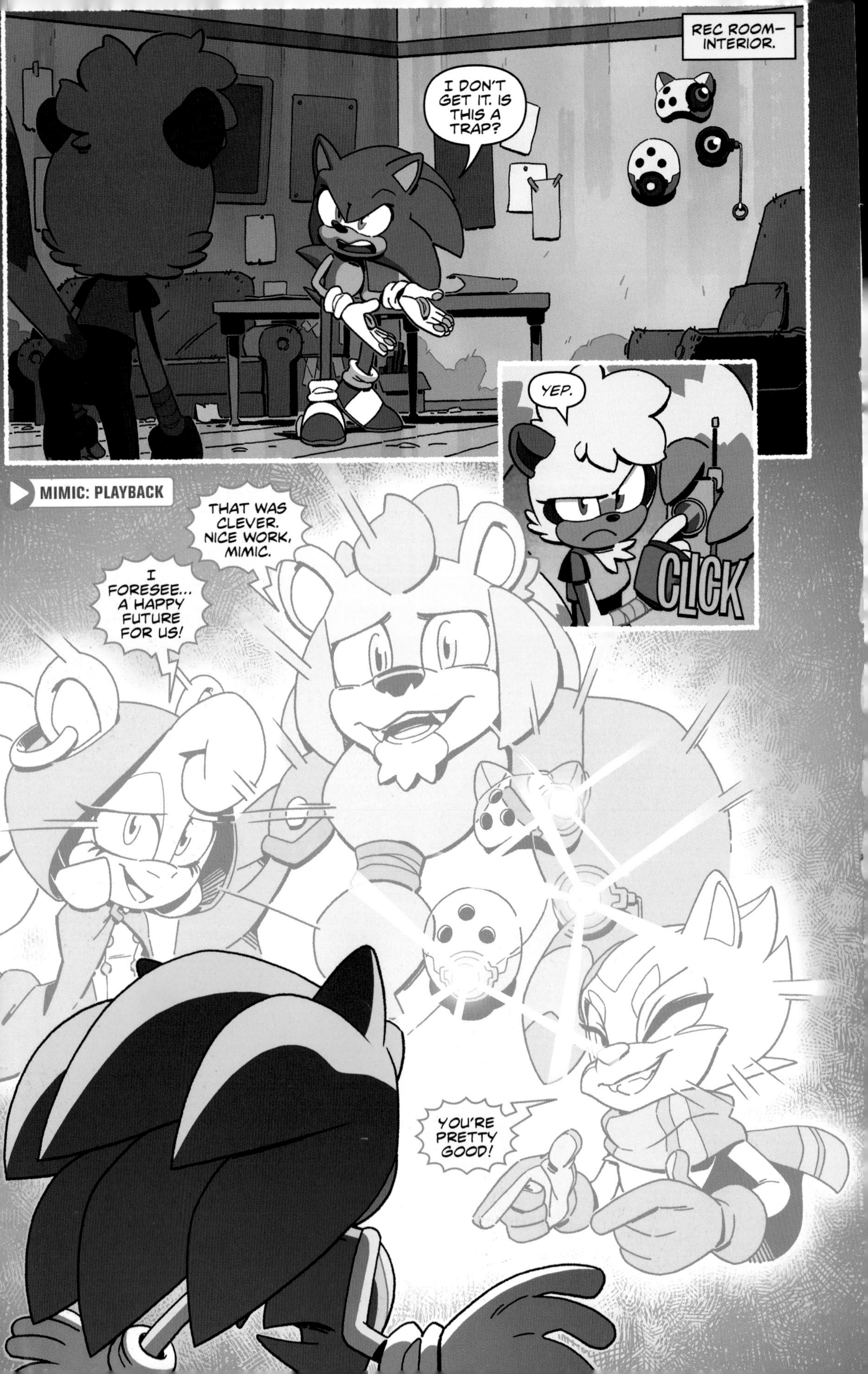
REC ROOM—INTERIOR.
I DON'T GET IT. IS THIS A TRAP?
YEP.
CLICK
MIMIC: PLAYBACK
THAT WAS CLEVER. NICE WORK, MIMIC.
I FORESEE... A HAPPY FUTURE FOR US!
YOU'RE PRETTY GOOD!

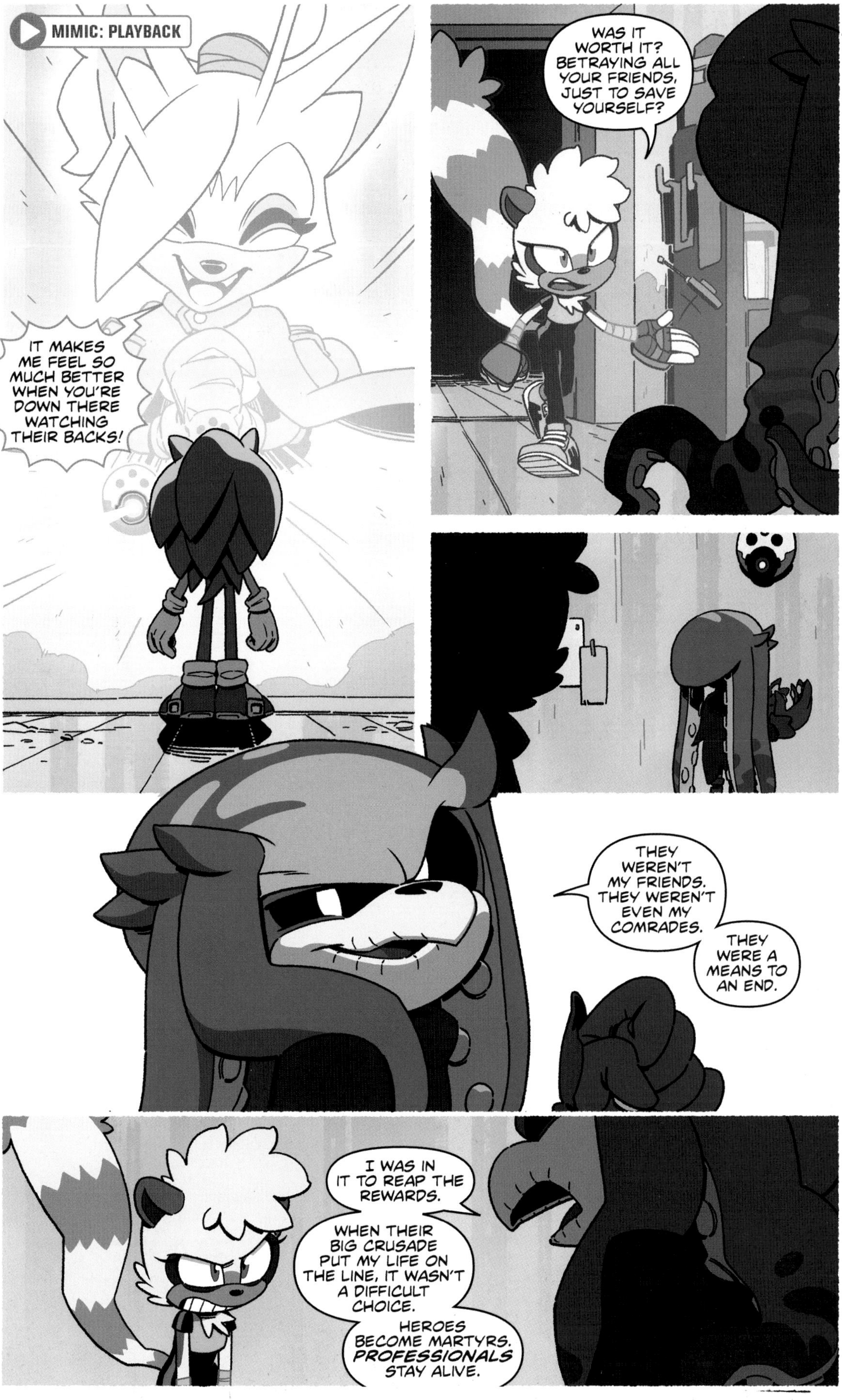
MIMIC: PLAYBACK
IT MAKES ME FEEL SO MUCH BETTER WHEN YOU'RE DOWN THERE WATCHING THEIR BACKS!
WAS IT WORTH IT? BETRAYING ALL YOUR FRIENDS, JUST TO SAVE YOURSELF?
THEY WEREN'T MY FRIENDS. THEY WEREN'T EVEN MY COMRADES.
THEY WERE A MEANS TO AN END.
I WAS IN IT TO REAP THE REWARDS.
WHEN THEIR BIG CRUSADE PUT MY LIFE ON THE LINE, IT WASN'T A DIFFICULT CHOICE.
HEROES BECOME MARTYRS. PROFESSIONALS STAY ALIVE.

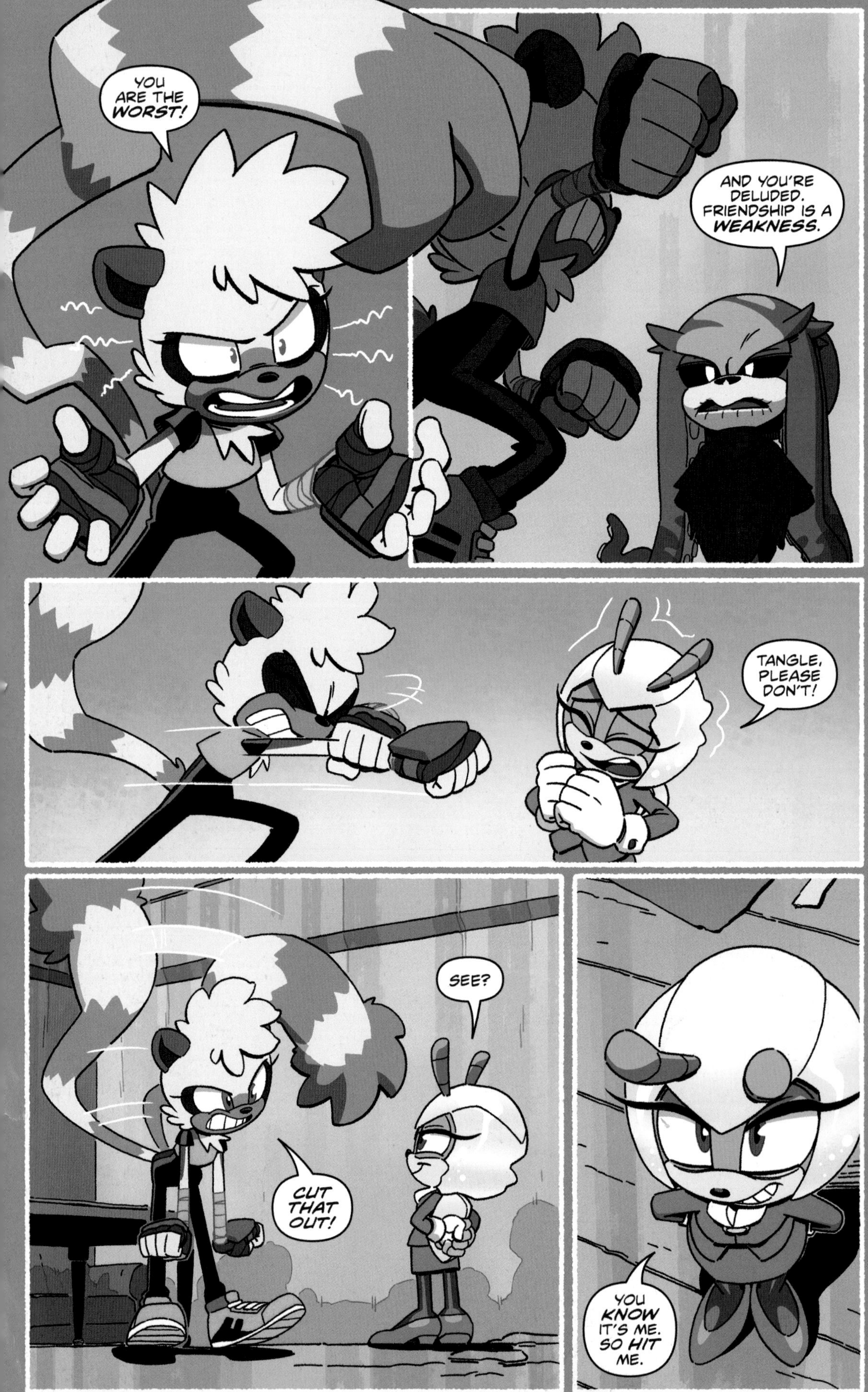
YOU ARE THE WORST!
AND YOU'RE DELUDED. FRIENDSHIP IS A WEAKNESS.
TANGLE, PLEASE DON'T!
SEE?
CUT THAT OUT!
YOU KNOW IT'S ME. SO HIT ME.

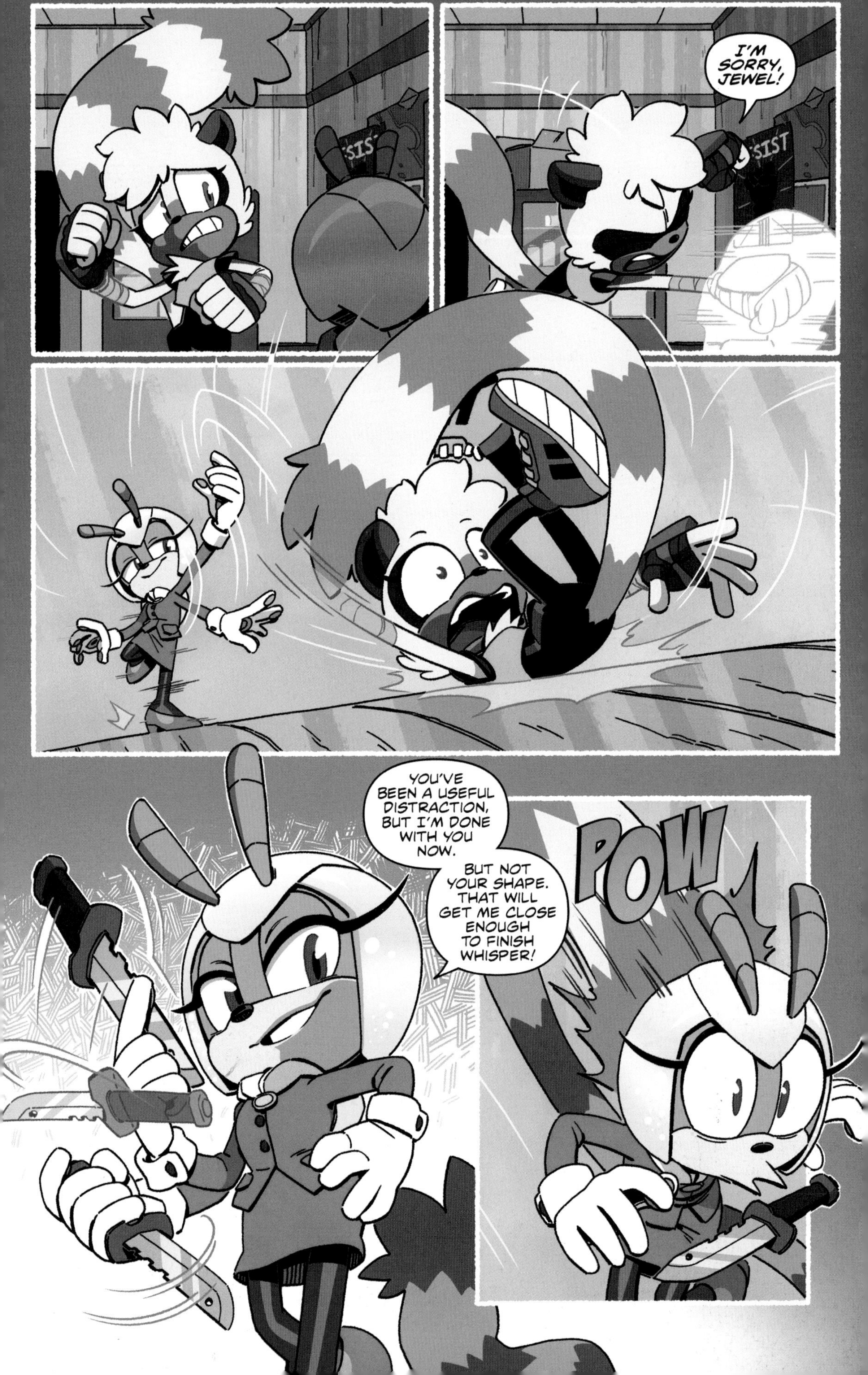
SIST
I'M SORRY, JEWEL!
SIST
YOU'VE BEEN A USEFUL DISTRACTION, BUT I'M DONE WITH YOU NOW.
BUT NOT YOUR SHAPE. THAT WILL GET ME CLOSE ENOUGH TO FINISH WHISPER!
POW

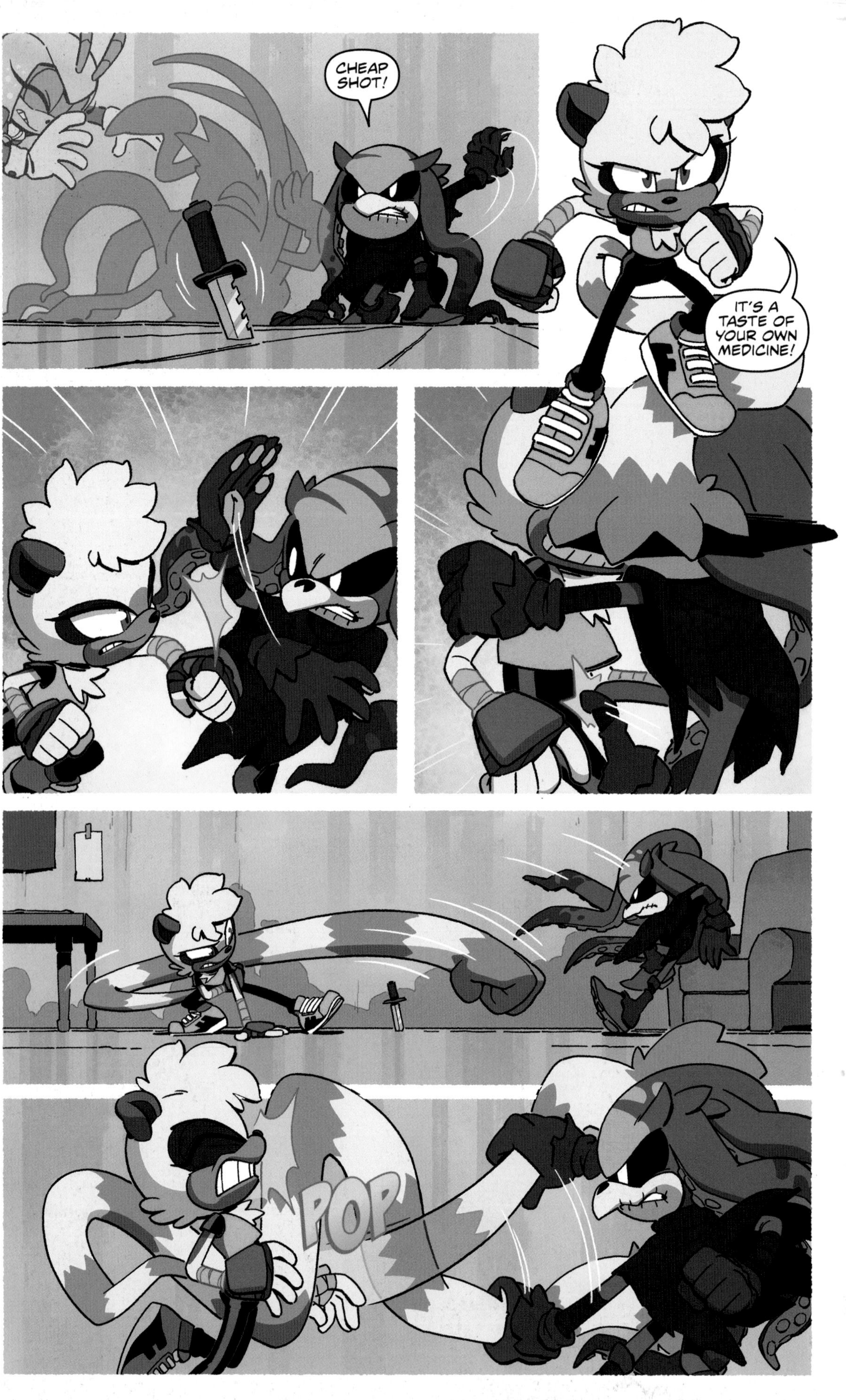
CHEAP SHOT!
IT'S A TASTE OF YOUR OWN MEDICINE!
POP

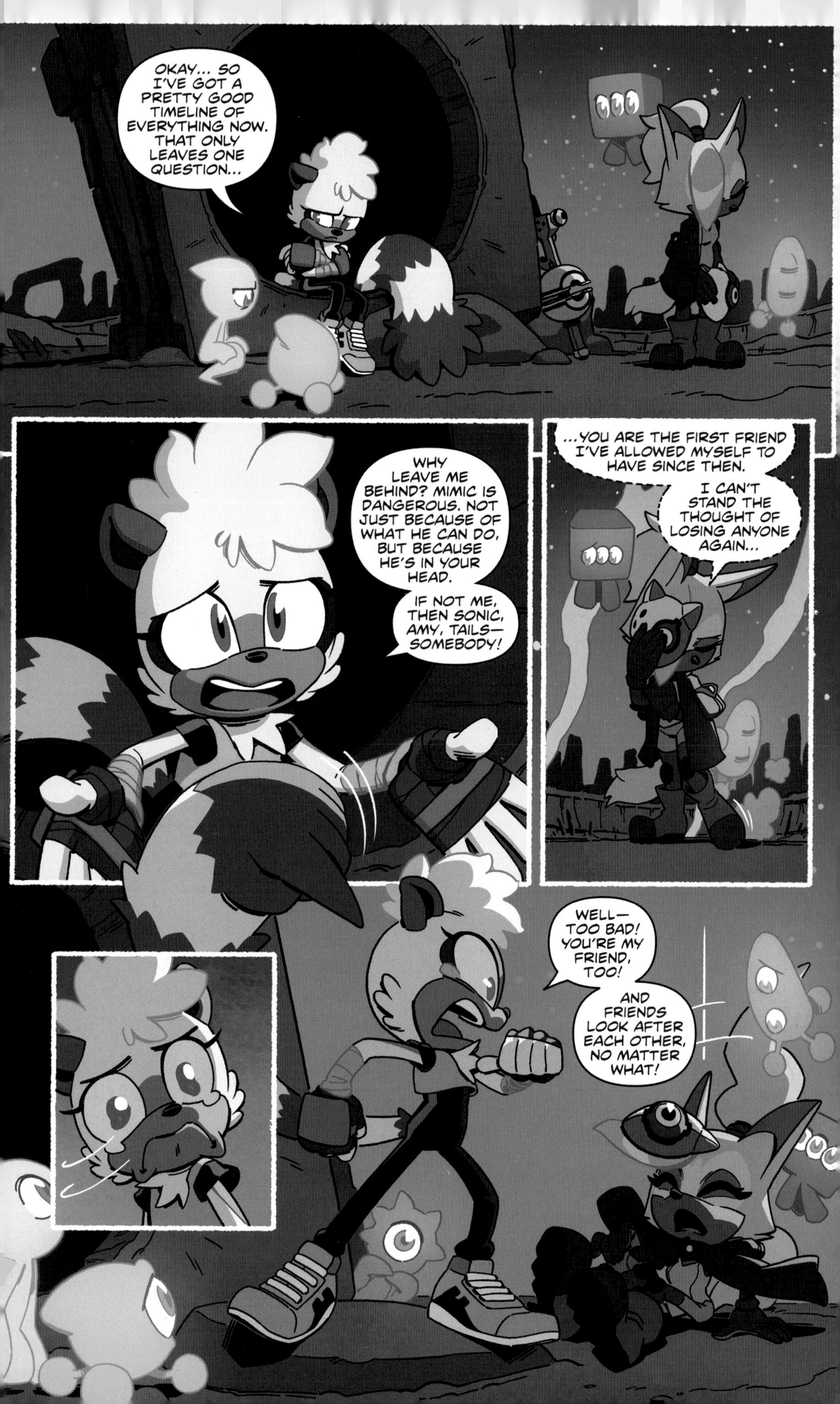
OKAY... SO I'VE GOT A PRETTY GOOD TIMELINE OF EVERYTHING NOW. THAT ONLY LEAVES ONE QUESTION...
WHY LEAVE ME BEHIND? MIMIC IS DANGEROUS. NOT JUST BECAUSE OF WHAT HE CAN DO, BUT BECAUSE HE'S IN YOUR HEAD.
IF NOT ME, THEN SONIC, AMY, TAILS—SOMEBODY!
...YOU ARE THE FIRST FRIEND I'VE ALLOWED MYSELF TO HAVE SINCE THEN.
I CAN'T STAND THE THOUGHT OF LOSING ANYONE AGAIN...
WELL—TOO BAD! YOU'RE MY FRIEND, TOO!
AND FRIENDS LOOK AFTER EACH OTHER, NO MATTER WHAT!

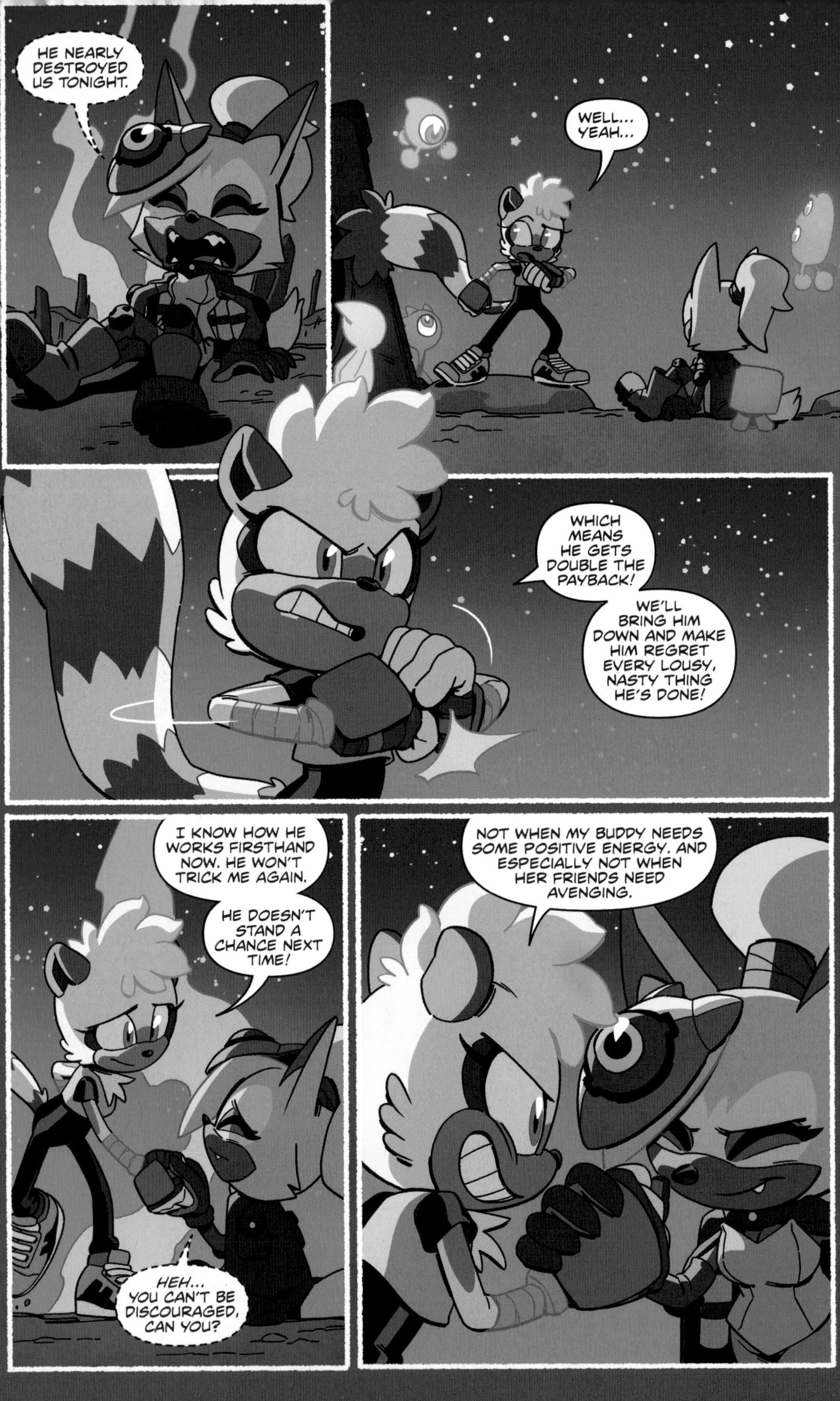
HE NEARLY DESTROYED US TONIGHT.
WELL... YEAH...
WHICH MEANS HE GETS DOUBLE THE PAYBACK!
WE'LL BRING HIM DOWN AND MAKE HIM REGRET EVERY LOUSY, NASTY THING HE'S DONE!
I KNOW HOW HE WORKS FIRSTHAND NOW. HE WON'T TRICK ME AGAIN.
HE DOESN'T STAND A CHANCE NEXT TIME!
HEH... YOU CAN'T BE DISCOURAGED, CAN YOU?
NOT WHEN MY BUDDY NEEDS SOME POSITIVE ENERGY. AND ESPECIALLY NOT WHEN HER FRIENDS NEED AVENGING.

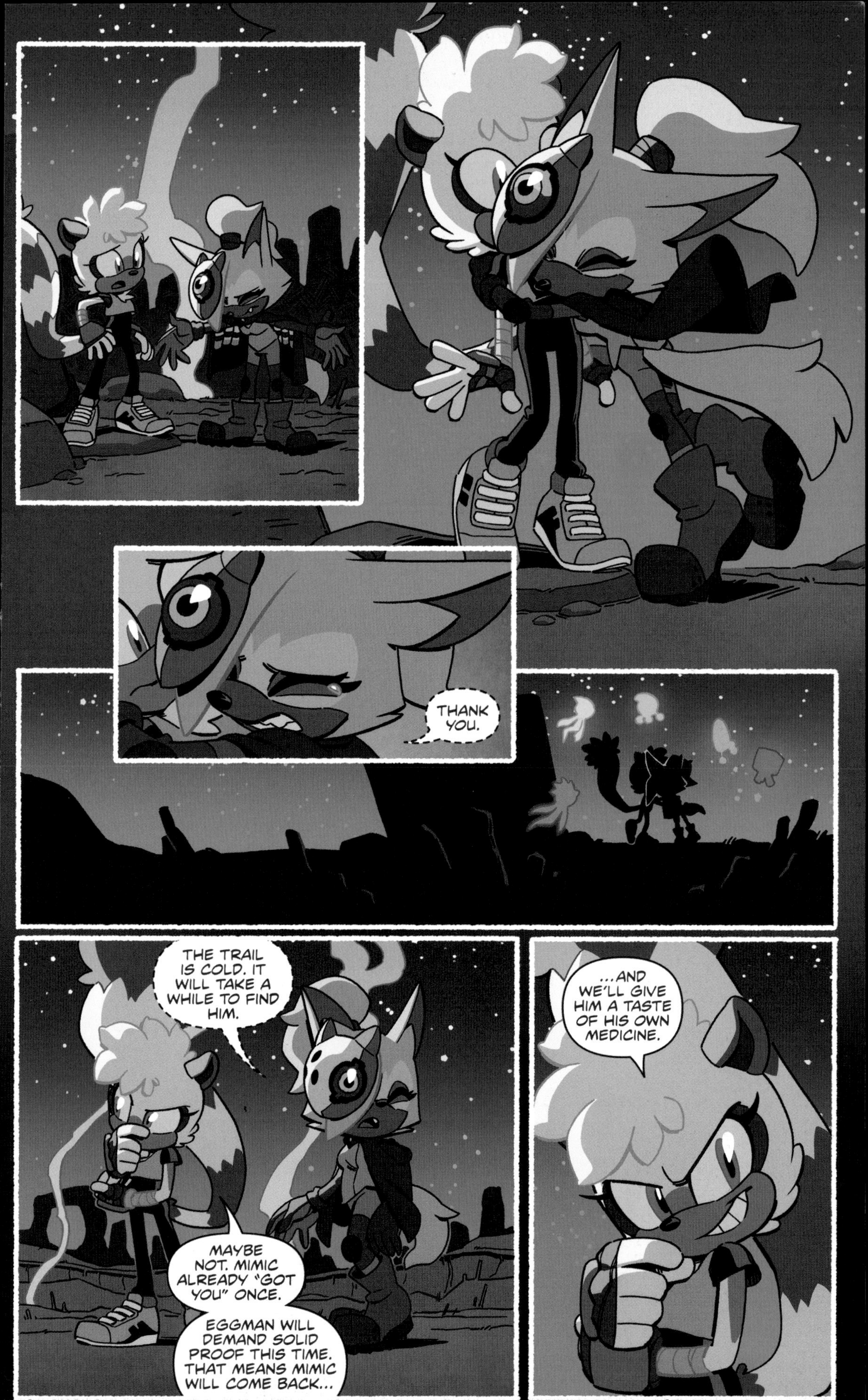
THANK YOU.
THE TRAIL IS COLD. IT WILL TAKE A WHILE TO FIND HIM.
MAYBE NOT. MIMIC ALREADY "GOT YOU" ONCE.
EGGMAN WILL DEMAND SOLID PROOF THIS TIME. THAT MEANS MIMIC WILL COME BACK...
...AND WE'LL GIVE HIM A TASTE OF HIS OWN MEDICINE.

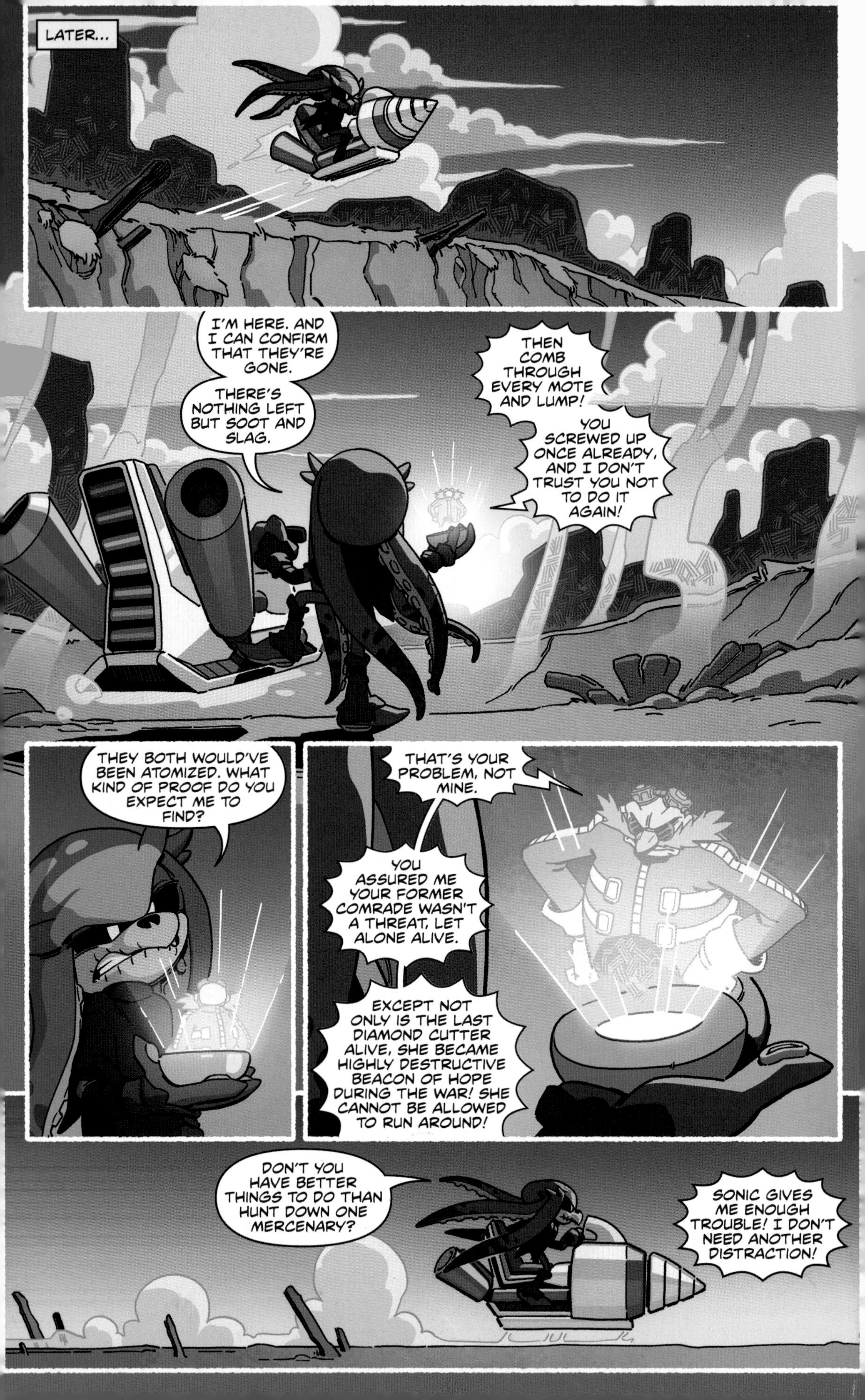
LATER...
I'M HERE. AND I CAN CONFIRM THAT THEY'RE GONE.
THERE'S NOTHING LEFT BUT SOOT AND SLAG.
THEN COMB THROUGH EVERY MOTE AND LUMP!
YOU SCREWED UP ONCE ALREADY, AND I DON'T TRUST YOU NOT TO DO IT AGAIN!
THEY BOTH WOULD'VE BEEN ATOMIZED. WHAT KIND OF PROOF DO YOU EXPECT ME TO FIND?
THAT'S YOUR PROBLEM, NOT MINE.
YOU ASSURED ME YOUR FORMER COMRADE WASN'T A THREAT, LET ALONE ALIVE.
EXCEPT NOT ONLY IS THE LAST DIAMOND CUTTER ALIVE, SHE BECAME HIGHLY DESTRUCTIVE BEACON OF HOPE DURING THE WAR! SHE CANNOT BE ALLOWED TO RUN AROUND!
DON'T YOU HAVE BETTER THINGS TO DO THAN HUNT DOWN ONE MERCENARY?
SONIC GIVES ME ENOUGH TROUBLE! I DON'T NEED ANOTHER DISTRACTION!

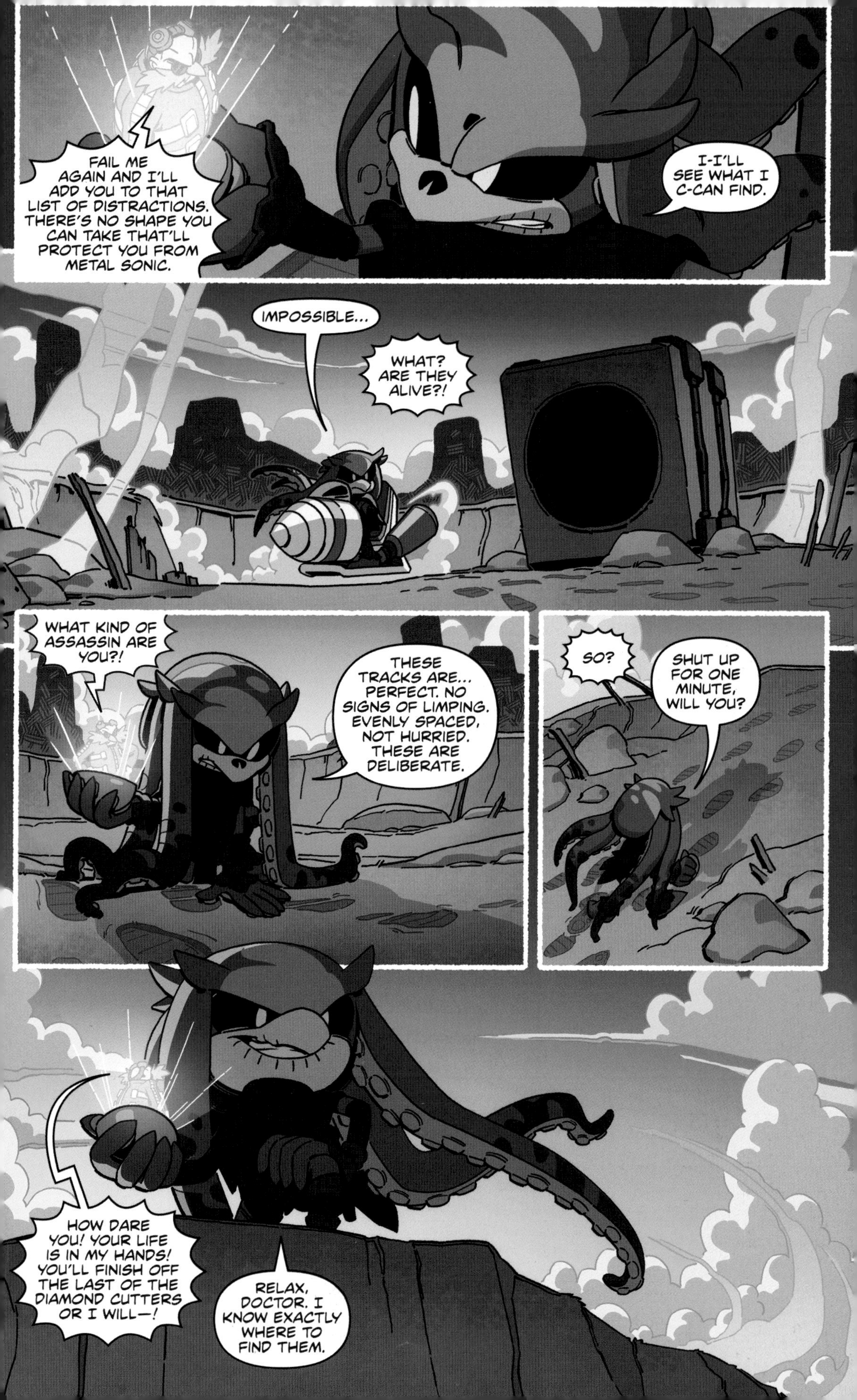
FAIL ME AGAIN AND I'LL ADD YOU TO THAT LIST OF DISTRACTIONS. THERE'S NO SHAPE YOU CAN TAKE THAT'LL PROTECT YOU FROM METAL SONIC.
I-I'LL SEE WHAT I C-CAN FIND.
IMPOSSIBLE...
WHAT? ARE THEY ALIVE?!
WHAT KIND OF ASSASSIN ARE YOU?!
THESE TRACKS ARE... PERFECT. NO SIGNS OF LIMPING. EVENLY SPACED, NOT HURRIED. THESE ARE DELIBERATE.
SO?
SHUT UP FOR ONE MINUTE, WILL YOU?
HOW DARE YOU! YOUR LIFE IS IN MY HANDS! YOU'LL FINISH OFF THE LAST OF THE DIAMOND CUTTERS OR I WILL—!
RELAX, DOCTOR. I KNOW EXACTLY WHERE TO FIND THEM.

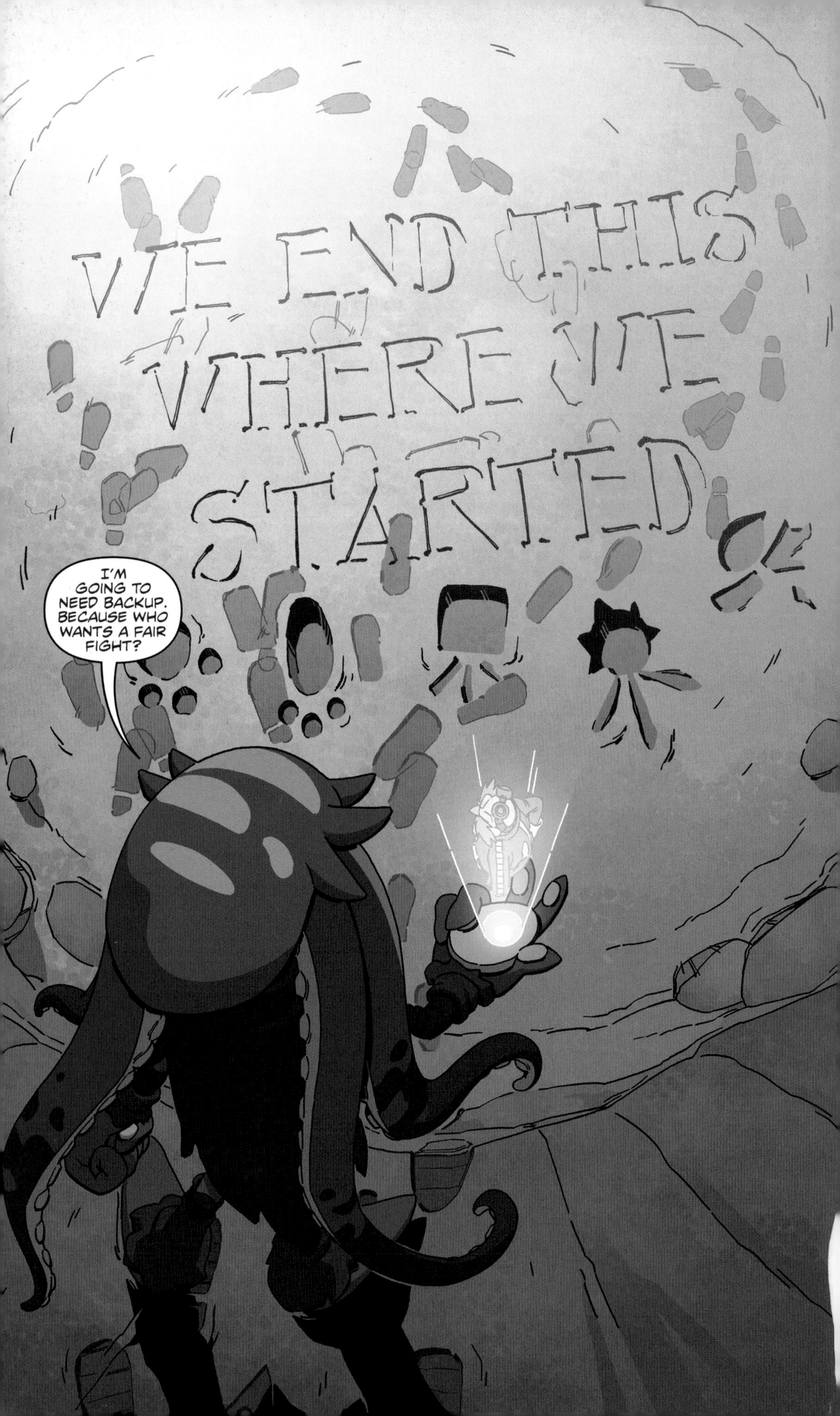
WE END THIS WHERE WE STARTED
I'M GOING TO NEED BACKUP. BECAUSE WHO WANTS A FAIR FIGHT?

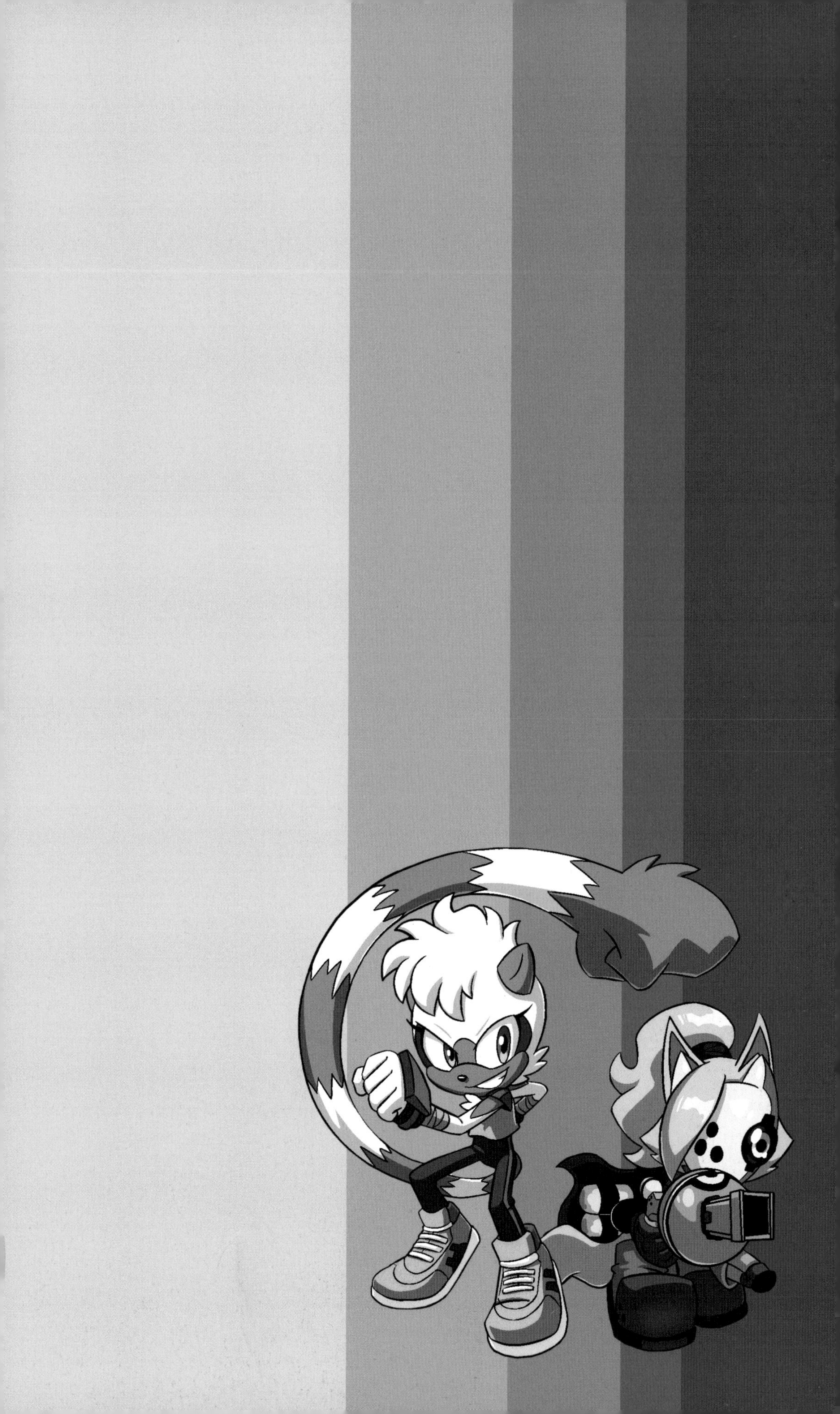

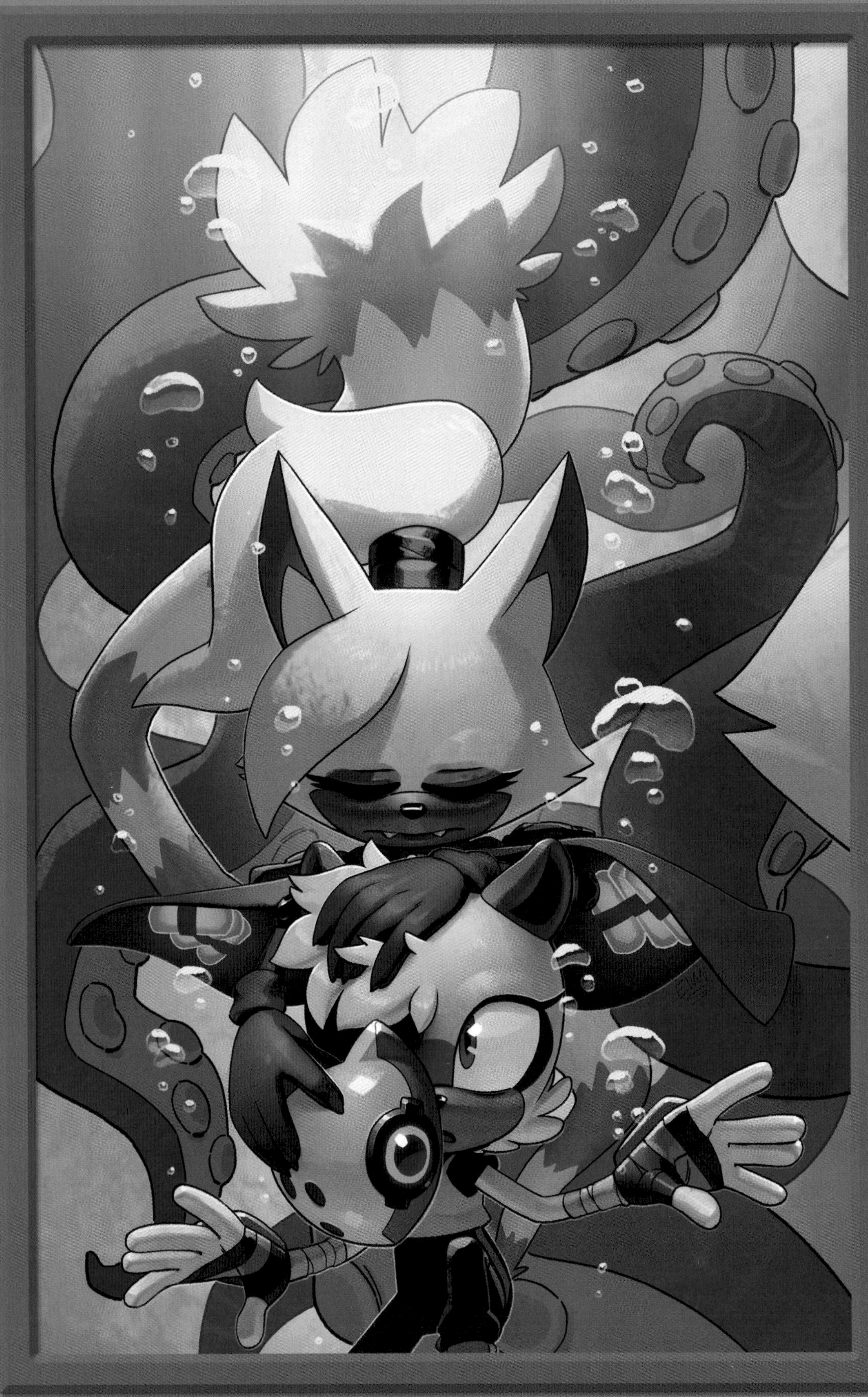

ART BY **EVAN STANLEY**

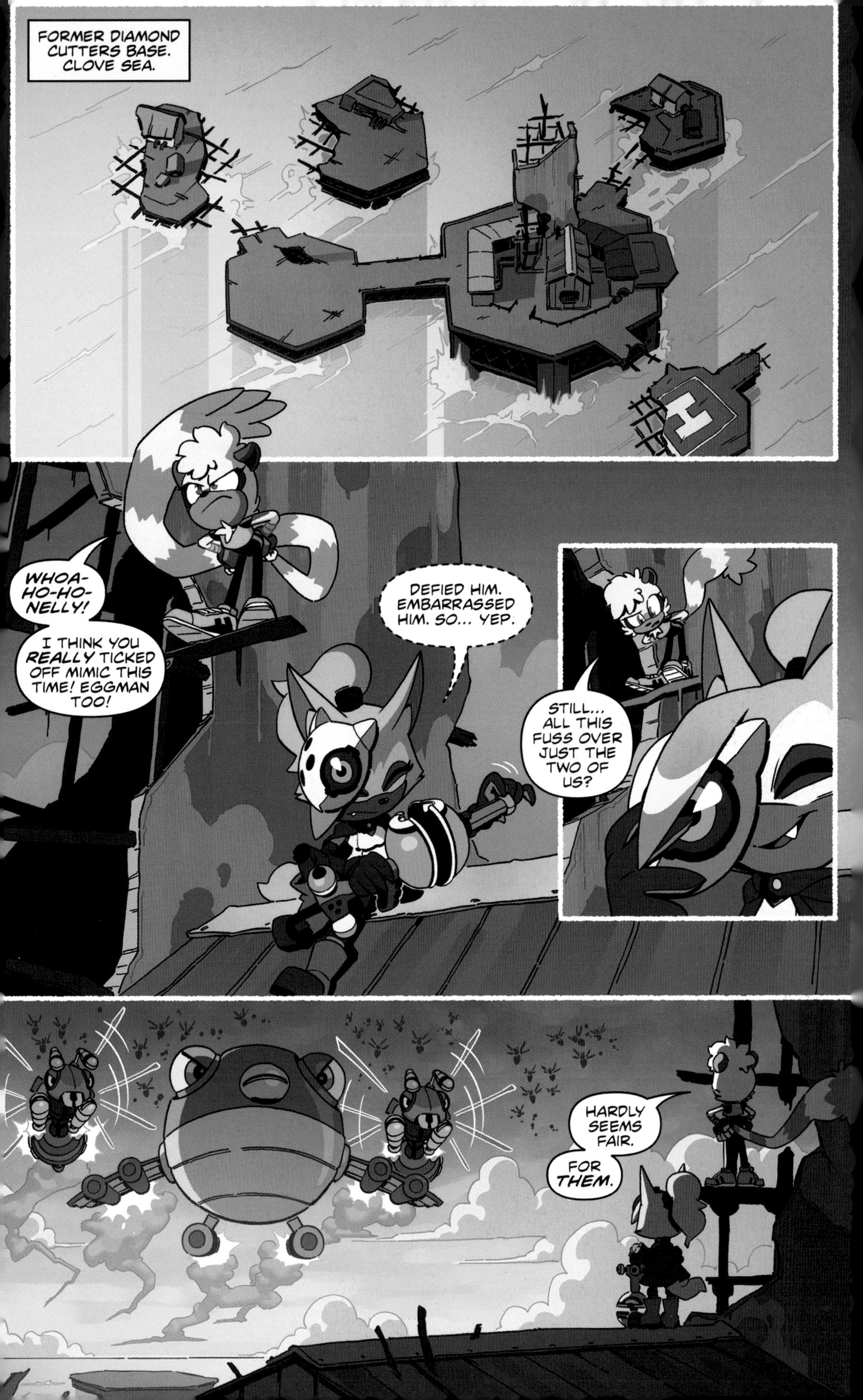
FORMER DIAMOND CUTTERS BASE. CLOVE SEA.
WHOA-HO-HO-NELLY!
I THINK YOU REALLY TICKED OFF MIMIC THIS TIME! EGGMAN TOO!
DEFIED HIM. EMBARRASSED HIM. SO... YEP.
STILL... ALL THIS FUSS OVER JUST THE TWO OF US?
HARDLY SEEMS FAIR.
FOR THEM.

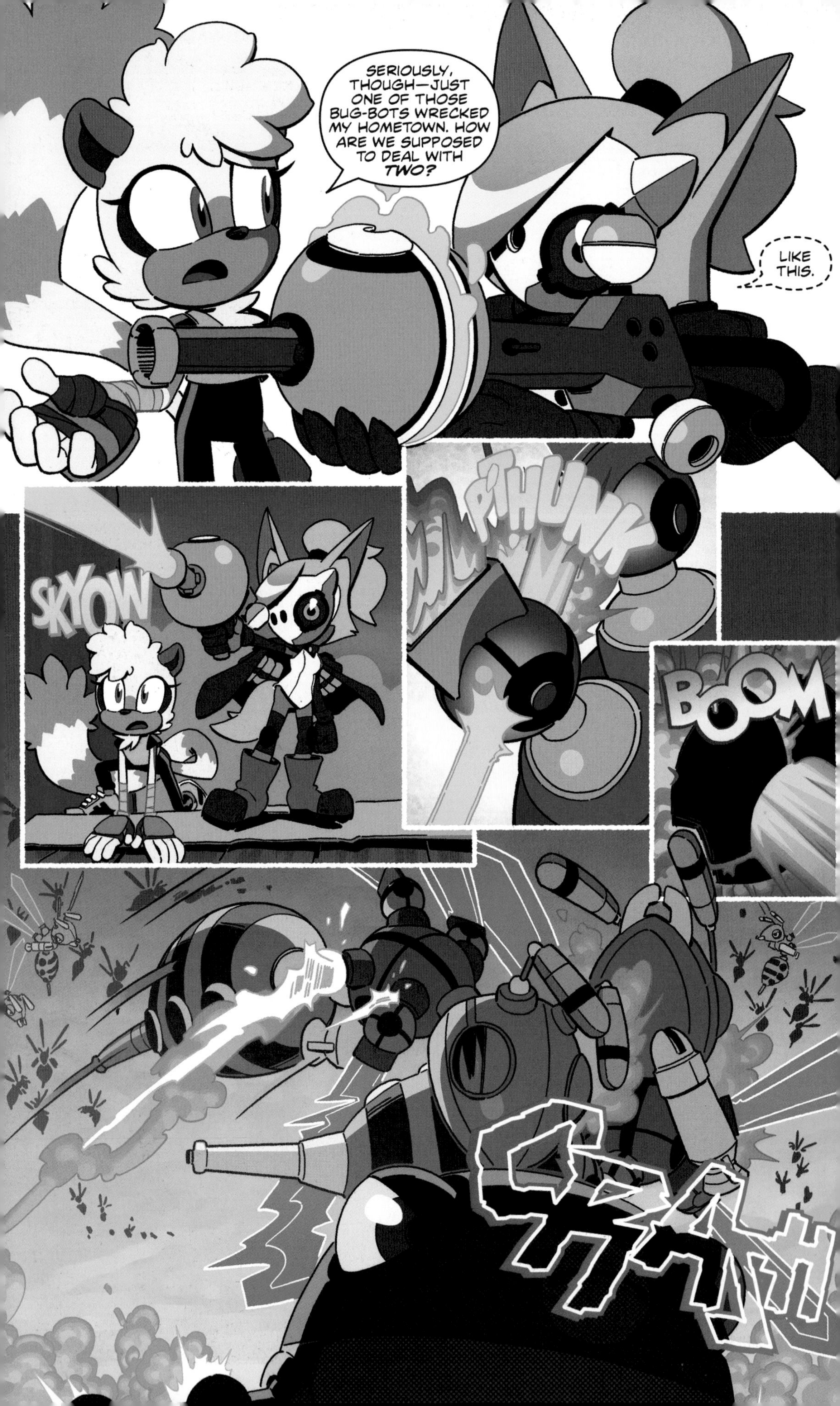
SERIOUSLY, THOUGH—JUST ONE OF THOSE BUG-BOTS WRECKED MY HOMETOWN. HOW ARE WE SUPPOSED TO DEAL WITH *TWO?*
LIKE THIS.
SKYOW
P'THUNK
BOOM

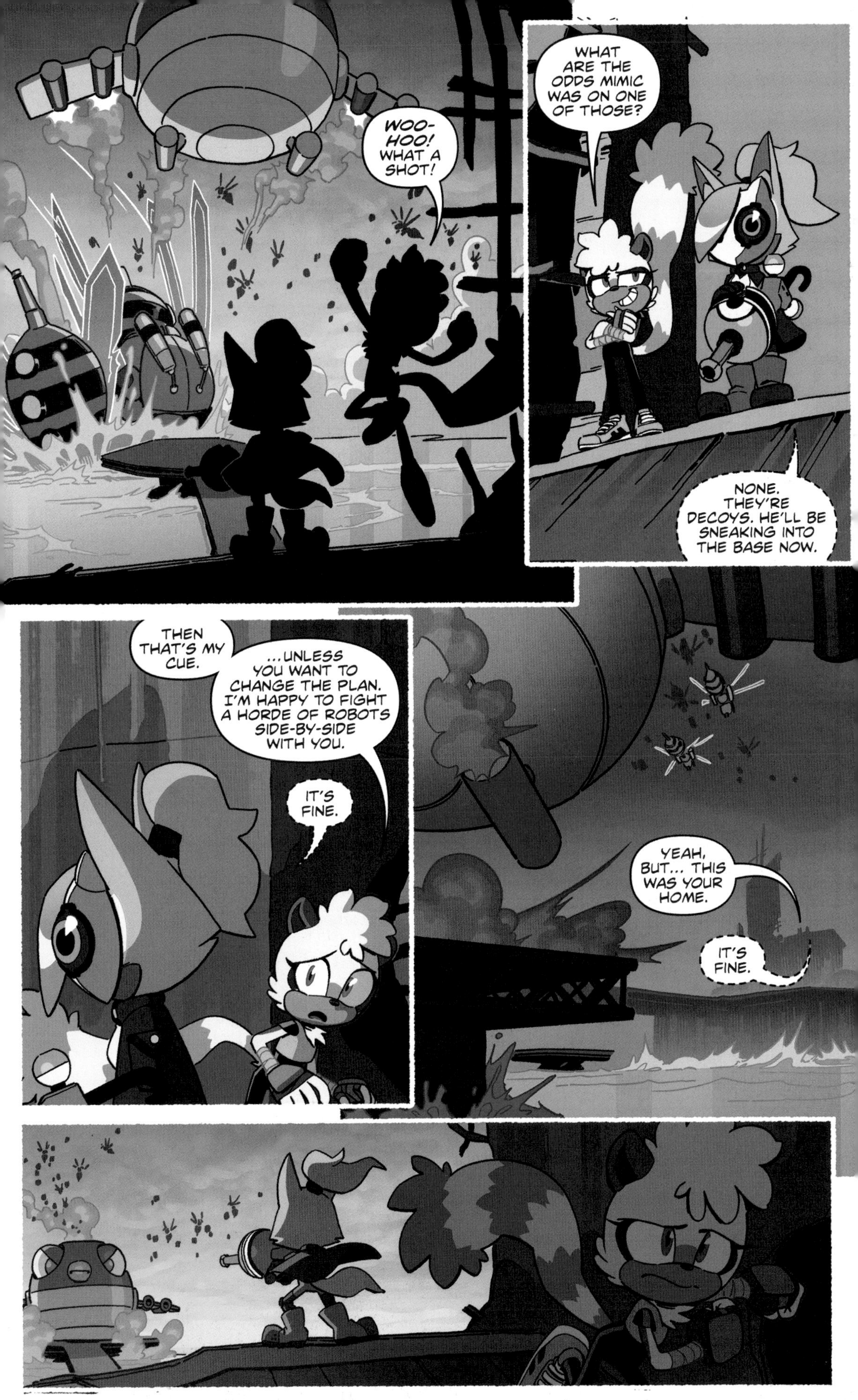
WOO-HOO! WHAT A SHOT!
WHAT ARE THE ODDS MIMIC WAS ON ONE OF THOSE?
NONE. THEY'RE DECOYS. HE'LL BE SNEAKING INTO THE BASE NOW.
THEN THAT'S MY CUE.
...UNLESS YOU WANT TO CHANGE THE PLAN. I'M HAPPY TO FIGHT A HORDE OF ROBOTS SIDE-BY-SIDE WITH YOU.
IT'S FINE.
YEAH, BUT... THIS WAS YOUR HOME.
IT'S FINE.

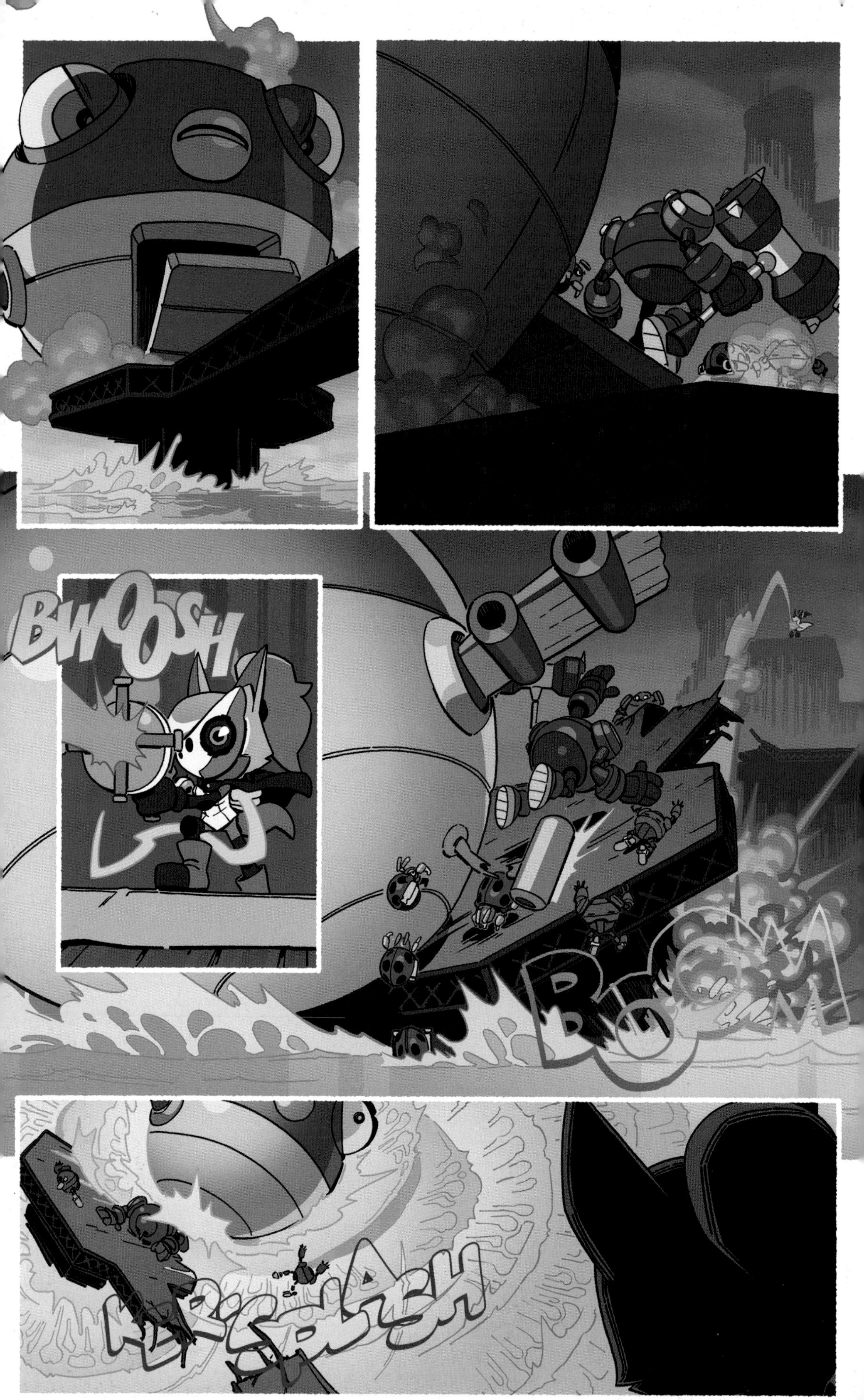
BWOOSH
BOOM
KRSPLASH

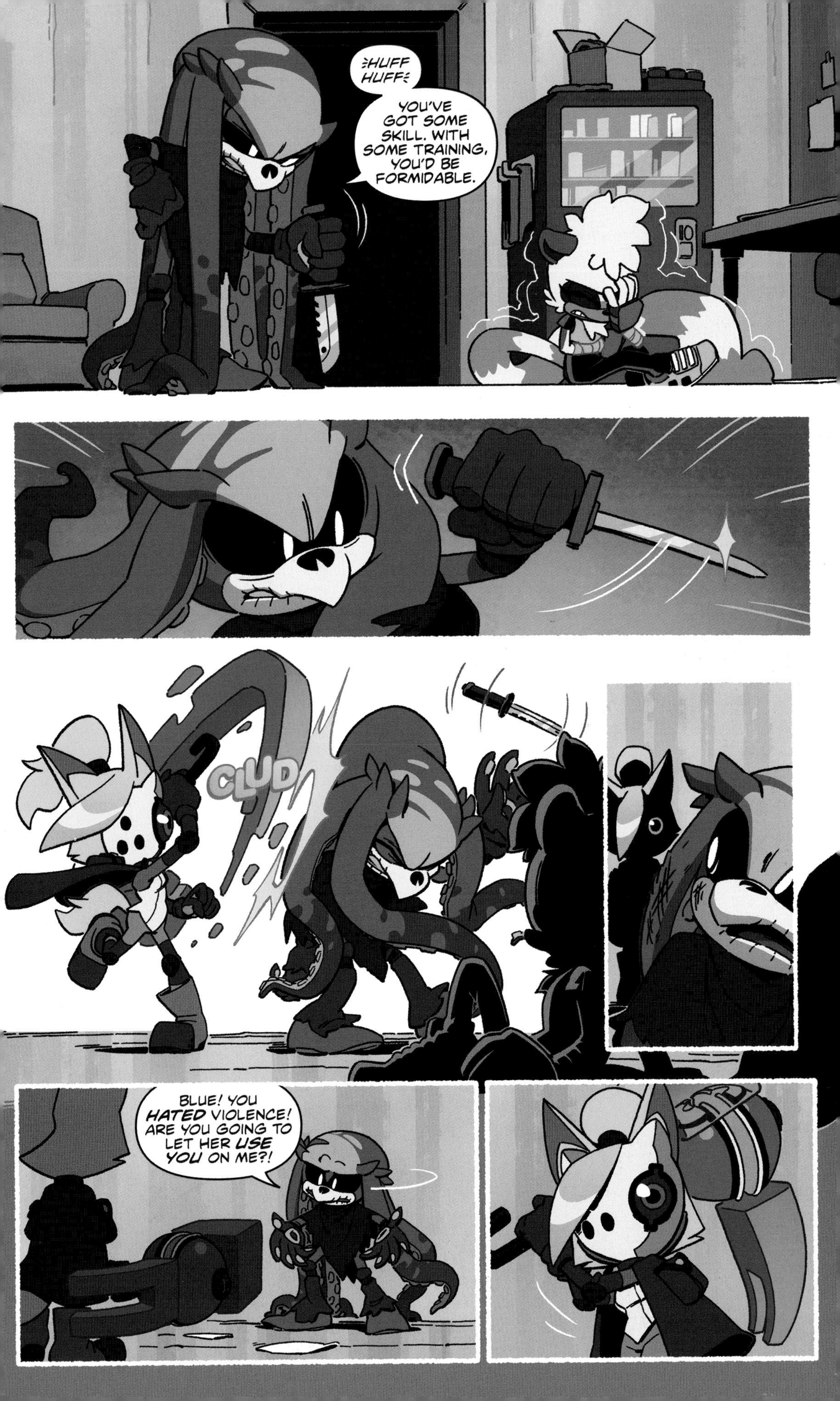
HUFF HUFF
YOU'VE GOT SOME SKILL. WITH SOME TRAINING, YOU'D BE FORMIDABLE.
CLUD
BLUE! YOU HATED VIOLENCE! ARE YOU GOING TO LET HER USE YOU ON ME?!

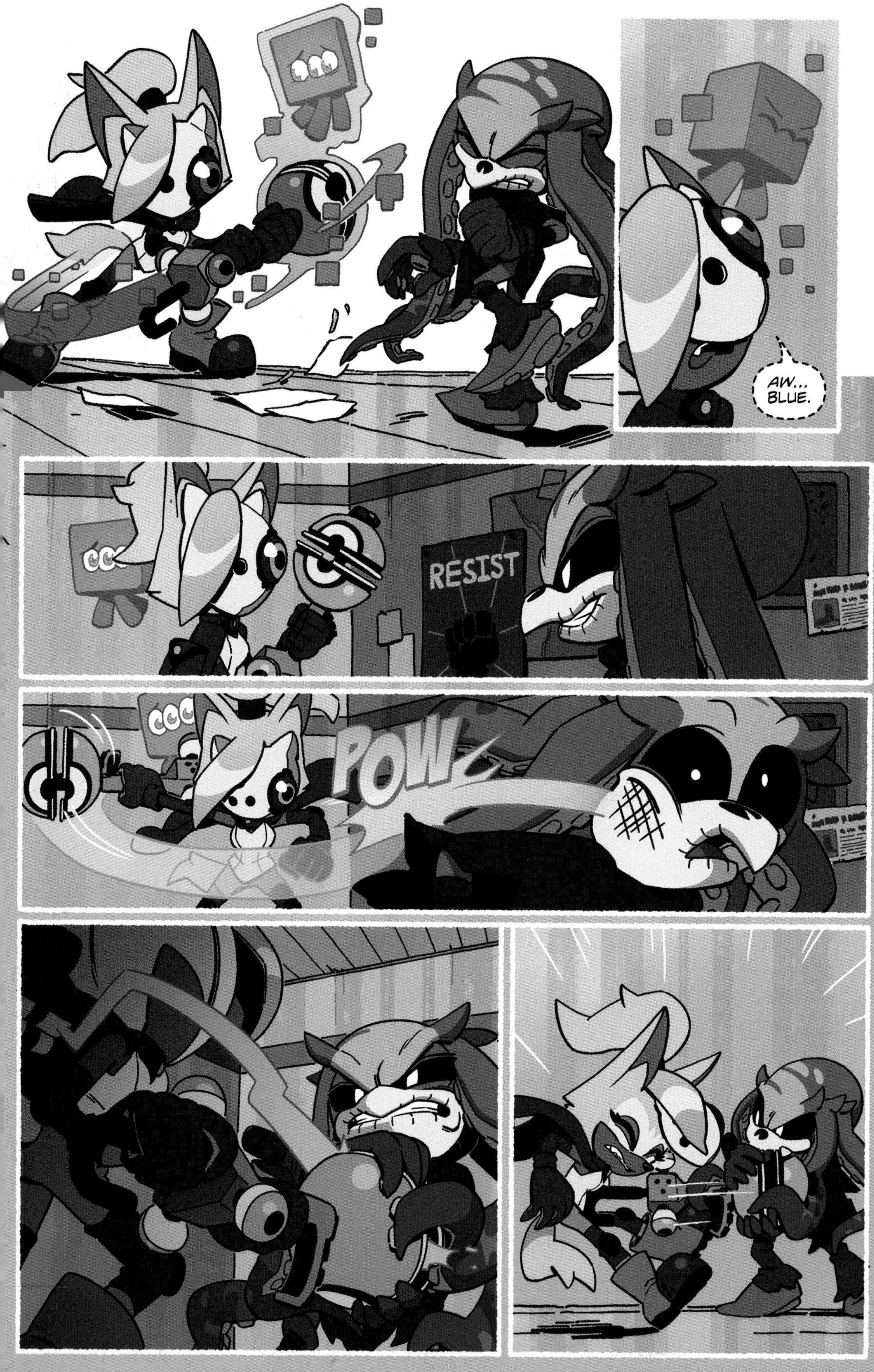
AW... BLUE.
RESIST
POW

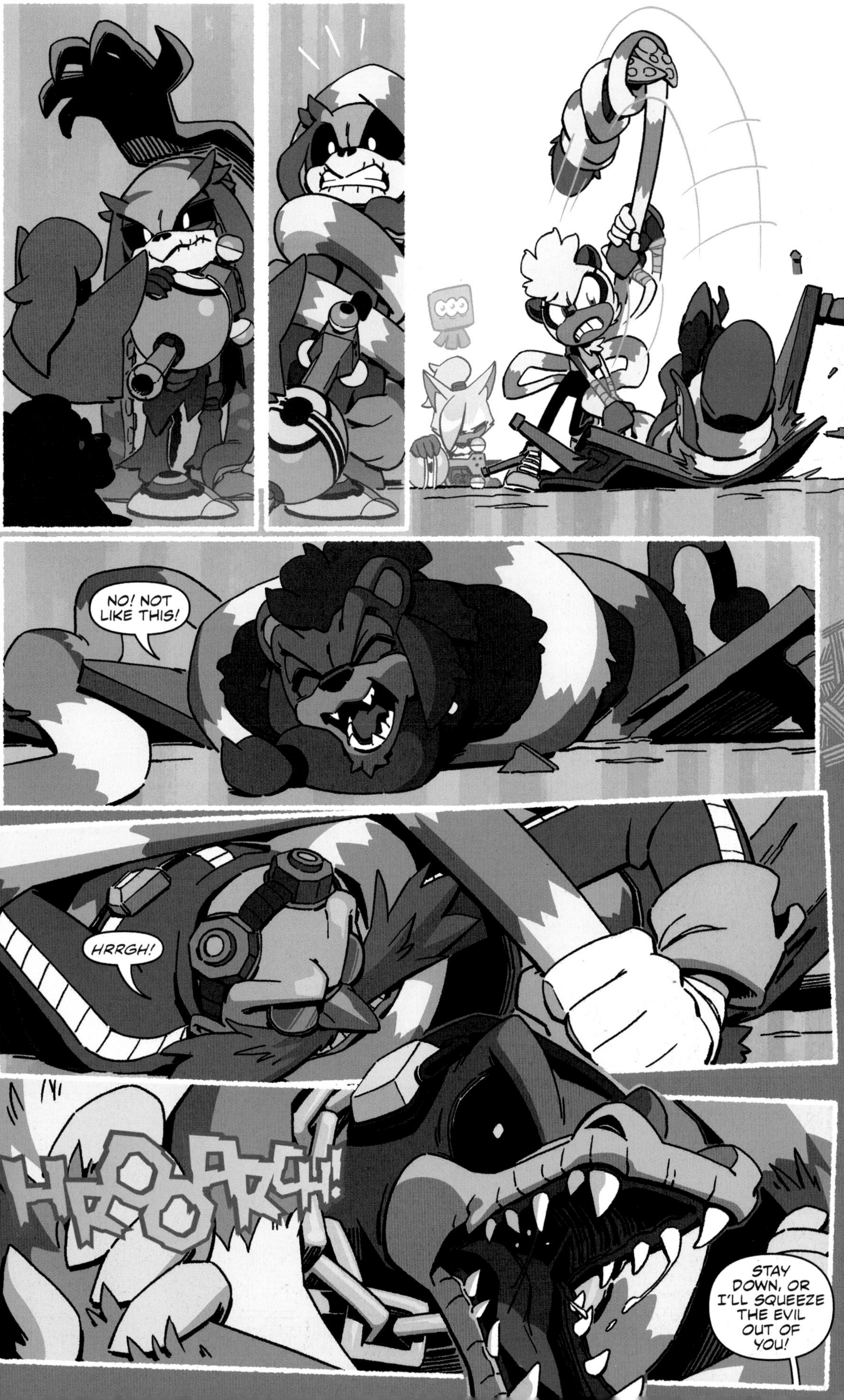
NO! NOT LIKE THIS!
HRRGH!
HROOARGH!
STAY DOWN, OR I'LL SQUEEZE THE EVIL OUT OF YOU!

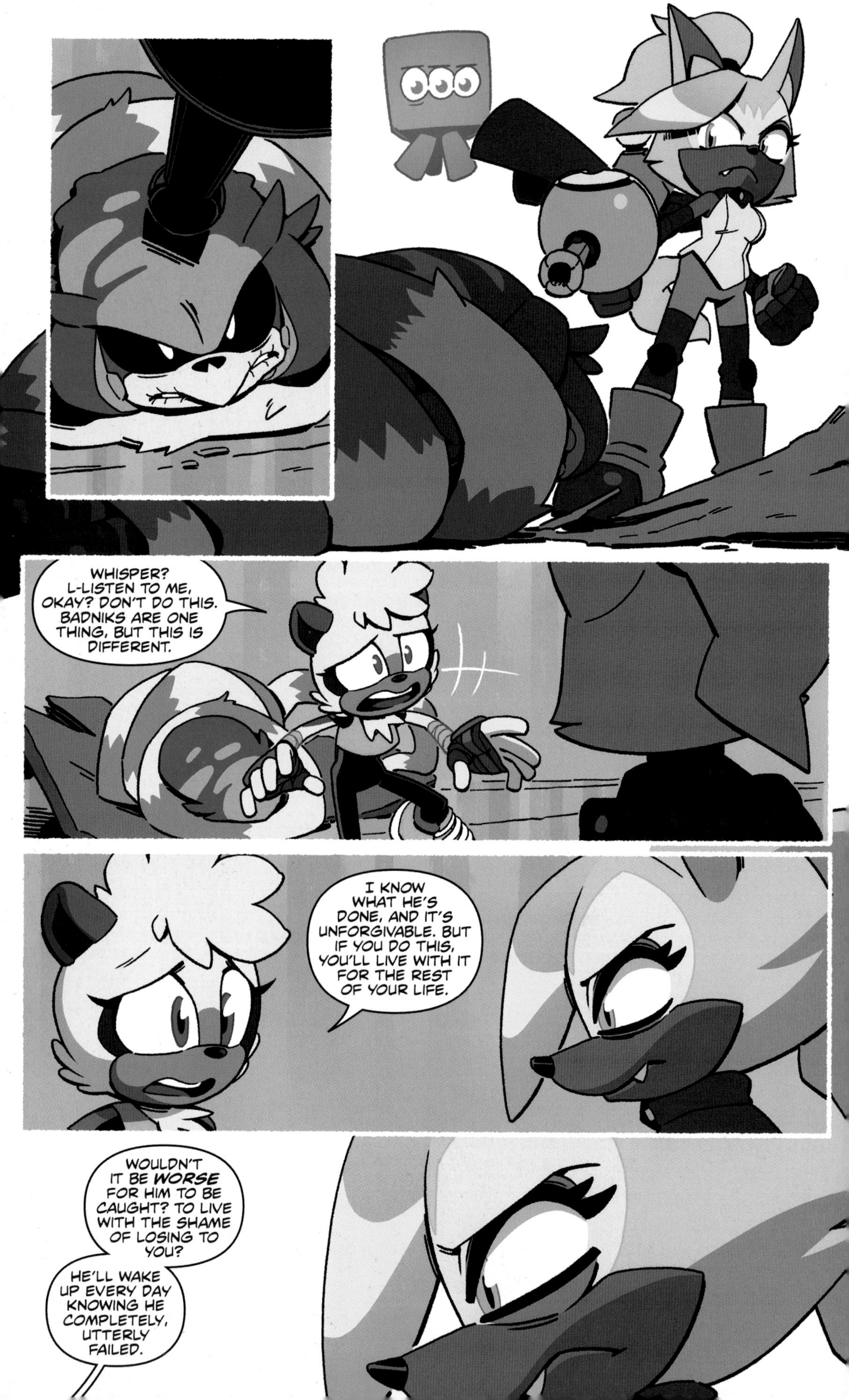
WHISPER? L-LISTEN TO ME, OKAY? DON'T DO THIS. BADNIKS ARE ONE THING, BUT THIS IS DIFFERENT.
I KNOW WHAT HE'S DONE, AND IT'S UNFORGIVABLE. BUT IF YOU DO THIS, YOU'LL LIVE WITH IT FOR THE REST OF YOUR LIFE.
WOULDN'T IT BE ***WORSE*** FOR HIM TO BE CAUGHT? TO LIVE WITH THE SHAME OF LOSING TO YOU?
HE'LL WAKE UP EVERY DAY KNOWING HE COMPLETELY, UTTERLY FAILED.

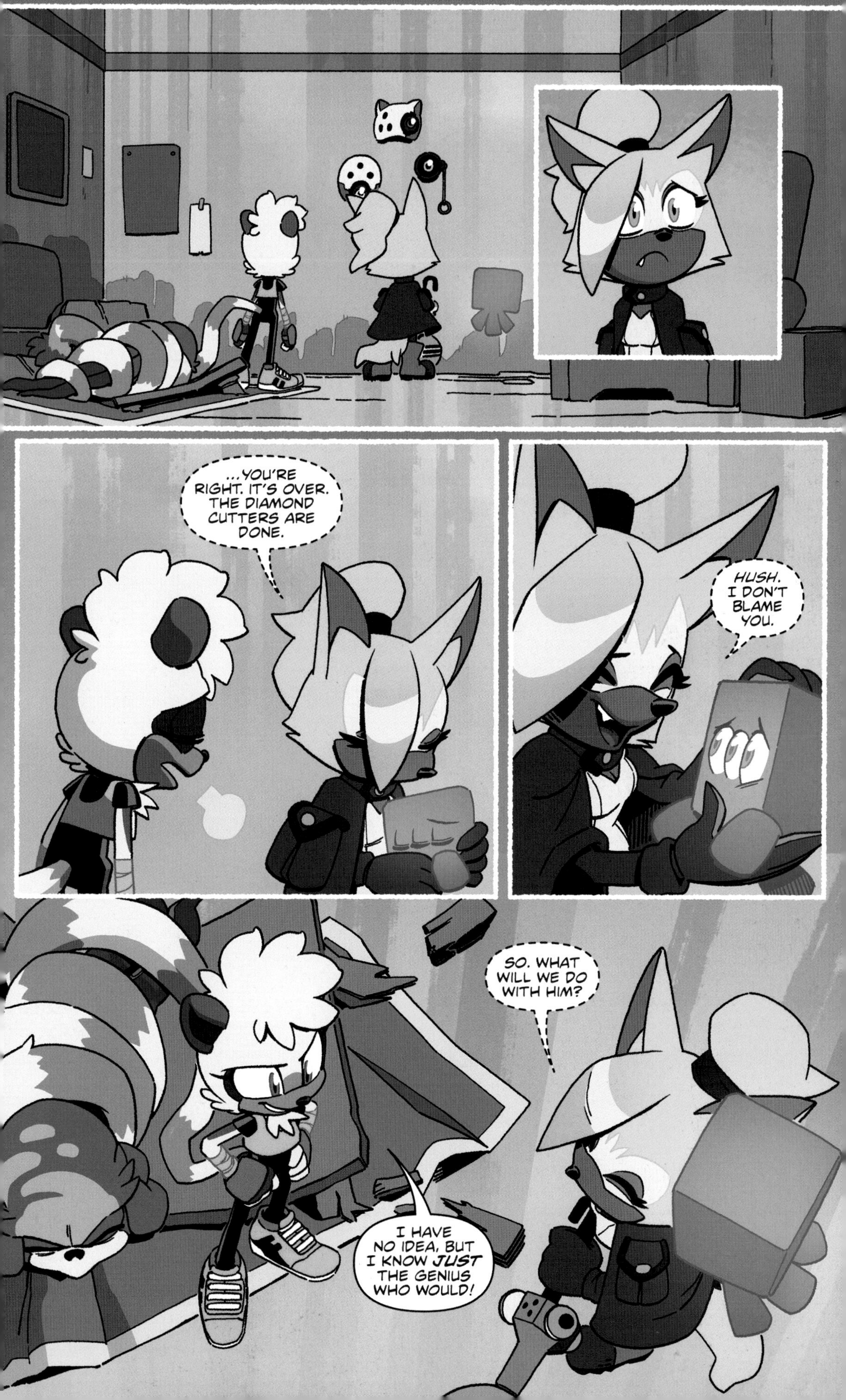
...YOU'RE RIGHT. IT'S OVER. THE DIAMOND CUTTERS ARE DONE.
HUSH. I DON'T BLAME YOU.
SO. WHAT WILL WE DO WITH HIM?
I HAVE NO IDEA, BUT I KNOW JUST THE GENIUS WHO WOULD!

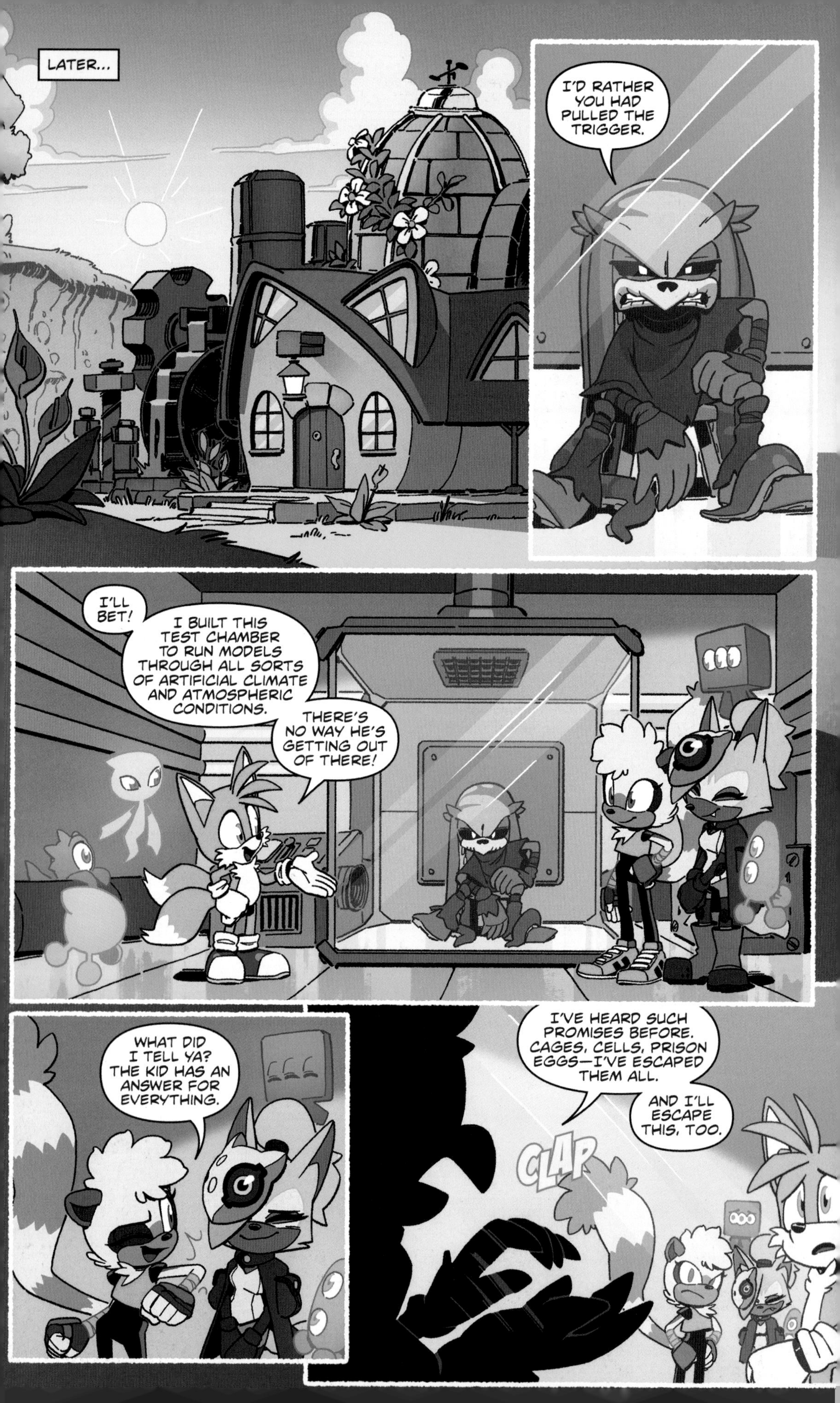
LATER...
I'D RATHER YOU HAD PULLED THE TRIGGER.
I'LL BET!
I BUILT THIS TEST CHAMBER TO RUN MODELS THROUGH ALL SORTS OF ARTIFICIAL CLIMATE AND ATMOSPHERIC CONDITIONS.
THERE'S NO WAY HE'S GETTING OUT OF THERE!
WHAT DID I TELL YA? THE KID HAS AN ANSWER FOR EVERYTHING.
I'VE HEARD SUCH PROMISES BEFORE. CAGES, CELLS, PRISON EGGS—I'VE ESCAPED THEM ALL.
AND I'LL ESCAPE THIS, TOO.
CLAP

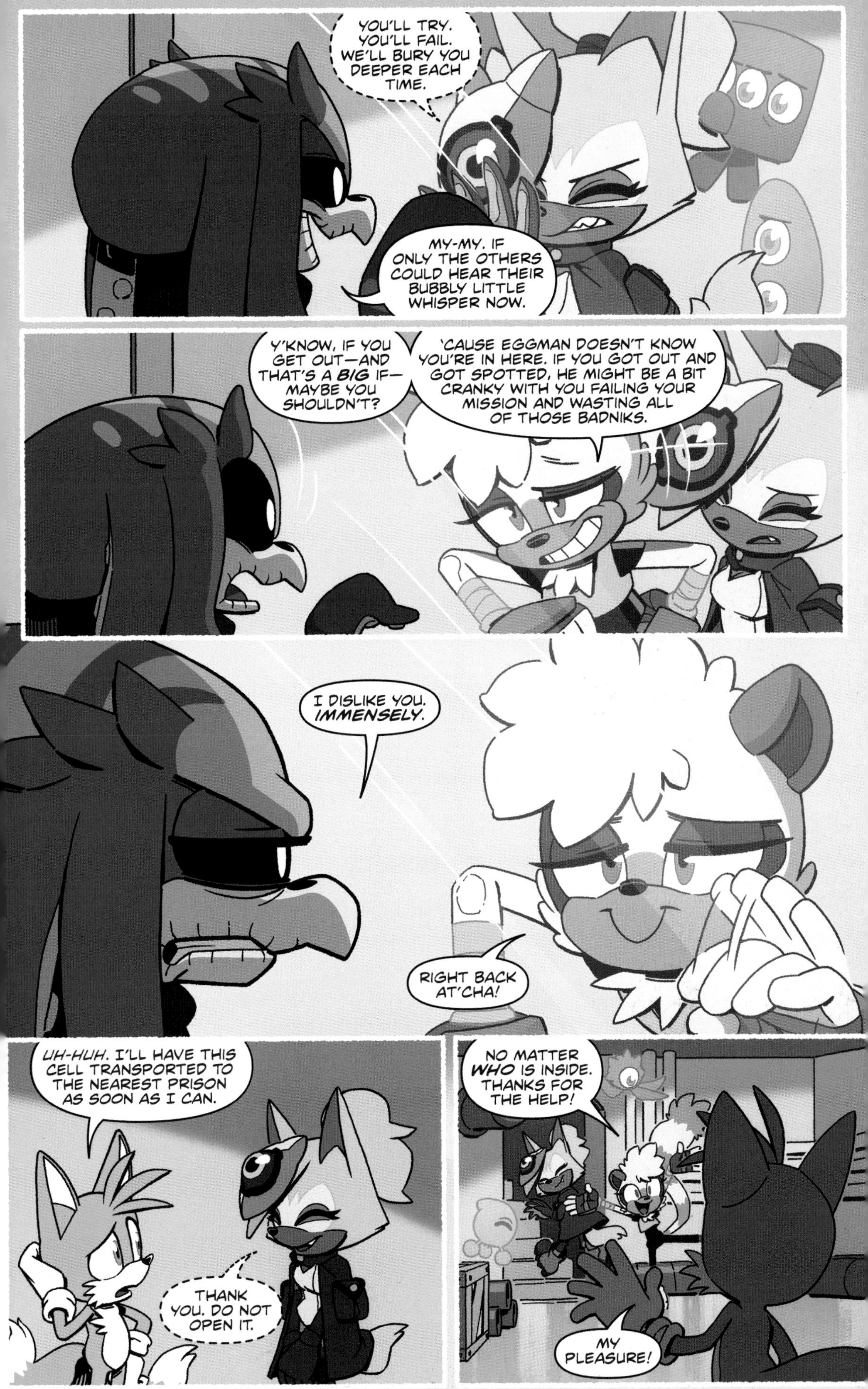
YOU'LL TRY. YOU'LL FAIL. WE'LL BURY YOU DEEPER EACH TIME.
MY-MY. IF ONLY THE OTHERS COULD HEAR THEIR BUBBLY LITTLE WHISPER NOW.
Y'KNOW, IF YOU GET OUT—AND THAT'S A *BIG* IF—MAYBE YOU SHOULDN'T?
'CAUSE EGGMAN DOESN'T KNOW YOU'RE IN HERE. IF YOU GOT OUT AND GOT SPOTTED, HE MIGHT BE A BIT CRANKY WITH YOU FAILING YOUR MISSION AND WASTING ALL OF THOSE BADNIKS.
I DISLIKE YOU. *IMMENSELY*.
RIGHT BACK AT'CHA!
UH-HUH. I'LL HAVE THIS CELL TRANSPORTED TO THE NEAREST PRISON AS SOON AS I CAN.
THANK YOU. DO NOT OPEN IT.
NO MATTER *WHO* IS INSIDE. THANKS FOR THE HELP!
MY PLEASURE!

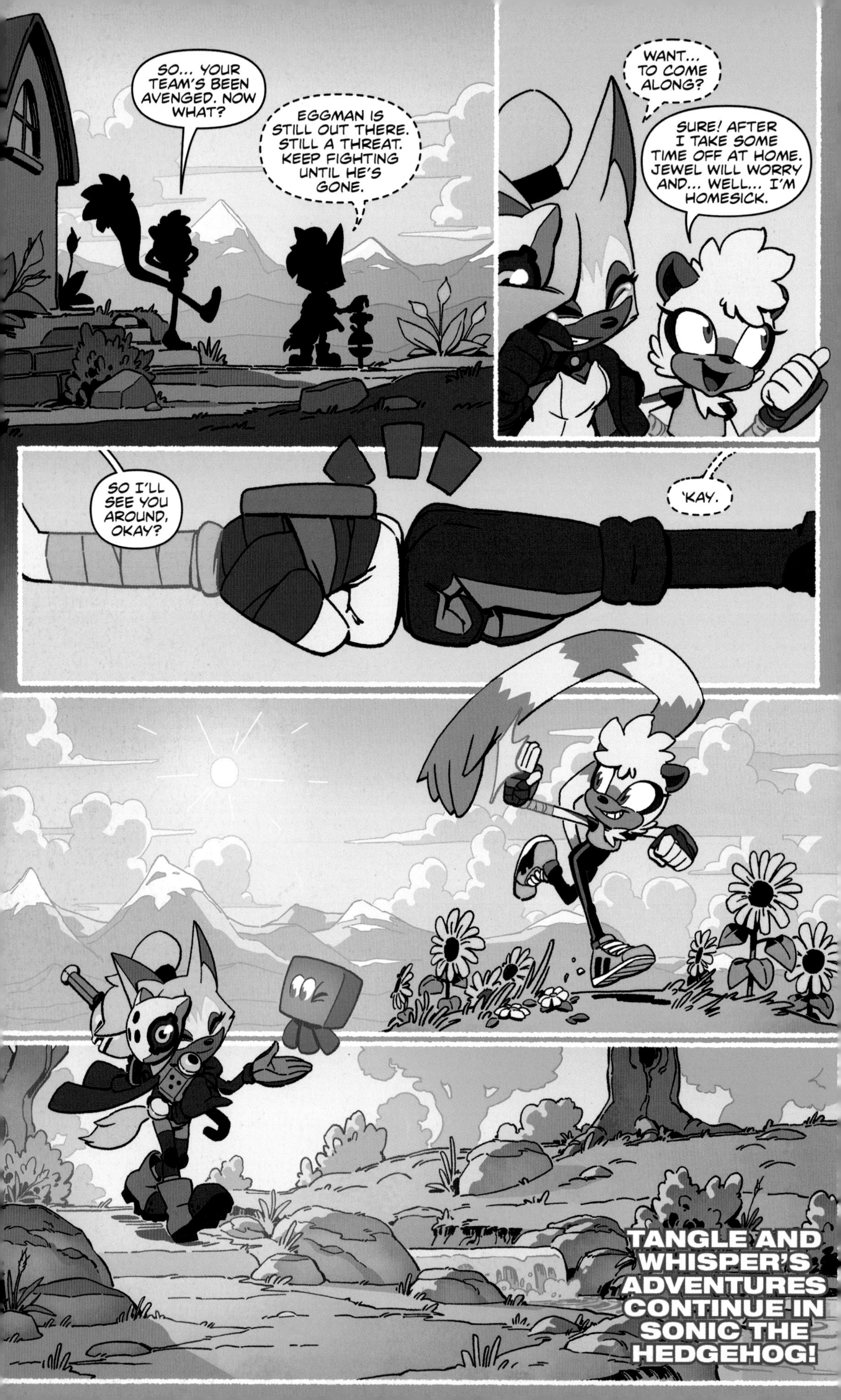
SO... YOUR TEAM'S BEEN AVENGED. NOW WHAT?
EGGMAN IS STILL OUT THERE. STILL A THREAT. KEEP FIGHTING UNTIL HE'S GONE.
WANT... TO COME ALONG?
SURE! AFTER I TAKE SOME TIME OFF AT HOME. JEWEL WILL WORRY AND... WELL... I'M HOMESICK.
SO I'LL SEE YOU AROUND, OKAY?
'KAY.
TANGLE AND WHISPER'S ADVENTURES CONTINUE IN SONIC THE HEDGEHOG!

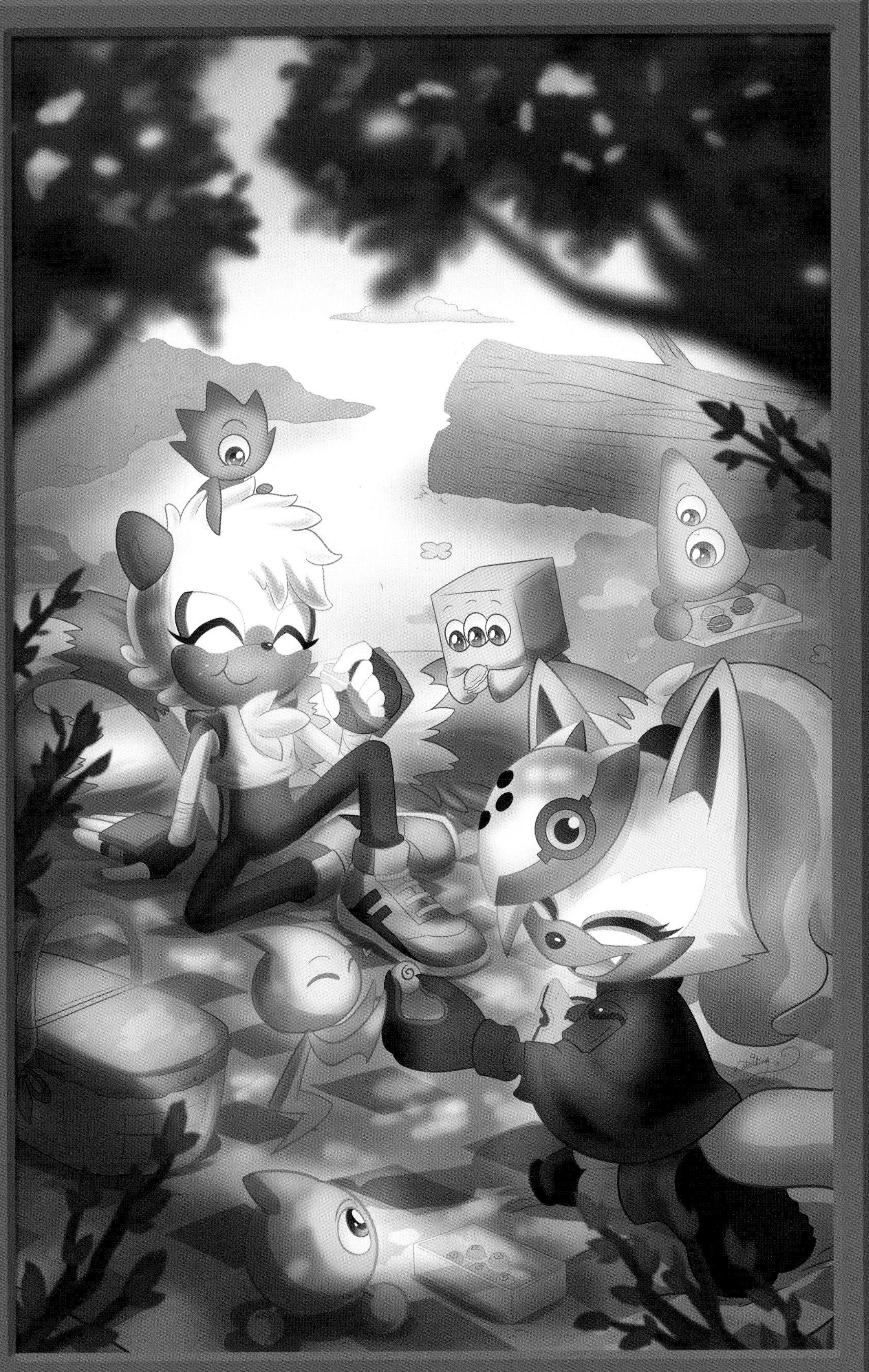

• ART BY **ABIGAIL STARLING** •

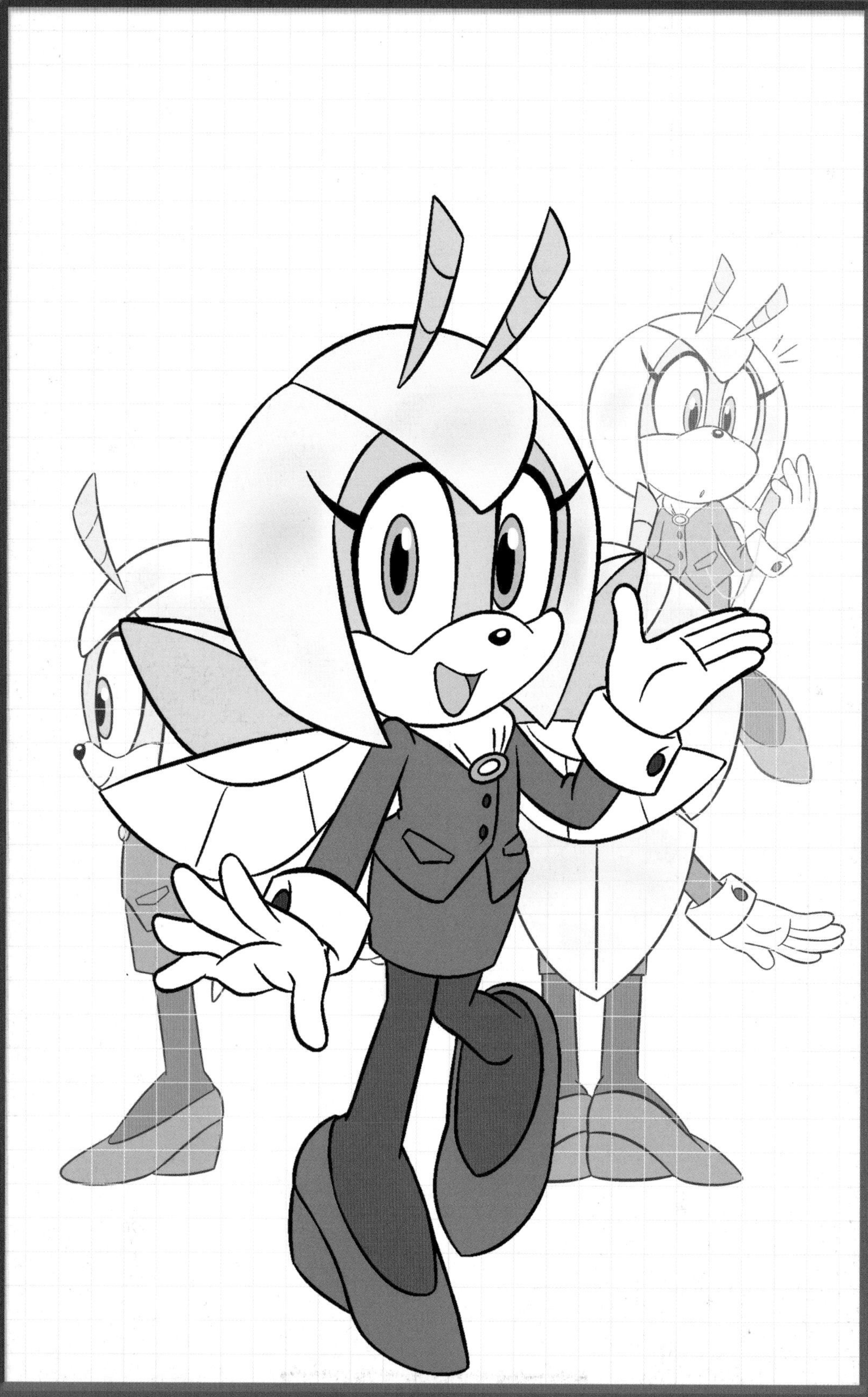

ART BY JENNIFER HERNANDEZ

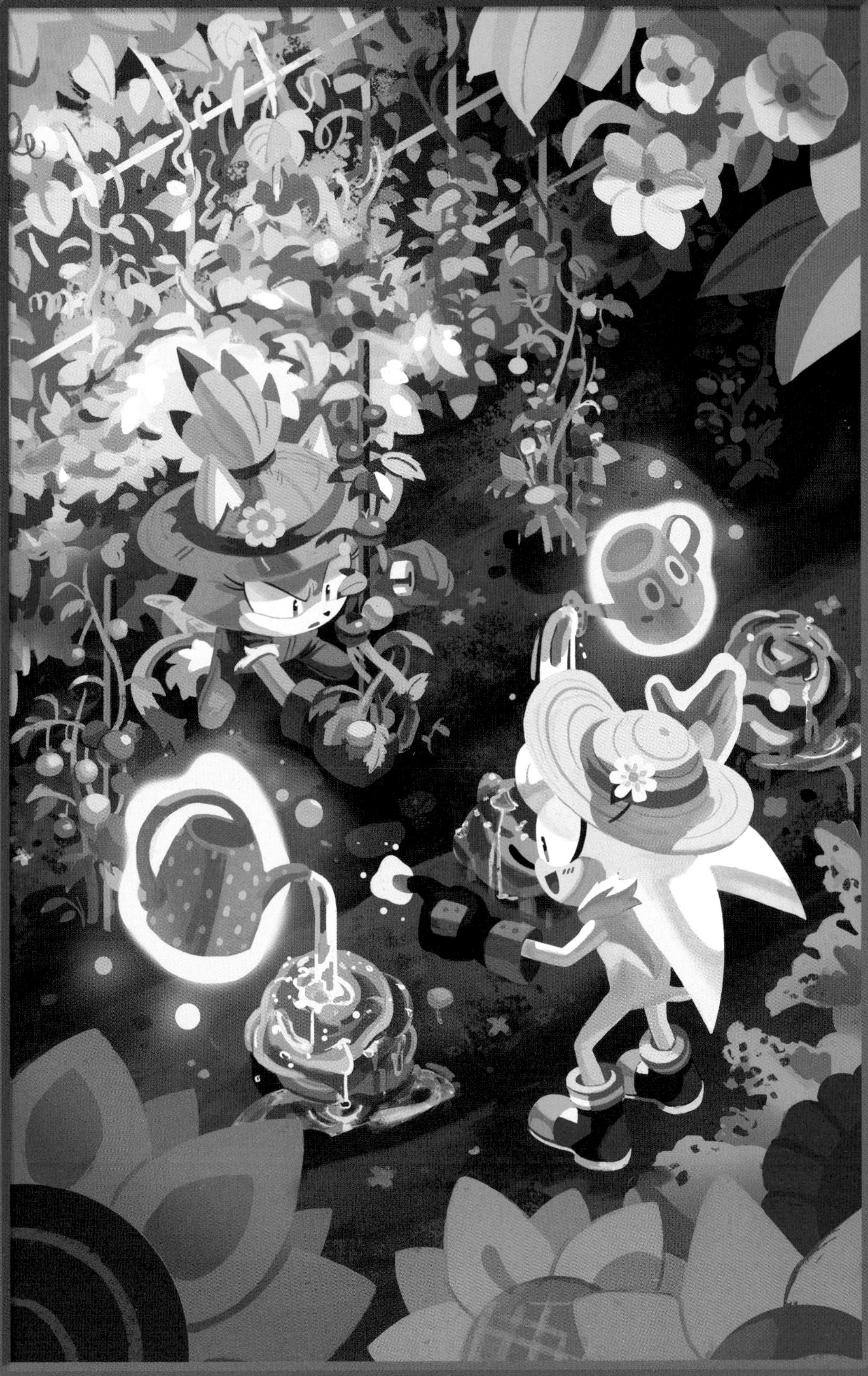

ART BY **NATHALIE FOURDRAINE**

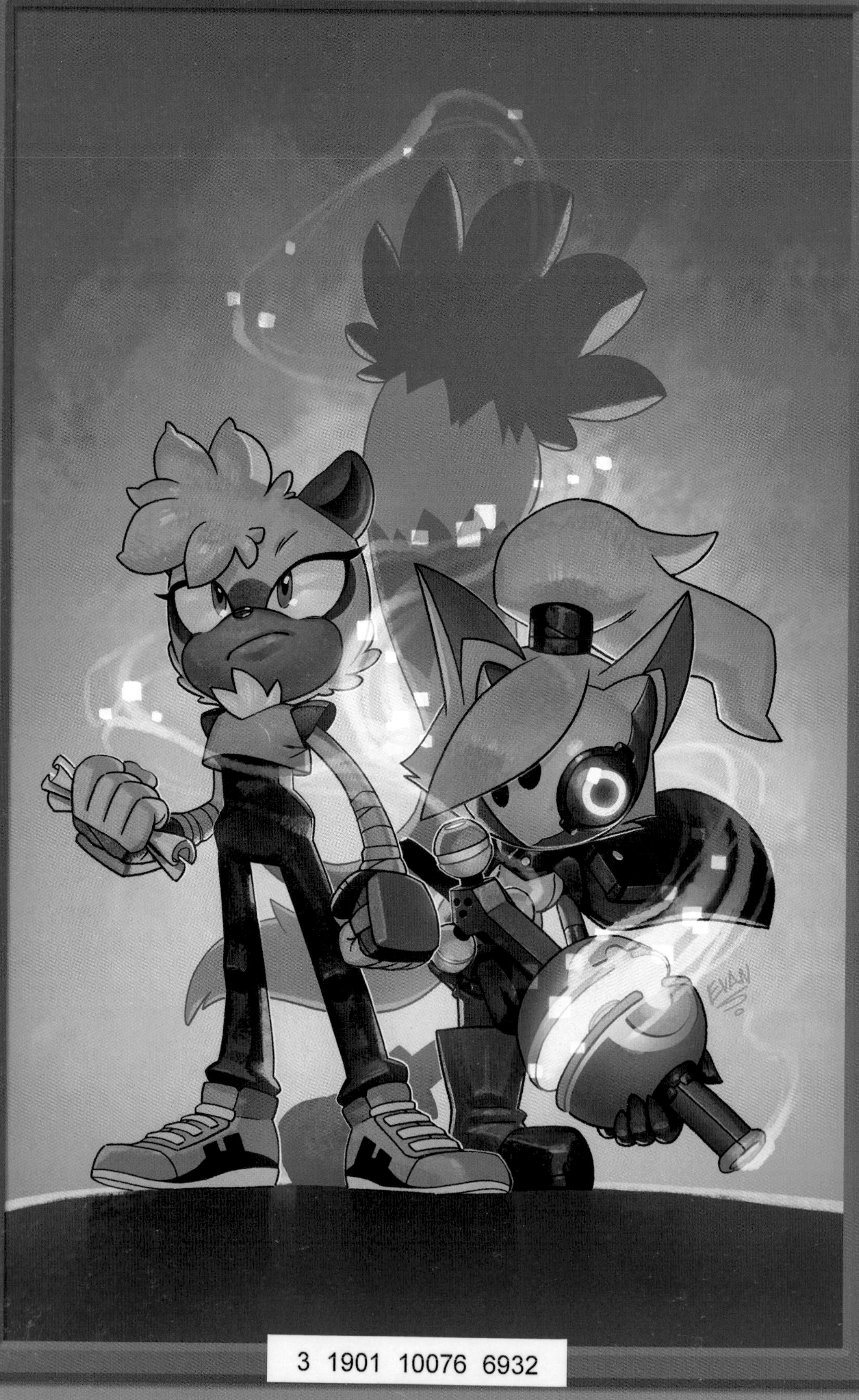
EVAN

ART BY EVAN STANLEY